bring doughnuts

mark szekely

PublishAmerica
Baltimore

First printing

ISBN: 1-4137-1969-4
PUBLISHED BY PUBLISHAMERICA, LLLP
www.publishamerica.com
Baltimore

Printed in the United States of America

To the four wonderful gals who rule my world!

Somehow … some way … anyone I ever met, by just meeting you, I'm pleased to say that I'm in your debt …

⌐ blast away ⌐

It is said, "that a single grain of wheat is like a reluctant will … sprouted from seed, it is nurtured and allowed to grow. Dependant upon the sun and the rain, it gains its form and character from nature and takes course at times headstrong against the wind.

"However, unless it yields and conforms as the rest of the field to be transformed, it will never have served its purpose … for the single grain can only flourish when it is harvested and becomes part of the flour. Like the grain of wheat, your independent will must succumb to the course set by God to gain its total worth."

"For Christ's sake, what a bunch of fucking horseshit," I said under my breath.

Twenty-five years ago, during a postmortem counseling session conducted by a priest with a B.S. in "b-s," Del Arroundo's *parting shot* pretty much summed up our general consensus, before the lot of us walked out the door, when he said, "Hey, Father, fuck you very much!"

Time may have tempered *our collective* anger, but *my independence* still fueled a fire of absolute candor and renegade attitude, especially when it came to that life-shaking event. A time of great anguish with little in the way of understanding, which harvested one hell of an *almighty spite* for the Almighty.

I'd sit and wonder and often found myself laughing until I cried about this freakish nightmare, that to this very day still renders me breathless and occasionally doubled up in pain.

I would deliberate … consider … and ponder almost everything related to this fiasco, and sought to be as impartial as humanly possible in trying to grasp onto some sort of logical answer, but I couldn't.

7

From the scientific findings of the professionals who were involved in the crime scene and investigation, to the futile attempts to comfort employed by the religious, everything in my mind pointed to one culprit ... "it was God's fault" ... plain and simple. That's right, I said it! "He fucked up!"

Is there a problem with me proclaiming this? For if there is a *responsibility factor* here, especially when it comes to having the ability to pull the right strings, "then who do you think wields the biggest stick?"

Let's face it, if truly *supernatural* and able to control destiny, wouldn't you think that his PR department could come up with something a little bit better than that *grain of wheat* bullshit, that was even hard for someone of my relative inexperience and impressionable age to swallow.

Believe me, I've tried to force-feed myself the nonsense that they were offering. I prayed, inquired, talked, conversed, begged, sought counsel and had often yelled into the night sky, but nothing ... not a damned thing ever came of it. No signs from above, no answers, no revelations and no divine interventions ... not a goddamned thing!

I began to realize that the teachings that I was reared on, had abandoned me when I needed them most. But, were these *teachings* or *classic punch lines* used to douse a simple need to question the faith?

I remembered my dad saying to me, "Mark, this is the time when you need the faith more than any other."

And I'd respond to him, "Dad, you always taught me not to be afraid to seek the truth, but what happens when you can't find it?"

"What are you trying to say, son?"

"How could a God ... your God ... our God permit this to happen? How can you believe in something ..." and as I began to tear up, muttered, "that you can't see, feel or touch?"

"Mark, granted you're pissed off because of what happened, but just because you don't know the hows, whats, wheres or whys behind it, don't assume that God dropped the ball.

"You have all of the talent in the world to be a great catcher, and the colleges are starting to take notice, but, boy, at this time, you're only a story."

"A story?"

"Yeah, to many of those scouts, you did something ... somewhere ... at sometime ... that's a story."

"Come on, Dad, those who are interested have either heard about me or have seen me play."

"Did you ever see Ty Cobb play," he asked.

"What?"

"DID YOU EVER SEE COBB PLAY?"

"Of course not."

"But he's supposedly the greatest hitter of all time?"

"So … what's yer point?!" I sarcastically bashed.

"How do you know that he was so great?"

"They have records, Dad. You know, statistics."

"You mean a story," he countered.

"No, Pop. Records, accounts, descriptions," I bellowed.

"Yeah, there are records, aren't there," he said while cocking his head toward the dust-covered Bible that was sitting on a doily over on the corner table.

"Hey, I get your drift, but I'm not doubting the existence of Jesus," I said.

"Then what are you doubting," he responded. "I don't want to confuse the issue here, but just because something's not visible, doesn't mean that it's not real.

"Mick's gone and if you're gonna try and pin this on God, you're barkin' up the wrong tree." Then he just looked out of the window for a moment before walking away.

I always loved and respected my dad, but this time his response was just too open-ended for me, and all of a sudden I found myself in an unfamiliar and scary place—alone.

Worse yet, both of my fathers, here and in Heaven seemed to be drifting away.

I'd lie in my room and wonder, if in *Him* we really do *trust*, shouldn't we have any recourse if that *trust* is broken?

Wasn't there any conducting of an appeal? Or was the only answer that "sometimes there is no answer … just faith."

Which I began to think was nothing more than the Church's way to keep those of us with half a conscience, in a slow burning state of compliance, while we internally try to *deal* with it? Would God really leave us twisting in the wind like this?

Oh, and don't think that my belligerence didn't earn me both ridicule and contempt from family and friends alike for even suggesting such blasphemy, and the issuing of the aforementioned statements. It colored me as a disbelieving prick, who was simply on the fast track to Hell.

Funny thing though, how those who had encouraged me "to question what others feared to ask," suddenly were yielding in their support. Not only was

I stunned and dismayed by the recent loss, but I was incredulous over the hypocrisy that surrounded me.

Yep, I basically pissed off everybody, from my folk and sis, to the aunts and uncles and just about every other person down the line, including our parish priest for taunting the *Almighty* and his Church.

Finding myself out on *that limb* was not the most pleasant of feelings, and though it's the same place that all of us sooner or later end up, rarely do we accomplish anything while we're there.

But this time I wanted—no, I needed—more than just the standard textbook response that this was *fate* or *His Providence*. For I had never before challenged or ever conceived the notion that I would; this concept of *destiny*, or what *the establishment* would want you to believe that meant. This time the *standard response*, that bullshit *grain of wheat* theory was not going to suffice.

"Trust in the Lord ..." no problem. "Don't question his ways ..." gotcha'. "Be a good little Catholic boy ..." whenever possible (except when needing to tell half-truths to girls) but that's where the shit had to stop!

He fucked up. At least to a certain extent, and *this one* was just a little bit more than usual aches and pains of the *growing games of life*. This was a *biggie*, and one that the Church didn't want to even screw with.

How else is one supposed to either explain or comprehend the inexplicable?

And if one more person was going to tell me that, "Hey, you're only sixteen years old ... and you don't know shit about shit," I was going to take a shot at them!

~ the one that got away ~

Let's face it, to find his eight-inch cloth and plastic scapular, timeworn and tattered, floating in a lake the size of Erie ... that minuscule religious artifact that was supposed to offer him protection and strength, recovered within forty-eight hours of commencing his search and to have no clue or notion of where his 5'10" frame was ... "how could that be ... how could this fucking happen?"

Erie is the shallowest of the Great Lakes and along its western basin, one could be adrift miles away from shore and only be in three feet of water. This is the Great Lake of which the locals profess that because of its lack of depth, "when two fart simultaneously along its shoreline, it will begin to thrash."

So how could it be that the only thing that could be initially linked to the recovery efforts was this small reminder of his professed Catholic *badge* of protection ... which in essence failed him?

It was a ten-square-mile nautical search for Mick's 150-pound lanky frame, spanning from the red and white beacon of the Detroit River Light, southward to the mouth of the Maumee River, and east bound just beyond West Sister Island. Initially, the hunt commanded all of the local resources from both the public and private sectors.

This normally quiet part of the lake had become a buzz with activity, with anyone having access to something that floated joining in on the cause. It was an operation that you could only imagine, went from an initial state of panic, to an official search and rescue mission ... to one that would end in despair.

As the days piled up, hope would subside, and what was once a positive mind-set quickly diminished into nothing more than a quest to recover.

Nothing went right. The weather wouldn't cooperate, the lake decided to whip up and God was keeping everybody in a suspenseful grip that was leading to an inevitable conclusion.

Not a goddamned thing would be found, nothing, that is, until the eighth day.

Caught in the seasonal thick and coarse seaweed, my best friend's disfigured and discolored body was finally removed from its temporary murky grave, dousing the fantasy that this was all staged. A master plan, if you will, to seek some sort of retribution over a legitimate insurance claim that saw Michigan Mutual "fuck his family over" a few years earlier, by paper working them to death over a workman's comp injury claim that caused his father injury, lost wages and financial ruin.

Instead, we found ourselves three days later in the arrears of an autopsy, gagging from the corpse's discharge, which emanated the most horrendous odor from within the confinements of the closed and supposed airtight casket.

The masses that came to the funeral home to pay their respects did so with heavy hearts, but many left literally sickened by the pungent remains.

On the day of burial even the mortician's suggestion that the three-eighths of a mile distance from their facility to the church, would probably best be negotiated in the form of an outdoor procession, drew little in the way of opposition. This certainly served multiple purposes far beyond exposing their hearse to the stench that their parlor had already encountered.

So with the police providing both a neighborhood blockade, the throng of family, friends and literally hundreds of others, including the local politicians and media cameras that were drawn into this saga made the trek down Martin Avenue.

Though silent from the disbelief that this was actually taking place, a collective weeping swelled from the gathering as Mick's favorite song, Bob Segar's "Main Street" was being blared along the procession route that ushered the casket toward the open doors of Our Lady Queen of Angels Church.

I had never witnessed more tears and disbelief over a situation than I did during this time, but quite honestly, I was cried out and had nothing left to give. Physically, I was hollowed out. Even as a pallbearer, it took all of my resolve and the dependence upon the five other fellas to help me pull my weight. But as defeated as I was in body, I remember being incredibly aware of everything around me and surprisingly keen to all that was associated with the past eleven days.

Within the stoic cathedral that was packed to the rafters, Farther Joseph Jankowski was attempting to console and provide understanding.

"It was God's will to take our brother Mick," he rendered.

God's will, huh? How in the good fuck do you know that, I thought as I shook my head in disgust. *Is there some sort of divine secret that they clued you in on at seminary, Father? Or, did you take this from the how to provide comfort manual that you were issued with your collar?*

Whatever shit he was shoveling, I just wasn't buying. His attempt at defining benevolence and the *unquestionable will* of his boss just wasn't making any sense. Was this really God's destiny for a good and productive son?

Or if it was human error, *then just fucking say it!*

Please … just don't bullshit us anymore … or maybe just don't bullshit ME anymore with prose and expect it to make everything better. Because, to be quite honest, I didn't see anyone around, either preaching from a pulpit or staring down from a crucifix, that was going to be able to give me comfort or answers about this one.

How could this have happened … and what the fuck were we doing here? One thing was for sure, blocking out the priest's sanctimonial bullshit was not going to be a difficult task.

Rowdy and ready, the seniors got out for the year on a Wednesday, while the rest of us had to *douche* the halls and rooms of St. Hedwig's smallish facility until the end of the week.

After the Thursday cleaning session at school, there were chores that would be waiting for me around the house, which I would intentionally embellish to avoid any additional duties that my dad may have imposed prior to dinner being served at the usual time of 5:30.

Dinner … hmm … I really don't think it deserved that *enticing* of a name, at least not in my mom's kitchen. This was not the place to come for a feeding frenzy or to indulge in rarities like taste.

Rather, it was *sustenance central*. A place to fill up in between spots where food actually had that thing called flavor.

I'm convinced that if it were not for Chinese takeout, McDonald's or Kentucky Fried Chicken, I doubt if I would have ever acquired any kind of taste buds. Therefore, dinner was more of a pit-stop that rarely invited or spurred on any type of conversation to prolong it.

Post-dinner activities on this particular evening found me leaning up against one of the brick walls of our front porch and watching the local traffic pass by. Across the way on the wide cement slab, sat my dad in his normal position on the glider, in a pair of Bermuda shorts, a short-sleeved collared shirt that was totally unbuttoned and a pair of opened-toed fuzzy slippers, that I swear were really my mom's.

On the window ledge next to him, sat his usual piping hot cup of coffee and his pocket-sized transistor radio, always tuned to AM 760 WJR.

"Here's the two-two pitch to Kemp, swing and a drive down the right field line, that's gonna be extra bases for Tiger star!" I could vision him lumbering around the bag at first and headed into second for a standup double.

"Yes," I exclaimed and raised my fist as longtime Tiger announcer Ernie Harwell continued, "that will easily chase Ron LeFlore home and give the Tiges a 2 to 1 lead over the Bosox."

"'Bout time that bum did something," jabbed my dad. Though he was happy that the Tigers took the lead, he always seemed to be pissed at Kaline's heir apparent.

At the same time, from within the house I could hear my mom bellow, "it's Mickey on the phone!" The Mickey she was referring to was my best friend, Mike Selby. I jumped at the opportunity to flee from what promised to be another verbal pounding of the Tiger star.

Though my dad and I were the best of friends, when it came to the Tigers, only his fair-haired boy, Jason Thompson, could measure up. Nobody else on the squad could advance the cause of the *old English D* other than *Jason boy*! To which I couldn't disagree, I liked Thompson too! But noooo way, he was my dad's *boy*, as if he had discovered him and made his trek into the majors possible.

In Georgie's mind, he was the only player that mattered, and the rest of the team as he often put it, "were nothing but a bunch of primadonnas."

Most of the time I would take the bait and come to Kemp's defense, becoming his un-retained agent, while Pops was the hard-lined *I know baseball* prosecutor, ready to once again make the Tiger left fielder his radio bitch.

"Geeezzzz, Dad, he's 2 for 3 with a run batted in again … what else do you want?"

He responded gruffly, "he makes a hundred and fifty thousand a year; the bum should get a hit every time up." Which immediately peaked the ire of Dad's porch-sitting accomplice, Mendhart Barber, a Hungarian immigrant who lived next door.

In his broken English, the elderly neighbor yelled, "Daaats right, Georgie, you tell da' kid!"

Knowing that this could only lead to trouble, I immediately thought that if it were not for the call waiting for me, that I would have considered heading up to my room, locking the door and contemplated masturbating myself to death to the thought of my sister's girlfriend, Rita, anything to get away from this!

Arriving in the kitchen, I found my mother talking to Mick's mom, Marianne, about the ensuing graduation party on Sunday. These two were cut from the same mold, card-playing *poker-holics* trapped in a domesticate's body.

Neither could cook worth a damn, but they were loving mothers who kept a clean house, did the laundry and the other chores associated with their stay-at-home positions, usually in anticipation of a big weekend game.

"Should I bring my change purse Sunday?" my mother inquired, which was just another way of asking, "would there be a game?" Despite, what I'm sure were a thousand details to cover before and during the party for Marianne, I already knew what the response was by the grin on Mom's face.

"Hey, I thought you said it was for me," I admonished.

"Well, Marianne, my Markie is here," and with that she passed me the receiver.

I was greeted with a hardy, "Hey, Moosie," a label placed on me by Mick's cousin, Alvin.

This *tag* was derived from our football get-togethers, where Al equated tackling me to trying to bring down a runaway moose. Believe me; I wasn't that good; though, from time to time, I dragged the occasional would-be tackler for a few extra yards.

"Whatever it is, if it's taking place right now, I'm in! I gotta get the fuck out of here tonight," I roared.

Laughing, Mick responded, "Sorry, sweetie, but how 'bout skipping school tomorrow and comin' fishin' with me and Cozzie?"

"Fishing … are you fucking nuts? No way," I barked.

"Well then, come out and work on your tan and throw down a few Red, White and Blues with us," he begged.

15

"As much as I like the sound of that, I gotta' a bunch of things to do, and besides, I got that tryout with the Legion team in Garden City."

"Oh, screw that," he shouted. "You know you're gonna make the team ... just get your ass out here."

"Naw, I'll be there either Saturday night or for the party on Sunday," I said.

"You pussy," he responded.

"I love you too; see ya later, asswipe," I concluded and quickly slammed the phone down in a playful manner which we had been doing for years, in effort to get in the *last word*.

Last word alright ... those were the last words I ever spoke to him.

Obviously there were no cell phones in 1977 and even if available, Mick would have never had one, especially when fishing. No, when he *dropped his line*, the only interruptions that he would tolerate was the casual conversation of whomever was tagging along, or the popping sound of the next cold one from his beaten-up green cooler.

But on this fateful Friday there were just too many things that were adding up to trouble, too many problems that *could have* and *should have* been taken care of, that were just *blown off* and as usual, taken for granted. A series of stupid and simple errors that would take the life of one, and haunt the survivors who were left in a wake of wonder.

It was a perfect mid-June morning. Erie was a sheet of glass and the sleepy cottage-type village of Estral Beach, which laid about half way between Motown and the Glass City of Toledo, was the perfect setting for a little angling.

Quiet prevailed, only interrupted by the occasional putting of a thirty horsepowered Merc, pushing yet another local to his favorite spot in the Breast Bay coves, or the faint echoes of passing seagulls.

As for Mick and yet another in his roster of cousins, Danny Cozgrove or "Cozzie," the checking of the gear was simplified to bait and beer. The beat-up and discolored white nineteen-foot Rinker, trimmed in light blue, was a floating *pig*. This was a craft that the Coast Guard should have placed in their maneuvers' firing range just off the coast Port Clinton, Ohio, and sunk it!

A post-tragedy inspection would detail some twenty-four violations of boating safety that probably contributed to Mick's eventual demise, and though I'm sure all were valid, the burning issue of how could this have happened still took precedence.

At 8:00 A.M. the two of them, by the accounts of others, were no more than a quarter of a mile northeast of the shore line's most noticeable landmark, the cooling towers of the Enrico Fermi Nuclear Power Plant. Regardless of season, safe warm water from the towers was discharged into the lake, adjacent to the mammoth facility on a daily basis. This seemed to have an immediate and magnetizing effect on the lake's fare, that lasted a couple of hours before the lake's natural cooling process kicked in. The local angling fraternity had used this to their advantage for years, and though youthful, Mick was *in* on this seasoned ploy.

The usual plan would either be to drop anchor in your favorite spot or to simply troll around in this area known as one of the world's best walleye catch basins. But, no anchor today because it was on loan to Louie Duremba, a neighbor who lived a few doors down.

Gas on this barge was usually the byproduct of the beer and whatever snacks that could have been scrounged up before leaving the dock. However, with a suspected quarter tank of petrol and an inoperative gage to boot, this, too, would play into the *plight* of this ill-fated trip.

Cozzie recalled asking Mick if there was enough fuel, only to get a smart-ass reply "Hey, if we run out, we'll just piss in the tank and that'll be enough to get us home … so don't worry about it."

The day's strategy was to get to a spot just north of the cooling towers and drift. A process that always began with a "morning toast to the barley gods" and the flipping on of the portable sound box to Rock Radio WRIF.

After an hour and a half of no bites and four beers each, Mick had decided to expand his slow motoring radius further from shore. Now about a mile and a half from the coastline, Cozzie said that he remembered Mick saying, "Cuz, you got to cast back upon the waters when you're runnin' a cold streak like ours."

So upon the urging of his cousin, Cosworth, the 290-pound human ball of ballast rose to his feet and like his relative, unzipped his pants and began to irrigate back upon the placid lake.

West Sister, though in the distance was now in sight, which was a cue to restart the engine and begin a new heading for a couple of reasons. A) Because it was simply too far from shore for today's stalk, and B) there were a lot of known shoals and rocky fiberglass eaters near the island.

Mick, with his line in one hand and his fifth brew in the other, moved to the driving counsel to flip on the ignition. Cozzie recalled that from sound alone, starting that piece of shit reminded him of trying to fire up a rusting V8, on a drained battery in the dead of a Michigan winter.

"You motherfucker," Mick thrashed out in anger after multiple attempts to start the drifting vessel.

Too far from the local cluster of fishermen to summon assistance by either flagging someone down or yelling for help, Mick's frustration grew. The ship to shore was taken off the boat a week earlier by Mick's dad for repair, because it was left exposed to the elements and a late evening deluge shorted it out.

They had a flare gun, but no flares, and the only traffic in the deeper open waters was either commercial trade or the massive Great Lakes Freighters, and they just didn't stop.

"Aw, fuck this, Cozzie, you know, I can make it in," Mick said as he looked toward the beach.

"Bullshit," the robust one replied.

"No...no, I can make it," Mick insisted in a slurred tone.

"Mick, don't. Let's just float. Who knows, maybe we'll end up at the bay?"

The bay he was referring to was Put-In-Bay, part of the Bass Island chain about sixteen miles east. Known in a historical perspective as a place of refuge during one of the great battles for our Nation's independence, by the renowned naval leader, Commodore Oliver Hazzard Perry.

Since, however, it had become a summertime retreat for families during the weekdays and the modern day *Sodom and Gomorra* for adult escapades on the weekends.

As Coz petitioned his cousin to sit tight, Mick's clothes began to shed.

"I'll swim into the shallows, get Lou's boat and be back with beer in no time, you big fat ass," Mick said in a playful mode.

"Come on, Mickey, it's too far," Coz insisted one last time.

They were now between two and a half and three miles out, when Mick, my sensible, smart and usually cautious friend, compounded his plight by diving into the still chilly waters of Erie, after shedding all of his clothes ... except for his Levi's. The one garment that he shouldn't have retained due to its absorption properties and the weight that it would force him to haul in his attempt to get back to shore. According to investigators, along with the alcohol, it would be one of the major factors that inevitably sealed his fate.

18

"At least take a life jacket," Cozzie pleaded.

"It'll just slow me down … just shut up and try to catch something."

At first, Coz recalled that Mick was progressing with long and fluid strokes. He was known as a terrific swimmer and had even received lifeguard certification through the Red Cross. But within minutes, his pace was slowing and it was apparent that he was grappling with the current.

"Coz," Mick yelled," I can't make it … throw me the ring," is the statement that the cousin gave to the police as the last thing he had heard from his doomed relative.

Panicking, Coz scurried around looking for the throwable preserver. Rocking the boat; he was becoming disorientated from the combination of the tension and alcohol. After stumbling and even falling a couple of times, he finally located the ring from its stowed location. Then, when he turned to fire it in the direction of his troubled cousin's distress call, he found nothing … only the emptiness of the glassy surface.

With bloodcurdling force, Coz screamed for his cousin repeatedly, only to have his worst fears realized, that his companion was gone and that there was little that he could do. This had now become a real-life nightmare.

It was concluded from the accounts of those who first arrived on the scene that Coz had either blacked out, or went into a state of shock over the incidents that were associated with Mick's disappearance. A little after 3:00 P.M., the distressed vessel, with its lone passenger was being towed in by a passing Searay.

Noticeably shaken, the bewildered and incoherent cousin was met by the local authorities who were summoned by the rescuing Samaritan by ship to shore. In turn, the police contacted Mick's parents and urged them to be on hand at the boat launch as soon as possible.

In this small village where insignificant news traveled at a heartbeat, something of this magnitude sent shock waves, especially when it became apparent that the Selby vessel was in tow with one passenger missing. The entire village seemed to be dockside upon its arrival.

Mimicking a military scramble, boats were dispatched and almost every personal craft became part of a civilian search and rescue. Panic spread up and down the cozy coastline, with wives calling their working husbands and urging them to hustle home to help join in on the mission.

Despite dusk and eventual darkness settling in, the lake was alive with activity. Coast Guard helicopters, crafts and divers were at the *point* of this mission, with support from the Monroe County Police and the local boating fraternity.

The media was also on hand to cover this search from land, sea and the skies as well.

The waters, as mentioned previously, were not deep, but were susceptible to any kind of boating traffic and generally sported a strong north to south and west to east current.

So despite the assistance that was being generated by the anxious folks of the community, the professionals were concerned that the vast amount of traffic would actually hinder efforts instead of helping.

Conceding that all hope was lost, they felt that the *stir* could dislodge the missing frame and place it into the swiftly moving current, thus, making an already grave situation, impossible.

By Saturday afternoon, the normally active fishing retreat was somber and listless.

Some twenty-four hours after being rescued and medically treated, Coz was returned to the Selby residence by the police, who had made him relive the entire incident via an all-night Q and A session. With no body and an elevated blood alcohol level, the police had no alternatives but to suspect Cozzie of some sort of foul play.

Understandably the rotund one was distraught, after having to relive this nightmare and was clueless that he was on the cusp of being charged for murder.

Now Sunday—graduation day, the aforementioned scapular was discovered some three miles west of shore and four miles south of his seaside home. When verified by Marianne, you could see the life drained from her already weakened body as she collapsed into her husband's arms. All of us now knew that it was over and all that remained was the recovery of the body and the determination of death.

There was absolutely no doubt in our collective minds that Cozzie was innocent of whatever the authorities had to suspect. There was no attorney retained to represent him, and Bob and Marianne strongly supported his innocence, despite the police department's procedural contention that he had to be scrutinized in connection with the disappearance.

To support that notion, the cops paid daily visits to the residence to check on him and to tactfully restrict his rights to travel.

The echoing words of the homily clashed with the somberness of the congregation and their continued crying.

"God's plan for us … all of us, is a divine mystery. A destiny … and it can never be questioned," pontificated the priest.

Then why… why in the good holy fuck did it take eight days to recover the body?

Who benefitted from that, God?

And if Mick's demise wasn't enough to deal with, please explain to me the virtue of making Coz witness this act *of destiny? What about the subsequent ordeal and burden of mind that Coz suffered through, until the autopsy finally determined that there was no foul play … was this ill fated* destiny *of one, supposed to torment the life of this innocent man? Did he really have to bear that cross?*

The experience *was life-altering enough, but for eight days, he was a suspect in a drama that he didn't deserve. What possibly could he have done in his youthful life that would have warranted being cast in this nightmare?*

And what about Bob and Marianne? Is there no more of a punishment greater in this world that you *have created, than to have a parent bury their child? Not to mention, having to suffer through the anguish of a prolonged recovery?*

I'm really having trouble with all of this destiny *and* free will *and* unquestionable plan *bullshit. I mean what is it?*

Granted, there were more things wrong with the boat than you could have shaken a stick at; and I'll give you the notion that everything should have been checked in advance … with safety first being paramount.

But, despite Mick's ego and the aforementioned indulgences, whose destiny was really being determined here?

When your son and his friends *fished, they didn't need flares or flotation devices and there was no ship to shore radios!*

In fact, if memory suits, didn't somebody have the ability to walk on water? And come on … if there's a destiny angle here, you couldn't give him a shot, by having him remove those jeans … those fucking, absorbing, weight-adding jeans.

Yeah, they drank and yeah, they were buzzed, but did death and the gut-wrenching witnessing of it have to be the punishment?

The nonsense from the altar continued and I found myself doubling up from the pain.

Where was Mick's trademark common sense that we used to rib him on ... why was it robbed of him on that day?

And, Lord, why did you spare me? Why wasn't I on that fucking boat to tackle him, to hold his ass down from attempting such a stupid stunt? At the very least, why wasn't I there to let him talk me into racing him into shore, to make a game out of it ... so that I could be my usual pussy *self, and though, I would have went into the water with him, you know me ... I would have taken a life vest!*

So why...why did you spare me? Could this have something to do with my destiny?

Should I be crying because I lost my best friend or am I really thankful that your example was made of him ... and not me?

I looked at Bob and Marianne and saw a transparency of my parents weeping for me. The *Mick* that Father Joe was referring to could have just as easily been George and Madelene's son.

All of a sudden, I found myself perplexed, yet at the same time relieved that my parents were not put into this situation, and thankful to the same *Being* that only moments ago I was condemning.

I felt funny, almost as if I were in the coffin being eulogized. In a peculiar, yet logical way, I believed that almost everybody in that church felt that a part of them was also being buried on this day.

Then again, maybe...just maybe we all deserved to be pissed at that Being that we were by ritual, seeking comfort from.

Maybe it was an interpretation problem, not only with the way Father Joe was delivering his message, but also with what we were trying to draw upon for solace from our being raised in the faith.

Whatever this was, it was not the same Providence that I was sold on growing up in the Church. I found myself in a fucking shell game with words: it's destiny ... no wait, it was Mick's free will, oh ... and remember, you can't question God's destiny for all of us ... because ... .

Because! Because why?

~ this was a good friend, well, sort of ~

I remember Mick saying to me, "Moosie, we all fuck up, but the great thing about life is that we all get second chances ... just don't get too greedy."

The thing about that son of a bitch that was so endearing was his persona. He was the poster boy for being sneaky and lovable, both at the same time. Which was a dangerous combination that always garnered him the benefit of the doubt. I would marvel at his ability to get out of trouble, almost as fast as he got into it.

He wasn't flamboyant and always downplayed recognition, though he loved dictating the scene. In fact, I can honestly say that he was the very first example of the *man behind the throne*, that I had ever encountered, and he probably played that role better than anyone that I had ever seen.

He was smooth. A great talker who could deflect criticism and simply frustrate the shit out of you. He would have made a great radio talk show psychiatrist, who would have made his listeners cry like babies, while selling them some self-confidence building, nonsensical bullshit book.

The girls at school or in the neighborhood would hang on his every word, and I would have bet my bottom dollar that he could have had any one of them.

And yes, I said lovable, but he wasn't the greatest looking guy, in fact, among the gang, he was probably the least attractive. Ahh ... but he was able to "level the old playing field" with that gift of gab.

Most of our little gang played in the same circles, baseball in the summer, football in the fall and hockey in the winter.

Mick loved hockey and was one of the smoothest skaters that I ever saw. His knack for instigation played well on the ice, because he could draw penalties against the other team at an incredible rate, which in hockey is great, because it would give us an odd man advantage or power plays against the other team.

A strong team has role players mixed in with their standouts. Mick's was not only one of our stronger players who could put the puck into the net, but he could bring that sneaky shit routine from his daily gig onto the ice.

We were in a tight game that had major implications on the standings and a possible playoff spot for our team. We played for a guy who owned an independent soft serve ice cream stand on Detroit's West Side. Stan Stankowicz, a robust and wonderful guy, who not only loved his business, but hockey and being coach of the team that he sponsored.

Our team was obviously named after his business, Whip and Whirl. But, besides being involved in sponsoring a community activity for the neighborhood kids, Stan had a passion to win and knew the strengths and limitations of his team.

We were playing Paddock Pools, the best team in the league and regarded as one of the top squads in the state. They always used to kick our asses and most games that we played against them were usually lopsided losses. The only good thing about playing Paddock was that the legendary Red Wing star and my all-time sports hero, Gordie Howe's son, Murray, played for them. So if the Wings were in town, that meant that Gordie would be on hand to see the game, which was more of a thrill seeing him in the crowd than actually playing the game.

Murray was a decent player, but he wasn't Paddock's standout. A kid who went by the name of Hines filled that role. This guy should have been playing with the elder Howe and not his son, he was just that good!

Somehow, late in the third period we were tied 3 to 3. We needed the two points that a win would give us and not the single point gained from a tie. Usually we were looking on the wrong side of a blowout against these guys, and would have pissed ourselves out of joy if we were able to gain a tie, but now we were trying to find a way to actually beat them.

During a stoppage in play for icing, Stan called our line over to the bench for some last second instructions. As the rest of us skated for the face-off circle deep in Paddock's zone, he grabbed Mick's jersey and whispered something to him. I noticed Mick nodding his head before skating toward the rest of us with a little smirk on his face.

"What's up," I asked Mick as he moved into the face-off circle against Hines.

"Nothin'," he said. "Just keep your eyes open."

He let Hines win the draw, which sent the puck deep into the corner. Hines chased the disc with another Paddock skater, as we countered with Mick, his younger brother, *ass and elbows* Robbie, and me. With the play piled up in the corner to the left side of the Paddock net, Robbie had Hines tied up and I had the other paddock player in a clinch.

Mick, in the mean time, came into the scrum and leveled a hard cross-checked to Hines in the back. As the talented star went down from the illegal but uncalled check, I heard Mick yell, "Hey Hines, that's just how I fucked your girlfriend last week ... from behind."

Mick skated away chasing the now loose puck, while the temporarily downed star was irate at the trash talk. But as focused as he was on the game, Hines was not sure who fired the verbal shot.

In the interim, Stan called for a line change on the *fly* and as we went to the bench to be replaced by fresh legs, Hines came barreling toward our area. Obviously aware that our line had just come off the ice, he targeted our seated positions.

Seeing it develop, I thought we were in for a little verbal byplay, but never expected what was to occur.

Like he was shot out of a cannon, Hines propelled himself over the boards and landed between Mick and his younger brother.

"You mother fucker, I heard what you said about my Jenny!"

With fists flying, Mick popped the star dead in the mouth with a short right, but knew that he wouldn't be able to hold this lunatic off for long. Just then, he said, "Besides, it wasn't me who said that shit ... it was him."

I found myself on my back, staring up at the rafters that supported the roof of the Jack Adams Arena. I knew that my nose was instantly broken from the first punch and that I was going to have a beautiful shiner on my right eye. Thank goodness for yet another Mark on our team, Mark Kowalcheck who tackled Hines and finally allowed me to get a couple of my own licks in. Usually this kind of fracas would have led to a bench-clearing brawl, but both teams instead ended up on our bench, with me seemingly on the bottom of everybody.

When the dust settled, four paddock players were ejected, Hines would receive an additional three-game-suspension for starting the whole thing, three of our guys got thrown out of the contest, including yours truly, who had to be helped off the ice surface by a summoned team of paramedics. A bloody mess, I skated toward the arena's first aid room to a throng of "boos" from the Paddock crowd.

"See what your rotten fucking mouth did," came from that son of a bitching instigator, Mick, as I was ushered from the rink.

"What?" I exclaimed. "You cock sucker!"

He was laughing his ass off, but said, "Moosie, he would have beat my ass to death, and would have killed Robbie twice; I knew you could handle him. Look, he's gone and you just got a little scratch."

Just then, I saw one of the paramedics furrow his brow as if to say, "You can't be buying this shit."

Not only did I buy it, but as I was getting stitched up, I heard this incredible roar from the crowd! With thirty-three seconds left, little Russ Bilinski scored on a rebound giving us the lead and the eventual victory! Stan's ploy and Mick's execution worked to a tee.

When I got back to the dressing room after the game, the boys were going crazy, thrilled about the victory. Looking as if I had gone a couple of rounds with the heavyweight champ, Mick came up to me and said, "Shit, Moosie, you look a mess."

"Fuck your mother," I responded.

To which he replied, "No, you fucked Jenny, buddy, Jenny!"

He then wrapped his arms around me and said, "We did it, sweetie, we did it!"

Ah, that ability to talk ... and "If shit could float ... well, I guess he would still be here!?"

But then again, maybe there are just some things that we just can't talk our way out of.

~ clocks cleaned leads to house cleaning ~

As if the effects of Mick's death didn't already diminish the prospects of our senior year, September at the corner of Michigan and Junction, was about to take on a whole new look.

Amidst the many oaks, elms and maples in the familiar courtyard that led to the diminutive school, there was something amiss. The main door was merely an entranceway that was noticeably empty. It was not decorated with any welcome back banners or the warmth that made you feel like you were coming back home.

For the past three years I was greeted with a hug and a smile from ... well, family.

Sister Emolina, our principal, *our shoulder and our guardian*, was not at her usual *first day back* post. Leading a reception line of her fellow penguin staffers and lay teachers who would genuinely be happy to see us, and eager to hear about our summer. And as corny as it seemed when it wasn't there, a hollow and empty feeling resulted.

Like Rosalind Russell's Mother Superior character in the movie classic, *The Trouble With Angels*, we were looking for Mother's homecoming, and it was distressing when she wasn't there.

"I miss her," a voice uttered.

"I know, it just doesn't feel right without her," still another wondered.

And though she's was gone, you'd think that the others who joined her in years past would have inherited such a wonderful custom, and would be waiting with opened arms in her absence.

A logical thought that would be answered soon enough.

—   —

If you got caught smoking a joint, you'd want to see Emolina. If you had a problem with one of the teachers, talk about it with Emolina. And if you were involved in a community-related incident, yeah ... it was Emolina whom you needed for counsel.

Though cloaked in her traditional I.H.M. (Immaculate Heart of Mary) garb, this five-foot-nothing dynamo was part nun, mother, lawyer, nurse, seamstress, carpenter and a world-class negotiator, who in retrospect, would have made one hell of a Secretary of State.

She was not only a respected commodity in the neighborhood, but also throughout Southwest Detroit as the bearer of olive branches, who didn't take any shit when it came to protecting *her family*, which was her faculty and students. The latter, often at the dismay of the stern male leadership of the parish.

But, she was first and foremost a teacher, and despite providing a refuge for those who were often guilty or looking to be exonerated, she had an incredible knack of being able to bring out the truth and even up the score.

She also had an enormous ability to get information before something would happen. If she would have exhibited even the tiniest interest in a little larceny, like getting the *skinny* on a game or boxing event, we could have made a killing! But she was incorruptibly honest.

Yet, leave no doubt, she stood for justice and though many tried, few if any students played her for the fool. She knew who was *snowing* her, and those guilty learned their lessons and paid the price.

Yeah, she often could get you off the hook of paying a heftier toll, but she stood for justice ... and eventually it would be served.

We often thought that, like a feline, she either had nine lives or had *something* on almost everyone in the neighborhood. Like a local syndicate boss, she seemed invincible and we were all glad to be a part of her family. Which makes the explanation of her *Waterloo* ... difficult.

—   —

It was a gloomy, cold and rainy mid-November Saturday afternoon. The

Knights (our school's nickname) football team was entrenched in a fourteen-game losing streak which encompassed most of the 1976 and the current '77 season. The streak really shouldn't have been that much of a surprise to those who followed Knight football with any regularity … if there were any!

We were bad! In fact, the surprising reality was that we were able to field a team.

Between the lack of interest, injuries from fatigue and getting our asses walloped, we deserved medals for combat. We were so bad; that Emolina actually instituted a policy to allow the football players to start school at 10:00 A.M. on the Mondays following a game, because we were so beat-up.

Unlike our rivals who were able to split their squads into an offensive, defensive and special teams unit, we were lucky to actually field eleven guys at the line of scrimmage for a play by season's end.

We played hard, and for a half could mix it up with the best of them, but by halftime we were *gassed* and often found it difficult just to get back to the locker room to take a breather. Unfortunately, the locker room for away games was usually our bus and it mirrored an emergency room's triage area, with bandages a plenty and a number system implemented for the oxygen tank.

Our average margin of defeat during the 1976 season was forty-six points. We managed to gain more than a hundred yards in offensive production only twice during the campaign, and were letting up on average more than 460 yards per game to our opponents.

A banner at our homecoming game read, "Have mercy on us."

Still another pleaded, "We need our players to show up to help us pay for the hall: so please don't hurt them."

Usually you schedule an opponent that you're confident that you can beat on this occasion, but there were no blind, handicapped and emaciated teams in the state. We lost the game 73 to nothing.

Our statisticians compiled the usual … including plays, penalties, yards gained, yards allowed and the infamous Hedwig categories: stitches received and bandages used.

A cold rain followed our bus on this final Saturday of the season all the way to Marine City, a small rural farming and harbor town off the banks of Lake St. Clair, some forty-five miles north of Detroit. Winless and with a roster of twelve, we had made the trek up I-94 to tackle the league's other winless team the Holy Cross Crusaders.

Like Consella's *field of dreams*, in the movie of the same name, this field was surrounded by some kind of unharvested crop, which I believe was corn to be used for animal feed ... "but what the hell did I know; I was kid from the streets of Detroit?"

What was apparent, however, was that this dump made our shitty home field look like the manicured surface of Tiger Stadium.

A half hour before game time, the stands were empty, and the aforementioned disaster of a field, despite being pummeled by the rain looked as if it had just got done hosting a tractor pull. And on a day like today, the best thing that we could have hoped was for the bus to have engine trouble even before we left the Hedwig's parking lot.

The eye-catching angle of the contest was the fact that not only were the Crusaders winless, but their last win was against us, in week six of the previous year (26 to 0). Which was the reason behind a short story in that day's edition of the Detroit Free Press, titled ... "Marine City to host Michigan's Prep Loser Bowl"... an event that in a peculiar way, lived up to its hype.

Our coach was Paul Owen, a huge individual who stood 6' 5" and weighed 270 pounds. He was an alumnus of Hedwig's who was about eight years our senior. A Detroit Firefighter by profession, he was part of Hedwig's last decent football era. As a coach, however, he seemed more interested in the perversion of our cheerleaders and how good he looked *chewing out* our asses after we fucked up a play.

After a miscue, he'd chew out whomever and then look over toward the cheerleaders to see whose attention he may have garnered. He was pompous, arrogant and always out for himself. If there was one good thing about our continued poor play, it was that it usually caused him to become hoarse by halftime.

It killed him to be associated with this losing streak, and in all honesty, his passions were probably more intense than his players ... which was a bad combination.

The byline of the game—"Whose streak would remain in tack?"

By the midpoint of the first quarter, that was a foregone conclusion. Holy Cross had scored on their first two possessions on a field that was such a fucking muddy mess that you couldn't tell one team from the other. Which the Crusaders took advantage of.

On our third series from scrimmage, we had a third and two to go from our own 37-yardline. All week long we had practiced on just this kind of scenario, a short yardage situation, which we expected Holy Cross to pack it in and bunch up the middle of the field expecting a quick *up the gut* hand off.

Our strategy was to surprise them with an *end around*.

Our quarterback, Tony Fernandez, was to hand the ball off to me for what appeared to be an off tackle run to the right side of the formation. In turn, I was to hand the ball off to J.J. Lambert, our split end and probably the fastest player on the team. This misdirection was to get their defense flowing in one direction and suddenly exploit it by letting J.J. hightail it in the other.

In practice, it was working pretty well, and on a day where the footing was not particularly good, this should have really caught them by surprise. But we didn't to get to the dubious level that we had achieved by executing plays properly. On the contrary, we could fuck up the proverbial wet dream.

It was if they knew exactly what play we were going to run ... and they did.

Game films would later show that because everybody was so caked with mud, that they actually sent a spy into our huddle, and when we broke for the line of scrimmage, he simply went back over to his defensive position, which, for Christ's sake, was the corner on the side that we were going to run the play.

When I got the hand off, this mole beat J.J. to the exchange point and instead of tackling me; combined with the fact that I assumed J.J. was going to be there, he took my hand off and scampered the 37 yards in the other direction into our end zone for the touchdown. Tripped up on the play and buried facemask down in the mud after the hand off, I could hear "yeah, baby, go!"

"Yeah ... touchdown!"

I thought, *No shit, it actually worked*! I pulled myself to my knees in a genuflecting position, looking down field in the direction that we were supposed to be going and saw nothing.

Then I looked up and saw a couple of our linemen and J.J., who just stood there laughing and said to me, "Way to go, asshole, you handed the ball off to the wrong fucking team." I joined in on the laughter conceding that when I got back to the sidelines, that Coach Paul would be tearing me a new asshole.

What's the frickin' difference? I thought, *what else could go wrong*?

Plenty!

In the second quarter we actually had the ball near the midfield stripe, but it was yet another three and out series for our inept offense.

"Punt," yelled Owen from our sideline. To which we lined up into punt formation.

I was the halfback in this spread, the guy who stands halfway between the front line and the punter. My responsibility was to call the formation and blocking assignments and to be the last line of defense to protect our punter, the hillbilly king, Tommy Campbell.

Tommy was the friendliest guy you'd ever know, but he was as dumb as a doorknob. He played the game because he liked to get hit … and the harder the better.

His normal position was an interior lineman on either side of scrimmage. Remember, we had a very slim roster so we played both ways.

Tommy's one asset was that he had a pretty good leg and could both punt and place kick pretty well.

So here we are, the mighty Knights in punt formation. The play was called, the assignments were understood and the cadence to snap the ball was being barked. With the rain still pelting down on a field that had little if any grass to start with, the ball was snapped.

Kyle Zeeb's delivery from center whizzed by me and into Tommy's awaiting hands. The Crusaders were on the attack trying to block the punt as I picked up the weak side rush. Our line seemed solid in picking up the rest of the blocking assignments, and we were following a standard punt team practice by stopping the initial rush, while counting to three before releasing downfield to go after the other team's receiver.

I'd usually go on the sound of the ball off of Tommy's foot, but today, his earlier punts were muffled by the sound of the rain falling and all of the sloshing around sounds. So, I'd launch my attack right after I would make my block.

But the sounds after this punt would be different … more so than we had heard all season.

For the sounds that we heard was of laughter, and not just casual laughter … no, I'm talking bust a gut laughter. It came from the stands, (what few decided to show up); the sidelines and even the referees got a laugh out of this one.

It was called the high school football highlight play of the year and was featured on every one of the local late night TV newscasts.

As Tommy presented the ball to his punting foot, his plant foot or the leg he pushes off of, due to the sloppy conditions simply gave way. This caused his ass and back to become parallel to the ground as if he were strapped in for launch at the Kennedy Space Center. Well, he caught the ball flush … and punted it twenty-five yards … in the opposite direction and into our own end zone.

The difficulty for Holy Cross was composing themselves from laughing so fucking hard and to run down and cover it for the six points. So while the Knights was running down field to cover the punt, the Crusaders were again off to the races in the other direction for yet another easy score.

In all honesty, we laughed so hard at the post-game film session the next week that we had a copy of it made and sent it into the Tonight Show, hoping that Johnny might use it in some sort of a blooper segment, but it never surfaced.

One last story about the first half. The biggest, most intimidating guy on our team was a fella by the name of Mike Whiting. He stood 6'-7" and already sported a full beard.

On size alone, he looked as if he should have been playing in the NFL, but he had the coordination of one of Jerry's kids.

Mike was a klutz and was simply all of the Three Stooges wrapped into one.

There we were already dealing with a huge deficit, the cold and rainy conditions, and a playing surface that was a virtual pigpen, when Owen decides to insert Mike in for the last forty-five seconds of the half.

He was the only player left on either bench that had not seen any action as of yet and looked like the Ajax White Knight. He threw off his poncho and came running on the field with the dexterity of drunken Clydesdale on roller skates.

In a style befitting to him, halfway between the bench and the huddle he tripped over his own feet and went sprawling headfirst into the mushy goings. The final piece to the first half joke had fallen into place and made a spectacular splash landing.

By half time we were trailing by 37 points and wanted no part of the second half of play ... and oh what a half it promised to be!

Among the small contingent of supporters that made the trip up to watch our team was Greg Cono, a graduate of the class of '75. During his prep career, he was dubbed golden boy and was a standout at whatever sports he performed. He either broke or set virtually every athletic record the school had and was frequently honored by being named to the different all league teams.

He and Owen were *asshole buddies* and were often seen together.

They shared many traits, such as womanizing and other forms of trying to gain the attention of the opposite sex, which was okay for Cono, being that he wasn't married, but it was really starting to piss off Owen's wife who had left him once before.

But the two of them were *asshole buddies* who believed that the team was a bunch of quitters and pansy-ass pussies.

Cono would often work his way down to the sidelines to criticize us during a game, and without any reservations or concerns from Owen.

The prospects of playing the other half in the shitty conditions, and on the wrong end of a lopsided score, didn't sit well with any of us. But contrary to both Owen and Cono, we weren't quitters and, despite being outmanned, fatigued and without much support, we wanted to give it our best shot.

Usually, we would have been getting another verbal pounding on the bus during the halftime session, but Owen was nowhere to be seen. Assistant coach, Len Herzack, was trying to encourage us while attending to our bumps and bruises with the student trainer.

Not much was being said, when all of a sudden, one of our linemen, Freddie Cholack elbowed me and said, "Moose, check this shit out."

The shit he was talking about was Coach Owen walking toward the bus with a new player, in a fresh and clean uniform. The two were about fifty yards from the locker room on wheels when all of a sudden, the player started running toward a vacant area of muddy land adjacent to the bus.

Like a pig taking to slop, this guy was diving headfirst into the mud, where he began to flop around like a pig in a pen. The object: to blend in with the rest of us.

The silent bus gawked at this display, knowing that we were witnessing the beginnings of a conspiracy. Stunned at the new depths that we were witnessing, Owen and Cono stepped into the bus.

"What's going on here," cried team captain Fernandez.

"Shut up, Tommy," barked Owen. "If you girls would execute better and have any desire at all, I wouldn't need to recruit to save your asses."

"Save us? From what," fired back the senior.

"Just shut your mouth. In fact, all of you keep quiet. I am so sick and tired of your losing and incompetence … and really fucking tired of being called the coach of this laughing stock of a team."

This had scandal written all over it. Not only were we getting our asses kicked, but also we were all about to become involved as accessories in a pretty serious infraction.

34

Our pleas not to "end it like this," fell on deaf ears. In fact, the more we bitched, the more steadfast Owen became.

"Screw this," said Fernandez. "I'm not playing."

This sentiment grew quickly among the team, when, all of a sudden, Owen said, "You will play ... and if you don't, you'll walk fucking back to Detroit, and I'll make each and every one of your lives a living hell ... and you know I'll do it."

Tired, weather-beaten, threatened and now betrayed, we reluctantly complied.

＊　＊

The art of the sneak attack is to catch your opponent off guard and to be able to gain something substantial by taking the risk, but to the contrary, there was nothing to gain.

The real stupidity of this ploy was that Owen was making Cono the object of every play.

Yes, he was still in shape and probably knew the playbook better than most of the team, but with every snap of the ball, we knew that trouble loomed.

An ineligible player, who, for Christ's sakes, was a graduate, was taking this whole scenario to a dangerously serious level. On offense, it was *hand the ball off to Greg here or throw the ball to Greg there*, it was a joke!

On defense, he was the freshest and most assertive player and simply looked out of place compared to the rest of us.

You didn't need spy satellites or the FBI to discern that there was an unscrupulous act being committed.

What really gave it away was that Owen must have told Cono to avoid going over toward the Holy Cross sideline, where longtime coach, Mike Lancaster, and staff could see who was really behind the mask.

Which Cono did ... to the extreme.

There was a sweep that the Crusaders ran off tackle that had the play going past their own bench. The ten trying but defeated legitimate souls that were on defense for us were beaten by the play, but Cono could have forced the ball carrier out of bounds from his roving free safety position. However, when he blatantly eased up on his effort to make the stop to conceal his identity, that's when Lancaster knew that something was up.

As the game began to wind down, the Holy Cross Athletic Director came over to our bench and demanded to see whom this player was. Remember, Cono was a standout during his playing days and was a known commodity. At the conclusion of the game, there was a one-way heated admonishment of Owen by the aforementioned A.D. from Holy Cross, who threatened to hang "Owen's ass out to dry."

But that was only going to be the beginning.

In a post-game conversation, Owen said that unbeknownst to him the team had actually employed luring Cono into uniform and mudding him up to blend in, and with the skewed conditions, he "didn't know that this was taking place."

Fucking Owen even intimidated some of the younger players to go along with this lie, but like the mud that we had played in, this would get deeper and murkier by the minute.

What should have been just another buried score in an already dismal season would become headline news. An investigation was immediately launched and a domino effect was starting to occur.

First were the players … the archdioceses decreed that we all were to be suspended from school. However, to ease our parents' collective concerns, Emolina made sure that we didn't lose any ground in our studies and informed the media who were now drawn into this saga, that not only would we would be back in school soon, "but it was believed that we were wrongfully involved in this unfortunate incident."

Next was Hedwig's Athletic Director, Wayne Frey. A great guy who let the likes of Owen walk over him one too many times.

He wasn't at the game due to personal reasons, but this was his domain and he had to eventually answer for all athletic department matters. Knowing that he would be fired and without a defense for the acts that took place, Mr. Frey resigned.

As for Owen, both he and Coach Herzack were suspended pending the league's findings.

Cono was basically unscathed, despite the fact that it was thought that the league would press charges against him, which surprisingly never occurred.

The Catholic League had its own problems knowing that it had to act swiftly and decisively to resolve this horrible blemish and to get the media out of the picture.

A week had passed and the players were finally allowed back in school, but were kept under a watchful eye.

Then came the day. A Tuesday, the last in November. The league held a press conference at their downtown offices. The results were swift and harsh. The main thing that the League Director said "Was that despite the fact that this incident did, in fact, take place, there was no smoking gun to determine who was behind it."

The ruling also held that though cooperative, "the school was responsible for all who represented it in any manner or endeavor." Therefore, the league had no alternative but to take the following actions. Though it was apparent that the players did participate in the contest, there was no reason to believe that they actually had petitioned Cono to play. However, because of their participation, they would be prohibited from playing in any athletic activity with Saint Hedwig's for a period of one year.

Owen maintained his defense that he really didn't know what was going on, despite being publicly admonished for "conduct unbecoming of a coach." The league and the State Athletic Commission suspended him from holding a coaching position for a period of three years, and in a diplomatic way, sent notice throughout the media that perhaps he shouldn't be put in this type of a position again.

Where he really got hit hard was in the community and at home. This rocked his already fragile marriage, and he was reprimanded and suspended by his employer for being a part of such a "poor public display."

As for the school, without any definitive place to point a finger, a comprehensive and immediate two-year probation on participating in any league or non-league sports was imposed. This was a death sentence, because any of us who had aspirations of trying to use athletics to advance our scholastic careers were now fucked.

We couldn't even field a team, and despite the school's recent ineptness on the gridiron, we were damn good in both girls' and boys' basketball and a serious contender for the state baseball crown.

Cono meanwhile had retained counsel and was instructed not to offer any information relating to his participation. The only penalty that the league imposed was to prohibit him from attending any Hedwig sporting events for a period of three years.

Like his entire career at Hedwig's, the golden boy got off unblemished … big fucking deal.

— ⁓

Less than her usual fighting self during this entire event, Emolina was protective but passive. She certainly didn't deserve this or most of the shit that was thrown her way, but as always, it was expected for her to save the day.

But this time, she didn't seem able to pull a rabbit out of her habit.

She refused to publicly scold Owen for what had taken place and seemed almost tolerant of his involvement. The other peculiar thing was that she seemed reclusive and remained out of sight.

The school was obviously rocked at what had taken place and rumor and innuendo was running rampant. Many of the athletes were ready to pack it in and head for refuge at either Holy Redeemer or Saint Andrews, in hopes of securing any athletic/academic future.

Speaking of future, the school's was literally at stake.

Parents were threatening to remove their kids from not only the high school, but Hedwig's elementary and middle as well. This was no longer just a sports-related incident; the parish's fate was now hanging in the balance.

Knowing the inevitable was about to occur, the sixty-eight-year-old solver of problems and healer of wounds was about to come to the rescue of her children and community one last time.

In a move that would shock almost everybody who became even remotely involved in this matter, the strong willed and uncontemptable nun cut a deal.

In what had all signs of a backroom cloak and dagger arrangement, she would singlehandedly author a resolution that would save reputations, satisfy inquiries, secure a marriage, and preserve something for the people she loved most … her kids.

She released a public statement, that "she had approached Owen and demanded that he do whatever necessary to resurrect," what was termed "that laughingstock of a football team."

She said that she further instructed him to "employ all means to assist our chances," especially after the paper had released the story about the game being tagged as the "loser bowl."

It said that Coach Owen "denounced her request," but that she indicated that "you either win, or you're out!"

She went on to say that she was ready to support any decision that he would have made, but "shamefully" did not come to his aid, when the story broke and the accusations began to fly.

The embellished confession went on to say that the student body, the parish and the community stood to lose everything, both in the short and long term because of her "shallow directive" and "wrongful demands."

She said that she was "ashamed of her actions and despite the involvement of many, she is solely responsible and at the root of the situation."

What she was doing was *righting a wrong by performing a wrong*, and confessed to a *sin* that she fabricated upon herself. In a place steeped in moral and intellectual fabric, she was breaking all of the rules and lending herself to sacrifice.

This was morally wrong! She would have never been a part of such an event and would have squashed even the thought of it. Yet in this public forum, she *wrongfully* admitted to endorsing the entire thing.

She had thrown herself on an already exploded bomb that had many and certain aftershocks. Like the unselfish and sacrificing soldier, she virtually took the bullet, so that the rest of the company could move on and that the common good could prevail.

This would stain a career that was unblemished and forever silence a voice that needed to be heard.

Somehow, she sadly pulled it off.

The Archdioceses and Catholic League, tongue in cheek, knew that if they didn't retract their earlier restrictions, a mass exodus would have taken place and that an already diminishing school enrollment and parish population would have been taken to the brink.

They bought into her hypocrisy, but considering the business ramifications, they had to.

An unknown and confusing part of this entire issue was the relationship between Owen and Emolina. Later it would be revealed that Owen's wife, Sandi, was the daughter of Emolina's brother, obviously making her a blood-related niece.

Emolina knew of the marital strife that the Owens were dealing with, and the fact that Sandi had left her husband on two other occasions. The scandal that was at hand would have been the proverbial straw that would have ended it.

With young children involved, she bought the lying son of a bitch one last chance to hold onto what should have been most important. However, despite being reinstated on the job and getting some fresh breath back into his marriage, Owen's ways finally would catch up with him, and within the year Sandi would leave him.

The restrictions would subsequently be lifted and despite some minor lingering issues, Hedwig's was reinstated back into the Catholic League with full privileges and a new lease on life. Albeit with a broken spirit, as the sacrificing nun was forced to step aside.

At a quiet and small farewell gathering, Emolina succumbing to our constant pressuring pulled a number of us into her office one last time. She knew what we wanted, but in her wisdom she waited until it was time to speak.

"As a postulant (a young woman studying to become a nun), some friends and I were caught cheating on an exam by the headmistress of instructors. Expulsion was imminent, until the Order's Reverend Mother, for no apparent reason, interceded with an embellished tale, that because of a special project that we had assisted her with, certain one-time liberties were unavoidable in respect to this matter.

"Knowing that this was untrue, we caught up with her later that evening and asked her why she deliberately lied for us?"

Emolina went onto say, "Mother ... Auntie, why?"

Her aunt responded, "Mary Beth," (Emolina's given name), "being a Christian means that one must be willing to sacrifice and do things truly inspired by the goodness of God's grace. Though we must follow the path that the Lord has set for us, we are only human ... and sometimes stray ... and bend the rules to help those in need.

"We learn from our mistakes and need to exhibit true virtue in a redeeming way, to always be able to restore righteousness and to make whatever possible whole again.

"Our Heavenly Father, if he chooses, can prevent mishaps; as for the rest of us, we gain our understanding, knowledge and merits through patience, understanding and experience."

"But, Auntie, we were wrong ... we did cheat and you're letting us get away with it."

"Oh, Mary, do you honestly think that Christ should have been sacrificed the way he was for the sins and corruption of others? It was his Father's will, and the benevolence of Heaven that dictated his fate, in the ultimate sacrifice, which was simply derived out of love.

"Likewise, you must believe that as brothers and sisters of Christ, you, too, must look past life's weaknesses and susceptibilities, and realize that the spirit of all God's children is always worth the sacrifice!

"I, too, must open my eyes to help those who may need a little extra direction, and at times regardless of what fate has in store. For to error is human ... and I need not to recite the rest."

"But Mother," the youthful Emolina inquired, "you...you lied!"

"My dear," she responded, "though you may view it as an untruth, I view it as a preventative choice, and a chance to save something very much worth saving, as once I needed to be saved ... as by fate we all need to be saved."

As Emolina smiled, we all began to cry.

"Sacrifice you see, has many different meanings ... and being right and doing what's righteous is a part of that creative understanding. Your mind can direct you to what's right, but only your heart can lead you. One day, the choice will be yours and when confronted by it ... you'll be amazed at what seems right ... and what is righteous.

"I did what I did for you ... and I did what I needed to do for me."

Then with one final gleam from her eye, she said, "Sometimes debts are resolved with those other than the original lender ... somehow I just paid Auntie back!"

It wasn't a crucifixion and not even close to the aforementioned sacrifice of the soldier who threw himself on the grenade, but it was a casualty none the less and "a life-altering lesson" from the woman who was our mother, maid, friend, nurse, judge and, most of all, our teacher.

Emolina quietly retired to the Mother house in upstate New York, and died eight months later. To those that she touched, she continues to live in our hearts.

She was guilty of only one thing, "teaching us the meaning ... to serve."

"Peace, Mary Beth."

～ picking sides ～

It was finally here, September of '77. The beginning of my senior year, and my time to kick ass and rule the roost. I had worked part of the summer at my grandmother's bar to save up for a car and didn't expect to get anything special or flashy, just something that would give me a little independence, while turning the occasional female head.

So, you can only imagine my surprise when my folks on my 17th birthday, back in May asked me how much I had for a down payment.

I had saved about $400 between the work and the occasional hot night at the poker table … more about that later.

"Well, that's not gonna get you into a new car," my dad said.

"No kidding," was my response, "what's your point?"

He handed me an envelope, which obviously contained my birthday card. I opened it expecting to find a couple of twenties, or maybe even a fifty, but found nothing … except a note which stated "We love you, son, let's make your first car a new car, Love, Mom and Dad."

With a half smile and a half-confused look on my face I looked up and asked, "How?"

We talked about the details and my dad simply said, "I'll match whatever you got and cosign for you, but you make the payments and pay for the insurance."

I shook his hand, then hugged him and my mom and asked when this was all going to happen.

The next day, I would be driving it!

$800 in 1977 was not a bad *down stroke* on a new set of wheels. I mean it wasn't Cadillac money, but it wasn't bad … I thought.

We went to a number of different dealerships and every time I saw something I liked, it wasn't either practical enough for my dad or stylish enough for me. We ended up at an AMC (American Motors) show room in River Rouge.

AMC was the renegade carmaker, with a vehicle in their product lineup that went by the same name, but their signature model was the Jeep.

Cool, I thought, *I could dig driving a Jeep around town*. But, when it came to the price, $4,700 was way out of my range, and my dad's position was that anything less than a sedan or a station wagon, hardly qualified as a car.

Almost ready to throw in the towel for the day, my dad said, "Hey, Mark, what do you think about this one?"

The one that he was talking about was AMC's newest product release, *the Pacer*.

"It's roomy," he insisted.

"Yeah, I'll give you that," I responded. Room wasn't the problem though. Style was, and this thing simply looked like the slang label it had received from those who reviewed it for the industry: "the aquarium on wheels."

The two-door model really looked like a gigantic fucking fish bowl, and I kind of cringed at his insistence that it was a "good looking set of wheels."

"Hey, Dad, you're kidding, right?"

"No," he said emphatically.

I just couldn't see myself in this mobile fish tank, but as I contemplated the used piece of crap that I was considering, compared with the prices of the nice new stuff that I couldn't afford, practicality was becoming more and more apparent.

Yes, it was new, and yes, it was certainly in my price range, but from where I was standing, all it was missing was some coral reef and a filter.

As we haggled back and forth with the salesmen, he asked, "For a couple of hundred dollars more, could I interest you in the four-door model?"

Great, I thought, *bigger size for bigger fish*.

But, to my amazement the four door model didn't look as bad. In fact, they showed me a "hot little red job" that they just got in that was in their back lot. Plus, it had a FM receiver and power steering.

I don't know what it was, but I was getting a little bit excited and within an hour and after my dad's colossal bargaining tactic to either "throw in floor mats or we'd walk," I was motoring down Jefferson Avenue to the sounds of the Doobie Brothers and enjoying the smell and feel of my new car.

Standing just inside the school's doorway, I leaned back against the wall and began to watch both familiar and new faces pass by. Even the euphoria of my new wheels and the freshness of the new school year couldn't diminish the fact that this place just felt different. Gone was that warm feeling of being welcomed back to a place that you considered a comfort zone. Gone were Emolina, the athletic department staff and any indication that this was going to be the senior year that I expected.

I just couldn't walk any further, knowing that each step would bring back a memory of what *was*, and I wasn't too interested just yet, in what was *to be*.

Instead, I walked back outside to get a breath of fresh air and immerse myself into something that was the same, and rarely changed.

It was the old neighborhood, predominantly Polish and Slovak, that featured two-storied dwellings that butted up against one another. The streets were narrow and everything seemed to be in the protective shadow of Hedwig's gothic spires.

The church, school and parish were everything to this neighborhood. It was there to welcome the newly born with baptism. It was the focal point of one's fifth year, which signified the beginning of school. You confessed your sins there, received your first communion, were confirmed, married and yes, even came full circle and were even sent to your final resting place from there.

But it was just a building…a building that led to other buildings on the relatively smallish campus. There was the parish office, which doubled as the priest's residence that flanked the church to its left. Across the way and separated by the parking lot was the convent, a huge building that was hardly being used to its capacity, due to dwindling nun population. Only eleven nuns were actively working in the schools and were taking up residence in a building that, at one time, had housed three times the personnel.

To the front of the church, Junction Avenue stretched from Michigan Avenue north to Fort Street. Mom and Pop stores lined the mature and ever aging local area, meeting the ethnic and local needs of the neighborhood that they served.

Across from the athletic field that was southeast of the campus, stood the ever-present and steely confines of the Clark Avenue Cadillac Assembly Plant, the source of income for many of the community's households. Though old, the area still was bustling with a mix of industrial and old world flavor that gave Detroit its character.

In fact, Motown was just that … many local sprawling neighborhoods that doubled as ethnic settlements supported by both light and heavy industry and smalltime shop owners who just tried to squeeze out an honest buck.

The high school was broken into two parts. An older building that was three stories high and housed the gym on the very top floor, with the remaining floors used for classrooms for the underclassmen. In addition, there was a new section that was built in the early 70s, that was two stories and accommodated the seniors, the administrative offices, the athletic department and all science related studies.

Both buildings were nestled in a courtyard that was surrounded by a brick and wrought iron wall, and a walkway that was arched by the majestic oaks and maples.

I found myself at that particular point staring toward the school and shaking my head, wondering what awaited me on the inside, and if this was going to be a ride that I'd never forget?

With a student population slightly more than three hundred, compared to one of the giant public schools that resided within the city, like neighboring Southwestern who boasted a student body close to two thousand, Hedwig's was just a blip on the screen. But for me, smaller was better.

Within a week or two, you'd get to know everyone, whether you wanted to or not.

The unknown this year, however, was not the new students, but rather the new principal and her administrative staff. Rumor had it, that Archdiocese, as part of the contingency to reestablish the trust that was fractured as a result of the prior year's scandal, demanded that a disciplinarian be installed.

That individual turned out to be a slender, featureless, forty-something-year-old, who seemed almost robot-like, due to the fact that her arms remained straight and pointed downward when she walked. She wore horn-rimmed glasses and had a strange look that really didn't qualify as a stare, and seemed quite fidgety like a nut-gathering squirrel. It was hard to imagine that she and Emolina were from the same order.

In an attempt to make herself visible and to let the students know who the new sheriff in town was, she stood at attention just outside her office door. In her *warm and fuzzy* way, if you looked in her direction, she'd nod to you at a pace that made you think that her head was on a piston.

This wasn't a person; this was a half-size edition of the robot from *Lost in Space*.

Her *taken* name was Ann and she was to become the instant leader of the *them* side, in what would become a *hundred-day conflict of us against them.*

Knowing that all nuns usually have some sort of quirks, I actually gave her a double take as I passed by, because I couldn't believe what I saw. Funny thing, I actually felt the pace of my gait pick up as I passed by her, as if I was in a Hitchcock flick becoming concerned that *it* might try to reach out and get me.

Fortunately, I was able to make a swift turn to the right into what I hoped to be the comfy confines of the senior hall.

The first door to the left was Sister Erasmus' math class. Though we were quite aware of one another, I never had a class with her. She taught everything from advanced algebra to trigonometry, which simply left me in the dark.

It was business math for me, or as it was belovedly referred to by the rest of the student body: Bookie Math.

It gave us just enough skills to figure out the point spreads on the weekend games and the payoff odds on a tote board at the track. And quite honestly, the nun who taught the class, Sister Bertina, would use inferences from the track and even brought in a felt fabric official sized rolled up diagram of a craps table, that I believe she obtained from Sister Loyola's brother who was a pit boss at Caesar's Palace in Vegas, to teach us about odds and probabilities.

It was understood that a furlong equaled one-eighth of a mile, so obviously eight furlongs equaled a mile, or once around the track at the old Detroit Race Course. Subsequently, while the Erasmus' brainiacs were learning about load bearing ratios and metric equivalencies, we understood that Denver was the *eight furlong high city* and that a trip to the moon was a *shit load* of distance races!

We even used the *Daily Racing Form* to chart horse's performances, their owner's earnings and the standings of both trainers and jockeys. In fact, if memory suits, I don't recall ever using a textbook for that class during the year.

Erasmus, or "Razzie" was a workaholic and one of Emolina's old lieutenants. She was old school who thought that homework assignments needed to take you deep into the morning hours; at least that's what I was told.

Next on the route to my new homeroom was the aforementioned Sister Loyola's language class. She taught Spanish, French and German, to those of us, in her words, "could barely handle English."

If love was what I felt about Emolina, then I adored Loyola.

Simply, "she was my buddy."

We had a wonderful give and take relationship—I'd give and she'd take.

I'd give her all kinds of shit and trouble and she'd take it with a grain of salt, and give me every conceivable benefit of the doubt, regardless of what I would do.

The tradeoff was that when she needed something, I was there for her.

I think the reason I gravitated to her, was due to the fact that she was the spitting image of my grandmother. This was verified by the look on my mom's face the first time that they met during an orientation, when I entered Hedwig's as a freshman. It was an uncanny likeness that stunned my mom, who was very close to her mother, who we lost in 1968.

I don't believe that she ever failed anyone who took her class, which was quite amazing, because none of us, especially the fellas in our little gang ever learned or retained anything from her classes.

Sessions with her was more like the learning of the fine art of bribing than anything to do with language. As another holdover lieutenant from the Emolina regime, she taught with her heart "with a bit of a twist."

Like a man, the way to Loyola's heart was through her stomach. It was amazing that she didn't weigh in excess of four hundred pounds, because every day we would bring her some little treat that would keep the focus on anything, but her proposed assignments or us.

She loved all culinary treats, but the thing that she craved the most—doughnuts.

Ahead, there was a gathering of *the gang* at the door of Mrs. Pawlak's room. She taught English composition and was responsible for creating the yearbook.

If there was such a thing as nutritional intake injustice, she was the opposite of Loyola. For as much as Loyola put it away and didn't show any effects of her Herculean appetite, Pawlak ate like a sparrow but looked like the first one in line at the trough.

She was huge and it took all of your intestinal fortitude not to cringe just at the sight of her labored breathing. She was repulsively overweight, yet, you truly felt sorry for her.

The mystery about Pawlak was how did she have time to do all of the things that she did and still give birth to seven kids?

Plus, just by sight alone, we'd often joke that two or three extra kids still remained inside.

So why the fuss by her classroom doorway? Pawlak was congenial, but not enough to spend any more time with her than you had to. Besides, as previously mentioned, she was kind of scary to look at for any prolonged period of time.

Upon my arrival, not much was said, but then again, no one knew that I had shown up, because of what they were fixated on.

Standing on my toes and supporting myself on the shoulder of fellow senior Danny Otto, I, too, turned my head toward this point of attention. Like Moses gazing at the burning bush, I now found myself in the clutches of what the rest had been engrossed with.

As if delivered by the gods of male fantasies, a breath of fresh and radiant air stood before us. She was 5'5", maybe 5'-6", a hundred and ten pounds, tops! Blonde hair and blue-eyed, this twenty-something-year-old became the subject of an immediate male gawk-a-thon.

Her name was Carol Gainer and if this was going to be God's trade-off for taking Emolina out of our lives, though our hearts felt her absence, other parts of our anatomies began to tingle with the trade-off and this new arrival!

How could this beauty be standing in the very spot, that only months before was occupied by a pig with a bad dye job and a dental problem?

Maybe this wasn't going to be such a bad year after all?

She turned and smiled at the contingent of youthful male vermin at her doorway, knowing too well, that all hormonal and testosterone levels had to be spiking the meters. It was a smile that had just the right mix of innocence and invitation.

She wore a pale yellow colored dress which was knee-length, pump heels which accented a very nice pair of legs, but if I had my way ... the shoes might have been the only thing left on that perfect frame in a cozier situation just for two.

As the bell rang, we dragged our semi-hard-ons and lustful attitudes next door to our new homeroom. There, too, we would confront another female newcomer, art teacher, Valerie Sheddow.

Unfortunately, our classroom didn't hit the good looking new young female teacher lottery. Sheddow had an aggressive look. She was a redhead, who didn't quite have freckles on her face; rather they looked to be blotches of some sort.

As far as body was concerned, she kind of looked like an out of training body builder ... male body builder at that. Her tits had kind of blended in with her biceps and shoulders, giving her an upside down pyramid shape, with an ass that just merged into her hips and belly.

Notice, I said belly, not "tummy" or stomach. For she had a full-fledged pot, that she either tried to harness inside of a girdle or some other kind of restraint.

Yep, wouldn't you know it … this was our new morning mama, while just on the other side of the blackboard wall was eye candy!

Sheddow came out swinging, laying out the ground rules in her gravely toned voice, and by the time she was finished, there was already a note circulating labeling her "shithole."

She did give some reason to believe, however, that if you didn't bother her, she wasn't going to bother you. Which was the perfect morning game plan for us, because we were a bunch of stragglers, slow starters and repelled any heavy early morning regiments.

~ eight by eight ~

At 6'-1" 175 pounds, I was considered to be one of the best athletes in the school. I was academically sound, a strong B student; but like many wanna-be professional athlete dreamers, I was frequently lost in the clouds concocting visions that I scored the winning goal in the seventh game of the Stanley Cup Finals or popped the game winning homer into the left center field bleachers that propelled the Tigers into the World Series.

In my sophomore year, I was named to the Class D (School's under 500 student enrollment) all state baseball team, as the starting catcher, which I'm proud to say was a rarity and quite the accomplishment for a tenth grader!

I also played basketball for the school, and though I played last season and received clearance to play in my senior year, I decided not to play for the Knight football team, which didn't go over very well with the new head football coach.

Perhaps my best attribute though, was the ability to size-up and analyze a situation and implement a plan of action if necessary. It also didn't hurt that I could bullshit with the best of them, a gift that I think that I gained from my mom and certainly refined through my friends.

The way that shithole had her room set up was pretty simplistic. Remember, she specialized in art, so the tables were those eight-foot long numbers and she coupled them into groups of two, making four pods of desks and seating areas that were 8 x 8 squares. That gave the motley crew that I hung out with plenty of space for our morning briefings and to complain about what the day had in store for us.

There was no assigned seating … yet, so joining me in the back right corner were both friends and foes alike.

The criteria to be associated in this little gathering, fell somewhere between worthy enough to *join in* and *too dangerous to trust*. It was a smallish contingent of four-year members, who basically grew to either depend on or fear … no, make that respect one another.

In this alliance, there were true friendships and some necessary acquaintances, sort of like a cross between being in a mob family to a membership in the United Nations.

Among the players was Alvin Semko, previously introduced as Mick Selby's cousin who dubbed me Moose. I knew Al just as long as I knew Mick and he easily inherited best friend status with Mick's passing.

He was a little fireplug who was just full of the devil, and resembled his old man. They were cut from the same mold and like his dad, Al was street smart and whenever he found the possibility to take advantage of something, he did. It was a nice little angle that he would occasionally use in his life. More on that to come.

He, too, was given a playful nickname, which was Hodge. Derived from a couple of different perspectives. Story has it that as a little one, he was infatuated with the movie *Ali Baba and the 40 Thieves*, And when asked what his favorite movie was, he'd respond, "Hodgie Baba."

Still, others will tell you that his style of play on the ice when we played hockey, reminded them a lot of a pro star of the day who played for the Boston Bruins, Ken Hodge.

Regardless, Al was a pretty carefree type whose main objective in school was encompassed between being an entertainment director and a bookie.

In other words, through his dad's connections you could get a bet down on just about anything, including the fact that he was the local distributor of football cards, or parlay betting slips that I used to help him run.

If you wanted to go to the track, he and his dad were glad to let you tag along, because they were either at the old Detroit Race Course for the thoroughbreds or across the bridge in neighboring Canada at Windsor Raceway for the trotters at least every other day.

And on Friday nights, well now … that was reserved for the *all-nighter*, a poker game, which usually started at about ten o'clock and simply went through night and sometimes well into the next evening.

Also on the friend's side of the ledger was Adam Baker. A 6'4" drinking machine whose goal in life was to work for the county, drive a Lincoln Town Car and to lick the feet of school dolly, Wendy Kutzko. Which I wouldn't have mind doing myself!

Adam was an ultra laid-back guy who always sported two things that became his trademarks. His big belt buckles and his Foster Grants. It could be raining in the wee hours of the morning and he'd either be wearing his shades or they'd be perched just above his hairline.

He even had a bogus letter composed from his parents confirming that for medical reasons (sensitivity to light) that he needed to be able to *don* the shades during class. Oddly enough, that was never challenged or researched by the old guard of school administrators. Everybody else knew it was bullshit, but he got away with it and frequently would lower them to catch up on his beauty rest.

Last on the friend's side was Del Arrondo, the chick magnet. He was sort of a linguistic marvel, who found more ways to incorporate the word fuck into a sentence, better than anyone I had ever known.

This *gift* was well known both in and outside of the school and though most of us really didn't give it much of a thought, the teachers would refuse to call on him in class; for fear that he'd start something that they couldn't stop.

Genius when you think about it. He never had to worry about being called upon for answers or going up to the board, which is something that the rest of envied.

Though we all thought that we had decent looks, it was pretty much conceded that Del had that department pretty much *sewn up*. He was the California surfer type, who somehow sprouted up in Motown.

Not only did Del have the *looks*, but he had the perverted mentality to match.

This is the guy, who, for a class assignment that required us to create a dialogue with a major corporation, actually sent a formal suggestion to Kellogg's to introduce a line of adult cereals, called "Nipples and Tits, Apple Jack-off's" and the less than appetizing "Corn-holed Flakes." None to my knowledge ever made it into the product line.

Among the foes was Maxie Boughton, who was simply a shit. He just always seemed to be in the right place at the right time. Which had to be linked to the fact that was going steady with Bonnie "big tits" Lorenz. She was genuinely a sweet gal, who must have lost a bet or found herself in a pre-arranged situation to find herself in a relationship with this asshole. But for some reason, she remained loyal to him and always displayed affection for the guy.

Then there was Ronnie Crooks, who was more of a friend of Del's and had worked his way into the mix. We called him Coma, because if he wasn't sleeping, he always seemed to be walking around in a daze.

Without a doubt, my main adversary was J.J. Lambert, J.J. being short for Joel James, of whom I had briefly introduced you to when describing the events that attributed to the football fiasco.

J.J. and I always seemed to end up in the same places.

Honestly, I couldn't give you the name of a person who actually trusted him with anything. He was a lying, fucking snake who was always telling a tall tale and constantly touting his fortunes with the ladies … which earned him the label "Assanova."

To the plus side though, he had a *smoking hot* sister who was about six to seven years older than the lot of us, and secretly I always had a little thing for her. In addition, both she and her mother, a widow, were sweethearts. How this asshole came from this absolutely lovely woman was beyond me.

They were French, but must have been from the Mediterranean side. Olive-skinned, J.J. never had a hair out of place and was always neat. He accessorized more than most of the senior girls and if I had to give him credit for anything, he was a perfectionist.

Most of the time you could expect him to take the easy way out, but in some strange way, if you needed to get something done, or needed to find out the "true shit behind a story," he'd be your man. Which, considering his M.O., was difficult to conceive?

I always thought he would have made a great CIA agent, because he was the sneakiest shit of all.

In sports, he was always the one who took the cheap shot. In the classroom, he cheated all the time, and in social situations, especially to cause trouble or to avoid responsibility, he'd rat on anyone he could.

Like most of us, he had that ability to talk his way both into and out of trouble. Granted, he had more charm than the entire school put together, but the best thing to do with him, was to keep him on a short leash.

Finally among the boys, there was Saint Hedwig's dark prince, Roger Frost.

To draw you a physical picture, he looked like the son of the Mythical figure Thor. He had a ruggedly handsome face, was without facial hair and had a shoulder length blond mane that half of the girls in school would have killed for.

He was about my height and build and seldom showed any emotion. He wasn't much of a conversationalist, except in respect to his Tonto, a smallish fella named Matt Pevia, who was the closest thing that I ever had seen that resembled an albino.

What you wanted to achieve with Frost was not necessarily a friendship, but rather an *understanding*.

You didn't want him on your bad side, for his version of retaliation went way beyond our practical jokes, and jumped right to scary! In retrospect, I'd hasten to say that these two were on the road to *bigger and badder* things, and Hedwig's was just a pit stop on their way to twenty-five years to life.

Prior to matriculating at Hedwig's, I went to middle school with him at a place called Wilson Junior High. One day while in the seventh grade, we were on a field trip that found us at a renowned bird sanctuary in southwestern Ontario, Canada, called Jack Minors.

Even then, Frost was a recluse who seemed to *dig* on the fringes of terrorism.

In this huge aviary refuge, there were places where you could watch a wide variety of our flying friend's nest, feed or just hang out. Or, for the adventurous types, you could even go to a special location where the birds would fly right up to you to be fed.

For some reason, Frost seemed to be interested in the seagulls. He kept inching his way apart from us and was throwing something round and white in the gulls' direction. This was not the standard feed that we were issued, but rather, looked like communion hosts. In actuality, they were Alka-Seltzer tablets and he had to toss at least thirty in the direction of the scavenger birds.

What was considered to be no big deal at first, quickly turned into a *Jonestown* scenario for birds.

The gulls had a problem digesting the antacid and when they went to the near by watering hole, the water they drank would trigger the tablets to start dissolving, which, in turn, caused the chemical composition of the product to expand.

Now I don't claim to be an expert on birds or their ability to pass gas or burp, but if something is building up inside of you, and it has nowhere to go, it's going to either find the nearest escape route or create its own.

In the distance, the gulls were exploding like rosin bags hitting the ground.

I must admit when I saw what was happening, at first I was shocked … and then began to laugh at this feathery fireworks display.

Well, it didn't go over too well back on the bus ride home or subsequently in the principal's office upon our return, where Frost was suspended from school … one of several times.

Suspecting that justice was served and that the teacher showed Roger who was boss, it was thought that this issue was "signed, sealed and delivered." We came to understand, or shall I say suspect that you just never ... ever count Roger out.

While serving his weeklong suspension, Roger was obviously nowhere to be found. But, one morning just after the second hour bell rang; it was accompanied by a loud blast that came from the teacher's parking lot. Instructor Harold Redding's six-month-old Ford pickup was no longer the deep blue color that was its original shade. Instead, it was transformed into a fiery red and yellow blaze and, by the second, was turning into a deep shade of charcoal black.

Everybody knew that it was Frost who did it, but, of course, nobody could prove it.

So, I knew the maniacal side of Frost and got a shiver up and down my spine whenever he and Pevia would cloister.

Two gals represented the fairer sex. First, there was Annie Vita, a playful but passive sort whose loins seemed to constantly be on *go*. She looked like the Underdog cartoon character Sweet Polly Purebred, with nice full lips and the cutest little body, who, without even putting much effort into it; was the "perfect little tease."

She always gave me the impression that I was a simple phone call away from oral bliss with her.

The one thing that irritated me about Annie was that she always wanted to know more about something than you wanted to give. Like a pit bull reporter, she'd keep pushing and prying for more details.

If just for conversational purposes, you ever started telling her about a dream that you had, the rest of your day was fucked ... she was on you like flies on shit for details or the perceived meaning.

And then there was Shelley...Shelley Hench. A great looker who had a one simple problem in life; there was no way that she was ever going to find anyone who would love her, more than she loved herself.

I am convinced that when she masturbated, she encouraged herself and passionately cried out her own name.

At this place and time, I know that she thought that we were all just guests pivoting through the revolving door of her *world*.

She probably could have had anyone she wanted and flaunted that fact as well. Standing about 5'4" and about a hundred and ten pounds, this dark haired, dark-eyed bitch had it all: a killer body with a tight little ass, a nice full set of tits and a face that you wanted to both "blow your load on and then slap the shit out of."

She was the perfect example of the *mistress*. Someone who you just wanted to fuck, and then drop off at the next corner.

If you could have just sewn her mouth shut, she may have been worth hanging around, but that attitude and her fucking sarcasm, they were just too much for me. If she ever had a softer side, she rarely displayed it, which is probably the reason why I never made a play for her.

She was a player though. Involved in the student council, she was also the senior class vice-president. But, I think her main platform was that she was captain of the cheerleading squad. Which besides a bedroom or the stage of a strip tease parlor, I figured was the only place where she could publicly, at least at this age … dance, flaunt, tease and scream all at the same time.

It was rumored, but I think a sure thing that Del had been banging her on a pretty regular basis, despite his denial.

Funny thing though, she'd just smile at the mention of them being together. Regardless, he might have been the only one who could have matched her in a war of words … if you know what I *fucking* mean?

I'm all for the adage that "if you got it, flaunt it." But this one pushed the envelope to the limit.

As if we were in mid-season form, the first day banter got right to the point and fast.

"Who was this new English teacher, and how does one get into her pants?"

"Fuck, Moosie, what a hot fuckin' babe," Del uttered, "Wouldn't ya love to fuck that?"

Smiles developed and eyebrows rose at the mere mention.

"In your fucking dreams," Hodgie responded. "She's gotta already be with somebody!"

Just by the nodding of heads, most seemed to agree with that logic, but even the remote possibility of being with her was worth the thought.

"Christ, could you imagine hookin' up with something like that," I injected.

Without skipping a beat, the cunt blurted out, "You said it dickhead, imagine, because that's the closest you'll ever get to her … only in your imagination. Oh yeah, and with the help of a box of Kleenex."

Her remarks reddened my face and brought out a hearty laughter among the group.

Pissed and with a crooked smile on my face, I responded, "Blow me, Shelley." To which, she fired back with a sinister little laugh, "another long shot that'll never happen in your life, needle dick," and as she strutted away the table, went into hysterics over the verbal beating that she gave me.

All of a sudden Frost called out to Shelley, "Alright, trench mouth, who in this group has the best chance to get her?" A query no one expected from him.

She looked back at him with a look of disgust and said, "Are you kidding me? Not a single one of you has a chance. She's a college grad, living on her own, who knows, at best, that you're nothing but a lesson plan for her. Maybe … just maybe she might cock tease you assholes, but that's it … so learn to live with it."

Then she offered, "Face it, the good ones …" and you could just see that she had included herself into that category, "can pick and choose the ones that we want."

And though she turned, she was compelled to do an about face when J.J. blurted out, "You mean she'll finger dip thinking about us too … like you do?"

The laughter peaked to a fever pitch and she just looked at him before flipping him "the bird."

To which J.J., fired right back, "Yeah right, that's the finger that I was talking about!"

She just turned away in disgust and went out in the hall to her locker.

"Ah, who are we kidding," I said. "She's a young teacher, fresh out of college, and I'm sure she's already got some guy … and we're here in fucking high school."

"Yeah, but everybody's got to start at the fucking bottom," Del reminded. "So she can start right down here, near my fucking bottom with the mother fucking drill master," he added as he grabbed his crotch.

Adam then looked in my direction and said, "Hey, man, if you think that mobile fish tank that you drive is going to woo her, think again."

Through the laughter, I fired back saying, "Hey, go fuck yourself, Captain Schwinn."

Baker would ten-speed his way to and from school on days that the weather permitted.

"I don't see her diggin' a ride on the handle bars of your ten speed, down Michigan any time soon."

Just then, as if all at once, it clicked into our heads at the same time, we all looked over at J.J., who over the summer became the owner of a new Pontiac Firebird, with the removable roof, (T-tops) leather seats, a great stereo system and with sleek lines ... the cars too.

I just looked out the window and thought, *of all the fucking people.*

Could this cock sucker, with his line of shit persuade this fantasy babe, and his high school English teacher yet, into a seductive situation? I mean, he's not the homeliest looking guy on the planet ... and yes, in comparing wheels ... well, there was no fucking comparison ... shit!

As the bell rang to start classes, everybody started to file out while I just sat, stared and wondered.

— when you're on the wrong side of the fence —

The first couple of weeks back were like the opening rounds of a prizefight, a feeling out process. Things were settling into a routine with little, if any fanfare. The new principal, though on the scene, was conspicuously keeping herself out of sight and remained tepid.

The Knight football team had a lot of new faces, from the coaching staff throughout the roster, but, unfortunately, the results remained the same.

They were playing under a lot of scrutiny and under the watchful eye of the Catholic League officials. Why though … was beyond most comprehensions, because this year's edition of the team was just as bad, if not worse than the past couple of editions.

And though I know that I shouldn't have been so critical, being that I refused to play, "fuck 'em," I was entitled to my opinion. Their dubious streak had now run to seventeen games and the forecast was for more of the same.

Academically, things sort of mellowed out quickly as well.

As a senior, you're warned to "Keep your grades up if you want to get into a good school." What they forgot to tell us was that the college recruiters start really paying attention to your transcripts dating back to your sophomore year…so "Thanks for the fucking head's up!"

Still, it didn't seem like many in the graduating class had much in the way of aspirations of going to college. Most seemed concerned with either finding a job that wouldn't screw up their weekend plans or advancing in the shitty counter jobs that they currently had.

As seniors, we didn't necessarily have a long day in the school itself. It would start at 8:10 A.M. and conclude right around the noon hour. A number of the seniors who had jobs would leave school; grab a quick bite to eat and then to work.

Still in all, the predominate attitude seemed to be, "Socially this place is cool, it's just the work load that's crampin' my style!"

For those of us whose parents allowed us to *play out* our prep careers, school was our work place to study, participate in sports and who am I kidding ... *getting ready for the weekend*!

The first Friday night poker game of the school year was upon us. But to the regulars, it wasn't that big of a deal, because it was just a continuation of the summer, and before that spring, and before that winter games.

You could set you internal clocks on these *sure things*.

Sunday mass was at 10:00 A.M. School started every weekday at 8:10 A.M. And the first hand was dealt every Friday night at Al's house at 10:00 P.M. Everything else in life was a crapshoot, but you could *bank on those institutions*.

The only modifications to the poker games, was on occasions some *sit-ins*, or temporary players to fill in for those who might have gone to either see the football team get thrashed during the fall, or if we had a late night hockey game in the winter or a softball game in the summer, or decided to catch the trotters at the track.

But if you were going to be absent, the best-case scenario was when you were on a pussy hunt and hopefully about to get lucky. Even then, however, the loyalty to the game was like being instructed by your folks to call if you're going to be out later than expected, which would happen.

There would, occasionally, be calls from one of the regulars to indicate that he would be a little late, "but to keep a seat warm for him."

One time we got a call from Del, who was in Toledo chasing this chick that he had met at the Fairlane Mall back in neighboring Dearborn. Knowing that he was about sixty miles away, he said that he was just about to "break the barrier," which meant that he was moments away from getting "some."

Recognizing that carnal bliss was not only the priority for most of the younger players, would have lead one to believe that he was going to be a "snatch scratch" for the night. But in his unique way, he said, "I'm gonna fuck her ... then get fucking rid of her; so I'll be there in a couple of hours."

Which he knew, meant that the game would just be warming up by the time he arrived.

The one unwritten law that had become adopted by the gang down through the years, and instituted by the *man* of the house, Al's dad, was that if you showed up late, you had to bring a snack for the players. This despite the fact that Al's mom, Lottie, always had a poker-playing banquet set up for the game in which we'd cut the pot (or take out a small portion) until we paid for all of the food.

"Where's the little son of a bitch at?" Koobs asked.

"Toledo," Al responded.

"How long's he going to be?"

Al answered, "A couple of hours."

While contemplating his current hand, Koobs looked across the table at me and said, "What do ya think, Moosie?"

I smiled back and knew what he was alluding to. I'm 100% Hungarian, and Toledo is home to the one and only Tony Pacco's and their world-renowned Hungarian hot dogs.

"I'll take two with the works, Papa," I said to the elder Semko.

"Sounds like a winner," he said back to me.

The total was an even dozen by the time Al tallied the count and sure enough, after a couple of hours our boy had "dipped his wick, dropped off the chick and delivered the goods ... what a great rule!"

Let me tell you a little more about Koobs. Physically, he was a cross between Bowery Boy, Huntz Hall and Popeye the Sailor Man. He was a good provider and made all of us feel like family. He was, in essence, a boy in a man's body, who loved hi-jinx, games and the fact that a youthful troupe enjoyed his company.

He promoted the benefits of a strong education on one hand, yet would often petition us to cut classes in lieu of an early lunch, and a couple of games of euchre before heading out to the track. Then, he'd make sure that dinner was waiting for us before demanding that our homework was complete, before he'd let me go home.

I didn't know if this was coddling or corruption. But these people were my second family, and often I found myself in their company just as much as my own family's.

It was the kind of relationship where I was expected to let myself into the house; take whatever I wanted out of the fridge and spend the night if I wanted.

The games were always played in the kitchen. The regulars were Koobs and Al, their neighbors Earl and his wife, Joan, who was a tough little cookie at the table, Del, occasionally Adam and me.

If we needed a sit in, Mick Selby's mom, Marianne, who was Lottie's sister would sit in, or Lottie herself.

Every once in a while, one of the gang from school or a friend of Kooba's from work would show up, and even my mom would leave her usual weekend game and show up if we were desperate.

The games always started out as nickel and dime events and were *always* on the *up and up*. Well, make that 99.9% of the time. There was a slight deviation for assholes that were either winning too much, or gloating about their play.

The rule was that regulars and family members were never targets, but for those *who asked for it*, they got it!

Prior to Mick's passing, the scam was perpetrated by Koobs, Al and Mick. But with Mick gone, I was next in line to join this elite force. I had been the target of this ploy in the past and was aware of its very humbling effects.

Any decent poker player knows that at some time or in some place, you will face the prospects of somebody who's trying to cheat the game. There are a thousand little tricks that have been pulled a thousand different ways, but if you're really going to *work* a game, true scam artists know that you target only one player and only one pot a night. One very strategic pot.

The object is to deal the targeted player such a good fucking hand that they just couldn't fold, no matter what the size of the pot was. But regardless of whatever the pawn had, you could bet your bottom dollar, which is what you did, that it was second best.

For either Al or I would be dealt the best hand by the *man* himself.

This is where I marveled about Koobs. His hands were noticeably affected by his many years on the job as a beer and pop deliveryman. In addition, arthritis had set in and had caused a disfiguration in both between the thumb and index finger.

At times, it looked as if he couldn't even hold a full deck, but make no mistake about it, he could set a hand up that would marvel even the slickest of *stackers, maskers and fixers of decks*.

Nothing seemed to be on for the night, until about the 2:00 A.M. hour. Being that the house was lit up, it wasn't surprising that just about anyone might show up.

This sting was going to be a no-brainer. Already half in the bag and flashing a decent wad of cash which included a couple of fifties, J.J. showed up of boasting tales about girls and good times, while constantly taking shots at, of all people, me.

My grandfather used to have a saying, "Feed the monkeys peanuts and watch 'em shit."

Or to translate, let this jerk-off just talk, because it's nothing but lies and nonsense.

Koobs subscribed to the treasured adage, "A fool and his money are soon parted."

J.J. was not only making an ass out of himself, but he was never one of Koobs' favorites to start with, which in this forum was a dangerous combination.

For an hour or so, J.J. was left unscathed and in fact, was doing pretty well. He was, as usual, both nicely dressed and groomed, which went hand and hand with his razor-sharp attitude.

"Hey, Marcus," he said as he looked in my direction.

"What can I do for ya?" I playfully responded.

"Guess who I was with tonight?"

I just shrugged my shoulders.

"Diiiiaaaannnnneeeee," he stated with glee.

The Diane that he was referring to was Diane Stankowicz, the daughter of our hockey coach and someone who everybody at the table knew that I had a little thing for as well.

I tried to act unimpressed, but it must have shown that he was getting under my skin.

"Eweeeeee, baby, she sure looked good, and by the way, sweetie, I told her about your new wheels," he said as he began to laugh in a sarcastic tone. "And she's really looking forward to seeing it," he continued as the intensity of his laughter grew.

I'm sure that the color of my face was an acting thermostat, because I was getting hotter by the moment.

"You know, Joel, if you'd like some toilet paper to wipe your lips up after all the shit that's come out of your mouth, I'd be happy to get some for you," Lottie said as she crocheted over in the corner. "Besides, I like my Moosie's car!"

"Thank you, love," I turned and said to her.

"Anyway J.J.," she continued, "you have a 'jig-mobile,' with those big tires and the holes in the roof."

I almost fell off my chair when I heard her say that, but just loved the anguished look of surprise on his face!

"Ma!" Al said in both a reprimanding and peace keeping way. "Watch how you say things!"

I, on the other hand, started to chuckle to myself, still shocked to have heard her mutter those words.

Meanwhile, Koobs interjected, "Leave her alone … it does look like a nigger's car," he said while studying the cards in his hand.

Again, Al and I seemed to be the only ones shocked to hear this kind of talk, because I knew, or at least I thought I knew that neither one of them had a prejudice bone in their bodies. In fact, I seen both of them open up their hearts and their home to Blacks, Hispanics and others in the past.

"But, Dad," Al interjected.

"Don't gimme any shit, Hodgie," Koobs said. "You know that I have nothing but respect for Jimmy Dobbs and Big Willie McRae down at the plant, and they're Black. They've been in this house and I've been to theirs, they're great people.

Niggers, on the other hand, are boastful, arrogant assholes who have no respect for anybody or anything. They can be any fuckin' size, shape or color … and they usually dress and act like him and drive cars like his," he continued as he raised his eyebrows while his bifocals slid down the bridge of his nose.

Al tried to quickly defuse the situation by changing the subject, but J.J. and the lot of us were still in a mild state of shock.

Then Joan spoke and indirectly would gut J.J. as she said to Lottie while letting a Pall Mall droop from her lips and examining her cards, "Sweetie, this one reminds me of why men are like cards."

Lottie smiled and petitioned, "Do tell, Joanie baby."

"Well," she uttered, "you need a heart to love 'em, a diamond to marry 'em, a club to beat 'em and a spade to bury 'em."

Some idle laughter just went through the room, but we got the meaning behind her dig.

A few minutes went by, when, all of the sudden, Koobs gave the signal by standing up and going into his back pocket to get his hanky. He would subsequently blow his nose and whatever back pocket that he would return the hanky to, the one of us who was on the side of the return, was going to be dealt the winning hand.

This, too, was going to be a no-brainer; I knew that he was going to give me the pleasure of sticking it to that swarthy cocksucker. Plus, he knew that J.J. was just aching to rub my face as deep as he could into the proverbial mud.

Koobs would set the deck up just the way it had to be. But Al's role was perhaps the most important, because he was the gas man. The term given to the guy who would simply fuel the pot by constantly raising.

So, everything was set and old fuck face, buzzed from the drink ... cocky from a number of winning hands ... and still pissed by both Lottie and Kooba's recent comments about his car, was about to get his best hand of the night ... albeit second best during this hand.

The betting was hot and even Earl was of the mind-set that he had a chance to win. The limits were now pretty much open and all of us were dipping into our reserves. After discarding and getting the back-end of the draw, the betting resumed at a fevered pace.

Within a matter of minutes, all of J.J.'s winnings, his original bankroll and an additional $45 that he pulled light or borrowed from the pot, were in the middle of the table. The fish was snagged; and all that remained now was to watch him squirm before reeling his ass in.

"I took out Diane earlier and I'm gonna to take you out right now, asswipe," he said as he smiled and looked right into my eyes.

It was moment of truth time and he revealed aces full of jacks (a full house).

I looked back at him and said, "Pretty good ... I just have two pairs."

To which, he began to smile while he looked over toward Al and said, "Two pairs ... do you believe this guy, Hodgie?"

As he reached to rake in the pot, I stopped his motion and said, "I told you that I had two pairs ... a pair of red deuces and a pair of black deuces."

The look on his face was payment enough.

"Wow, that's a tough beat, J.J.," Koobs sarcastically fired into his direction. "Oh, by the way; you owe the pot forty-five bucks. So why don't you either call Diane up and have her bring it over for you, or jump in that Neeeegro car and get it from your mommy."

He fell back into his seat and seemed to sober up by the second.

J.J. was bust in both spirit and in stake, which is what we ate with our eggs and hash browns at the end of the game while we split up the money that was creatively separated from dickweed, and divied up by the coalition.

I could hardly wait for next Friday!

~ let the games begin ~

The pursuit of Miss Gainer continued in conversation, but the conception of actually scoring with her was dampened by the word that she was *involved* with a medical resident at the University of Michigan. Which explained the fresh floral arrangements that would grace the corner of her desk at the start of each new week.

But we were seventeen- and eighteen-year-old sex-starved (except for Del) and cum-filled deviants, who were swimming around in a tank with this *angel fish*, and sooner or later, something had to give.

With this in mind, I turn to the Biblical reference and quote "And a babe shall lead them." Well, more like a boob in this case.

The composition class that I was in with Gainer was predominately filled with seniors, but had a few juniors also. Those juniors who were in the class, however, deserved to be there through merit and because they were exceeding their peers in academic proficiency.

The exception, however, was that somehow Bobby Selby got into this class ... which was like trying to figure out the mystery behind the Immaculate Conception.

If the name now seems familiar to you, you're correct in assuming that this was the other son of Bob and Marianne and the brother of Mick.

Bobby was the complete opposite of his departed brother. Where Mick was neat and clean, Bobby was a slob. If Mick was cunning and the smart one, Bobby was the attention seeker who would purposely brag about things that he shouldn't have, and couldn't back up.

He was stupid and needed remedial help in hygiene, let alone all of his studies.

For those of us who knew both he and his deceased sibling, it was hard to believe that these two were from the same mother.

But he possessed something that far exceeded his brother's abilities; Bobby had *balls* and a well-earned reputation for reckless abandon. If a stunt was possible, Bobby was in. If it promoted childish antics and trouble, more than likely he was at the core of it.

For example, he had a run-in with a couple of the female lay teachers about something ridiculous and purposely got himself relegated the next day, to after-school cleanup duties. He then volunteered to faculty bathroom cleanup, and after he scrubbed the toilets, basins and the facility down ... he went on the attack.

It was a simple mission, but one that would be effective and have definite results.

He took clear polyethylene food wrap, like something you would seal your kid's sandwiches in, and stretched it as tight as possible across the opening of the toilet bowl. Well, unless you examined the opening with precision, you couldn't tell if the drop was open, or as in this case, not.

Suffice to say, the next morning Mrs. Jennings, the Health teacher and target of his attack, went for her morning constitutional and instead of executing the *perfect drop*, found her *deposits* deflected into her unmentionables and garments that were positioned at her ankles. It was a good laugh, but all trails lead to Bobby and he would just get himself into deeper trouble.

He was nicknamed the Muskie after the warrior fish, because like the namesake, he had an incredible mouthful of teeth and would put up one hell of a fight.

The other less than endearing thing that could be said about Bobby concerned his appearance. Unfortunately, he had hit the ugly trifecta at birth, and it didn't get any better as he matured.

Let me try to paint an image. I really think that *Mad Magazine* used his face for their poster boy, Alfred E. Newman. Mix in a little of the Bugger character from the *Revenge of the Nerds* movies and a dash of the Schultz's *Peanuts'* regular Pig Pen, and there you have it ... our Bobby.

He was anything but subtle and hygiene was definitely not one of his strengths. In fact, he would sleep in the clothes that he was going to wear the next day, just to gain a few extra minutes of sleep the next morning.

Adam Baker once provided the definitive copulation of Bobby. "He was a walking Petri dish, who doubled as an unmade bed and combed his hair semi-annually."

It was a rather grayish looking day outside and the leaves that had been dislodged from the trees were being blown around by a rather stiff autumn wind.

Gainer was going over an assignment that she had been discussing over the past couple of days, when all of a sudden, she went to the board in the front of the room and began to write something. After completing her illustration, she asked for a volunteer to come up to the board to break down some kind of proper grammatical bullshit.

Without hesitation, Bobby sprung to his feet and quick stepped it to the front of the class.

"Oh," said Gainer in a halfhearted response to his appearance on the scene, "well, okay then, Bobby, you'll do."

Her surprise was due to the fact that Bobby never volunteered for anything, especially if it had any type of scholastic relationship. He was as out of place at that board, as Pavarotti would have been in a spittoon-leaden speakeasy in Alabama.

He was obviously there for the attention and to be close to the *honey pot*.

So, when he shocked the world and actually got the desired results, the class became dumbfounded over this display, of what could only be termed divine intervention.

With a furrowed brow, Del, who sat a seat in front of me and a row to my left looked back at me and said, "Did we just witness a miracle?"

Meanwhile, Gainer approached Bobby to congratulate him and gave him a simple pat on the shoulder. To which the Muskie looked back at her and stated, "I think I deserve more than that ... don't you?"

An instant look of confusion came over her face, followed by a disconcerting laugh, "I'm sorry Mr. Selby?"

"Come on, baby," he said, "gimme a little sugar."

And like a bear coveting and smothering his prey, the Musk had grabbed the beauty and proceeded to give her one hell of a *lip job*, while simultaneously squeezing a generous portion of her ass.

As the guys in the room urged on the *beast*, the girls were screaming and being repulsed by this vision, of what I'm sure was a reoccurring nightmare that each one of them had had in the past ... not being ravaged per say ... but being ravaged by Bobby.

Gainer was putting up a valiant struggle, but the Musk was winning this scrum.

The sight of this was too much for some, including goodie-two-shoes junior, Missy Galevich, who streaked out of the class and down toward the office to get the cavalry.

By the time Ann and Nazi football coach, Stu Lynch, arrived on the scene, Bobby was beaming those muscovite teeth and receiving high fives from the fellas in the room.

Gainer had exited and had subsequently made her way to the teacher's lounge.

Bobby was now being hauled down to Ann's lair, as well as the seven of us who were caught offering him kudos for *breaking down the barrier*.

As we sat outside Ann's office awaiting some sort of obvious punishment, Lynch, who as mentioned earlier was really pissed at me for not coming out for football, looked in my direction and said, "Didn't you have the balls to stop him from doing this?"

I looked right back at him and said, "No, but I'd like to ask him where he got 'em so that I could pick up a pair."

"You little smart ass," he issued back at me while pointing. "If you had the guts to come out for football, you wouldn't have this kind of attitude."

I just smiled to myself and said, "Yes, sergeant!"

"You're all talk and no action … aren't you, smart-ass?" he barked back.

Just then Dickie Gracie, one of the seven who was dragged down to the office said, "Why are you getting on him, coach?"

"Quiet, Grace," Lynch responded.

"It's Gracie," Dickie replied.

"No, the way you play, it's Grace," he fired back at him. To which, you could just see Dickie say to himself, "I'm gonna get that fucking prick."

And Dickie was just one of the *dynamic duo*. When he and his twin brother, Kiki, got together … *danger*. More about them to come.

Lynch returned his stare to my direction, to which I just looked back while wearing a shit-eating grin.

Marianne and Bob would end up making the first of what would be many trips to pick up their ill-fated son for some sort of infraction. This one was worth a week's detention and the cleaning of all bathrooms in the school for another week, which occurred after classes upon his return. Which makes one wonder, *Didn't they learn anything from his last stint in their bathrooms?*

While being escorted off campus by his parents, his dad was just shook his head in disgust, while Marianne berated him with admonishments, followed by an occasional slap.

But the look on his face said it all; there was this half smile that simply stated, *Hey it was worth it!*

Furthermore, despite all of our claims and talk about what we wanted to do to the sweet looking instructor, he knew that he was "one up on the field … a big one!"

A funny side bar to this story, and one that raised Gainer's stock in our opinion of her, was that the very next day, she not only was able to shake this incident off, but she gave the exact same task to another guy in the class. However, before she allowed him to start, she went into her personal cloakroom at the back of the class and when she reappeared, she was wearing a Hedwig football helmet, face mask and all.

Without saying a word, the class broke into hysterics upon seeing her and gave her a standing ovation for being a good sport about this whole thing.

I think she knew that she had gained much more than our carnal schoolboy desires … she had really gained our respect.

Bobby's heralded but sort of stupid preemptive move set the administration and faculty on high alert. But what the new leadership didn't understand was that the student body wasn't an aggressive group, that wasn't our style.

The seniors, especially our little band were more of a reactionary bunch. If you didn't move on us, we wouldn't move on you. But try to cut the knees out from underneath us, and expect an answer.

Hopefully there wouldn't be much of a need for an adversarial position on the part of the different sides, however, if they were going to start a Cold War period … then so be it. We weren't going to be the first to blink!

On the second floor of the newer wing of the school were the science rooms, comprised of chemistry and biology. The rooms sat next to one another and were connected by a little hallway that was divided by a steel door without windows. This department, too, was restructured with a new breed of instructors.

The chemistry teacher was a guy by the name of Charlie Fuji, a strange guy with an even stranger name. It wasn't that Fuji was obscure, but this guy didn't have a hint of Asiatic heritage to him. And if you asked him about the origin of his sire name, he'd just look back at you with a dopey expression on his face and shrug his shoulders. Which, according to most of the students that had him for class, was sort of the way he taught.

It quickly became apparent that he really didn't know what the hell he was doing, which made him a perfect fit in this school.

He had a full, flat head of jet-black hair and a beard/mustache combination that was the type that one grows, without ever attempting to shave in his life. You know what I mean; the facial hair was just as soft and smooth as the hair on his head. He didn't have one coarse strand from the neck up.

His colleague next door was a dude named James Ball. Dude was the operative word in describing this one, because he was deposited here right out of the shooting acid days of Hippy flower-powered love.

He had the Jesus look down to a tee, with just the right dash of John Lennon's specs for style.

He only had two pair of shoes, earth shoes that he wore when it snowed, and sandals that he wore all of the rest of the time. Occasionally with the sandals he would wear either a soiled pair of white or gray stockings on those days where he must have considered it too cold for bare feet and too hot for the ugly earth cold-hoppers.

Also, he'd either wear a pair of black or brown corduroy pants … always wrinkled and seldom cleaned.

This was the kind of guy, that *if* he washed his clothes in college, when he went to the campus Laundromat, and would wear one of the two outfits that he owned, while the other was going through the cycle … and when that was done, he'd change in the establishment's washroom and repeated the process with the other outfit.

But in the case of Ball, the word if was paramount.

This guy made Robbie Selby look as if he just stepped out of the pages of *GQ Magazine*.

Oh, and one other thing about Ball, he stunk, and not just a little. In fact, I don't know how he got through the interview process for this job, because he reeked from Day One.

Ball was the student body's response or example, when a faculty member would question the hygienic practices of Muskie. We'd fire back and say, "Hey, what about *clear the hall* Ball?" Discussion over!

Chemistry class, even in the most guarded of places is a risky proposition at best, but at Saint Hedwig's the need for concern was heightened due to the presence of the Gracie brothers: Kiki and Dickie.

Fraternal twins, these two were dangerous not because of their intellect, but rather in the manner of how they conducted their experiments. They never tried to purposely cause harm or danger to anyone, but if you were in their immediate vicinity, you were at risk.

Like the wonderful Greek heritage and the great chefs of their background, the boys tended to subscribe to Mama Gracie's "pinch of this and dash of that" theory of chemical composition, or to coin the old typing cliché, they "hunted and pecked" their way through the periodic table and never ever went by the book.

When separated, they were bad enough, but put them together, and it was a certainty that they'd taunt and dare each other into trouble. So putting them anywhere in the proximity of hazardous materials was more than just a calculated risk.

Small fires, toxic smells and minor explosions were almost daily occurrences for the dynamic duo, and despite an anxiety for all who were in class with these two, both the third hour chemistry and biology classes appreciated the fact, that if they needed some sort of interruption or early dismissal, that we could count on a "Gracie bomb." Which would be something with just enough *oomph* to it, to command a brief evacuation. It was a perfect way to screw up a lesson plan or to cause a diversion.

Dickie got what little brains that were passed on through Mama and Papa's DNA, but Kiki was fearless to the point where he didn't even care about the need to be inconspicuous if they were plotting something. The other thing about him was that he had a very short fuse.

Even Fuji knew that in the interest of safety and higher insurance premiums, these two had to be in opposite ends of the room. But even then, they'd either signal one another or have some sort of cadence to joust from afar. In essence, it was still a pretty loose voyage around the chemical world for the Brothers Grim, until ... green rub.

Both of the twins played on the current year's edition of futility in motion, the football team. Like most of the guys on the squad, they were pissed at the fact that they were the laughing stock of both the Catholic League and pretty much the entire ranks of prep football throughout the metropolitan Detroit area.

The twins, if nothing else, were committed to trying to turn the fate of our gridiron heros around, and in doing so, brought some of the principles that they learned in the classroom into the locker room.

For instance, the team's tail back, Benny Menendez, had a horrible tendency of fumbling the ball … on average of four times a game.

The coaches did everything within the rules to help him with this problem, which included an application of stick-'em, a substance that was supposed to help him hold onto the ball … but it didn't.

To the rescue, our Greek chefs of disaster, who created their own version of stick-'em that was a bit on the extra goopy side. So much in fact, that after being tackled for his league lagging 1/3 of a yard average, the ball would be difficult to extract from his arms. When the officials asked for the ball to be replaced at the line of scrimmage, Benny couldn't hand it over to them.

Needless to say, the one series experiment didn't go over to well. But, at least Benny didn't cough up the pigskin!

Still another brainstorm of the twins was to coat up the jerseys of the team's entire front line, of which Kiki was a part of, with white lithium grease. The object here was to do just the opposite to the opposing team's linemen than the desired results with Benny … make their hands slippery, so that they couldn't grab on to or tackle any of our players.

Now this one had promise, until our training staff couldn't get the grease and grime out of the jerseys when they tried to clean them. In fact, there was so much of a build up of stains and ground-in dirt that the entire line's jerseys remained noticeably discolored compared to the rest of the team's for the remainder of the season.

They were dirty looking even before games, despite whatever cleaning techniques or solutions used to get rid of the stains. This, too, was another shelved gridiron experiment.

The twins certainly had the right intentions and the will; they just couldn't put all of the pieces together.

Ridiculed by Coach Lynch for both their inept play and unethical means of deception, the brothers were verbally hung out to dry.

Unlike his predecessor, Lynch was quite small and a little bit on the pudgy side. He had a head full of curly brownish-blond hair, and according to the guys on the team, enough body hair to make a bear envious.

But you really didn't need to hear that from the fellas to gather that Lynch had went to the hair buffet one too many times. He always wore a short sleeved, undersized T-shirt with some sort of school logo on it. This provided more than enough evidence to validate Lynch's excess mane.

It was as if this guy was part of the evolutionary chart, in line with some of the other creatures just as man was learning how to stand up right.

He honestly had so much hair packed into so little clothing, that he looked like an exploded Brillo pad, the way the hair protruded out of the neck and armholes of his shirt.

Like his display against me in the waiting area of the principal's office when Muskie made that move on Gainer, Lynch usually employed a battlefield diplomacy; he yelled all of the time.

Needless to say, that gets tiring awfully fast, and to the guys on the team, even before the halfway point in the season, they had just about had it.

But Lynch liked fucking with the twins, which many of us thought was sort of a death wish. He would verbally beat them up on the sidelines, during practice and in the halls during class changes.

He would effeminize his voice and call them Grace just to piss them off … which would just irk the shit out of Kiki.

Like the old cliché goes, however, "You can only go to the well so often," and Lynch dipped on the twins one too many times.

October saw a rapid return to cooler weather, and a common practice among the football team was to apply a moisturizing and warming substance to your skin, before going out into the cold, called green rub. It would allow you to wear less layers of clothing and still keep you comfortable in the face of the cooler elements. This was not only a player's aid, but was also incorporated by the coaches.

Usually, one would self apply the formula generously on their body, but for the areas that were hard to reach, one would employ the help of one of the trainers to complete the process.

Lynch also made green rub part of his outdoor preparation, and had it applied by the head trainer during a pre-practice rub down that he routinely received.

Unlike their normal fly by the seat of your pants classroom methods; the twins were about to gain their revenge on the unsuspecting coach, via a thoughtful and methodical scheme.

Prior to what promised to be a normal after school practice, Kiki, as was his habit, would go into the training area to have his ankles taped for additional support. Then he would meet Dickie in the weight room for a little pre-practice lift session. However on this day, the boys staged a pre-taping get together in the weight room that would purposely see them get into an altercation.

Kiki was to be the aggressive one, which he normally was, but this needed to be embellished beyond normal expectations. This had to be a performance that was going to captivate and gain the attentions of their targets. And though the twins probably would have had volunteers lined up to join in on this one, they took little to chance and wanted this to remain as covert as possible.

The scuffle broke out with the sounds of objects being thrown, cursing and all that was needed to command a lot of attention. Meanwhile, Lynch and head trainer, Bob Collins, were about to commence the coach's rub down. But the sounds of trouble would compel them to rush to the scene and try to quell the combatants.

Though a few players in the weight room were separating the twins, Lynch and Collins were now on site to intervene.

Kiki, as planned was relentless. "You fucking pussy," he screamed at his brother, "if you would only work as hard as coach asked, we'd be able to turn things around, but you're nothing but a fucking complainer!"

"Oh fuck you, you kiss ass motherfucker! You gotta stick your head up his ass like he's something special, he's just a fucking coach," Dickie lashed out, "and a shitty one at that!"

That didn't sit too well with Lynch who went toward Dickie and grabbed him in effort to help separate the two.

Lynch was actually encouraged to at least get a little support and see a "fire burn in the bellies" of a couple of his players. But hearing Dickie's rather negative attack on him, compelled Lynch to pull Dickie aside to address him first.

He actually strong-armed and bullied Dickie out of the training area and down the hall quite a spell to his office. Before leaving, Lynch looked over his shoulder back toward Kiki and said in a friendly way, "Kiki, you okay, fella?"

When Kiki responded affirmatively, Lynch instructed Collins to look after him until he got back. Things obviously cooled down, which is just what the twins planned. Stage Two was about to commence.

For this to work, a little outside help was necessary. With Collins now attending to Kiki, he asked if he wanted to get his taping done while he cooled off. Kiki agreed and Collins began the process. The trainer was employing small talk and some consoling efforts, when all of a sudden, a compensated underclassmen, Marty Bresheski rushed into the training room yelling for help.

"Mr. Collins ... Mr. Collins!"

"What's wrong?" answered the guinea pig.

"It's my sister, Julie, I think she broke her ankle or something," he said in a rushed and breathy manner.

She was a cheerleader who had a thing for Dickie, and faked a sprained ankle during their practice that was taking place in the third floor gym.

Injuries took precedence over all else, so Collins grabbed his bag and left Kiki ... all alone ... and with absolutely no one else around. The smile hit Kiki's face as soon as Collins hit the door ... Stage Three.

Kiki went into his locker and removed a gallon container of what was soon to be known as "Gracie's green rub."

First, he went to Collins cabinet that was open and accessible. Of the eleven eight-ounce bottles of green rub that was in the cabinet, he dumped all of their contents down the drain except for three that were earmarked for the players, so that Collins couldn't draw upon that now limited supply.

He then took Lynch's supply from four bottles, down to two. Again dumping the contents and reloading it with the special brew.

Next, to leave no trace that tampering took place; he ditched the empty bottles with Marty, who dumped them off campus. He then proceeded to refill the coach's stash with the class-made concoction that he and Dickie had created earlier in the day.

The player's dosage of the liniment was usually potent enough to do the trick, but it was known that Lynch, like Paul Owen before him, liked a little additional heat to juice up their already ornery dispositions. This was done by adding another component after the green rub, sort of an alcohol base item with much more of a kick. If it got too hot, one could always cut or lessen the effect, with yet a different product.

One last thing needed to be done. For this, Kiki went into his duffel bag for a wrench and some sort of foreign substance and would soon proceed to the showers. He quickly modified the closest showerhead knowing that time was of the essence.

Everything was now in place. The products were where they were supposed to be and the *players* were now coming back into play.

Kiki went to the taping table and leaned back in a relaxed position, as if to catch a quick catnap. Lynch came back into the locker room area and found Kiki relaxed on the table.

In an uncommon tone, the coach said, "Hey, son, you okay?"

A play-acting groggy Kiki responded, "Umm, yeah, Coach, I'm fine."

"I really appreciate the way you're believing in the system. If we had more of an attitude like yours around here, we'd be kicking some ass. I always knew I could count on you.

He continued, "I sent your brother on a two-mile run to clear his fucking head, so maybe that will cool him off."

Kiki just sat up and said, "You did the right thing, Coach."

Shortly, Collins showed up. "Sorry, Coach, hope you didn't have to wait too long."

"Where did you go?" the human pecker-head inquired.

"Just to the gym. That cute little junior, Erica Bresheski," to which he was interrupted by Lynch who said, "Oh yeah, the one with the cute little ass?"

"Yeah," Collins responded. "She sprained her ankle, so I had to bandage it up."

"Nice," said Lynch, "I would have liked to have had that assignment," and the two perverts broke into laughter.

"Let's get you going here," said the trainer.

Lynch liked to be worked on from feet ascending to shoulders, and starting with his backside. Story has it, that Collins was applying the solution generously, just as Lynch liked it.

Kiki, meanwhile, was back on the taping table waiting to be finished and continued observing.

"It's a cold one out there today Bobby, so hit me with some extra heat," the ill-fated coach requested. On cue, the trainer started to mix in the heating agent and began to work it in tandem with the twin's product.

"Let's hustle up here, Bob, or practice is gonna start late," Lynch demanded.

So the trainer picked up his pace and got the coach to turn over for the frontal application.

"Goddamn, Bobby, this shit is a little too hot today … you're going to have to cut it down."

All of a sudden on cue, Erica Francis, the cheerleading coach, summoned Collins for yet another faked injury, this time performed by Amy Bogdanski, Julie's friend. From just outside of the locker room you heard the screams, "Mr. Collins, are you there? We need your help upstairs again!"

"What now?" he said.

Kiki then issued, "I'm going to go get something to drink." Knowing full well of what was about to come.

"Coach, I gotta go," the trainer issued.

"Goddamn it already … okay go for Christ's sake," the coach barked. "I'll have to cut this shit myself."

Collins again grabbed his bag and scooted off to help.

Lynch, who was now covered in the twin's version of the green rub, was unaware of a couple of variables in the mix.

First, the twin's version had a nice supply of resins and hardening components that were quickly forming into a sealant, making the mixture unforgiving when applied to hair. Next to "turn up the heat," the cutting agent was actually an acidic based formula that when sealed by the liniment, had nowhere to go and couldn't be washed away.

Suffice to say, Lynch who was rapidly changing shades was beginning to measure pain, not by simple discomfort, but rather in degrees of burn.

Alone, *on fire* and now becoming affixed to the training table, Kiki said he could hear the chemically challenged coach moaning and wrestling to free himself from this pain.

"Son of a bitch," Lynch screamed as he extricated himself from the table in a ripping sound that was to surely leave some body hair behind.

Now confronted with deciding what was the lesser of two evils, to rip more hair and get to the showers for cooling relief, or to stay put and suffer until help could arrive, the coach became perplexed.

In what can only be described as an attempt to clean and jerk in lieu of the watery cool down, the tough guy, in one full swoop raised himself to his feet and made a beeline to the showers.

Kiki could now only hope that his *heated* antagonist would go for the first showerhead to seek relief. If so, it would be known quickly and without question that the entire plan had been worked to perfection.

He heard the water kick on and the sounds of comfort that Lynch was seeking. This was not the desired last result.

Just as he was about to concede that they had not quite taken it to the desired level, he heard a bloodcurdling, "M O T H E R F U C K E R!"

With that, he knew that they had experienced total success. For within the shower head and activated by the water, was the nicest, brightest color of red that you had ever seen. From head to toe, Lynch was covered in the off color that was mixed in with the previous substance that would *gum up* just about every hair on his stout frame … inevitably requiring some major attention!

Game, set and match ... twins!

Coach was not seen for a couple of days, and upon his return, everything seemed to appear normal. The dye was gone except for in his cuticles and maybe in some of the wrinkles of his face and hands.

As far as those who may have gotten a glimpse of a little more of him, it was said "that's where most of the damage was done." The furry layer that the bastard once possessed was gone ...betcha' it would have made a nice coat!

Neither brother was tabbed for any involvement, and in fact, the administration really couldn't do much of anything. Funny thing was that Lynch initially pointed the finger at the trainer for this, but that, too, couldn't stick. There was no evidence ... not even a hair.

— when the law strikes back —

If the Gracies tormented the senior Chemistry lab, then the world of Biology belonged to the aforementioned Roger Frost. It was nothing to walk into the lab and see a taxidermied squirrel with a lit cigarette in its mouth, or a yet-to-be-dissected frog piloting a remote-controlled car down the hall.

Adolescent … sure, funny … without a doubt, but to Frost, these were nothing but icebreakers.

Now on the other hand, Mr. Ball the instructor saw them as nasty boon-dogglings and was going to catch the perpetrator. This was not going to take the NASA think tank to come up with whom the responsible party was, and quite frankly, Frost wanted to be caught. It was suspected, however, that Ball didn't want to look in Roger's direction out of fear of reprisals.

The straw that broke the camel's back however, was when Ball's prized stuffed Osprey Eagle found new life and was flying … well, make that suspended, from the rooftop, just outside of the lab's windows.

This eagle was Ball's forbidden Garden of Eden apple tree—off limits!

And though he knew who the responsible party was, this time he had to face up to it.

When Sister Ann arrived on the scene, there was an unmistakable association to Frost on the bird, his scarf … and after retrieving the decked out dummy, Roger was whisked off to the main office.

But in Hedwig's standards this was a misdemeanor at best, and all he received was a passive warning. This, however, also opened up Frost to more scrutiny from both Ball and the principal, and made him first in line to be questioned for any wrongdoings related to the Biology lab.

What did this mean for the rest of us? It was a free pass to do whatever we wanted, knowing full well that Roger probably would be ending up as the fall guy, but as I mentioned before, woe be the stupid ass who crossed him.

Then again, how could we resist?

Plus, Roger practically encouraged us to try to get away with anything we could. So the occasional overflowing of sinks, the redecorating of the room with that white shit that comes out of the fire extinguisher or even the locking of Ball's cloak room and throwing away the key were our collective contributions, in which Frostie was a decoy.

Then came the day when all of the tension came to a head.

While Ball was writing some kind of bullshit on the board, a chalk-filled eraser came flying from Roger's vicinity and bopped the transplanted hippy in the back of the noodle. The perpetrator was not Frost, but rather Adam Baker. However, like a thoroughbred whose trainer has put blinkers on him to focus, Ball grabbed his woodened pointer and steamed toward the snickering Frost.

"Did you do this?" Ball ranted.

Calmly Roger responded, "No."

"Liar," Ball insisted, and in his best feminine stroke, cracked Roger across his knuckles. I don't care who wielded the stick, across the knuckles ... that hurts!

"Ouch," Frost screamed. Then he quickly rose to his feet saying, "You faggot motherfucker!" Then he lunged at Ball, just missing the cowering teacher.

Now realizing that this was an error of epic proportions, Ball streaked for the door. With Roger right on his heals and the class now urging him on to catch his prey, the teacher was first through the door and ran screaming like a thirteen-year-old girl down the hallway.

"Kick his ass, Thor," was the cheers that came from all of us as we raced to the door to see the student chase the teacher. Class was over for the day, with the two of them ending up in the principal's office.

Upon arrival to class the next day, Sister Ann was poised at the front of the room about to issue a decree. Flanked by her beatnik staffer, she spoke in a firm and decisive tone.

"I have had it with you seniors. You are unruly, crude and think that you run this school ... my school! I have had enough of your shenanigans and you are all going to quickly come to understand that I'm not the weak and undisciplined person that had this position last year."

When she said that, you could just sense the ire of the entire room begin to build. In fact, I saw out of the corner of my eye that Hodgie was about to lash back at her for making that comment, so I quickly reached out for his arm and tried to steady him.

This was not the place to address her verbal bullshit. But across the room, you could see some of the girls getting choked up and were dismayed at her comments about our beloved Emolina.

"I will have my eye on all of you. You will not mislead or misguide the underclassmen in any fashion as long as I'm here, and if I had my way, none of you would have ever returned here for the twelfth grade.

"I just hope that this year flies by so that we can extricate our problems. All of my teachers have been instructed to have a zero tolerance with your collective behaviors, and disobedience will result in immediate suspensions!"

She then paused, and with a glint in her eye lashed out, "I now have become your biggest problem … understood?"

And the room stood silent. "I said, was that understood?"

In unison there was a composed "Yes, sister." But as I looked around the room, I noticed a look on many of the guy's faces that you may have won the battle, "But oooooh, baby … get ready for the war!"

"Proceed, Mr. Ball, the class room is yours." And with that, she began to step backwards toward the door eyeing us like one of Hitler's field marshals.

Frequently, she would peer in the window of a variety of classroom doors, inciting even the least of situations.

When we tried to talk in between classes, she'd break us up. If we were in a class and genuinely tried to seek the assistance of, or provide the same to someone else, if she were within ear or eye shot, she'd reprimand and admonish on the spot.

She was definitely becoming a pain in the ass and wasn't just trying to put the clamps on us; she was trying to break our collective spirits.

⌐ school is school, but business is business ⌐

As little as five years ago, a normal day at Saint Hedwig's started within the magnificent cathedral, as the entire school would celebrate morning mass. Since, however, such a daily gathering had been scaled back significantly, which, in retrospect, I thought was a bad choice.

So the celebration of the mass for the students was modified to include only holy days of obligation and fortunately all Fridays.

Each grade level sat in a designated location, with the seniors occupying the front pews just to the left of the altar if you were viewing from the back of the church. We'd be followed in order by the juniors, sophomores and obviously conclude with the freshmen. To illustrate the enormity of the church compared to the student body, we hardly filled an eighth of the facility. Even with the addition of both the middle and grade schools, we'd occupy less than a quarter of the total cathedral.

The church was truly awe-inspiring even for the casual on looker or an infrequent visitor.

Like many of the great shrines of its era, it was the size that just blew you away. I'd often sit and wonder that if I were to punt a football, say from the altar, if I could ever hit the ceiling with it?

I'd also be amazed at the detail and splendor of the renderings and heavenly scapes painted by those latter day commissioned artists, who would never get the acknowledgment or accolades of their profession's Babe Ruth … Michelangelo.

How they could create such beauty in the difficult places was beyond my comprehension.

Those coved ceilings and obscure architecture had to cause them problems, but somehow they were able to create images and duplicate the lore of the faith that not only captivated audiences, but helped to provide understanding of the faith.

This shrine and others like it spread throughout metropolitan Detroit were absolute treasures that often were taken for granted.

On Fridays, I'd marvel at all of this beauty while stationed at the back of the church, as the student body would independently file in and meet up with the respective classes.

It was at this time when Al and I would inconspicuously collect envelopes from a significant number of the student body who were themselves risk takers, or runners for their folks dropping off past amounts owed or this week's bet slips and monies wagered.

Like ushers at Sunday mass, we'd collect a nice offering, but unlike those servants of the church, the take collected here was not going for the proliferation of the faith.

Being stationed in the back of the church was more than just a convenience for us, it was a duty. For the third year running, Hodgie and I were honored with the privilege of ringing the bells prior to the start of mass. A task granted us by our old buddy, Sister Loyola, who again was in charge of assigning chapel duties, and aware related of dealings.

Now, aside from business, this chore was far from an easy gig. Though it did have its thrilling aspects, there was muscle that was needed to make the towers chimes ring out.

The ropes that led directly to the bell tower were massive and resembled the lines that you'd see down on the river securing a tug or large commercial vessel. So hanging on them would be no trouble at all.

Now considering the distance involved which had to be a dozen stories, the size of the bells and the single rod axle that the huge bells rested on, a lot of force went into getting the bells to sing.

There were dedicated openings in ceilings and structural bypasses that allowed the ropes to hang freely, but to get this bitch started, one of us would have to go up to the choir loft grab a tight hold and jump through a trap door toward the main level. This would lift the other guy back into the loft, thus causing one hell of a thrill ride!

We'd milk this for a couple of minutes before allowing the bells' own momentum to take over. When done right, they would basically ring themselves out, as the celebrant and the altar servers would process towards the altar to the accompaniment of the opening hymn.

This would allow Hodgie and me just the right amount of time to work our way into the church's basement and into a seldom used underground tunnel that would lead us right to our last stop before splitting the scene, the Janitor's room just inside the school.

It was there that we would conclude our Friday morning tasks, by dropping off one large envelope to Wally Wilzack, who was the school's janitor. Wally was sort of a distribution agent for us, who doubled as our teller and would have the payoff envelopes for those who enjoyed success from the previous week's wagering. It was clean, safe and the perfect little system. Hey, it was business!

Even Ann's dictorial reign couldn't stop the ingenuity and spirit of the iron-willed, risk-taking Catholic."

After meeting up and settling up with Wally, it was an easy trek to the car and off we continued on our trek.

The next stop would be to a little dive restaurant, which sat in a section of Michigan Avenue called Coney Row. Senate Coney Island and was nothing more than a greasy spoon, that was by far Detroit's best coney joint!

Now the Chamber of Commerce may have had you believe that Lafayette Coney Island was Motown's best, but that was a bunch of horseshit. True Detroiters who indulged in the finer fillings of the dog and bun, either frequented Senate's or one of the other coney joints on the Row.

It was the visitors and those who lived in the suburbs, who were jerked into patronizing Lafayette's, because it was located downtown and near the city's business district.

Senates was always open! Even on Christmas day, the lights were on and people would filtering through for a quick *dog* on the way to their relatives for the holiday feast.

You were always be met by long time owner Joey "the hunch" Cavelo, who was either at the grill or on the register. He was well aware that we were cutting classes, but also knew all of the circumstances that were related to our visit.

"Boys, how's it hangin'?"

A simple wave was all that was required to honor the proprietor, to which he'd signal Angie "Do," the hostess, to let her know that we needed our usual table.

The "Do" who was named for the unique way that she would have her hair done up, would make sure that we were isolated and to let Hodgie's sister, Claudia, know that we were here. Claude would then come over; greet us with a kiss and head up to Joey to get our breakfast.

Like clock work, she'd come back to the table with her hands and arms full of dishes. She had my two eggs over easy, which were set on a huge plate with five strips of bacon and a nice helping of hash browns, garnished with a little parsley, a slice of orange and rye toast.

Then for her brother, it was scrambled eggs, sausage and on another plate, a heaping stack of pancakes smothered in butter.

A copy of the *Free Press* was always there waiting for us and we'd each grab a section and scan the headlines to see what was happening in the world, as in the background we'd listen to Detroit's legendary funny morning radio guy, Dick Purtin.

Before too long passed, Koobs would drop in to join us for a cup of coffee and to pick up *the* envelope; containing money and bet slips on action of anything from whatever major sports were in play to the daily *numbers* ... which was simply a lottery.

It was so much a part of the neighborhood, that not only were the parents of the students getting down some action, but some of the *religious*, including Loyola, a couple of the nuns and even the associate pastor was on occasion placing a bet ... on Notre Dame, of course, which sort of legitimized the whole fucking thing.

We'd hand over anywhere from a grand to fifteen hundred a week during the school season, which was a nice chunk of change! Payouts were rarely more than three to four hundred dollars, so everything was in line.

"Those fuckin' Lions, they're bums," Koobs would mumble as he thumbed his way through the sports section. He'd then announce that he was going to be track bound around two o'clock and though no one committed to anything, there was usually a good chance that we'd meet at his house, grab a quick bite and split for the ponies with him.

Whatever, we all knew where we would eventually end up that night ... hey, it was poker night!

Koobs would then go into the envelope and give each of us our *taste*, or little kickback for picking up and delivering. Alvin did most of the work, so he obviously got more than I did.

I'd get anything between forty and sixty bucks and Al would take a little, but usually settled up with his old man at home.

The other thing that the house allowed us to do was to make one bet a week for a *quarter*, or twenty-five bucks, which was great because we could end up with another fifty bucks or even more if we hooked into a little parlay. Regardless, we couldn't lose, which was a nice little fringe.

Koobs would soon leave to make his end of the *drop*, before being off to his morning calls. However, before he left, he'd put a twenty on the counter near Joey, smile and just walk out the door.

"Well, Moosie, you ready to get back?" Al asked.

"What do you think?" I responded.

He then raised six fingers in the air to Claudia and without missing a beat, she'd yell, "Bag me eighteen with everything, with six chili fries."

To which Joey replied, "Them fuckin' penguins are sure hungry today … ay, boys?" Which brought out the hardiest of laughter from the group at the counter, which even included the neighborhood's beat cop, Andy Gogleshcheski.

Call it business, corruption, or whatever you want, but it was simply Hedwig's economics at its best. There was a little of something for everybody. Koobs and his connections, of course, got the lion's share of the receipts, which they deserved.

Claudia got a nice little tip for her usual service and for being the sister.

Joey got the little *dish* from Koobs on his way out, and an automatic order to go for the nuns from the menu, every Friday afternoon. Sure, he'd discount the shit out of it, knowing that we were using it as a bribe to skip out of the mass and to meet up with Koobs, but at the very least, he was making something and was rotating his inventory.

Besides, we were always coming in to grab something; we all ran tabs there and paid religiously. So we were a steady source of income for him, and "why fuck with a good thing?"

He would always say to us on our way back to school, "Tell the nuns to say a little prayer for me," which I firmly believe that he was serious about, whether it had something to do with luck, superstitions or the belief that "what could it hurt?"

The nuns, of course, got another free lunch, and even Ann would indulge in the bounty not really knowing how they got to her table, only that it was the *gift* of a kind member of the community.

And, of course, there was Hodgie and me. We got to skip out of mass, have a free breakfast, get paid and were able to help make some people happy.

The wealth was spread around ... everybody got what they wanted, and a little larceny of the heart and soul was waged.

Nothing really ... that three Our Fathers, two Hail Mary's and an Act of Contrition couldn't take care of ... until next Friday.

~ he shoots ... he scores! ~

I believe that most seniors go through a stage of indecisiveness at one point or another in their final year. They worry about the real world, work, college and that sinking feeling that free room and board at home is about to come to an end.

The world of the comfort zone, begins to meet up with the realization that being an adult means that besides independence kicking in, so do things like bills and responsibilities that put shitty looks upon your face, like your parents have ... so the question begs to be asked, "Do I really want to take the next step?"

Even under Ann's dictatorship and all of the Nazi-like changes that had taken place at school, "Better the devil you know." For my tastes, desires and tolerance levels were all within the range. I didn't mind the schoolwork, I just didn't want too much of it.

I looked forward to preserving my free room and board privileges that collegiate matriculation would have assured, but I wanted more money and that meant getting a job. And though millions of high school seniors and college students work their way through that time in their lives that would have cramped my spoiled ass style.

Besides, I was always told by my folks to enjoy this time in my life because it was only going to get tougher from here. "So fuck it!"

Between now and June, whatever the Chinese had earlier declared this year to be in their mythical salutes, from this point on this was going to be the year of the Moose.

Anyway, there was an even greater issue to tackle here, my glands were at DEFCOM 3 and my needs for pussy were registering at dangerously low levels.

Despite Hedwig's fem-fatal population being worthy of both mind and penis expansion, the connection for me just wasn't there. I was interested in a number of the girls in my class and a couple of the underclass babes as well, but not enough to get involved. With the emphasis being on involved.

For me, a relationship even the most casual, was more than adhering to Del's school of thought, of *dinner, do her and done*! Which I still don't know if that should be considered a weakness or strength.

So while Del and Adam and a few of the others were stockpiling notches in their respective gun belts, by spilling their little swimming fishies, I was a part of the contrarian contingent who was stockpiling *fish* and had an empty gun belt.

Fridays were etched in stone for poker, but on Saturday nights, I kind of broke away on my own. At midnight, a group of guys ranging in age from sixteen to those in the 40s, would gather at a suburban ice rink called the Ice Box for a couple of hours of pick up hockey and beer.

It was a good group of fellas who played a decent level of the game, with some minor checking and little in the way of any rough stuff. Afterwards, one of the older guys would bring in a couple cases of beer to pass out and it was a fun way for one to pass a couple of hours for only five bucks.

The bad part was the locker room talk after the session. The older guys, those both married and single would talk about this broad's snatch and that one who went down on him, as if they were picking them off some pussy tree in a hockey player's Garden of Eden.

I'd sit there, thankfully all sweated up from all of the action on the ice, with my jersey off, skates loosened and in those oversized hockey pants, with a beer in one hand and trying to suppress a hard-on while listening to their stories. Fortunately, the last thing to shed from all of the equipment we wore was the cup and jock strap, which was my last line of defense from having all these guys know that their real life stories were the inspirations for my late night erections.

There was this one guy, Mike Phelps who probably was in his mid to late 30s, who was an extremely good player and a genuinely nice guy. Without fail, at this late hour on a Saturday night, he would show up to the rink with his wife, a very attractive girl named Beverly.

Prior to him going to the locker room, she would give him an incredible bedroom kiss, and a little pat on the ass as he would make his way to getting dressed. In addition, she would make her way to the stands where she would have a cup of coffee and a book in hand to occupy her time while we played. She'd often be the only one in the building besides the cleanup crew and those of us who were on the ice.

She was a striking brunette who always wore jeans that were tucked inside of her boots. She would remove her parka and use that for a seat cushion and then wrap the coat back around herself as she settled in for the next couple of hours.

Nothing would rattle her. If a great play was made on the ice surface or if tempers got a little heated, she would just remained focused on her book.

Like clockwork, however, every time Mike was on the ice and there was a stoppage in play, she'd look down at him while he peered back at her. Then he'd wink and she'd lick her lips as if she were savoring some sort of heavenly nectar. Just the sight of her doing that would conger up so many nasty fucking visions of things that I would have enjoyed her doing to me.

One of the guys who used to play in goal named Mick, would always pull me aside and say, "Mark, I'd eat a yard of her shit just to sniff her pussy."

Regardless what steps one would endeavor to gain her attention or affections, she was certainly worth the trouble, but inevitably a one-man woman.

As she continued to be part of the Saturday night mix, she began to greet certain individuals with either a smile or a "hello," that in itself was worth a warm little felling in the loins.

Then one Saturday before the two of them showed up, there was some locker room chatter that she and Mike were rather liberal when it came to their sex lives. Now understand, things said among this group are either the Gospel truth, or the biggest fucking tale that you ever heard. So being able to decode what's fact or fiction was part of the night's activities.

"She likes sucking cock while he watches," said Billy Jessup, a regular who was single and in his thirties.

I was just walking in when he said this and placed my sticks in the rack by the door, with everybody else's. When I heard the actual words, I must have looked like a bumbling fool making his way into a sophisticated party.

I immediately looked up at him with a goofy fucking look on my face, when all of a sudden the sticks went crashing and I tripped over my equipment bag and went head over heels onto the floor. The room broke into hysterics over my entrance and when I regained my sense of direction, I turned to him and said, "who likes sucking cock?"

Still laughing, and with me now on the floor, Billy said, "In that position, we may be talking about you." Well, even I had to laugh at that one as I gathered myself and my gear to find a seat.

Pockets of regular chatter commenced as I found a seat next to this guy named Vick, who elaborated on what Billy was talking about.

"So what's this shit Billy's spilling," I asked.

"Story has it that Mike told Donnie," another guy who plays on Saturday and works with Mike, "that Beverly enjoys giving head to strangers and Mike doesn't mind, just as long as he can watch."

Like a deer affixed on a set of headlights I responded, "No shit?"

As I disrobed, I found myself drifting into thought that maybe, perhaps by some fucking wild chance, I could be that someone.

I mean, I wasn't exactly ringing the bell in the gettin' any department, so why not. I'm decent looking, well, better than most of the assholes in this room. I got a decent-sized member, not a tool that you might find in a porno, but it's loaded and ready to fire ... and I'm young.

"Uhh, young," I thought. A high school kid getting head from this thirty-year-old honey, who I really don't even know ... not likely.

About an hour into the skate, we usually took a break to either take a piss or sometimes they'd distribute a case of brew a little early to wet our whistles. I just happened to be sitting up on the ledge of the boards catching a breather and wiping off my face.

In a relaxed manner, Mike comes skating up to me and leans on the boards where I'm sitting. "Hey, man," he said, "good skate so far."

"Yeah, it is," I said.

Then he looked up in the stands for his next dose of motivation and blew her *the kiss*.

As she returned the volley with her patented tongue shot, I laughed and just shook my head and said, "Michael, you're a lucky fucking stiff."

"Yeah, my man ... I am that," he followed.

"She's a beauty, no doubt about that," I rambled.

And just before he skated away, he looked back at me and said, "She is pretty, isn't she? ... and she thinks the world about you."

As he quickly skated away, I became dumbfounded at what he just laid on me.

I zoomed in on her with a million fucking thoughts going through my head, and was so shocked to hear him say that after the comments in the locker room, that I lost my balance and fell backwards into the bench area.

92

Ironically, nobody saw my boob of a move except for Bev, who laughed playfully and then waved at me.

Oh my fucking God, I thought ... *me? Could I be in line for a blowjob from this hot chick?*

I'd have to let Mike watch, but who the fuck cares! Shit, I'd let the whole fucking arena watch.

I suddenly found myself skating with an intensity that I usually didn't bring to this kind of a casual skate around. My adrenaline level had to be spiking the meter and I wanted her to notice the hunter in me.

Every shift on the ice I tried to stand out, while every time I hit the bench, I just found myself in thought about her going down between my legs.

After the skate we all hit the showers. As if I was ODing on uppers, I ran the soap over me in a highspeed piston-like fashion.

First in the shower and first out tonight, I was flying to get into that lobby to play off of any little thing that I possibly could to gain her confidence. I hardly toweled off and raced to put on my clothes.

"Hey, Mark, what's the rush?" one of the guys yelled.

Yet another offered, "The kid's in a rush ... I smell pusssssssy," to which the rest of them laughed.

Go ahead, I thought, *laugh all the way home to your ugly fucking wives and girlfriends, I'm going to get some real sweetness!*

I bolted from the room leaving even her husband in my wake. With my gear and my sticks weighing me down, I began to think, *what am I going to say to her? We've only exchanged simple hellos, so what am I going to say? Something stupid like "Hey, I'm ready to get my cock sucked!*

Suddenly I found myself at a snail's pace not really wanting to go any further. I didn't want to return to the locker room, because I knew that I'd be the brunt of all of their jokes. I wanted to proceed to the lobby to see her, but I really didn't know how to handle the situation.

I *mean I think I got a big shot here, so why not? Then again, I'm a horny senior who has thought about making the trek out to California because I thought that half the girls in Playboy were posing just to please me ... personally.*

Fuck ... I found myself frozen in my tracks, I wanted to go on, but was becoming fearful that I was about to over play my hand, and going back ... well, that wasn't an option.

Just then from around the corner, Mike appears.

"Hey, I'm glad I caught up to you," he says.

"Oh yeah," I said in a sheepish way.

"Yeah, come on and follow me."

This was it! I was about to score the winning goal in overtime for the Stanley Cup of blowjobs! Holy shit, I didn't know how to contain myself.

When we got to the lobby, Bev was waiting in her usual corner. "Hi, baby," she said to her hubby.

They kissed and groped for a second when all of a sudden, Mike turned to me and said, "Hey buddy, Bev has something she wants to ask you."

I got this big smile on my face, and was ready to blurt out "yes" before she even asked.

"Hey, Mark, Mike and I were wondering if you would be interested in ..."

It was like being in a porno flick. I was crossing over into Del's world and was about to have this beautiful woman, in front of her husband ask to suck my dick! No pre-coursers and no strings attached just sex and go ... I was breaking through!

"... something that you might enjoy. You see, we're pretty open-minded when it comes to certain things and well, we would like to invite you to ... umm ..."

She began to struggle to say what I wanted to hear.

"... join us."

"Forrrrr ..." I playfully inquired.

"A little fun," she said. "You see, I really like you, and I wouldn't let Mike bring just anybody into our private lives, unless I thought he would be right. We both like you, and if Mike is going to do this, I want him to do it with someone that he likes too."

My brow began to furrow as I thought she mispoke herself, when she said, "If Mike was going to do this," and I contemplated, *big fucking deal ... all he's gonna do is watch. You're the one who's going to go bobbing.*

I just smiled and said, "Look there's not a guy in that locker room who hasn't thought of doing this. I'm just freaked out that you thought so much of me!"

She just smiled back at me and said, "I'm just so excited to watch Mike do this."

From my postured position that saw me contort from placing my hands in my back pockets, to arms now folded across my chest, I responded with a little laughter and said, "You meant to say, have Mike watch ... right?"

But, there was no laughter when I said that.

"Noooo," she sternly injected, "Mike wants to perform, and I want to watch."

"Watch what?"

"Well, him performing oral on you, silly," she countered.

Expressionless ... I looked at her ... then at him and then back at her again.

"Are you fucking nuts?" I said. "I ain't into guys. I thought you liked to go down on strangers while he watched?"

She began to laugh and said, "Honey, I don't know where you got wires crossed, but I'm faithful. All I'm trying to do is let my baby explore his fantasies and to enjoy a little show."

"Well, I don't star with fellas in any kind of show," and I turned to Mike and blasted, "and where do you come off thinking that I'm some sort of a faggot, you motherfucker!"

He cut me a little smile and pointed his finger behind me. Stunned and incredulous, I knew what awaited me before I even looked back.

I had been "had," and there, behind the glass doors were all of the guys, and when I finally turn around to take my medicine, they let out one hell of a blast of gut-wrenching laughter.

Supposedly, they had set this up for months. Everybody was in on it, and I was so hot and horny that I just took the bait ... hook, line and sinker.

In the crossfire of all of the laughter, Bev turned to me and said, "I really do think you're adorable."

She then gave me a kiss on the cheek, a hug and my ass a squeeze much the same way she had done to her hubby in the past.

Mike then followed with a Stroh's in his hand as an olive branch.

"Fuck you, Mike."

"Sorry, man, but I couldn't back down from the challenge; plus, they promised to buy Bev and I dinner if we could pull it off."

In hindsight, it was the perfect play. Mike didn't have a gay bone in his body, he and his Mrs. were as advertised ... hot for one another, and I must have just been hanging on every sexual connotation to give the boys enough reason to think that they could hook me... which they did.

"That's alright," I responded, "we'll see what you say when one day you walk in on Bev really going down on me."

He just laughed at me, shook his head and said, "Keep dreamin', man ... everybody needs a dream."

― if she chokes on carrots ―

Despite the cleansing from Mike, Bev and the rest of the hockey crowd, I still enjoyed Saturday night on ice.

The pre-skate routine usually saw Mom burn something for dinner prior to exiting for an all-night game with her regular poker crowd.

Dad would be happy with a full tummy and a promise from one of us to bring home a late night snack, before he would set out on one of his magical journeys. Magical, because he would be able to focus on three things at one time.

My dad loved to read westerns and always had one near by. In addition, his love of sports was incredible … he pretty much loved it all. It was because of that and without actually knowing what he was doing; my dad invented what is now known as simulcasting.

During the colder weather months, he would turn the TV on to Hockey Night in Canada, while tuning into the Detroit Pistons on his transistor, which he had an earpiece for an effort not to disturb others if they were near by.

So, he'd watch a game and listen to another while simultaneously being whisked away by another Zane Grey novel. He was quite the sight.

As for my sister Rose, nine years my senior, she would come home from work, primp for an hour and hightail it with either her steady fella Mike, or hook up with her friends from the office.

"Karen's sweet sixteen is tonight … you should stop by," my mom encouraged me. I was torn at the thought.

Karen my cousin was my dad's brother's daughter, who I really loved, but being around her and her friends was not my idea of having fun. "Kare" as I affectionately called her was a bit too athletic for me. In fact, I think she competed harder than I did, and I hated to lose.

Plus, there was the butch factor. Her friends were tougher than mine and probably could have kicked their asses too.

Now I don't think that Karen was dykie, but I know that some of her friends were. Which really didn't bother me … in fact, it kind of turned me on, but they looked more like guys than girls and that bothered me plenty.

So being in the midst of this party was not my idea of *the* place to be on a Saturday night.

The upside was that this was on the way to hockey and her mom, my Aunt Stephanie was one of the world's greatest cooks. That in and of itself was reason enough to make the trip.

"And don't wear jeans, dress up for a change," Mom insisted. "Who knows, you might meet someone there."

Just then I looked over at my dad, to see his crooked smile and raised eyebrows. I just snickered at him and laughed. "And don't forget to say hi to my brother for me," he said.

To which I responded, "Why don't you just call him yourself?"

"Just go and find a girl," he wailed in a sarcastic tone.

If he only knew how badly I wanted one … if he only knew.

I didn't wear jeans, but rather khaki slacks with a loose fitting denim shirt, which for me and on a Saturday night was formal attire.

While driving, I found myself developing scenarios for a quick exit. They knew that I usually played hockey during this time, but didn't start until midnight. So dropping in to say "hi," snatching something from the buffet table and planning a quick exit, was probably not in the cards. Besides, they had admonished me enough in the past for not coming by more frequently.

Maybe I could say that I was picking up a friend or had to run an errand for my mom … but they'd probably call me on that one. I even thought that I could have someone like my sister call and say that there was an emergency or something like her car broke down.

"Yeah, she'd do that for me!"

So before I drove any further, I stopped by a pay phone to call back to the house to set up my alibi.

"Hello"

"Hey, Dad it's me."

"What's the matter?" he asked.

"Nothin' ... is Rosie still there?"

I could hear him yell upstairs, "Roooooseee, phone!"

She had an extension in her room, and at twenty-six, she should have. In fact, what the hell was she still living at home for? Besides having no confidence in herself, she needed to have her head half way up Mommy and Daddy's asses. She was such a pussy and usually afraid of her own shadow.

As I waited for her to tear herself away from the mirror, I started to wonder if this was really a good idea? Because she was not only a wimp, she was terribly forgetful and always late for everything.

"Hello," she said.

"Hey, sis, what's going on?"

"What do you want, lil brother?" she inquired. "And if it's money, you can forget it."

"I don't want any of your money, but I do need a favor."

"What is it?" she asked reluctantly.

"Wait a minute," I responded.

I didn't recall hearing my dad hang up the downstairs phone, which he had a habit of frequently doing. Not out forgetfulness mind you, but rather to eavesdrop on us ... as if he already didn't have enough shit plugged into his ears.

"Dad," I screamed, "hang up the phone!"

I must have startled the shit out of him, because I heard the receiver crash to the floor, which provided Rose and I with a good chuckle. It was irritating, but cute.

"I need you to do me a favor," I said.

"What?"

"In about an hour, I want you to call over to Aunt Steph's and Uncle Richard's and say that you have a flat tire or some kind of car trouble and that you need my help."

"Why?"

"Because I don't want to be stuck there all night for Kare's lame sixteenth birthday party."

"Ah ... afraid of being around all those girls," she teased.

"Girls no, she-males yes," I blurted, "just do this for me."

"What's in this for me?" she insisted.

"For you? What's the big deal, just make the call?!"

"Nawww," she responded, "if I do that, something bad will end up happening."

"Nothing bad is going to happen, quit being so frickin' negative," I said.

"Nope, not until you tell me what's in this for me."

"For Christ's sake, why does there always have to be a price tag on something with you?"

"You can vacuum my car out tomorrow," she offered.

"Are you kidding me?"

"Take it or leave it," she bartered.

I found myself shaking my head in the cold night wind, "OK ... OK, in one hour, and don't be late!"

So I created my escape and felt better about this obligation.

I quickly stopped in at a drug store along the way to pick something up as a gift. There were no flowers, but there was plenty of candy, this, however, is something she didn't need.

Karen was a great girl who had a wonderful heart, but she was cursed with pretty face syndrome. The dreaded affliction that usually attacks at least one girl in almost every extended family, and seems to be most prevalent amongst cousins and nieces. These are usually girls who are overweight and don't have a snowball's chance of getting a date.

And like with other causes, such as Jerry Lewis with the Muscular Dystrophy Association, spokespeople are necessary to promote and assist the foundation.

No different here. Usually it's an aunt or sometimes an uncle who tries to soft sell the related heifer not necessarily into a date mind you, but rather into a meeting.

The routine or pitch commences after the spokesperson targets a potential candidate, who could be anybody from a friend of a family member, to an unsuspecting schmoe who's either a relative of a neighbor, or worse yet ... someone from the church.

After the initial scouting process, which could entail a comprehensive check ... no less than if you were applying for a mortgage, an extensive Q & A session would follow, that would rival a criminal interrogation.

It was as if they were prearranging a marriage for a gorgeous princess and not the side of beef that was waiting in the meat locker.

Continuing, the process would find one of them asking the age-old question, "so tell me about yourself."

This would lead to a dialogue that would range from the prospect's current relationship status, to his occupation or scholastic endeavors, and would eventually delve into what his plans were for the future. When in essence, all they really needed to ascertain was whether or not the guy was breathing and how good his vision was.

But don't under estimate the "babas" (aunts) because they were good … very good in fact.

They'd dazzle you and sell the sizzle, focusing on the girl's best features and sugar coating her less than marketable ones … like everything from the neck down.

The thing that always amazed me about the guys that they'd corner to pitch the pig, is that if this angel, this blossom, or this living doll were everything that you said she was, why would she need you to represent her? I mean the way they touted her, she should have been beating them off with a stick!

The climax of this rite of passage is when the *baba* says to the guy, "You two should meet." This is the aunt's last-ditch effort and blatant attempt to broker such a deal and to create a debt that the girl's parents could never repay.

Now it's the guy's turn to starting asking questions about this mysterious diamond in the rough. Really there's only one question … "Tell me about this great girl?"

Well, you just know what the first thing out of their mouth's going to be.

"Well … she got a pretty face."

"Bam!" Right there you should be countering with every escape line and excuse that you ever heard, because they just gave you the *skinny on the fatty*.

They didn't say that she had a great body or a set of tits that would drive you crazy, they stayed on the face, and they'll continue to stay in that vicinity! "Oh yeah, and she's got beautiful eyes and a lovely smile. Do you like beautiful eyes?"

Well what the fuck is the guy supposed to say?

"No, I'm into chicks with some sort of pigmentosa problem."

Come on, this is not the time to soft sell your product. You have to lie, and I mean big time to hook somebody up that has pretty face syndrome. Let's face it, if the guy were to ever get a predate peek at this type of girl, you'd either have to pay him to take her out, or have something on his ass like a major gambling debt that would force him into this predicament.

Truth be told, Karen really did have a pretty face and an incredible personality, but that wasn't going to help her romantically down the road.

Anyway, "fuck it," at this hour on a Saturday night, whether she needed it or not, it was going to be candy and a card.

Driving up to the house, you could hear the music blaring from the basement. Every light was lit and the screams and shouts of teenaged girls emanated from within. And though we've established that my glands were deficient in female fondling, my brain was saying, "Stop, asshole, turn around and run! These girls are different, and most of them probably pee standing up!"

All visitors report to the side door at Aunt Steph's house. The Pope couldn't even make it past the front door. For as long as I could remember, that room was off limits. The furniture was never sat on, the china cabinet was never opened and the carpet never showed any signs of wear. That room was a fucking enigma, and was watched over as if it housed the Holy Grail.

I recall that when we were younger, we happened to run in there for what seemed to be a split second … and holy shit, did we get our asses chewed out. Never again did I ever set foot in that room. Christ, I was even afraid to look in there!

I opened the door and stepped foot onto the landing, "Hey nephew!"

It was my dad's brother, Richard, "Hey unc'."

"Hockey tonight," he said.

"Yep," I replied while nodding … or would there be? For out of the corner of my eye, I was compelled to look down to the basement, where I saw the most beautiful sight that I had ever laid eyes on.

"What the hell?" That doesn't look like any of the Murder's Row gang that Karen usually hung out with? This girl was beautiful, and not just in face. She had a cute little body, a nice perky set of tits … and a beautiful face, with bright blue eyes, a golden mane that shined like the sun, and a smile that froze me in my tracks.

Unfortunately, she couldn't eat, stare and smile at the same time.

As she looked up at me, the sliced carrot that she was chewing on must have gone down the wrong pipe, and she began to gag on it. As serious as this could have potentially become, I found it a bit flattering that she did this while staring at me. Plus, it was kind of funny to see how she tried to maintain her composure while her eyes teared up and she tried to dislodge the veggie.

She had the presence of mind to make her way out of sight, probably for vanity purposes and not to allow me to see her in distress, rather than clearing her passageway.

If she was trying to advertise her future oral skills, she was not off to a good start.

I wanted to go to her aid, but was literally dragged off of the landing and into the kitchen by my aunt, who was a tiny, but strong as a bull.

"Give me a big fat kiss, you handsome devil," she said, to which I certainly did and followed it up with a huge hug. Next was my uncle. In his house, the youth always kissed the elderly, which I always thought was a nice little custom and a show of respect.

Then, out of the family room ran little Stevie in a full out sprint. "Markie," he yelled as he leaped into my arms and playfully began to wrestle with me.

We chatted for a while and as custom, she put a plate in front of me at the kitchen table, loaded up with traditional favorites, like stuffed cabbage, pork chops and all the trimmings. The food was great, the conversation was tolerable, but I had trouble trying to remain focused, wanting to find out about the cute blonde at the bottom of the stairs.

"Some pretty girls down there, nephew," Uncle Richard said.

To which, I casually smiled and nodded in agreement. Between his inquiries into life back in the city and how my dad was, the anticipation of what was really important and getting into that basement was killing me.

I scarfed down the rest of the chow on my plate and decided to make a quick pit stop in the bathroom before heading down. For someone who had dreaded the thought of being here, my anxiety was now based on fear of my appearance … not theirs.

I found myself tearing through the drawers in their bathroom, looking for a comb, cologne or anything that I thought would help me look my best. I was glancing at myself in the mirror and going through a mental checklist: *hair, OK*, cupping my hands around my mouth, *breath … ditto*, and then stretching my head from side to side like a turtle to check my under arms. Finally it was a quick peek at the compartment that I eventually wanted open, but not at first sight.

I began my trek down the stairs and with each step felt my heart rate increase.

This is gonna be alright, stud, I said to myself, *just be cool…just be cool.*

With an insignificant gift in hand, I turned the corner and over the music I heard "Cuzzzzzzzz!" Karen had raced over with a big smile and bear hugged me.

"Hi, kiddo" I said, and as I handed her the gift and said, "Happy sweet 16th!"

Before I could utter another word, she grabbed me close, acted as if she was giving me an extended greeting and whispered in my ear, "Her name is Laura ... the blonde you saw when you walked in ... it's Laura."

I tried to put on this suave and sophisticated look as if to indicate, *Are you talking to me?*

Me, Mr. Wonderful, the one who has women usually just dripping off of him, when in essence, I was about to piss my pants, partly out of fear that I might embarrass myself because I was so excited to meet her!

Surveying the room, the place was packed with wool! Blondes, brunettes and redheads alike, and I must admit, most of them were not hard on the eyes. It was as if Karen had dual memberships of friends ... the athletic dykes, and the girls you wanted to bring home to meet Mama. But this Laura was the one that stood out. She was the one that I had to meet.

She was sitting with another group of girls, away from where Karen was leading me. And despite my attempt to be gracious during this flurry of introductions, I found myself stealing peeks into her direction and caught her doing the same in return.

Oddly enough, I failed to notice that I was the only guy there ... *Holy shit; I had hit the cute suburban girl jackpot, and didn't recognize what the hell I was in the middle of.*

But I knew where I wanted to be and it was next to the cute little blonde in the white painter's pants and blue and white small-checkered shirt.

Finally, after being ushered around I was about to come face to face with her.

"Cuz, these are my friends," and as she introduced them one after another in this little huddle, but none of them clicked until she said, "and this is Laura."

I stuck my hand out and thought that I was going to faint as soon as she were to touch it.

Then all of a sudden I got this burst of coolness and said, "Oh yeah ... the choker I presume," and I pulled her close and said, "You're alright, aren't you?"

Then I thought to myself, *stupid ass, why didn't you say something like, "I was worried about you" or "I wanted to come to your rescue."*

I began to think, *way to go dumb fuck, "the choker I presume"... what an asinine thing to say. She probably thinks it was some stupid tie into "cock sucking" or "blow jobs."*

She just smiled and said, "Hi, Mark, I've heard a lot of great things about you … would you like to sit down?" In unison, the group gathered around in a gleeful and playful manner said, "Eweeeeeeee."

I found myself feeling as if I were putty, not just in her hands, but because I was really seemed the center of attention. This emotional roller coaster ride began to make me fidget, sweat and really feel uncomfortable. I thought that if I didn't get any fresh air, and soon, that I would explode. But on the other hand, I knew that if I left now, I'd probably blow it with her and never get a second chance.

Just then, little Stevie came running down and tugged on my sleeve, "Markie, it's Woesie. She said it was an oui … an oui," and I interrupted him and said, "Settle down, buddy, what are you trying to say?"

He was having difficulty talking over the music and all of the commotion.

"Ouimergency," he yelled, and then it hit me … *oh shit, the excuse.*

I got up and pulled him aside, "Buddy, get on the phone and tell Rosie that Markie said to forget about it, and just hang up the phone … OK?"

"Okay," he said and he rushed off to disconnect my sister.

I snuck myself back into the group where Laura was and she asked me, "Is everything alright?"

I just smiled back and whispered into her ear, "It's nothing … and remind me one day to tell you what that was all about."

I tried to build in a reason for needing to talk to her in the future by saying that, as if this secret would someday save the world.

"But he said that it was an emergency?"

"Naw, it's just a little game between my sister and me," I responded.

"Are you sure?" she issued.

"Trust me," I laughingly responded.

The next fifteen minutes were pure bliss. We just talked about … well … nothing. It was insignificant, but it was wonderful.

Soon my aunt and uncle had joined in the activity and saw that I was really enjoying myself. Even little Stevie wasn't a bother when he came down a second time and whispered in my ear, "It's Woesie again."

I whispered back to him, "Don't even speak to her, and just go hang up the phone."

Then I gave him a little kiss on the cheek and sent him on his way. Nothing was going to get in my way continuing this conversation. I even conceded to myself that there was not going to be any hockey tonight.

Suddenly, a girl came over to Laura and said, "we better get going."

This was not funny ... not in the slightest! In fact, if I had access to a gun, I would have considered taking hostages just to prolong the evening.

"I'm sorry ... do I know you?" I asked.

"Mark, this is my twin sister, Cindy."

"Twin?" They were fraternal and didn't look anything alike.

Cindy said, "Yeah, I just met you over there twenty minutes ago."

I just smiled and said, "oh yeah."

Laura looked at her twin and said in a disappointed voice, "do we really have to?"

Karen interceded and said, "Laura, why don't you call your folks and see if you can stay a little longer?"

Then I immediately blurted out, "And if you have to go, maybe I could drive you home?"

She looked right at me and with the biggest grin said, "That would be nice ... but I'd have to ask."

It was one of those soldier in the foxhole moments, as I silently asked God to fill this favor, and if he did, I'd take back everything I said bad about him as it related to Mick's death.

Please, God ... let her dad say yes ... please!

When she returned to the basement after her appeal, I knew the answer before she could say on apologetic word. "I came with my friends and my dad said that I have to go back with them."

Despite my hormonal disdain for the decision, I said, "That's a smart move on your dad's part."

She looked somewhat surprised and disappointed with my response, as if she wanted my inner James Dean to come to the forefront and say something sarcastically like, "Parents ... what a drag." But, I wasn't raised like that and quite frankly, I didn't have the balls to say something like that, especially at a first meeting.

Her facial expression seemed to exude a certain finality and she muttered, "Well ... I guess I better get going."

I was suspended in the moment. On one hand, I was frightened that I might never see her again, yet somewhat relieved that this was about to end without me getting slapped in the face by anyone.

Besides, I was somewhat still in control. Especially after all of the anxiety of not wanting to be there, then thanking my lucky stars that I was and most of all getting the chance to meet Laura.

So I stood up, offered her my hand and said, "Maybe we could see each other again?"

Her answer was in her smile as she nodded in the affirmative!

———   ———

Some of the guys after that evening's skate remarked that I played as if I was possessed.

"What got into you, asshole," were among some of the remarks that I endured.

"Nothing, I just found a new gear, fellas…I just found a new gear."

I decided to head over to White Castles to pick a sack of enemas in a bun for the trip home and some for Dad. When I arrived at about 3:15 A.M., the usual dark house was fairly lit up. I walked in with the goods and was greeted by my dad and sister with a drilling, "Where the hell have you been?"

Puzzled I said, "At hockey … what's the big mystery?"

Rose then roared, "I called for help, you little bastard."

"Yeah … I know and I appreciate it, so ease up," I responded.

"No, pecker head, I really needed your help, my car broke down."

"What?"

"My car broke down," she rifled.

"Sorry, sis, I just thought you were trying to get me off of the hook."

Just then, my dad looked at my sister in a distressed manner, "Off the hook?" he asked.

"It's nothing, Dad, just a little something between her and I."

"Were the two of you playing games with my brother?"

"No, Dad, honestly," and I proceeded to tell him the story.

Seemed that my nitwit sister left her lights on at one of the stops that she made earlier in the evening and ran down the battery. That forced her to call on my dad when I blew her off, thinking that it was nothing but the alibi call.

The explanation helped, but the burgers really did the trick as Pops let this one slide by, though my sister got a bit of an ass chewing for the whole lights to dead battery thing that forced Dad out of his comfort zone for the evening.

"Honestly, I didn't deserve that brow beating," I said to the two of them. "And on top of that, I brought home sliders."

My dad said, "you're right, my son, we owe you one. How 'bout I take your wheels over to the car wash after Mass in the morning and have it washed for you?"

106

"Great," I responded.

He followed that up by saying, "and your sister can clean the inside out for you after she's done with mine."

I just smiled and continued eating away.

Rose on the other hand, gave me a death look and grabbed the crackers from the pantry. She then turned and marched upstairs for what I assumed was for the night, but instead proceeded to my room where she crush the whole box of saltines evenly between my sheets and blanket ... *the bitch!*

Needless to say, I slept on the couch that evening, which probably cost me a jerk session that I would have privately had thinking about Laura.

⌐ he needs to grow a set ⌐

Believe it or not, for the next six weeks I lost all confidence in myself and feared Laura's possible rejection of me. But what really kept me away from her was *the voice*.

It was deep, resonating and more than I could deal with at this tender age. It was the voice of authority and one that conjured up visions of gloom, pain or death, if I ever did her wrong. Every father should be issued a voice like this to scare the shit out of those would be swarthy suitors of their daughters.

Every time I called, *the voice* would answer.

"Helloooooo," would bellow from the receiver, and I would just freeze thinking that I was about to ask the gatekeeper if I could talk to his daughter. I really wanted to be with her, but this David wasn't prepared to go through Goliath.

For Christ's sake, didn't anybody else answer the phone in this house?

I thought about asking Rose to make the call and ask for Laura, but phone activities between my sister and me hadn't yet recovered from the last incident yet.

I considered asking Karen to make the call, but that would show a kink in my armor and I wasn't about to expose my deficiencies in ego to her. So, I had come to a crossroads, keep whacking off again or confront the monster?

It was another Friday night that I found myself full of excuses and with no Laura. Even the allure of the all-night poker game was far down the list of things that I wanted to do. So come hell or high water I decided to head over to Farrar Field, home of the Trenton Trojans and Laura's high school, for their Wolverine "A" gridiron contest against the Belleville Tigers. This was a very good brand of high school football and not that faggot league shit that Hedwig's was a part of. The players were fast and talented behemoths, of which many were being scouted for collegiate play.

The atmosphere at one of these games was electric. In the suburbs, practically the whole city comes out, because in one way or the other, almost everybody's attached with the school.

Trenton's enrollment ballooned over 2,400 students, so with mix of parents, relatives, friends, neighbors and the rest of the locals joining in, it was nothing to see crowds in excess of 4 or 5,000 at the game.

In comparison to a Hedwig game, where there were so few who showed up, that drug deals used to go down in the stands because the dealers felt that it was a secluded enough, and that nobody would be around to ID them. Besides, the only crime that was taking place was on the field, in the play of our beloved Knights.

I, too, was on a recruiting mission, combing the stands for that smile, those eyes and that yet to be discovered sweet little body. Like a cross between an anxious Secret Service Agent and a stalker, I watched the crowd while they watch the game.

Thoughts were running rampant in my head, *What if she's not here ... or worse yet, what if she is, and with somebody else?*

Worse yet, what if she's involved with one of those monsters on the field?

I deserved the self-torment, due to the fact that I was a pussy for not following through with any of those earlier calls. Walking through the hoards was like battling through the discount rack at a Hudson's Department Store Christmas sale. No way was I going to find her.

My pace slowed as the third quarter approached and I began to hear the faint echoes of cards being shuffled in the distance.

"Are you lost, little boy?"

I turned with a puzzled look on my face to see who had said that to me in this dense crowd. I purposely turned slow as if I were being caught heisting a box of Milk Duds from the local store. "Could it be?"

Yes! There was that smile that glimmer and beamed. But instead of continuing with the pleasantries, she began to frown and said, "Why haven't you called me?"

In the coolest style I could muster, I lowered my head, just thrilled knowing that she was next to me, and remained silent for a moment before saying, "I've been on a secret mission for the government and believe it or not, I was needed to save the world."

She burst into laughter and *that smile* just made me want to take her ... right there and right now!

"Honestly though," she responded with a much more serious look on her face, "why?"

I suddenly realized that she was no longer interested in jokes or tap dancing away from the issues. How was I going to tell her that I was too embarrassed to call? Afraid of her possible rejection and most of all terrified of *the voice*.

"I've been busy with school and stuff," I said in a hesitant tone that was being shuffled around by a lying your ass off posture.

"But I did come here to see you tonight," I quickly followed up.

"Really," she said, and I began to see those eyes soften again and that smile start to melt its way through.

"Any chance of me taking you out for a little something before running you home," I inquired.

With brows furrowed she replied, "Probably not," and then she paused and said, "I'm here with somebody."

"I knew it ... I just fucking knew it!" I felt my heart sink into my shoes and was ready to cry, when all of a sudden one of her friends from Karen's party came up from behind her and said, "Hey, your Kare's cousin, aren't you?"

Laura just smiled and pointed her thumb back in her friend's direction and said, "My date for tonight." The two of them just laughed and I joined in with a partial snicker and a sigh of relief that it wasn't some suburban stud.

"If I promise to call," and she looked at me in a disbelieving glare, "I mean ... I promise to call ... and soon."

"You better ... I mean, that would be nice," she followed.

Then she reached out and grabbed my forearm as if to reinforce her command.

"I'm gonna run now, but I'll be waiting for your call," and before disappearing into the sea of people, she looked back at me and waved.

With my back to the field, trying to get one more glimpse at her, I stood there relieved and feeling redeemed. I thought, *Okay, asshole, no more excuses, you gotta make that call!*

I became absorbed with the thought that no matter who answered that phone, I was going to ask for her. But, I found myself trying to build up the courage to still go through with it, and role-playing how the *asking for her* might go.

I was consumed with this as if I was going in front of a parole board and needed to have every word come out just right.

While driving, I would talk it out and passersby would look at me as if I were crazy.

In the bathtub, I would whisper to myself what I thought I should say, and I know I was having night sweats and insomnia, worrying about simply saying, "Hello, is Laura there?"

What's the big fucking deal all about? It's a girl, for Christ's sake, and regardless of what her father sounds like, there's great looking pussy at the other end of this mental moat.

Monday, Tuesday and now Wednesday was about to pass again and I began to start to freak out over the possibilities of asking for her.

Why was this so tough and why was I anguishing so much?

Like a revelation, I gained a Herculean burst of confidence unlike ever before. *I can do this! What the hell was I worried about?*

I reached for the phone, picked up the entire unit and began to dial the number. The rotary spindle couldn't go fast enough for me. I was now supercharged and ready to stake my claim. With each number I dialed, I paced back and forth like a prizefighter waiting for the opening bell.

I had hit my stride and nothing was going to stop me now … except for my own strength.

I had dialed the complete number and found myself psyched and ready. *You know what to do, babe, this is your time … bring on the fucking monster,* I coaxed myself.

My mom had appeared in the kitchen, "Who you calling?"

Sarcastically I fired back, "None of your business … can I just have a little privacy, please?"

She looked back at me and said, "Keep that attitude up and you'll have plenty of that."

Then she preceded to hand me the other end of the phone line that I had unknowingly ripped from the wall. I was so caught up in my newfound confidence that I knocked myself off line. "Goddamn it!"

Rose's phone, I thought. So I rushed upstairs to her room, only to find that she had the ability to unplug the whole base … and being as paranoid as she was, hide the phone to avoid me from using it when she wasn't around.

My energy level was fading fast and I fell back upon her bed and thought to myself, *Is somebody trying to tell me something?* So, another emotional roller coaster ride with the same results … no call … and Laura.

When I arrived home from school on Thursday, the guy from Bell was just finishing up reinstalling the phone. So, I grabbed something from the fridge, threw my books on the dining room table and decided to blow out what little homework that I had, just to get it out of the way.

I had become frustrated with this whole Laura thing, that between my apprehensions, *the voice* and simply no luck, this was more of a chore instead of something that I should have been looking forward to. I had no burning desire to make one of the most important calls of my life.

But sometimes when you get fed up enough, when that tolerance level has hit its mark, you knee jerk your way into doing what you have to do.

It was now about 3:00 P.M., Mom had gone to the store, Dad and Rose were still at work and the house was all mine. For some reason, I found myself marching straight to the phone and without any reservation, started dialing the number.

I used to have consult the sheet of paper that I originally wrote the number on to dial it, but I had tried and bailed so many times that I think I knew it better than my own number.

Something was different this time. Something besides my fraidy-cat demons were in control of my mood and direction.

The dial tone didn't sound like a prolonged dirge of death. The rotary phone dial suddenly didn't feel as if I was towing a Mack truck up hill for ten miles, and the ringing of her phone was not like prior feelings of standing next to Big Ben at the strike of noon.

I had spent enough time pissing myself off enough into making this call, that I finally knew that I was ready for anything.

"Helloooooo," it bellowed from its depths, permeating its way through my no shit force field.

As if I had just reached the top of Cedar Point's latest thrill roller coaster, not knowing what to expect, but ready to shit myself out of fear of the big drop, I wanted to again bail out of this call.

But, in what can only be described as the good angel on my right shoulder finally getting the best of that little devil on my left, I quivered, but said, "Ummm … ummm … is Laura available?"

"Hold on," it said. It actually said "hold on!" It knew other words!

And I was still breathing! I now found myself looking at my hands as if they had just caught the winning pass in overtime of the Super Bowl, when all they did was dial a phone.

"Lauuuurrrrraaaa, telephone," it yelled. Funny, but the volume when he yelled for her sounded the same when he answered the phone over the past month and a half.

"Who is it," I heard her shout back.

"It's a boy."

"Dad, get out of here," she responded.

Something … some kind of commotion was now taking place as the mouthpiece was covered and there sounded like a crowd of people gathering around the other end.

"Hello," she said.

"I'm tall, dark and handsome and live in Detroit," I said without realizing that I could have just described half of the male population, regardless of pigmentation.

I could feel her smile as she said, "Hi, how are you!"

You could tell that she was trying to jockey for position and distance herself from others within earshot, who were trying to get some sort of idea of what we were talking about.

We enjoyed some small talk for a while, and then I just came right out and asked, "Would you like to catch a movie and get a bite to eat on Saturday night?"

Again I could hear the excitement in her voice as she said, "Hold on."

Fifteen seconds went by … then thirty and I began to wonder what could they be discussing? Now forty-five seconds had passed and I thought she was trying to get some sort of security clearance.

This just isn't going to happen, I thought.

She had released her hand from its muffling position and uttered, "What should I wear?"

Yes! It was actually happening. "Just casual, nothing special and I'll pick you up at about six … if that's okay with you?"

She agreed and we ended up small talking ourselves into goodbyes.

I know it's unfair of me to make this comparison, but I could only imagine both the joy and exhaustion that women feel after going through labor and the process of delivering a baby. I found myself in a pool of sweat, smiling at my accomplishment, but ready for a nap.

Now mid-Saturday afternoon, I bathed and was starting to spruce myself up. I had blow-dried my hair, Right Guarded my underarms and Old Spiced my face. Clean underwear was a must, though I conceded that I had little chance of exposing them later that evening.

I put on a denim shirt and my best jeans and my penny loafers and was raring to go.

When I got downstairs, my parents were poised like two drill sergeants waiting for inspection.

"Uh uhhhh, no way, buddy, there is no way you're wearing that," my dad roared.

"You look like a bum," my mom said in a concurring tone.

"Gimme a break, we're just catching a movie," I fired back.

"What are her parents going to say when they see you?" she said.

"Mom, don't worry about it. We agreed to go very casual." But I knew that I didn't have a chance. Somehow, some way she was going to influence my appearance tonight.

Mom had a wonderful way of getting results with me. First, she tried logic and conversation, which in and of itself was enough to drive you crazy.

Next she'd threaten not to cook any meals for a week, which even my dad knew was more of a reward than a punishment. When I showed my disregard, she just threw her hands into the air and retired to the kitchen.

Meanwhile, Dad tried to soft sell me on the reasoning that this was really not the way to show up for a date, but despite his best efforts, he wasn't going to change my mind.

Which leads us to an iron clad axiom, "Don't send Dad to do a Mama's job." Because sooner or later, we all come to the realization that Mama may not always know best, but she usually gets her way.

"Well, I don't approve," she yelled from the kitchen, "but at least come in here and let me give you a good luck kiss."

This was cool, because I would not only get her blessings, but she'd usually place a quick ten spot in my hands, just to make sure that I had enough cash on me. Maybe she'd even throw a twenty in my direction tonight, because she knew how much that this really meant to me.

In what can only be described as "don't fuck with mama" was about to come to pass.

I should of expected something from her oldie but a goodie arsenal, for as I turned the corner, instead of greeting me with encouragement and luck, I was bombarded with the combination of leftover coffee and ice cold pickle juice.

Standing there drenched in both wardrobe and spirit, the only thought that came to mind, was that for the first time in my life, I saw her have a triumph with food.

"I'm late for cards," she said, "hope you have a good time tonight, honey," and she proceeded to make her way out the door, leaving me no alternatives but to clean the mess and myself up, before changing into something a little more upscale.

As I passed my dad on my way back upstairs, he just looked at me and said, "I see she convinced you."

Attire was now the least of my problems, I was going to be late ... and I knew that I was going to have to deal with the next stage of discomfort, meeting Laura's parents.

Laura would later confide in me that many skewed thoughts had entered her parents' collective thoughts. Concerns that I was from Detroit and playing off of her description that I was tall, dark and handsome, led her father to the assumption that I was Black.

"He's Karen's cousin, come on already," she argued.

"Well, you never know," he would respond.

"And why do you have to date somebody from Detroit anyway?" her mom petitioned.

"What does it matter where he's from?" Laura would defend.

But the best one had to be after that initial meeting, when both of them commented to her the day after, "Is he in the mafia?"

Thanks to my mother's last minute acts of desperation to force me into a change of attire, I sported a nice pair of dark gray dress slacks, a gray dress shirt, a black v-necked sweater, a pair of highly polished, black Florshie wing tips, with a knee-length, black wool overcoat. My hair was slicked back and come to think of it, all I was missing was the fedora to complete my Michael Corleone look.

So I could see their point, except for one major flaw. The car that I was picking her up in wasn't a Cadillac or Lincoln; it was the good ole' red fish tank ... hardly Cosonostra material.

I thought I would try to score some extra points by winning her mother over, so I picked up a simple bouquet to present to Laura's mom upon arrival.

It seemed as if everyone on Woodside Street was aware that Laura was going to have a date that night. How else could you explain the fact that it was November and dark out, yet some of the neighbors were screwing around with their lawns as if it were mid-May.

One of their neighbors, Harry Brumback from directly across the street was sitting on his porch with a pipe sticking out of the left edge of his mouth, a libation in his left hand and a section of the daily paper in the other. Furthermore, he was in his robe, bare legged with a pair of slippers.

Now, I may be a bit naive, and will concede the fact that this guy may have had night vision and was able to read in the dark, but unless he had antifreeze in that glass, it was too cold to be out dressed as he was.

Besides, when I stepped out of the car he looked over at me and said, "Are those for me?"

To which my response was "Not unless you shave and put on a dress." Which got me a pretty good laugh from both Harry and the others who were within earshot.

I was both excited and scared when I got to the door. After ringing the bell, I was greeted by her twin Cindy, "Hey, come on in!"

"How's it going?" I responded.

She nodded positively and said, "Laura has been looking forward to this ever since she saw you at Karen's party."

I just raised my eyebrows and thought, *Hmm. She's been waiting for me?*

As the two of us just chitchatted in the living room, from an adjacent hallway, Laura's mother appears and said, "Hi, Mike!"

"Mom, it's Mark," Cindy scorned.

"Oh, I'm sorry," she said and started to both laugh and grimace.

Hmm, I thought, "who's Mike?"

"Don't you look nice all dressed up," she said.

"Oh me, well thanks ..." and I paused for a minute and said, "Oh by the way, these are for you."

She beamed and gladly accepted the flowers.

The house was on the smallish side, but extremely clean and well kept.

As the three of us continued to just shoot the breeze, Cindy excused herself and ran down the hallway. The only thing that I could surmise was that she went to inform Laura that I had redefined casual.

I heard a surprised "What?" coming from what I expected was Laura's room, followed by some scrambling.

All seemed to be going as well as could be expected, when suddenly I heard an ascending march of footsteps from the basement area. The steps led up from the lower level and into the kitchen at the rear of the house.

As *its* appearance drew closer, my heart again began to race! The moment was at hand.

From around the corner, appeared this bull of a man, standing every bit of 6'1", he was about two hundred pounds and had a rugged and imposing look. He had sandy blonde hair, a thick mustache and a five o'clock shadow that made Nixon's, during the Kennedy debates look as smooth as a baby's bottom.

The other thing that was mesmerizing, were his eyes. One seemed perfectly normal, and the other, though not ghastly, seemed to be a little off center. I found myself looking at them pretty intently, as he extended his hand to me and said, "Hello, Mark. I'm Bill."

"Pleasure, sir," I said.

Actually, his name was John … John William Locke. Bill I assumed was just used to condense his middle name, which again, I assumed he used?

I would latter come to learn that his wife also called him "Billy, Rick and son of a bitch."

He was in jeans without a belt that sagged just above his hips, a white T-shirt that was partially tucked in and a pair of white sweat socks.

"What are your intentions with my daughter tonight?"

Still captivated by that eye, but searching for some sort of icebreaker to take the edge off of things, I responded like the smart ass seventeen-year-old that I was, "Just dinner, maybe a movie and a quick jaunt to the Caribbean, sir." Which, in hindsight, probably wasn't the answer that this forty-four-year-old man was waiting to hear from my smart-ass seventeen-year-old mouth.

His grip on my hand got noticeably stronger as did his ire. Fortunately her mother said, "Look Rick," as she showed him the flowers, "Mark brought these."

He just raised his brow at me and seemed to approve. Then his face got a steely look on it as he said, "Eleven o'clock and no later."

This time there would be no sarcasm, "Yes, sir," I said, and I just kept my mouth shut.

Finally he let my hand go and I think that he felt that he was successful in instilling just the right amount of fear into my life … which he had.

On cue, Laura appeared with a look of curiosity and disbelief on her face concerning my attire. I just shrugged my shoulders back at her and said, "You look great."

She just flashed *the smile* and said, "Ready?"

Which made me hightail it toward the door to a chorus of "Have a great time."

I was only step away from escaping this visit into teen hell, and though this was not my first official date, it was my first dating inquisition, which had all of the appeal of a root canal.

We went to a place call the Showboat Theater to see the Gene Wilder and Richard Pryor flick, *Silver Streak*. Though it was an enjoyable way to kill an hour and a half, it was just a backdrop to try to get more acquainted.

We held hands and she laughed at my off the cuff comments about the movie. We were both a little nervous and obviously careful not to say the wrong thing to offend the other person, but I think we quickly gained each other's confidence!

After the movie, it was off to Big Boy's Restaurant for a tantalizing shit burger, which again, was to be nothing more than a place to hang out while we tried to get to know one another a little better.

"You know ... I've got to ask you, why so dressed?" she inquired.

"I'd rather not say," I responded.

"Don't get me wrong, I like it," she followed up.

With about an hour to go before I had to return her back to the lair, I asked, "Would you like to go somewhere a little more private and talk?"

"Talk huh?" she said with a sly look on her face.

I was beginning to think that I was overstepping my bounds with her, when she suddenly said, "How 'bout down by the water?"

Trenton is wonderfully positioned on a channel that is part of the Detroit River just before it empties into Lake Erie. Across from its banks is the quaint and exclusive island community of Grosse Isle.

There were plenty of places to park and watch the moon reflect off of the water. We just happened to duck into a retirement community's parking lot for the continuation of our late night talk session and what I hoped to be the beginning of some physical activities.

Trying to put up a suave front, but awkwardly going about it in the bucket seats of the fish bowl, while trying to reposition myself, I accidentally elbowed her in the forehead with enough intensity that if during a hockey game, I would have received a two-minute elbowing penalty. I made a wise crack about the hockey analogy, to which she replied, "Maybe one day you could show me what butt ending is all about?"

I laughed so hard at her comment and had such a stunned look on my face that I could only imagine how fucking goofy that I really looked. But I thought that this was the perfect time to move in for our first kiss. We both seemed relaxed, poised and ready.

I pulled her closer as she got into a nice position for final approach. Just as we were about to hit pay dirt, my left elbow hit the steering column, which subsequently set off the horn … and not just a little toot, but rather the sitcom version where the horn is stuck and sends out this blaring and attention focusing sound.

Every window in the old foggie home seemed to have an observer now trying to find out who was disturbing their Saturday night sleep-a-thon.

Looking at the wheel like I was trying to petition a baby to stop crying, Laura yelled out, "Can't you get that to stop?"

I looked back and said, "You're kidding, right? I can hardly drive this damn thing and you want me to fix it?"

We began to laugh at one another, but realized that the cop's arrival was imminent, and that we should get the hell out of there.

Midway back to her house, I stopped into a service station, where a frail guy undoubtedly irritated by that incessant fucking horn, motioned me to pop the hood. I complied and almost instantly, either a wire was yanked or something was reset to stop the noise. We sat there finally in silence looking out toward the hood of the car, where the guy just politely closed it back up, gave us a wink and proceeded to walk away.

At 10:52 P.M., we were parked in front of her house, mildly concerned that her folks were going to peek outside of their windows, or that Harry from across the street might come out to the porch to start *War and Peace*. I decided not to press the passionate goodnight kiss issue, but thankfully, Laura did.

Holy shit, what a kiss … I had wet dreams about her for the next two weeks, which was the next time that we went out.

~ a funny thing happened in wally's toilet ~

Despite Sister Ann's attempt to enforce a new iron grip on everything that occurred within the walls of Hedwig's, there was an underground counter movement that was not going to allow her to fuck up our senior year.

We understood that we brought a lot of the shit that she was trying to impose on ourselves, so we expected some rather unpleasant medicine, but we were only going to tolerate so much.

I mean, let's face it, despite our antics; she was the new kid on the block. We knew that the reins were going to be pulled in, but in the parlance of the sport of kings, she wasn't going to geld us.

Among the little things that a small group of us used to enjoy was the second period shuffle. Basically, it was a chance to head down to Walt the janitor's cubby, to read either the *Free Press* or whatever magazine he had hoarded away from Jimmy's Barber Shop on Livernois.

Walt would usually be at lunch at this time, which I guess was normal considering that his day started at 4:30 A.M. He knew that a few of the seniors would take this liberty to perform our morning constitutional, and all that was required, was to keep it quiet, clean and smoke free.

It was one of those cool and damp late November days, where even the weathermen didn't know what to predict. It felt like snow, but this is Michigan where twenty minutes later you could be shedding sweaters.

Adam Baker had just come back from taking one of his legendary bowel movements that usually lasted about a half hour. He not only stunk the joint up from his deposits, he would also defy Walt's request and usually light up while he was unloading. Nobody wanted to follow him in, but, "when you gotta go ... you gotta go!"

There was no paper when I got in there, because Adam heisted it to look at the football and basketball betting lines, plus, he liked to read the funnies and do the crosswords. Therefore, I found myself rummaging around for whatever other kind of rags he had in the bin.

There was *Popular Mechanics* ... "read it," *Sports Illustrated* ... "read it," even *Good Housekeeping* and "I had read that too." Still thumbing my way through the stack, blah, blah, blah, blah ... ahhhh, "wait a minute ... what is this?" *Penthouse*! What the fuck is this doing here? Way to go, Wally! Hmm, wonder if Del has been here yet?"

Naw ... the pages would be sticky ... eweeeee, how gross would that fucking be?

Unlike *Playboy*, *Penthouse* had those incredible forum letters that stirred up so many fantastic visions! Plus they had just a little bit more of the racy stuff you wanted to see, like two chicks getting it on, the occasional threesome or some other kind of kinky masturbation jumpstart material.

I would usually build up some momentum when thumbing through a *Penthouse*, by reading some of the letters and letting my mind expand, before other parts of my body would follow suit. But in this edition the letters were pretty blasé, so I decided to head directly to the layouts.

This was so cool, because I never remember Walt stashing away any pussy mags. In fact, there was always a weak notion that maybe Walt fancied fellas in the privacy of his own little corner of the world. So seeing this was not only exciting, but sort of a relief as well.

The first pictorial was of this fresh faced babe who was cute, but wasn't Kleenex material if you know what I mean?

Next was the Pet of the month, and this one was worthy of the title. A dark-haired beauty with a nice body and a great set of tits. I could see this one in contention for Pet of the year! And when I look at one of these spreads, it's more than just the physical attributes that turn me on. I like the little things.

For example, it's when the model accents the photo with a little more tease that makes all the difference in the world. It could be how she arches her back or positions a leg. Or maybe licks her lips or runs her tongue along her teeth to give it that, "Hey, I want you to fuck me look."

Unlike some of the other guys in Hedwig's, who were ready to drop their loads at the drop of a top, I always needed a little more to get my motor running. Call it what you will, but at a very young age, I was very much aware that the mind, and not the loins was the true G spot.

Yeah, I wanted to fuck just as much as the next guy, but like most things in this world, half the battle with accomplishing anything is fought between your ears. And let's face it; everybody knows that there is a direct link between a guy's mind and his cock. Though it sometimes gets bypassed when a fella thinks with the head between his legs instead of the one on his shoulders.

However, I must have been blessed by being put into that select group, where I actually used the head on my shoulders, even to spur on little Richard.

Simply, I liked to be mind-fucked as an appetizer to the real deal!

Anyway, this *Pet* did that for me. She knew how to play the camera and the pictorial was pretty moving. If it wasn't for the lack of toilet paper to complete my current excrement, I may have indulged?

As I continued on, there was this little note paper clipped to the page that started pictorial number three. It said, "Walt, here is my favorite part," and it was signed C.G.

It was a shot of two chicks together in a hot tub. "Goddamn, was this hot!"

The first couple of pages showed them on the edge of the hot tub, exquisitely positioned. Then you would see them looking into each other's eyes on the verge of kissing and, of course, that would lead to breast fondling, the licking of nipples and last but certainly not least, the two of them going down on one another!

"Fuck," I saw myself in the middle of these two enjoying both the pleasures of observation and participation.

This was not good, because I was now seriously considering forgoing the "cleaning part, in lieu of capturing."

I know, there are some of you true artists would have worked, jerked and unloaded in the pot, but that just wasn't my style. I needed the soft feel of two plies for all of my business beneath the belt, and this was pressing the issue.

How does someone get a gig photographing this stuff, I thought. I could see Del doing this for a living.

With every turn of the page, these two were taking me to places that I visited in my mind, oh so many times before. "Sweet Jesus!"

But who was C.G.? I thought for a second when suddenly I heard "Walter, you in there?"

It was Carl Gnieweck, the boiler operator of the entire campus. "No, Carl. It's me, Mark."

"Oh, Moose man, you know where Wally's at?"

"Sorry, man," I said, "but I don't."

"Well ... okay then, if you see him tell him I want that ... uh schematic back."

"Schematic, what the hell are you talking about?"

"He'll know what I'm talking about." Then he said, "Take it easy, man," before he left the area.

You kinky motherfucker I thought. Carl digs two chicks doing it to one another like the rest of us. And if you saw his wife, you'd know that any strange pussy would light his fire.

Then I thought, *alright Wally's not gay, but am I'm in the same boat as he and Carl?*

For Christ's sake, if I like the same shit as these guys do, am I destined to end up like them? I mean, we liked the same perversions and I sure didn't want to find myself talking about the wonders of lesbianism with these two fucking losers. Suddenly, my urge to follow through with this mind experience with the two hot tub sisters just wasn't going to happen.

Perhaps this was one of those tests that God plays upon good little Catholic boys who have bad little fantasies? Whatever, it sure beat the shit out of the *Free Press* and gave me more to think about

On Friday of that week, I thought that I'd visit Wally to see if I could take the dynamic hot tub duo home with me for the weekend, and asked if I could borrow the issue.

"Marcus, what's up?"

"Oh, a little of this and not much of that, Walt," I responded. "Hey, buddy, that *Penthouse* I thumbed through the other day in the head, can I borrow it for the weekend?"

He just smiled at me and said, "Why don't you go get the real thing for yourself?" Then he laughingly followed up by saying, "Besides, I had to give it back."

"Oh," I said in a dejected manner, "Well, okay then, catch ya later."

Desperate for another glimpse at those two, I headed over to Carl's office, which was actually located under the church. A longish walk, but one that I considered worthwhile.

Upon arrival at his office, I said, "Hey Mr. G., what's up?"

"Moose man, how are you?"

"Not bad my man, not bad. Hey, Carl, this is a little awkward, but that issue of *Penthouse* you let Walt peek at earlier in the week, you think that I can borrow it over the weekend?

"There's this chick that looks like the cousin of a friend of mine, and I just wanted to show him the likeness."

"Yeah right," he laughed. "Anyway, I don't know what you're talking about. I didn't have any *Penthouse*. Besides, if I did have a copy, do you really think that I let that pervert Wally at it?"

We both laughed, but soon my smile diminished as I not only came to grips that I was not going to have the girls to view this weekend, but who in the hell was C.G.?

~ wham, bam, see ya, ann ~

With a third of the school year now completed, there was an obvious gap in communications between most of the upperclassmen and a large portion of the administration and faculty.

Certainly all schools have their renegades on both sides of the fence, but Hedwig's was small and always family like, and a wedge of division was driven in, and that wedge was spearheaded by Sister Ann.

The odd thing was that not only were those of us who had been here a while having troubles conforming to Ann's regime, but so were some of nuns who were holdovers from Emolina's régime. For they would nurture and guide us in somewhat of a maternal way, and though they expected us to perform both our academic and catholic duties, they used just the right mix of discipline and compassion to facilitate our development.

So Ann's rule had its effect on not only a large portion of the students, but also on a small and wiley group of her faculty as well. She was undoubtedly in control and beginning to see her grip strengthen on a daily basis.

You could feel it building, like the components of a large storm that were coming together … stirring, developing and ready to unleash its purpose.

Suddenly a decree had been put into effect to curb any preschool gatherings. First, she staggered admittance into the school.

The freshmen and sophomores had to quickly and quietly disrobe their outer wraps, put what they didn't need in their lockers and get into their homerooms, where they were given early morning assignments. This was the easy part, because this impressionable group was easy to mold, which was exactly what Ann wanted to accomplish with them.

It was the upperclassmen where the resistance existed, but make no mistake about it, we, too, were in line to have our attitudes curbed, and she had her beady little sights set on us.

Were we bad? Within reason … maybe. But if we were, it was all in good fun and never malicious. At least never before.

What was odd about this iron curtain approach was that the lay teachers really got into it, while the cloth resented this activity. Also, it was apparent that Ann's group used the underclassmen as operatives to gather as much information about us that they could.

So the divisions were set, Emolina's holdovers and the upperclassmen against Ann, who was now becoming known as Adolph, her field marshals and the rest of the future Nazis that she was trying to mold.

In addition, there seemed to be an agenda now in place to weed out any longstanding problems. One of those issues had to deal with the ever-diminishing hemline that saw most of the senior and junior girls' skirts inch their way up toward their ass cheeks. The senior girls thought that this was a little too harsh, especially when they were now being stopped in the hallways to actually be measured.

Now, never let it be said that those of us in the male fraternity didn't actively support those issues that meant so much to our female counterparts. If they felt that this hemline issue infringed upon their rights, then we were going to get as close as we could to give them what they wanted.

A note was passed around by Shelley and the sweet looking Kinevoch twins and a few of their gal pals, requesting an after-school get-together at Jeff D's, a local greasy spoon a couple of blocks off campus. I must be honest, this was considered a hangout of the goodie two shoes crowd and I seldom frequented the place.

All of the fellas indicated though that they were going to show up, if for nothing else than to claim that they were there for the girls *when it counted*. But their real motivation was trying to get pussy, and this was just a process in the hunt.

Though the girls wanted to keep this as secret as possible, you just knew that somebody was going to spill the beans, and Ann was somehow going to be a part of this scene.

Her demeanor was getting more stringent by the day and she had everybody … and I mean everybody looking over their shoulder.

On the morning of the day of the meeting, Al, Del and I were making our way down the senior hall, when, all of a sudden, Sister Loyola called us into her room.

"I have it on good authority that your principal has convinced some of your very own classmates to report back to her on the meeting that you're going to have later today."

"What meeting would that be, Sister?" I responded.

"Don't get funny with me, mister," she barked at me while extending her index finger. "I'm trying to help you and you're being smart with me."

"Sorry, Sister," I said, "but lately we don't know who to trust."

She took a step back toward the door and sternly slammed it shut. "Why you little … how dare you treat me like that? You know that I have always cared for you and have given you privileges not extended to other students … and you say that to me?"

I felt like an asshole and said in a sheepish way, "Sorry, Sister, I was wrong."

"That Ann," she said as she cringed her face and bit her lip, "she's a back stabber and trying to get most of the order transferred out of here. She wants an all-young and lay staff that she can control. Well, we're not going to let her put us out to pasture just yet," and she seemed to catch herself just before it sounded as if she was going to cry.

She composed herself then continued, "I don't know who the stoolies are going to be, but I also understand that Ann arranged to have Gainer and that fat Sheddow …" and we bust out laughing when she said that.

"Sister," Del interrupted.

She fired back, "oh, you hush, Arroundo, did you expect to use your "f' word," and our snickering continued.

"Anyway, those two are going to be in the kitchen of that restaurant and will also report back to Ann and Roberta."

The Roberta that she was referring to was Sister Roberta, Ann's Assistant Principal and a defector from Emolina's old staff.

"Be careful," she insisted, "they're going after rabble-rousers and you three are on their list."

"But, Sister," Al said, "it's really not even a meeting."

"Listen," she countered, "the girls are worried about vanity, but you boys … my boys can do the right thing."

"Do the right thing, Sis?" Del inquired.

"I'll give you sis," she said as she raised her hand in his direction.

He cowered and replied, "Sorry, Sister ... but take it easy."

"Sister," I said in a serious way, "what do you mean about doing the right thing?"

"The older staff is well aware of your abilities and how you boys care for us. This is our life, to teach and see you develop into adults. But we also realize that fun is also a part of that development, and there hasn't been much of that around here this year."

"Sister, what are you suggesting?" Hodgie said.

"I'm not suggesting anything, but I do know that when challenged, you boys can usually rise to the occasion."

Then she gave us some ammunition. "In two weeks, a representative from the Mother House and one from the Arch Dioceses, will be here to inspect the school under Ann's leadership. It seems that our new principal has a past."

"Oh yeah," Del said with a breaking smile on his face.

"A few years back, she was the principal at an elementary school in Minnesota, and there were reports of excessive acts of discipline. Some of the kids had to receive counseling because of the things that she did to them, and nobody knows what happened?"

"That cun ..." and Al caught himself just in the nick of time.

"What did you say, Mr. Semko," she said in a forceful manner.

Quickly Al looked at me, opened his mouth and began to choke on his own gibberish.

"Ahhhh," he said, "caaa—cunning woman," I assisted and he looked at me in a thankful gasp, as I just rolled my eyes back at him.

"Cunning woman, huh? Well, you just watch your language, mister," she said while now waving her finger at him.

"So, Sister, you were saying," I interjected.

"I said it before and I'll say it again ... when you boys are challenged, interesting things can happen. If something strange were to happen ... let's say at just the right time ..." and the conniving old penguin raised an eyebrow and cracked a small but sinister grin.

The three of us just looked at each other and cracked some smiles of our own.

As we walked toward the door, she cleared her voice and said, "Boys, some ribs would sure hit the spot on Saturday." And we raised our hands as if to say, "Order received."

With this new information, things had to be modified. The three of us were able to pull Shelley and the Kinovich twins aside to give them the heads up that the heat was on.

"That fucking bitch," Shelley gunned. "Well now she's gone and done it! I'm so pissed! I'm gonna get that bitch!"

"Yes, you are … we all will, but for now, were going to give her the impression that she's right and that we're going to comply like good little Catholic boys and girls," I said.

"Hey, Mark, go fuck yourself," the feisty little brunette fired back at me.

"Listen, you," Del jumped, "cool your jets! You'll get your fuckin' chance … just clam up and listen."

We proceeded to inform them about the information that Loyola passed on to us. Our mission was to remain the same, how we would go about getting it done was the thing that was going to be modified.

First, the meeting had to go on as scheduled. We had to present a front that showed that there was some dissent among the ranks and that Ann's policies and regiment were taking their toll on us.

Next, we made a pact that from this point on that only a small circle of just the right people would be let in on what we had to accomplish, and after today, no more public get-togethers.

We convinced Shelley to take things in stride and to resign herself that Ann's ways were currently the right ways.

To my surprise, Jeff D's was jammed when I arrived. Practically all of the senior and most of the junior class were there, with a sprinkling of underclassmen.

Though we had an idea of who the turncoats were among our own, we really couldn't say for sure. Besides, we wanted Ann to feel that she had the upper hand. In addition, Jeff D's daughter, Eva, who Del was probably bangin' gave us the nod that Beauty and the Beast were stationed in the kitchen with their eyes and ears wide open.

"Wow, I'm glad every one could show up," said Billy Bednarick, our class president.

"It's obvious that hem lengths pose a greater concern than other issues that this board regularly deals with, like community service, the year book or planning for the prom."

Now Billy was a straight A student, and sort of born to lead. I say sort of, because he seemed beyond contempt. He'd never be seen participating in activities that were considered less than proper. But in that same respect, he had garnered the support of all of the different cliques, just because he was a get-along kind of guy.

He'd show up for everything, and seemed to have this political persona to be the clean-cut guy that you could always trust to do the right thing … very vanilla. But he deserved to be the class president. His only problem was that his administration, though nice to gaze at (Shelley, VP and the twins, Sue, treasurer and Laurie, secretary), didn't share his same convictions or work ethic.

Billy wanted to not only put this title on his college applications, but he genuinely seemed to want to make good things happen. The girls, on the other hand, probably thought that the positions came with a 10 percent discount at certain stores at the mall.

Actually, Shelley would occasionally throw her title around as if it came with some sort of regal clout.

I remember Del often saying to her, "Hey, dildo cowgirl, you're the vice president of our senior class, not the Queen of Detroit."

Billy, unaware of the bubbling undercurrent and uninformed that the girls were not going to challenge Ann's decree, turned the floor over to Shelley, whose prior hard line views against Ann were about to take a public about-face.

"A few days ago when I first heard of the rule change the hem length of our skirts at school, I thought enough was enough. But, in talking to many of the girls in the senior and junior classes, we understand that Sister Ann is trying to return the school to better times."

Puzzled looks were growing among those in attendance at a quick rate.

Shelley continued, "I know it's hard to understand, but sacrifice is everybody's responsibility so that Sister's goals can be reached."

Listening to Shelley give this address was like listening to my mom teach a cooking class … it just wasn't r.ght? The crowd was looking at her as if she had been brain washed and comments of "what do you mean" and "you must be crazy," were being fired back into Shelley's direction. But she remained the trooper and stayed the course.

"We, the senior class officials, strongly agree with Sister Ann's new direction for the school and advise everyone to follow to form. Therefore, girls, we ask you to follow this new rule and all of the new rules that will be coming from Sister Ann. Thanks for coming."

Despite receiving obscenities, I must admit that the bitch's performance went over better than those of us in the know could have hoped for. The crowd was noticeably pissed and those finks in the crowd and the two that were in the kitchen were left high and dry. But perhaps most importantly, the bait was set.

Next, we had to set an atmosphere of total compliance, which was not going to be easy.

We needed to relax Ann and her band's concerns that this was just a day or two of abstinence from hi-jinx. Our behavior surged beyond unprecedented levels; our work habits were textbook and even Robbie Selby bathed and combed his hair.

It was like a trainer seeing that his attempt to break the new colts was finally paying off. The guard of Hedwig's Third Reich was noticeably more relaxed and was still being fed this daily compliance tranquilizer that we were in line.

The transformation had become complete and the administration was ready for their inspection and to show the powers that be that things had been clamped down.

The day to showcase Ann's application to the Discipline Hall of Fame had arrived. The moon and all of the stars were in line, the students were in check and the school was cleaned to an inch of its life. But as the wheels had turned for preparing Ann's presentation, so were the same efforts being fine-tuned to counter her regime.

It was confirmed a few days prior to the dignitaries' arrival that they would be on campus promptly at 10:30 A.M. So, despite the behind the scenes' last minute prepping of the counterattack, things on the surface appeared to be running smoothly.

If there was doubt to those who wondered if we really needed to take the strides to prepare a response to the current dictatorship, Ann, during her morning briefing over the public address gave us fuel for the fire.

"Though we have made tremendous strides in recent weeks, there is still a long way to go. Your efforts to help present this institution, though leaving a lot to be desired, will have to do."

While sitting next to Del, I heard him remark about her comments, "That fucking cunt, you just can't please her."

As Ann continued, I could see the faces around the homeroom, both those who knew what was going to take place and those who didn't have a clue, just cringe at her every word.

"You will go about your business today, and no one will talk unless asked. The faculty has been instructed on how to handle any nonconformity.

"You will not let me down today, because if you do, I will personally bring to an end your scholastic career here at Saint Hedwig's. I will be watching ... and you can count on that."

I looked at the speaker and thought, *She'll be watching, alright ... in fucking disbelief!*

As I recall, it was about 5:00 A.M. and like a well-trained militia the fifteen of us who planned this counter act for liberation, met well before the crack of dawn.

Who else but Roger Frost, was our field commander and had a look of exuberance on his face that could only be described as Christmas morning. From the simplest of tasks, he had outlined the entire day.

You have heard of the saying, "a fish taking to water," well that was Frost. We were about to watch a *specialist* at work.

We each had our assignments and the beauty of this, was that everything was made so simple. Roger had even had a replica of Wally the janitor's key made, so all that we had to do was to walk right in the front door.

It started with our lookouts. Shelley and the twins covered every angle of the convent that Ann or any of her henchmen would have come from. In addition, to make sure that Ann went in the night before and didn't come out, Frost, Pevia and the Gracie brothers took shifts in the school bus that was always parked right outside of the convent doors, to make absolutely sure that she was accounted for. So, without fail we knew where she was.

Pevia's brother was an electrician who worked for Michigan Bell. He fooled around on the side with radio bands and walkie-talkies, to which the girls, Frost and me were provided one to keep abreast of all communications and happenings.

When we got into the school, Roger, his *Friday* and the Gracie brothers, with flashlights in hand, made their way to the upper level. The remainder of us, which included, Del, Adam, Hodgie, Muskie, J.J. and me, along with recruited Junior's Terry Smith and half pint Irish Billy O'Brien, who could contort his frame like a human Gumby toy, had details to perform on the main level.

Arroundo and Baker handled the main office area. Del's father was a master carpenter by trade, so he commandeered some of his tools to reconfigure some of the main office's furniture and equipment.

First thing on their agenda was to saw the legs off of the sofa in Ann's office, and then lightly glue them back into place to provide for a startling arousal for those who would be invited to sit. Likewise, a similar fate was in store for the legs of Ann's antique desk.

Her phone was super-glued, receiver to handset. The door handles to her office were loosened to the point where the cotter pins were barely holding on. And for good measure, fresh dog shit from Adam's German Shepherd was placed inside of the vents of her office, for that perfect aromatic ingredient.

Meanwhile, Hodgie and Muskie loosened all handles and knobs on all senior and junior classroom doors and replace all the chalk in those rooms with look-a-like candy cigarettes. They also pulled all of the pins that held the hinges of the teacher's closets doors in place, just to cause the right amount of a chaotic diversion.

Smith and Irish Mickey caught and killed rodents to subsequently place them into individual rotating slots of vending machines in the teacher's lounge and in the senior hallway. In addition, they plugged up every toilet on the main level and whatever was to be deposited, was either staying or overflowing … but nothing was going down.

As for yours truly, I was joined by J.J., who assisted me in redecorating and rearranging the Athletic Director's office. It was a given that he never showed up until the late morning hours, so upon her inspection and tour of the facility, we wanted to make sure that Ann and her guests would be greeted in a very unique way.

We traded a mutual acquaintance for a Soviet flag, and an oversized picture of Hitler inspecting his troops that he had. Then, J.J. somehow superimposed Ann's face on the centerfold of some raunchy large women's nuddie magazine … it was wonderfully gross.

But this was pretty adolescent stuff compared to what the *four terrorists* were planning on the level above. Kiki and Dickie were assigned to their domain, Fuji's room.

They began by loosening all of the fittings on the plumbing beneath the sinks throughout the room. This was going to be timing issue, because Fuji didn't have his first class until 10:30 on Thursdays.

It also had to be rigged just right to avoid leaking prior to use, and then as soon as the valves were opened ... bam ... water every where!

In addition, the bonus here was that they couldn't just shut the valve down to stop the water's flow. The twins had managed to again rig the on/off valves to disassemble, thus impeding the ability of the unsuspecting user to shut it down. In fact, said user would end up with the valve coming off in their hand.

To accentuate and parlay the beauty of the Gracies' actions, was that the eventual recipient of the overflow was going to be Sheddow and her entire fucking room, just as a wonderful group of freshmen would be coloring away.

The still unknown factor to all of this was what was taking place in Ball's room. Roger was adamant that this room remained off limits to everyone except he and Pevia.

"God help us all!"

By 6:45, we were all at a local Denny's enjoying breakfast, confirming alibis and counting the minutes.

At 8:00, we staggered in under Ann's martial law and a skeptical eye, and as planned small doses of chaos that we allowed them to find were being dealt with.

"Whatever's going on here, I know that you probably had something to do with it ... so I'm warning you, confess now or this will be your last day here at Saint Hedwig's," the fidgety principal said.

Without giving her any satisfaction, I just looked back at her and said, "Day off to a bad start, Sister?"

Both Wally and Carl were scurrying around to re-secure doors without cotter pins and were petitioning the female students for nail polish remover, to try and dislodge Ann's super-glued phone. But this was just the calm before the storm.

In our individual homerooms, playing the obedient roles that she had hoped for, we got a visit from the jumpy principal.

"I expect each and every one of you to cooperate with what will be happening around here today. And though we have not ..." and she paused for a moment "... gotten off to a smooth start, you will mind your business and keep to task." Then she said in a harsh tone, "Is that understood?"

Meekly, the class responded, "Yes, Sister."

Then like a disbelieving Drill Sergeant, she again shouted, "Is that understood?"

With a bit more vigor, we acknowledged her question, as she intently looked at a number of us before heading over to her lieutenant Sheddow, for some obvious last minute instructions.

What she should have done was to cancel the day's activities and sweep the school for problems ... but the *iron penguin* was not to be denied ... or so she thought!

You could sense that she felt that surprises could be waiting around every corner, and it was a given that she was instructing her soldiers to keep a watchful eye out for a select group of us ... all day long.

We looked at her as she kept her back to us and quietly conferred with the pig. Then the horn-rimmed penguin took one last look in our direction and waddled off to her next pulpit.

We got word to Loyola to pass along to the friendly habit wearers of certain places and the times to avoid them.

When the bell sounded to head toward our first period classes, both Walt and Carl were seen running with mops and buckets in hand to the different restroom areas that were experiencing toilet problems. As we quietly went about our business, we were smiling to one another knowing that the best was yet to come.

In about a half hour, it was expected that the teachers' lounge would get their first taste of trouble, as J.J. slipped about a quarter box of Ex-lax into Sheddow's morning cup of java. And, though we couldn't enjoy the actual execution of that one, we did enjoy Wally's later accounts of his battle with dealing with the smell and the free flow of her constitution.

There was just the right amount of diversions that were taking place to keep Ann and her dizzy crew busy, as *the hour* had now come upon us. The visitors had arrived and were greeted by Ann, Roberta and senior faculty staffer, Loyola.

The five of them adjourned to Ann's office for the pre-inspection formalities, and according to Loyola's accounts, the fun began!

While standing in between Ann's desk and furniture, they chitchatted while waiting for coffee to be served. Loyola indicated that "pungent" smells emanating from the vent that put curious looks on everyone's faces.

When the refreshments arrived, they each went to a designated area, with Ann heading for her usual seat at the corner of her desk. Like clockwork,

Loyola indicated that once Ann had adjusted her posture, the desk's corner leg gave way, sending coffee flying in one direction and Ann free falling to the floor in the other.

Loyola said it was a frightened scream that accompanied Ann's spill, and though she wouldn't approve of our methods, as she was recapping, you could tell that she enjoyed the results.

When everybody tried to rise to assist the now prone nun, Roberta and Loyola were able to get to their feet without difficulties from their chairs, but the two visitors' initial momentum to rise caused the rear legs of the sofa to give way, propelling the couch and the visitors head over heels toward the back wall. Even Loyola couldn't keep from laughing while she explained the accounts of that one.

Meanwhile, shirks of noises started to come from Sheddow's room as the Gracie brothers' internal rain forest commenced. Panic was now full scale in the senior hall as the water started flowing at full peak upon the Art room, and its current dwellers had to flee for cover.

Wally was still dealing with the cleanup in the teacher's lounge; doors were falling off of their hinges, board assignments were not being completed due to the chalk replacement and Ann was trying to compose herself from the mishaps that were taking place in her own office.

When word came of the problem in the Art room, Roberta left to intercede and head off that situation, while Ann tried to explain the comedy of errors that was happening around them.

Wally and Carl were now being adamantly summoned to address the issues in Sheddow's room, leaving other problems unresolved. Meanwhile, a now shaken and distressed Ann was leading the visitors toward the AD's office and away from suspected trouble.

Even Loyola admonished us for what they saw in the AD's office. The screams of terror and shock prevailed as they saw the symbols of dictorial Europe and Ann's "puss" plastered on the obese porno's "puss...y"

To those of us who were hearing the accounts of what we had planned, it was hilarious but painful, due to the fact that we couldn't actually witness what we had devised. This however, was relatively nothing compared to what was ticking away in Ball's room.

Hardly recognized for their concern for the well-being and welfare of others, Frost and Pevia had planned the grand finale, and had done so to avoid anybody being within harm's way.

Roger's work had a double-edged implication, due to the fact that, it was not only going to cause Ann trouble, but it would even the score with Ball.

Everybody knew of Ball's infatuation with tropical fish and the habitat that he had created for them in this huge saltwater aquarium in his room. This was his pride and joy and while pandemonium was running rampant the floor below him, at 11:05, Ball was enjoying a "quiet free period" and eating a sandwich at his desk.

Ann, meanwhile, was still trying to explain the perversion of the AD's office, and fighting a losing battle. During her futile attempt to formulate answers, the coup de gras, Roger's flying fish show, was about to occur.

In the non-submerged portion of the aquarium's filter, was a device that was on a timed detonator. At quarter past the hour, the explosion was just as Frost had planned. Muffled by the water for the most part, glass and sea life flew halfway across the room. It was Ball's girlish bloodcurdling scream that resonated throughout the facility and *announced* loud and clear that Roger's Pearl Harbor had been successful.

School was closed for the rest of the day and for the remainder of the week as an internal and police investigation took place. On Saturday, many of us with our parents were called in for questioning, but when all of this occurred, we were on the other side of the building in class and in front of a teacher. Our alibis were airtight and despite Ann's insistence that we had to be involved, even Ann's top aids couldn't refute our whereabouts.

Not a trace was to be found.

The ribs promised to Loyola and some of her friends from the prior week were finally delivered, and when asked about the delay we simply responded, "Sorry, Sisters, but our plans to get these to you sooner, sort of blew up."

Many of the nuns who were in the convent's kitchen when we arrived with the goodies sheepishly smiled.

The usually refined Sister Carol looked back at us and said, "I understand … there seems to be a lot of that going on around here."

～ when birds of a feather try to nest together ～

The obvious fallout from the well-planned attack was a continued daily monitoring of the entire student body. The beauty was that they still couldn't prove anything and the perpetrators pact not to squeal was iron clad ... except for ...

... Shelley. She was fearless, brash and possessed loose lips that, when not wrapped around a cock, had the habit and reputation of "sinking ships."

She was warned about the troubles that bragging could bring and she assured us that this time, "mum was the word."

As weeks passed and as the dust from that "dark Thursday" settled, a subtle relationship seemed to be developing between the captain of the cheerleaders and some of the women lay teachers. It was nothing startling, but due to the exchange of some courtesies and noticeable liberties, it was worth scrutinizing.

During breaks in the day, you would see the brazen bitch conversing with the enemy. Which again seemed nothing more than a senior trying to make *in roads* after her high school days. However, that changed and one late morning when Shelley was seen in the company of Gainer, Sheddow and Sister Ann, our fears raised to a code red status!

News of this summit spread quickly among those of us who were involved in Ann's *display day fiasco*. Especially when Sue Kinovich told us that there was laughter among this budding alliance.

Could an *immunity for special liberties* deal be on Shelley's plate?

Later in the day, a few of us finally had a chance to corner her and question these get-togethers.

"Hey, Shell, wait the fuck up," yelled Del.

"Fellas," she smiled back at Del, J.J. and myself.

Del fired back, "you've been hangin' out a lot with Gainer, shithole and the prin, what the fuck is goin' on?"

Taking a defensive posture, with hands now on hips, she responded, "Nothing, I'm just showing them that at least one of us can be trusted."

"Well, don't get to close to them," J.J. retorted.

"Fuck off, limp dick," she replied and she brashly walked between Del and me, rubbing her tight little body against us to escape any further questioning.

"I don't like this," J.J. said as we all watched her disappear down the hall.

Basketball season was in its early stages and those of us who were either shut out from football or decided not to play, decided to indulge on the *hardwood*. Most of us had a pretty extensive extracurricular after-school schedule, with homework, jobs, basketball, hockey and, most importantly, the pursuit of sex.

Now unlike Hedwig's ineptness on the football field, we were a decent, middle of the pack basketball squad. And considering the fact that the basketball roster equaled in size to the football team, is it any wonder why we sucked with the pigskin?

Funny thing, despite being the same size in number of players to the football team, we were not allowed to take the school bus for any road games. We were forced to usually hook up with three or four guys per car and drive ourselves, which probably was for the best.

It was an early December Friday night and the schedule had us traveling to Waterford Our Lady of the Lakes, an equally small school located in the shadows of the new Pontiac Silverdome, some fifty-five miles away from our neighborhood.

In what was a close game throughout, Joey Ochuba's baseline jumper at the buzzer found the bottom of the net and allowed us to escape with a slim two-point victory.

Back in the victorious post game locker room, after coach gave us the "way to go, but there's still a lot of work to be done" speech, the conversation focused on the fact that the lovely Miss Gainer was in attendance at the game!

This was strange because, not only didn't she not attend any of the football games earlier in the year, but out of our first five basketball games, this was the only one that she attended, and it was more than fifty miles away from our home gym and about seventy miles away from her apartment.

She sat in our fan section or as they were commonly referred to … the "the six additional cheerleaders."

Our roster numbers not only mimicked those of the football squad, but we shared similar fan support.

Besides being in attendance, she was noticeably chummy with the cheerleaders all game long … especially with the captain!

Showering, the banter continued, "She's here for my cock," Adam Baker said.

"In your dreams, asshole," I responded.

"You fuckers just won't believe me, but I'm telling you that something's up," J.J. added.

"Oh stop with that shit, J.J.," I said.

"Alright, you just wait and see, Shelley and that broad are up to something and we're gonna get caught in the middle of it."

We left him in the showers by himself, lamenting his feelings and preceded to get dressed for the ride home. After exiting the locker room, we were greeted by those few who came out to root us on. There was small talk and the occasional pats on the shoulder and even Gainer was in the mix to offer congratulations.

"Nice game, Mark, you really looked good out there," she said with a smile.

"Well thanks, Miss Gainer, it was nice of you to come out and see us," I responded as I thought my dick was going to jump out of its pants. All of a sudden Gainer said, "Well, Shell, are you and the gang ready?"

"Shell? What the fuck?" Adam, J.J. and I looked at one another and J.J. got this "I told you, motherfuckers" look on his face.

We quickly headed into J.J.'s car and ignored the inquiries of some of the other guys on the team who tried to see where they could meet up with us for a post-game bite to eat.

"Do you believe this fucking shit? Did I tell you that they were going to recruit her for information against us," J.J. whaled.

"Just cool your fucking jets and don't let them out of your sight," I said. I didn't want to admit it, but I was now beginning to think that J.J. was right about his suspicions.

Shelley, two junior cheerleaders and Gainer all piled into the teacher's car for the trek home. As we tracked them from a distance, our collective anticipation … make that fear increased all the way down I-75.

"Maybe Gainer is finally chilling out and realizes that we're cool," I offered.

"Quit being so fucking naïve. Shelley's a rat and Gainer should be with people her own fucking age," J.J. argued.

When we arrived back in the neighborhood, we stopped just shy of the campus parking lot, but within view of what was happening. We saw Shelley jump out of the car and released the back seat to allow the two juniors to get out of the back. After saying their good-byes, Shelley had jumped back into Gainer's car and off they sped.

It was as if we had all seen a ghost. "What do you two assholes think now?" J.J. said.

"Just shut up and drive dickhead," Adam responded.

The chase was on.

"Hey, you know what. Fuck this. Just drop me off at Koobs, I'm going to play some cards," I begged.

"The fuck you are," Baker scorned, "it's musketeer time and you're coming!"

As we drove down Michigan Avenue, it looked as they were heading in the direction of the Big Boy Restaurant, a usual gathering place. But soon, we were some ten miles past the Dearborn hangout and on the fringes of hitting Livonia.

Now at the intersection of Seven Mile and Middlebelt Roads, the two of them pulled into the parking lot of what appeared to be a bar. Even more startling, was that when Shelley exited the car, she was no longer in her *cutsie* cheerleader's outfit, but rather a nice pair of slacks, heals and an ass-length leather jacket.

"What the fuck," I said. "She can't go in there … she's not old enough."

"Well, if she's going in … we're going in," J.J. issued.

"Now wait a minute," I said. "At least she's with Gainer; we're all under age and with no IDs to prove otherwise."

In a blink of an eye, both Adam and J.J. produced fake IDs from their wallets and made me feel like Cinderella with no invite to the ball.

"Holy shit, where did you guys get these?"

They just both snickered at me as if I had just fallen off of the turnip truck, and continued to tell me that they have been barhopping with these forged IDs for over a year. I was more out of the loop than I had thought.

"Well I guess that I'm the odd man out," I declared.

"You're right," J.J. said, "but if you both go in," I fumbled, and they both looked at me as if to say, "Yes?"

"Ah fuck it, just go and let me know what you find out? But, leave me the keys so I can drive over to that Burger King for a bite to eat."

"I'm going to leave you my car keys," he laughed, "think again."

"Oh fuck, come on ... I'm hungry, and it's cold out here."

Adam interceded, "Just leave him the keys, but you gotta get something for all of us and be back in this lot in ten minutes to pick us up."

So after giving me their orders and money, they went one way for "burgers" and I drove off in the other for ... well, sort of the same thing.

I got out and went to the counter to place the order, all the while keeping an eye open across the street. Within five to six minutes, I was back in the car, food in hand and making my way back to the bar's lot.

Moments after I parked and started to indulge in my part of the order, the two of them were walking back toward the car. J.J. opened the passenger's side door and allowed Adam to climb into the back, before hustling into the car and trying to collect himself.

"Well," I said, "is it a nice place?"

Adam looked at me through the rear view mirror and responded, "Nice, who gives a flying fuck if it's nice?"

"Well, what about the talent? Some good looking pussy in there?" I said while chowing down.

The two of them just looked at each other as if I was speaking in a foreign language.

"Well, is somebody going to tell me what the fuck's going on?"

J.J. looked at me and put his hand on my arm as if to say, "Shut up." He then said, "They were dancing."

"You mean to tell me that they were already picked up?"

Again they just looked at each other in amazement.

I continued, "Plus, isn't Gainer going with a doctor or intern or some fucking thing like that? And that fucking Shelley, you expect me to be surprised that she's already picked up some guy ... fuck, she'll have her lips wrapped around his cock in no time," I laughed and proceeded to take another bite out of my burger.

"Shut up, stupid," Baker said. "They were dancing with each other ... slowly and passionately French kissing!"

I went blank for a moment and with a mouth full of food, tried to regain my composure and said, "Fok ya, mudderfokers,"

"What was that?" J.J. asked.

"You heard me," I said after swallowing the mouthful, "don't fuck with me."

J.J. just shook his head and said, "We're not. They were dancing and making out with each other at the same fucking time."

I looked in the mirror and saw Adam nodding his head in the affirmative.

"And they were doing this in front of guys?"

J.J. followed, "We were the only two guys in the whole fucking joint."

"It's a dyke joint," I laughed in amazement. "Oh my fucking God!"

"Moose, you wouldn't believe it," Adam said. "When we walked in, there was this Amazon at the front door who could play middle line backer for the Lions. She asked me what we wanted and I said "A couple of beers."

Then she looked back at me and said, "Honey, do you know where you're at?"

He continued, "The next thing I knew, dickhead over here was tugging on my sleeve and speaking in some foreign fucking language. I just looked around and thought I was fuckin' already tanked. There were chicks everywhere, chicks with chicks and over on the crowed dance floor, our two friends were as close as close can be."

"I don't believe this," I said. "Do you mean to tell me that Shelley is a lez?" And that fucking honey pot Gainer ... she's into pussy too?"

"I know," J.J. smiled, "can you believe it? I'm getting a chubby just thinking about it!"

"Down, boy," I urged. Then I paused and smiled.

"What?" Adam inquired.

"You know ... this is great," I said in a matter of fact tone.

"I know, motherfucker. Wouldn't you like to be in the middle of that sandwich?" J.J. hollered.

I thought for a moment ... "Yes!" Then said, "No ... wait a minute and just listen. They're obviously trying to hide this thing and keep it in a spot where they can control it. If we had any concerns about Shelley spilling the beans on us for what we did, we could ... ya know, use this against her?

"In addition, I wonder if Carol baby would want this to get out that she's a closet dyke?"

Adam climbed on board and said, "Yeah, and I wonder how it would look that an underaged high school girl was being harbored by of all fucking people, her teacher?

"Just think, fellas, Gainer's career just fell into our laps and we're on the verge of adding lezbo onto Shelley's resume."

"But it's our word against theirs," Adam raised issue.

"We need a camera or something for proof," J.J. pondered.

Adam responded, "You're nuts if you think that we're gonna get by that huge bitch at the door ... with a camera no less."

"She was that big?" I inquired. To which, they both nodded yes in a vigorous manner.

I thought for a moment and said, "I need a phone."

"For what?" J.J. asked.

"Don't ask questions, just get me to a pay phone ... but first, drive by Gainer's car."

J.J. and I exchanged positions and he followed my instructions by first passing by the teacher's blue Datsun, so that I could copy down her license's plate number.

"Gentlemen, there's a pay phone across the street at that gas station. I'm going to walk over and make a call. Park the car somewhere over there in the dark and let the air out of her tires and knock out that windshield."

While they got started on my request, I called the police and informed them that there was a "situation" and where "it" was taking place.

Our source of proof was on its way. I flagged them over to the gas station and got back into the car. Within minutes, two patrol cars were in the lot surveying the situation.

Management obviously must have been made aware that there was trouble with the flashing lights of the cop cars on their property, and soon many of the patrons were filing out to check on their wheels.

Gainer was now by her car and noticeably upset to have seen what had happened. Shelley could be seen just outside of the front door, trying to see if everything was all right with her girlfriend.

At 11:48 P.M., the police report was being taken, this was also known as proof! Proof that would soon be on the public record, for "anyone to obtain a copy of it."

Though it would have been fun to have stayed around to see what the two *special friends* did next; logic, fatigue and poker were calling in the distance.

The next day, J.J. placed a timely call to Shelley mentioning that a friend who had some "unique qualities," happened to see her getting quite cozy with this attractive blonde at the Two of a Kind Lounge in Livonia last night. He went on to say that her silence, pretty much "spoke volumes."

Then on Monday, I went straight to Walt the Janitor's cubby and asked, "Where's that *Penthouse* that C. G., or shall I say Carol Gainer loaned to you, and made that comment about those two chicks getting it on in the hot tub?"

He just smiled back at me and said, "C.G., you know who C.G. is?"

I just shook my head yes and urged, "Just hand it over."

He forked over the magazine and I left him to go to the library, to type myself a little note that read, "Perhaps the caption on this should be ... hot tub fun with Carol and Shelley."

The note went on to say, "We know more about you than you think, but nothing needs to be said ... we hope!"

I proceeded to slip that note into the location where the pictorial was in the magazine and sealed the whole thing in a manila envelope, and placed it indiscriminately on her desk.

Though many of us fantasized about the two of them together, their bond seemed to diminish with the same speed that Shelley seemed ready to give all of us up over the *issues* that rocked Ann's stranglehold over our senior year.

And yes, J.J. was right about Shelley being ready to rat us out, but this was a pretty firm insurance policy to protect this from ever happening.

There was much to be thankful for as we approached the Turkey Day weekend.

～ it's the most wonderful and confusing time of the year ～

As indicated earlier, J.J. and I had a strange relationship. There was a certain camaraderie that we had, sprinkled with a little respect and a whole lot of distrust. But what really stood out between us was a lot of competition and a shit load of spite.

Perhaps Mario Puzzo summed up our relationship best, when he allowed Michael Corleone to say to say to Frank Pantangoli, "My father always told me ... keep your friends close, but your enemies closer."

J.J. was not what I would call book smart, but he was cunning and street smart.

Despite everything that you could nail him on, coupled with the fact that he was a living and breathing Simon Lagreed, you wanted him on your side because he could always, somehow manage results.

He was jumpy and was always talking some kind of bullshit. He'd never do anything without expecting something in return, and you always thought that he was mixed up in something underhanded, wherever it might have been. He would have made a great CIA gent.

As the holidays approached, all grades were expected to become involved in a charitable event that would benefit a couple of families who had been down on their luck. What it basically boiled down to was that teams of us within the school would get the "needy" family a tree with all of the trimmings, interview them to see what kinds of things that Santa could bring for the kids, and make sure that they would have enough comfort and food to last throughout the season. It was dubbed as our "Advent sacrifice and seasonal gift."

In years past, I'd never see J.J. participate in this event, knowing all along that he was nothing more than the J.J. that I always knew … a self-serving, on the take prick.

I'd shake my head at him, knowing that if he could pilfer something from these people in need, he'd do so in an instant … the motherfucker!

I found myself trying to do a lot of things at once, with time becoming limited before Christmas. I was running errands for my mom, picking up things for my dad, hunting down items for the nuns and trying to assist in getting this project done before we hit the eleventh hour. All this and I had not focused on my new and most important priority … Laura.

I had a carload of things when I decided to run over to Fairlane Mall to try to get something for her. Out of the corner of my eye, I catch J.J. driving in a panicked rush in the same direction that I was going, so I thought that maybe I could catch him in an act of deceit, and have something on the bastard.

Besides, I was in my dad's car, so I didn't think that he knew it was me, as I was tailing from a distance.

Nearing the mall, J.J. made a sudden turn south bound on the Southfield Freeway and really began to pick up his pace. I was thinking that this was getting too juicy to resist now and was going to see this adventure through.

About five miles down the road, he exits on Oakwood Boulevard and races toward Oakwood Hospital. I found myself about five car lengths behind him and when I got into the parking lot, he was already running toward the emergency room doors. All of a sudden, I thought that he has a genuine problem and all I was there to do was to see the cocksucker get into trouble.

"Shit, maybe it was his mom or God forbid, that sweet looking sister of his?" Whatever, I felt compelled to cross the line and to go into the ER to snoop.

I found myself a little corner and began to observe just whom it was that he had rushed to see.

I saw no signs of his mom or anyone else that I could have linked him to, but was drawn to a few kids that were sobbing inconsolably. As I repositioned myself, I saw three little ones, somewhere between the ages of six and twelve, who began to cling to J.J. as if he were their father … *Wait, could he? Naw, what the fuck was I thinking?*

The kids seemed to be petrified at whatever was going on and only seemed to be more at ease with J.J. I couldn't tell what his involvement was, or who was the one that the kids were upset about.

Then a representative of the hospital came to J.J. and the children and took the four of them to a separate area, allowing me to head into the waiting room for a better vantage point.

Suddenly a woman, probably in her 30s, but looking haggard enough to look twenty years older, came from a room with what looked to be a doctor trying to console her.

She seemed distant, unsure and unable to speak. Then at the sight of J.J., she surrendered herself into his arms and literally broke down, screaming, "He's gone J.J. He's gone."

"I know, sweetheart, but we're gonna make it … I promise ya … we're gonna make it."

"And the kids … oh, J.J., those poor children!"

Again he comforted by saying, "I know, sweetheart, I know," and you could hear his voice start to crack.

In a reassuring act, J.J. grabbed her with steadfast strength and promised her that everything was going to work out, and that he'd make sure that they had whatever they needed.

Then a nurse appeared, gathered them all together and took them to another private area.

As the situation calmed, I worked my way to the nurse's station and asked, "Can you tell me anything about the people or their problems who were just here?"

"Are you a family member?" a staffer asked. And as much as I wanted to say yes, I just couldn't bring myself to doing so. I just shook my head and headed back toward the waiting room.

About forty minutes had passed and there was no sight of J.J. or the surviving family members, so I decided to go about my business and leave. Despite my curiosity, I really had nothing to go on and felt like I had hit a brick wall.

Besides, I really didn't deserve to know anything about this situation.

The thing that was so compelling however was that I had this cold and hollow feeling inside, that I tried to catch J.J. at something and ended up seeing a side to this nemesis that I had never seen before. The cold and

calculating prick was compassionate and providing hope and comfort ...
while all I was interested in, was trying to see what kind of shit he was about
to cause.

I left the facility troubled and somewhat ashamed.

A couple of days later, while assigned to pick up some hams for the gift
baskets, I ran into J.J.'s sister, Monique. The stunning twenty-six-year old
beauty was one of the most feminine and gracious women I ever met. She
epitomized kindness and always had a pleasant disposition. I never met a
princess, but as far as I was concerned ... she had the pedigree to be one.

"Hi, Monny," a nickname that she answered to.

"Hi, Mark," she said with one of those incredible smiles and she offered
me a hug as she always did. "Have your Christmas shopping done?"

"No, But I'm getting there," I said. "Listen though, can I confess
something to you and also ask you a question?"

She got a puzzled look on her face, but nodded to the affirmative.

"The other night I saw your brother racing down Michigan, and don't ask
me why, but I followed him." She just grinned at me as if to say, "When will
you two ever leave the other one alone?"

"He went to Oakwood Hospital and being the asshole that I am, I just had
to follow him." She shook her head as if to say, "I know all about it."

I continued, "I saw all of them crying from a concealed area, and quite
frankly, left after a lengthy time of not seeing him or any of the others.
Monny, what happened?"

She pulled me aside and sat me down and began to tell me this story.

"Barbara and Neal used to live down the street from us. As we grew up,
Neal and J.J. would talk about sports or you know ... those guy things." She
continued, "Neil became sort of a big brother to J.J. and kind of took over
where my dad left off."

J.J. lost his father at a very young age to heart failure.

"When Neal got laid off about a year and a half ago, he started to drink and
they began to have some major financial troubles. He was able to pick up
some odd jobs, but they were never able to catch up, even with Barbara trying
to help out.

"Well, it hit J.J. kind of hard to see them tumble like that and they
eventually couldn't afford to stay where they were.

"They went on State Aid and welfare but things just got worse. Neal's drinking continued and though they didn't say anything out of pride, we eventually found out that they were living out of their car, when Neil refused to comply with his parent's requests to stop the drinking.

"His parents said that they would care for the kids, but would not allow Neal and Barb to stay as long as his drinking persisted. A fight resulted, hurtful things were said and Neal gathered their meager belongings and the kids and left."

She began to shed a tear, but continued.

"They became homeless and still didn't hit rock bottom. J.J. would get them some odds and ends, made arrangements for them to check into a hotel and tried to get Neal enrolled and become focused on a recovery program through AA. Unfortunately, Neal just wasn't interested in turning things around and expected others, including J.J. to continue to do things for them.

"The other day ... the day that you saw them, he had come off of an all-night drunk, ran a red light and blindsided two teenagers in a small car."

Her tears became more evident and you could tell that this had a profound effect upon her as well.

Then I thought, *The kids, those were the kids that they were talking about ... oh, for Christ's sake.*

She composed herself and talked through the tears, "The two kids were killed immediately and after going through the windshield, Neal was pronounced Dead On Arrival."

I saw that she was about to break down again so I took her in my arms and just wondered about all of the lives that were going to be affected by this whole thing ... Merry fucking Christmas.

"J.J. was the only one that Barb and the kids could turn to, and that's basically where you caught up to them."

I felt like shit when she said that, despite the fact that she meant no harm. We hugged again and small talked ourselves toward an exit and wished each other ... a happy holiday. Can you believe I told her to have a happy holiday? What an asshole I was.

I went home and called Billy Bednarick and told him the entire story, and to appeal to him to see if there was any way that we could dip into our class dues to sponsor this family and to get them housed, fed and somehow into the holiday spirit.

Billy said that he'd do what he could, but not to expect much considering that Neal's actions caused so much grief to the survivors. This was not going to be an easy chore.

On the 23rd, two days before the birth of the Christ child, the two teens were buried in separate morning ceremonies and Barb had J.J. take her to both, in effort of trying to apologize for the actions of her noncompliant husband.

Then, later that afternoon in a simple ceremony, Neal was remembered. Only a handful of people showed, including his widow, their children, J.J.'s mom and Monny, two others that I didn't know, J.J., and in the back … me.

Not even Neal's parents would come to honor the memory of their own son.

The two youngest children clung tightly to their mother, who was meagerly attired and noticeably defeated. The eldest boy just sat in a somber state like a soldier with little, if any of a future. J.J. was sitting next to him ready to offer an arm of comfort, but careful not to infringe upon his pride.

I don't know why I attended? It really wasn't for Neal, though I was torn over his demise.

Of course, I was left empty over the void he left in his family, perhaps more prior to his death than afterwards. And, of course, I was disgusted over the fact that he was pathetically weak and the hole that he left them in … that they probably would never be able to climb out of.

As I sat in silence, I began to concede that it wasn't for Barbara either. I was sad for her situation, but honestly I just felt emotionless for her.

Certainly I felt for the kids, but hoped that despite the next few years that would be filled with pain, that there was going to be some sort of light at the end of their respective tunnels.

So, that left J.J…who I disdained, questioned and blatantly thought was a first-class asshole.

Problem was that I so often questioned his skeptical ways that I never really considered what it was like to walk in his shoes.

For the son of a bitch wasn't the best man, but today he was just the better man.

He wasn't the best Catholic, just the better Christian.

And the motherfucker didn't have all of the answers; he just had enough of the right ones at the right time.

I honestly think of J.J. every Christmas, not just because of his heroism, but because he showed me what the true gift of meaning was all about.

From the competitive standpoint that seemed to mark our time together, I was hardly in his league.

"Merry Christmas, you prick … no make that Joyeux Noel Joel!"

~ a glimpse into christmas present and christmas future ~

With Laura, the holidays were a little bit more strenuous than usual. Reason being the formalities of either introducing her to my extended family, or being introduced to hers.

Then there were all of the "have to dos." You know, we have to go to my grandma's, or aunt's, or we have to go see this display or that ... just always enough of something to screw up your chance of watching a bowl game. And there is nothing more upsetting than placing a bet on a game and not being able to watch it.

Especially if the thing that's keeping you from the game has something to do with sitting around people that you don't know, don't like, or don't care to listen to. But, that's what you do when you're in love—let me rephrase that—that's what you do when you're *chasing new pussy*.

Because let's face it, you can tell who's *hunting* especially during the holidays, not necessarily by the things that they buy the ones that they're chasing, but rather how the prey subtly subdues the hunter into becoming nothing more than a smiling and sitting pigeon.

He's the one who goes and sits next to the girl and says "he's perfectly content" to be right there, when every other guy who walks in the door, streaks through the room of women like he's running a fly pattern in the Rose Bowl. He's the same one who lets the kids go in one direction, and doesn't see the wife until either half time or until the kids break something.

He proceeds to either the den or basement where the *boys* are, who have already bagged their prey—or shall I say—have whipped themselves into a temporary stay of continued execution.

They have nothing left to prove and are allowed to meet up with these other retired hunters for a session of beer drinking, cussing at the game and watching their extra cash pass from their pockets into their bookies.

Meanwhile, you sit there all gentlemanly and act like you really care about what's being discussed, when secretly you're trying to decode everything coming from the other room and simultaneously incorporating that into the *spread*.

This is when you officially become a circus performer, due to the fact that you are now juggling.

Your mind is on the game, your persona is in play with the women folk, and your desires are on that sweet little girl that you have been lying to all along by saying that you're really having a great time.

But, truth be told, she knows that you're lying and insists that you go and watch the game! But in the hope of carnal knowledge, you call her bluff with one of your own ... and decide to stay the course.

Now, here's where it gets tricky. You want to go and watch the game but the entire gang who's already watching it, knows what you're up to ... and are just aching to give you just enough of a razzing to make you feel uncomfortable ... and if that was all you had to endure, "no big deal."

But also in that room is her dad ... in this case, *the voice*, and he suddenly goes from really enjoying the game, to staring you down, because he knows what your *true intentions* are.

So then you're now in the place that you wanted to be ... but you wish you weren't there because you know that you're ruining her father's enjoyment of the game ... because you know that he knows ... that all you really want is his daughter's pussy.

Besides, guys like bragging how much they got on the game, but if you *spill the beans*, then that's going to lead to visions of ... "oh great, she's in love with a deadbeat gambler who she'll marry ... he'll piss away all of their money and they'll have to move back in with us, until they divorce."

"So how did you make these delicious Christmas cookies?"

Isn't Christmas wonderful?

~ out with the old garb and in with the new ~

For those of us at Saint Hedwig's, Christmas really didn't come until after we got back from the holiday break. Standing at the front door upon our return was the old guard, the nuns from Emolina's reign who had been working under duress with Ann.

They had smiles on their faces and were welcoming us back with hugs and genuine interest in how we spent our holiday.

Did Ann see the ghost of Christmas past, present and future and have a revelation? Did the events of that black Thursday temper her outlook on the school? Or was there a Christmas coup that knocked her administration off? Whatever it was, she was nowhere to be seen and there was an air of looseness and liberation throughout the hallways.

I walked up to Loyola and said, "What's going on?"

She just smiled at me and said, "She's gone."

"Who?"

"What do you mean who?" she playfully scorned. "Ann ... that's who."

"What? ... that's great ... What happened?"

"We all went back to the mother house for the holiday, and between Christmas and New Year's, she not only resigned her position, but left the order."

"What? She's no longer a nun?"

"That's right, she packed her bags and left."

Without the need for sentries at every corner of every hallway, we orderly filed into our respective homerooms and were ready to start back to the conclusion of the school year.

Ann's exodus was obviously the topic of conversation, but there was really an indifferent attitude about her leaving, especially among those of us who considered her to be an adversary.

So, with Loyola now given the reigns of control for the rest of the school year, the only ones who now seemed to be out of place, were the lay teachers who so adamantly supported Ann's ways.

For the seniors, thoughts turned to the fact that our time here was now going to be winding down. So we started to concern ourselves with plans for Spring Break, the prom and life after Hedwig's.

Fortunately, I didn't have to worry about employment while in high school. My dad encouraged my involvement in sports and maintaining a good GPA in effort of getting into college, and without exhausting too much of an effort, I was able to meet his expectations.

Laura and I were making nice progress, but remained celibate, though we indulged in other fruits of carnal knowledge. But the respect was in place and I had such *a thing* for her that I really didn't press her for the *sweet spot*, until she was absolutely ready.

Basketball and hockey remained the current diversions during the cold weather months, but I must admit, I was eagerly awaiting the return of baseball. In all modesty, I was a standout in baseball and was expecting my senior year to be an ass-kicking sensation that would allow me to write my own ticket into college!

But getting to that point ... especially in Michigan, during January and February, was like *doing time*.

Winter in the Great Lakes State is dreary as shit. It's cold, the sun never shines and in Detroit, it hardly snows. And what little we get is not white ... it's sort of gray and once it hits the pavement, it turns into a dirty, slushy pile of shit. It's simply a climatological prison.

Therefore, the focus during homeroom's morning briefings started to turn more and more toward sunny Florida ... and Spring Break!

Daytona Beach or Fort Lauderdale, flying or driving, nice room, the YMCA or the backseat of your car, were all initial topics of conversation. Incorporated into the mix would then come traveling partners. Due to the fact that money was of a premium, most needed to drive and many needed to offset some of the cost of transportation by sharing the ride, rooms and whatever else could possibly pop up?

The problem was ... who your partner(s) was going to be, because popularity didn't always equate into financial means. So, there would be sessions that would have you scratching you head wondering if you would have to travel with an asshole just to make ends meet.

It was like the trading deadline for teams in the thick of the pennant race. One moment your team is set, and the next it's divided because one person can't get along with someone else.

The one thing that everybody could agree on was the need to win the annual Hedwig interschool competition known as "All Stars." A weeklong event that combined scholastic achievements, community service and a multitude of different athletic events.

It also was a Lenten Rite of passage with us that in some way tried to promote commitment, sacrifice and good will.

For parody sake, the seniors were teamed up with the freshmen, while the juniors and sophomores were coupled for the competition. The angle here was that the winning team would get three additional days off during the Spring Break, while the losing team had to perform school and church spring-cleaning duties, during half-day sessions of that same three-day period. So, in our menial world, the stakes were high!

If you were trying to handicap this series, the edge would have been given to the juniors and sophomores. They were more compatible in mind, body and attitudes than the freshmen and us, who seemed to be further apart than in just years and the other aforementioned qualities.

They were babies and I don't mean that in just attitude, but rather in the fact that we intimidated them, and it was difficult to conceive how they were going to be able to contribute to the cause.

When we were freshmen, we wilted in the presence of the seniors and were total fuck-ups during the All Stars battle.

Motivating them with three extra days or the Florida scenario was futile, because they just didn't have the same motivation to get away as we did. Threats or drill sergeant techniques were also a waste of time, because they would just freeze up and be on the verge of tears. So we took the big brother and big sister approach.

The senior girls were especially good at this task. Their involvement made the freshmen girls feel as if they had an older sister looking out for them, while they made the boys feel that they had some sort of interest in them, and that they were cute and had a certain allure to an older woman.

The basic objectives were to make sure that the freshmen had all of their assigned work brought up-to-date, which really wasn't that much of a problem, considering that most of them were impressionable and still within the clutches of Ann's "do your work or else doctrine."

Despite the senior's chicanery and focus on life after high school, our overall work ethic was pretty good, so we were confident that our academic requirements of this competition would be met.

Besides, the other side had Robbie Selby, who had Incompletes dating back to Kindergarten, which warranted the thought, how did he make it this far? Let's just call it the power of tuition and the blindness of a Catholic education.

Yet another portion of the competition dealt with all team members, performing some act of kindness … for the community service part of the event. This didn't mean picking up a piece of paper blowing around on the lawn or helping an old woman cross the street.

No, it had to be something of at least three hours in duration, verifiable, and needed to benefit someone other than the individual who was providing the service.

I had yet to find any activity to satisfy this requirement and was starting to get pressured by the senior team leaders to get something accomplished. I thought about going to the track and picking up losing tickets in between the races that I was going to bet, but that suggestion didn't go over very well.

As I was about to exit Spanish class, Loyola beckoned me, "Stay here, I want to talk to you."

I obviously began to wonder what this was going to lead to, since it was still too early for a lunch order.

Walking by with her little clique, Shelley whispered in my direction, "Hey, limp dick, it's finally going to happen … she wants your bod."

I simply looked back at her, put two fingers in a "V" formation up to my mouth and stuck my tongue in between my fingers as if to replicate that I was eating pussy. As I raised my eyebrows, she just flipped me the bird and walked out of the room.

With just the two of us there, she spoke, "I want you to do something for me."

Without saying a word, my facial expression signified, "What?"

"The nuns are hosting an early Easter party for the residents of the Norman Home," she said. This was a care facility for the mentally challenged which was near our campus, but off limits, simply because most of the student population didn't want to bother with these people.

She continued, "I want you to come and help us out."

"But, Sister, I already have a community service thing that I'm scheduled to do," which was simply me lying my ass off.

"I don't care about that," she interrupted. "I need you there … and you will be there for me!"

She knew that I wouldn't turn her down, so in an exasperated tone I asked, "when?"

"Saturday, at the Romanowski Hall, it starts at ten … you be there at nine."

"Ahh, Sister, not Saturday," I begged. I had planned to forego cards and hopefully spend a late evening with Laura, but I could see it in her eyes, that my plans were about to change.

"Can't you get somebody else for this?" I asked.

"Probably," she responded, "but I want you. And I'll be calling your parents to assure your appearance, so you be a good boy and go on … get out of here."

Call my parents, what a joke. The only reason she called was to ask my mom to pick up some specialty items for her and a few of the older nuns the next time she ran to Hudson's.

"Alright, alright, I'll be there, but it might not be until 9:30."

To which she fired right back, "better make it 8:30, I might have a few extra things that I'll need you to do."

"Shit," I said.

"Don't you use that tone with me, mister," she barked. "Make it 8:00 now."

I looked at her with a pissed look on my face and she frowned back at me and said, "Do you want to go for 7:30?"

I just turned and headed for the door.

"By the way," she said, "where are you off to?"

"Biology," I quipped, "why? Am I going to get penalized for that too?"

"Go on you little smart ass," she said with a smile, "and take it easy on Ball … don't let Frost make him cry."

———   ———

Here it was, a Friday night and Laura's parents decided to turn in early giving us the whole basement to ourselves! My urges were on overdrive and she was extremely playful.

The only problem was that I couldn't get Loyola out of my friggin' head and I knew that if I indulged with Laura and *popped my gun* that I wouldn't make it on time to Loyola's early morning event.

"Come on, baby," she said to me with that innocent little look, while she left-handed my member through my jeans. She began to become more intent on getting her way and was starting to work me into a frenzy.

"Don't you think that we should bring Richard (her pet name for my dick) out to play."

Then she laid a French kiss on me that by itself made my cock rock hard and said, "I think he'd like me to kiss him just like that too."

Fuck, I thought as I tried to restrain her hand.

She just laughed at me and worked her head into my crotch, and said, "But you good little Catholic boys have to do your duty … don't you?"

Then she sat up next to me, stuck her hand inside of her own jeans and began to give me a little show, with the gyrations, moaning and all … and when she was done, she brought those two moist fingers up to my lips and rubbed one of them on my mouth.

As I extended my tongue to get the full compliment of taste, she pulled her hand away and said in an incredibly teasing way, "Sorry, but dessert is only for those who do their work."

Then she put the two fingers in her own mouth and I thought I was going to cum in my pants on the spot.

I had never seen her so provocative and kinky before!

Then she sighed and uttered, "Mmm, now that's sweet … you don't know what you're missing."

Screw Loyola, this had now gone to a whole different level and I wasn't about to miss this opportunity. I went for her top and was about to go for her tits, when all of a sudden, as if some angel had come to fuck up my night, I hear footsteps on the upper level and a throat being cleared at the top of the stairs.

"You kids mind if I come down and watch Carson, I can't sleep."

"Sure, Dad, come on down we're just talking anyways."

Ain't this a bitch, I thought. *I was already to grab myself a nice* little piece of pie, *and now this. Friggin' Loyola must have prayed that I get shut out tonight.*

Believe me when I tell you that it was not a comfortable ride home … and on top of everything I missed poker!

I arrived at Romanowski Hall at 9:00 A.M., clad in jeans, a sweatshirt, my ball cap and tennis shoes, with a big fucking chip on my shoulder. When I walked in the entrance … with what else, a large box of doughnuts that Loyola instructed my parents to have me pick up last night, there she was, with a smug look on her puss, standing with some of the other penguins, and to my surprise, my hockey coach and local business proprietor, Stan Stankowicz.

"Morning all," I said as I got to the group. Then I continued, "Coach, what are you doing here?"

"Hey, Mark," he offered, "there's a little something here for you, but I'll let the good sisters explain that … I've gotta run." He shook my hand and quickly made a dash for the door.

Then Loyola said, "Come here and help us set up."

"Wait a minute," I responded, "you got me out of bed on a Saturday morning to set tables?"

"No," the interim principal said, "but until otherwise, you mind your manners, mister."

I saw four of the nuns from Hedwig's assist two of the elder members of the hall set up tables and place chairs, and regardless of my attitude, I just couldn't let them do all of the heavy moving without taking the lead. So we set up for about a hundred and twenty-five guests.

I was still unaware of what was going on and what role I was supposed to play, but I thought, *the hell with it, with Palm Sunday tomorrow, maybe this was my cross to bear?*

Besides, whether Loyola liked it or not, this was going to be my act of community service for All Stars.

After the setup was complete and most of the morning had passed, I found myself now sitting in the wings watching the nuns greet these retarded weenies of all ages, their caretakers and families.

And though it was touching to see a little joy brought into their lives, this just wasn't for me. I felt uncomfortable and really didn't want to be there.

They were flailing around and had all of these goofy looks on their faces, and for Christ's sake … they were scary!

The nuns and their caretakers should have thrown a party for these people, because they were the only ones who could stand to be around them for any length of time.

I thought to myself, *They'd have to spoon feed me too, if I had to spend any real amounts of time with these … idiots.*

Sister Erasmus summoned me to help serve soft drinks and munchies to each of the tables and I felt like a two-bit freshmen.

Oh boy, look at me, waiter to retards.

It even freaked me out to get within reaching distance of them, fearing that if they touched me, some of that goofy shit might rub off.

As I continued schlepping eats and drinks, I was amazed at how the nuns thought nothing of hugging and showing affection to these weirdos.

Then, out of the corner of my eye, I saw the school Glee Club start to file in through the front door.

Great, I thought, *I'll be seen by these nerds here on a Saturday.*

They started to set up in a vacant corner when their director, Mrs. Karl, a middle-aged, slightly plump, but attractive woman, who was always kind and a bit provocative toward me, came up and said, "Hey you, what are you doing here on a Saturday morning?"

No shit, I thought to myself. Then I countered in a sarcastic tone, "I'm the official waiter of the fruit and nuts club."

"Now, now, sweetie," she said, "this is for a good cause."

I continued on my rounds and occasionally peeked in the direction of the Glee Club where I'd occasionally get a wave or a smirk from one of their members.

As I went into the kitchen to get a towel to clean up a spill, I heard over the hall's sound system, "Good morning, everyone … Happy almost Easter! Are you ready for music, fun and games?"

And I thought, *God Almighty, most of them don't even know where they're at … let's get on with this shit already!*

I found myself gazing into the abyss not only counting this as credit toward my community service, but also figuring that God owed me one, and was going to have to let me get into Laura's pants for enduring this bullshit.

They soon began singing songs and playing their little games, which actually became quite hilarious watching these *basket cases* floundering around.

Then the kitchen counter opened, and hot dogs and a variety of salads were about to be served.

Great, it was time to get back into the game … and serve.

Loyola came strolling in my direction, and I thought I'd beat her to the punch and said, "I know ... I know, time to dish out the dogs."

"No," she said, "you follow me."

Now what, I thought. I followed her into what seemed to be a small storage room.

She turned to me and said, "Are you wearing anything under that sweat shirt?"

I laughed for a moment and said, "I beg your pardon."

"Oh you, don't you get smart with me, young man." Then she asked again, "Well?"

"Yeah," I responded, "a tee-shirt ... why?"

"Then take the sweat shirt off," she ordered.

"Now wait a minute," I said, "what's going on?"

She looked at me and grabbed my cheeks, "You know that you're one of my favorites, and I know that I can always count on you, especially when things get difficult."

Suddenly I thought the old girl was going to ask me to do something that I couldn't do if Christ himself came down off the cross and asked me.

I started to get a little sweaty and thought, *This just couldn't be happening?*

I don't mind telling you that I was getting concerned that she was having trouble asking me to do something, especially considering that we were in a relatively secluded and private area.

Then, over the P.A. I hear, "Soon our guest of honor will be here, are you all ready for Peter Cottontail?"

She then looked at me, smiled and said, "That's you."

Relived in one aspect that my runaway thoughts were not going to come to pass, it hit me what she meant.

"Ohhhhh noooooo wayyyyyy, Sister. I'll serve the food ... clean up ... anything ... but not that!"

I now knew why Stan was there. He owned a soft serve ice cream parlor in the neighborhood and had one of those big bunny suits specifically for the Easter season. Sort of a "come out and see the Easter bunny, buy one sundae and get the other one at half price," shtick.

She held this big furry jump suit in front of me and pointed, "In you go!"

I couldn't believe it, but I was about to shed the last few remains of dignity that I had to become this fluffy six-foot fucking rodent.

I found myself engulfed in this bunny jail cell, when she handed me the gigantic plaster and fur covered head ... ears and all.

She just looked at me and said, "I'm proud of you."

My response, "It took me to dress up like this for you to finally say that to me?"

She then took the head and placed it in position to complete this humiliating scene. I could see her through the eyes of the headdress and issued, "You owe me one."

She just continued to smile and urged me to stay put and to wait for my introduction.

To be totally honest with you, I was praying for one of those hundred-year storms to take out the building … at least I would have died with some shred of dignity.

I was in there for what seemed to be decades and hoping that the door would suddenly swell and jam shut, imprisoning me until after Easter Sunday. Then I heard, "Is everybody ready?

"He's here! Let's give a big welcome to Peterrrrr Cottontailllll, the one … the only … Eeeeeaster Bunnyyyyyy!"

Then I heard the piano start the accompaniment for the Glee Club, as they began to sing, "Here comes Peter Cottontail, hopping down the bunny trail, hippity, hoppitey Easter's on it's way …"

The "nutty buddy" club was cheering like I was the President for Christ's sake and even the cute girls in the Glee Club were waiving to me with smiles and playful excitement. I thought to myself … make a fool out of me … I'll give you a foolish performance.

I'd shake my tail, hop around and every time I did something that I thought was contemptuous, I'd get this incredible roar from everyone in attendance.

Suddenly, it was becoming quite the rush, but I still had a plenty of sarcasm left in me!

When I went past one of the old timers who was a member of the Hall, he said, "Quit hamming it up, and let's get this fiasco over with."

Fortunately, the outfit came with big and roomy mittens, which allowed me to "flip the old fuck off," for making those comments, but all he saw was a friendly backhanded wave.

Then Loyola grabbed me and I thought, *uh oh, she's going to kick my ass.*

Instead, she led me toward the stage and to a special chair saying, "You're doing great!"

She then pulled me close and said, "Mark, I'm glad that you're having fun, but I wanted you to know that this was never meant to be a punishment, but rather a reward.

"Now continue to play it up or I'll make you wear this suit all next week at school."

I just paused for a moment, turned to her and wiggled my tail in a gesture to tell her to kiss my ass, but what the crowd got out of it, was a friendly little gesture from the "big ole bunny."

She just smiled and said, "OK, I'll take that for what it's worth."

I was only in this costume for about five minutes and was already wringing wet! I was roasting in this motherfucker and genuinely wondered how long I was going to be able to manage?

What I didn't know was that she was about to fulfill a promise that I never imagined that she could keep.

From my guest of honor position on the stage, I noticed the "loony tunes" lining up and holding the hands of those that they trusted, with many also holding onto trinkets of some sort.

These items seemed to be drawings and pasted objects and other tattered items that at best, could only be characterized as junk.

But incredibly, from the very first goon who came up to me, I suddenly began to realize that these were not just gifts, but treasures. Something genuine, made from the heart with only one condition attached, "that it was to be remembered whom it was from."

Something was happening to me … from my confined burlap chamber I began to feel and see things change.

"Hi, Easter Bunny … this is Tommy, he's twenty-two and he has a special gift for you," said his chaperone.

I reached out and took the drawing in my hand and had problems distinguishing what it actually was. It was some kind of doodling … some kind scribbling … it was … junk … and it was just about the most beautiful thing that I had ever laid eyes on.

I held it next to my heart and found myself crying as I heard him turn to this caretaker and say, "He likes it." … and he began to clap his hands and said, "I knew you'd like it, Peter. I just knew it!"

Then this man … this "boy-man" … this "troubled angel" sitting in my lap proceeded to hug the furry façade that was shrouded around me saying, "Peter, I love you, and I promised to be a good boy."

Then he asked the image "to forgive him" and promised to be a "good boy" if I'd deliver a special surprise for him on Easter Sunday.

I found myself nodding yes, not realizing what kind of promises that I was making, but hoping that like the mythical power of Santa, that someone special would be able to *make it good*.

Instructed not to speak, I took Tommy's hand in mine and placed it over my heart, and suddenly made a connection that I had never known was possible.

Even if I wanted to, I couldn't speak, because this feeling was beyond words. I was just left in a quivering state, silently crying because these incredibly special children of God opened my eyes, by opening their hearts to an unworthy soul who was masquerading as trusted friend in a furry façade.

For whatever nonsense I first thought this was, they overwhelmed my sarcasm and scorn with genuine affection, hope, and contrition that simply permeated my heart.

They didn't understand hate or revenge, no ... their logic was based on simplistic measures known as trust and truthfulness, and their challenge in life was just trying to be understood.

With each new friend that passed my way, I realized that their work was their play and that their play was their work.

For acceptance in their world was an invitation to share and give, where I always measured it in ways that I could gain or acquire.

Yes ... their minds were simple, because so much went into their hearts, that I was convinced that God couldn't fit anything else in!

And for two hours I never had experienced the presence of the Almighty, like I did with these incredible beings.

I often heard the term "unconditional love," but I was at a level beyond that ... fringing upon something heavenly, and given a unique glimpse at the world that I believe few have ever experienced.

I was privileged, connected and for a brief period enjoyed uncompromised sight.

As my performance concluded, I labored back toward the storage room.

I was stopped along the way by many who were close to these special angels, who pulled me close and thanked me for what I had done for them today ... if they only knew who really benefitted from this.

How I equated dignity with certain criteria in life. The type of car you drove or house you lived in ... were standards that I had become not only introduced to, but compelled with.

Those impressive outfits worn by lawyers, doctors, businessmen, political and military leaders ... now those were measuring sticks of success!

Or those time-honored uniforms that measured one's worth ... the old English "D" of the Tigers, Yankee pinstripes or the green and white cloverleaf of the Celtics ... now those were impressive threads!

But in some strange way, I was standing in the most dignified garb that I had ever been in, or could hope to be a part of.

For those that I *touched* didn't measure me on what I was driving or how much I was worth, but simply on how good it felt to brush up against my furry frame and to get a hug from a *reliable* six-foot, buck-toothed, long-eared storybook image.

I was lifted beyond the degree of success and though emotionally drained, more refreshed than I could ever imagine.

I was … yeah … an idol, albeit for a fleeting moment, loved unconditionally and without anything to prove, from those who had absolutely nothing to gain.

I was in the midst of something life-altering … and in a time and place that I would never forget.

Perspective, it can be a pretty enlightening thing … considering your perspective.

Unexpectedly, I was turned around in a forceful manner and greeted by the she-devil herself, who said to me, "Bunny, if could find it, I'd squeeze that little carrot of yours … you're okay, Markie!"

As I grabbed her in my arms, I responded, "You know what bunnies do a lot of … don't you, Shell?"

"In your dreams, Cottontail … in your dreams."

"That's Peter, baby … you can call me Biggggg Peter!"

She just laughed her way back to the choir.

I finally got to the storage room and with the help of my dearest Loyola, shed the outfit and stood there in a pool of my own sweat and tears.

She wiped my brow and said, "I see you enjoyed your reward?"

I laughed, paused and then started crying again, before embracing her and said, "Thanks."

~ all stars ~

It was a strange time around campus; with an expected solemn mood prevailing as we were in the midst of Holy Week, even the now liberal interim administration stressed that we exhibit a more subdued and contrite behavior in respect of the period. However, the heart of the All Stars competition was upon us, and those additional few days off were on the line. So despite the somber climate, work had to be done.

With the acts of charity performed and classroom details in a satisfactory state, the two days of All Star competition dealt with athletic events from the conventional to the obscure.

In all earnest, the freshmen despite their size, fragile emotions and limited abilities, were really trying hard ... but their efforts weren't measuring up. So, if we were going to be successful and pull this thing off, we were going to have to get creative.

I can't say for sure, but I believe it was former baseball great, Ty Cobb, who said, "I hate to cheat ... 'cept when winning is involved ... and I always want to win!"

Though we were not publicly going to adopt this war cry, deep down we knew it was the only way that we had a chance to prevail.

Day One of the athletic events was a complete bust for our side. In the coed basketball game, a 5'-9" sophomore girl, name Felicia Evans scored fourteen points and singlehandedly embarrassed the few seniors that we had on the floor. She should have been playing for the varsity boy's team! Ironically, she transferred to a Detroit public school, and two years later led them to the girl's state basketball title.

During halftime of the basketball game, the tug-o-war event took place on court. Each class had to be represented with four students and two had to be girls, so the freshmen once again, served as little help in this effort. Besides, junior Eric "the cow" Cobelenz was the other team's anchor.

He was given that moniker because of his eating habits and his appearance … need I say more? This kid was so huge that he couldn't fit into a desk, so every class that he was in, they had to sit him in the back, at a long table with a separate and heavy-duty chair. He would also be five to ten minutes late for each class, because he just didn't move too swiftly, and though he was a pretty pitiful specimen, on this day, he was a "tug-o-war-god-sent!"

The event was a joke as the juniors and sophomores again … kicked our butts.

Down two events with only three to go, we had to run the table or forego our chances of the additional time off.

The final event of the day one was a seven-and-a-half-mile run. With our backs against the wall, this effort called for strategy, cunningness and that "Cobb edict" to help us prevail.

Actually our freshmen entrant was the strength of our team. His name was Louis Agiar, a lanky string bean of a kid who had a distinct edge.

You see, away from school, he was part of an independent track and field organization and had excelled in long distance events. So, it was a given that he was going to fare well in the event and we really needed for him to come through for us!

In addition, his father, Hector, was a champion runner in his native Panama. He was pretty cool too, as we petitioned him for advice on how to plan out our strategy for this event. When asked how he gained his champion status, he replied with a smile, "I remember my papa saying that having the cops chase me would never lead to anything but trouble … he was right … and a little wrong."

In that mix and match format that tried to even things out, our problem was that the seniors needed to provide a female to make up the other half of this running tandem. This task was difficult, not only because it was forecasted to be cold and damp, but most of the senior chicks dreaded the thought of driving the distance, let alone running it.

"When you don't have the ability, you have to find other means," Hector said.

We knew what the route was going to be and needed to figure something out to finish "one–two" in the race.

The course was laid out with safety paramount in the planning. We examined the route in detail and came across an interesting angle we thought we could exploit.

The motto and angle here was the old real estate cliché, "location, location, location!"

It was just after the race's halfway point, where we noticed that the route went down Demeter Street. A part of the path that had a large bend in the road and just happened to be where Sue and Laurie Kinovich, the sweet looking senior twins lived.

Normally beyond contempt, the two Polish beauties probably would have never considered what we were about to ask them to perform. But considering it meant some extra time off, and knowing that Laurie's college boyfriend was also Florida bound, we knew that she had aspirations of getting away with him for some *special* alone time.

The problem was Sue, though she was also southbound, she was not in any hurry; so she needed a bit more enticement to have her interest peeked.

So Adam, Hodgie and I met with the twins to lay the groundwork for yet another "less than Christian" scheme to meet our needs.

Though reluctant at first, Laurie came to our defense and petitioned her sis to join in, especially when it meant a little more time for her to "shack up" with Sammy "six-packs," her boyfriend who was an alum from rival St. Andrew's and always was seen walking around with a six-pack of beer.

The enticement, considering our ages and financial situations usually went hand and hand with dollar deficiencies, something that the twins were susceptible to. In addition, the look-a-likes were alluding that they were going to spend their break in Fort Lauderdale, which many considered a higher-priced ticket in the battle of Sunshine State spring break capitals.

Hearing their plight, Hodgie bolted to his feet and asked to use the phone for an important call. Seemed his sister Claudia, knew a person who worked in hotel management in Lauderdale, and Al was determined to secure the right carrot to dangle in front of the girls.

Mr. Kinovich, seeing all of the commotion finally spoke up, "Hey, boy," he said to Hodge, "you're not calling Mexico or something like that, are you?"

Hodge just waved him off and said, "No, sir, but I am trying to get help from a Mexican … if that's any consolation to you," and Al kind of grinned at him and got a stoned-faced look in return.

Finally after multiple calls, his connections were able to get the twins a waterfront view room, for only $35 a night! Sue suddenly found no problem in justifying a little participation in the advantage-rendering plot.

Now with the twins "bought off," we were able to refine our strategy.

The obvious key for our side in this scheme was that the twins were identical in every feature. Both were fit and active, but Sue was a little more "adapt in the realm of athletics" than her sister. Thus, making all the pieces come together at the precise time was going to be our "pickle."

Plus, the opposition was formidable.

The junior's hope in the event was a guy by the name of Phil "Nuts" Barda. A moniker derived from the incredible amount of times that he ended up "taking a shot to his balls."

From doorknobs to baseballs, or errant books being carried around a blind corner, if he was anywhere in the vicinity, there was a better than even money chance that he'd end up "taking one in the jewels." It was uncanny how many times this dope got popped in the nuts!

But this guy loved to run and would often do so, both to and from school. And if you're wondering, yes … he once did step on a rake and "pounded his pud."

The thing about Phil was that the seniors razzed him so much about his less than glorious reputation that he would frequently break out into a tirade about how he despised us and one day would "get us all." It was sort of creepy the way he would look back in our direction, and I always thought that he was just one comment away from going off the deep end.

That weakness, however, was what we needed to play off of, hoping that he'd become flustered and would lose focus. So, as race time neared, we bombard him with visions, such as jock straps and athletic cups at his desks and with other homemade notes and teases referring to his dick. And when the notes came from some of the senior girls, well … that drove Nuts … nuts.

The tenth grade entrant on the junior/sophomore team was a cute little blond by the name of Kelly Pixter. She had a serious crush on Alvin, so the play here was simple. Hodgie was deployed to her house the night before the race to keep her "active" and tire her sweet little ass out. There was no hanky or panky, at least nothing that he would admit to, but he assured us that she would be "off her game," come race time.

Now we wanted to finish 1–2 in the race, but in essence, all we really needed was to finish 2–3 to capture the event's points and position ourselves to win the entire shebang.

Early on race day, the twin's mom was dooped into believing Sue was not feeling well and subsequently called into the school to confirm that she wouldn't be attending.

Next was outfit coordination. They needed identical outfits to continue our ploy, which was really not a big deal to handle. The only problem that we could possibly experience was in the actual pass by timing.

The race was set for noon, upon request from the seniors, citing that Laurie needed to be at work by 4:30 that afternoon. So, considering the race and all of the post event preparations to get ready for work, Loyola and those monitoring the event agreed.

Now part of timing issue was to get the twin's mother out of the house around 1:30, which was about an hour and a half into the race. The play here was that Mrs. Kinovich worked part time as a cashier at Farmer Jack's, and was scheduled to start work about that time.

The coolish day was actually great for the competitors and even better for our girls to camouflage themselves. Laurie was dressed in runner's shorts, a gray T-shirt, white socks, running shoes, with a blue hooded sweatshirt and a dark blue baseball cap.

To the cheers of their classmates, from both the starting point and classroom windows, the quartet was sent on their way. Disappearing from sight, the boys were already distancing themselves from the girls.

From Louis' perspective, he was planning to lay off of Nuts' pace and try to run him down at the wire. But, we wanted to assist our little Spanish friend in his plight, so along the route before school, Del, J.J. and Roger hung subtitle reminders to Nuts about the little things in life that had meaning to him. Such as dildos with band-aids on them, underwear with the blood-like (ketchup) wounds dripping from the crotch and other little trinkets to steam up his demeanor.

According to Louis, Nuts would jump at all reminders to rip them down and was just furious at the sight of these reminders.

Despite Hodge's promise to lessen the chances of the little freshmen, reports had her anywhere from a half to a whole block ahead of Laurie.

"I thought you said that you were gonna soften her up, asshole," I said to him after hearing the report from the station monitors who were conversing on walkie-talkies.

"Just remember what you said," he replied.

"What the fuck is that supposed to mean," I said.

"Don't worry," and he winked at me and walked away.

The actual pace of the race was going faster than expected, and at 1:10 the two girls were approaching the halfway point of the race. Positioned there was perhaps the biggest kid … Koobs and though not feeling all that well, he was eager enough to be involved in this plot.

He was our lookout and when the two girls passed, that was his que to call Sue at her house and to inform her that the two of them were on their way.

So, Koobs dialed the number and instead of Sue answering the phone, her father, all congested answers and says, "Hello."

Always quick on his feet, Koobs says, "Uhh, yeah … is Sue there?"

"Who's calling?"

"Umm, this is Bill from work."

"Bill," her dad asked inquisitively, "I thought she said the guy she works with wazzzzz … now what was that name … .oh Steve!"

"Well, I'm in payroll and she forgot to punch out the other day. Just need her toooo … ummm, uhhhh … come in and clarify the matter."

"Oh sure, Mr. Kinovich said, "hold on. In fact, she's homesick from school today. By the way, how did you know to call?"

Perplexed, Koobs said, "Well … umm … I'm actually filling in this week and didn't know she was a student."

"Man, you're either really efficient or damn lucky, aren't you?"

With a hesitant laugh, Koobs responded, "oh, yes, sir!"

After being handed the phone, she answered timidly, "Hello."

"They're on their way … what's the story; are you ready?"

"Oh yes, Shirley, you need me to work?"

"No," Koobs shouted, "I said I was Bill … from Payroll with a clock punching problem."

"Ohh," she corrected, "this is Bill and you need me to come in and fix the clock?"

She would later tell us how her father looked strangely at her when she botched up the lie that Koobs had started.

"Now wait a minute," her father said in the background. "You can't go in when you're not feeling well."

"You need me immediately," she said, while looking at her frowning father.

"What's going on?" Koobs inquired.

"You can't go in … and if you do go, you can't go dressed like that," her dad stressed, and it was now evident that chaos was at hand.

"Dad, I gotta," she insisted.

"You let me talk to that fella," her father demanded.

"No," she screamed.

Meanwhile, the sophomore had passed the twins' house and was pulling away from a tiring Laurie and our hopes seemed to be fading just as fast. The tenth grader was about to run us out of the entire competition, and even with the impending switch and fresh legs it didn't look like we were going to be able to make up that kind of distance.

As Laurie approached her house, Sue shucked and jived, but finally made it out of the house, to inform her tired twin in a hurried manner, "that Dad's home sick from work and you gotta act like you're me going to work to handle some kind of goddamned clock issue or something like that ... so you can't go into the house!" and she sprinted to try to get us back into the race.

"What?" her tired and breathless sister said.

"Just don't go inside for a while ... go for a walk," Sue yelled from halfway down the block.

The fresh twin, wearing the identical clothes was launching her assault, but as previously mentioned, the sophomore just had too much of a lead ... or did she?

⌐   ⌐

"After all we did to plan this thing ... and all you had to do was to slow down Kelly! Nice fuck up, asshole," I blasted to Al.

You could see him now starting to become concerned, as he appeared to fail in his attempt to derail the young blonde.

"I just don't understand it," he said to himself.

"What," I inquired.

"Nothing man...shit!"

After a while, a number of us started to gather outside in anticipation of the two guys arriving. When we saw them in the distance turn for home, Nuts was about fifty yards ahead the freshmen and not showing signs of quitting. When, all of a sudden, Nuts seemed to have his attention suddenly diverted and he bolted out of sight and down an alley. Louis unexpectedly inherited the lead and simply strolled home, the uncontested winner.

But what happened to Nuts?

Louis gave us his account.

He saw Nutsie chasing J.J. down the aforementioned alley, for holding a pornographic picture of a guy on her knees ready to give a blow job another guy, who J.J. superimposed a photo of Nuts' face on.

It was the proverbial straw ... and Nut's went ballistic and chased J.J. for blocks in the opposite direction before he realized that he had blown his team's total chances.

But that was only half of the needed results. Some twelve minutes later, around that same bend, Sue came lumbering and again … it was without any competition?

Where was the sophomore? I thought.

We were about to finish 1–2, when it was once conceded that we might not even "dress" a senior to compete! As she crossed the finish line, a group of us huddled around her in celebration and to conceal the fact that it was Sue and not Laurie.

"Where's the blonde?" she asked in a breathy voice.

"What do you mean?" I asked. "You beat her … and by the looks of it, beat her bad."

"I what?" she said with a blank look on her face.

"You passed her, right," I asked.

She just shook her head in a negative motion.

I looked at Del and Adam and they just shrugged their shoulders as they looked back at me. Then out of the corner of my eye, Alvin comes strolling up whistling, with his hands in his pockets, "What happened?" he asked.

"We won," Del said in an incredulous tone.

"Nooooo shit," Alvin responded. "No, make that plenty of shit."

With eyes brows now furrowed, we collectively looked in Al's direction and saw him laughing his ass off.

"What?" I asked.

He motioned us to the parking lot, where Koobs sat in his car reading the paper. "Like father … like son," the two of them started to laugh it up.

"Go 'head … tell 'em," Alvin encouraged his father.

"What?" Del pleaded.

"Last time I saw her, she was in a bush between a couple of houses, looking for something to wipe herself with I suppose."

"What?" Sue said in amazement.

"Oh my fucking God," Adam said, as we all started to laugh.

"What can I say? She thinks chocolate gives her energy," Al offered. "She told me last night. So today before the race, I went to wish her luck … and while I was eating a Hershey Bar, I offered her a piece for luck and she accepted." The father and son duo again began to snicker when the younger one said, "Oh, I had Hershey and she had a nice thick piece of Exlax."

"Jesus H. Christ, are you kidding me?" I said. "Fucking Hodgie, you're a genius!"

"Naw … he is," as the son deferred to the father.

"Come on, Sue, let's get you out of here," Koobs said, and she hopped in his car and he drove her back home to once again exchange spots with her sister.

By the way, it was later learned that her father went to sleep and was no wiser about the entire situation.

We were back in this competition and ready to roll for the top prize!

The final day of All Stars was a combination of circus games of chance and other bullshit that didn't quite fit into anyone's agenda except for the freshmen, because they seemed to be still amused by popping balloons with darts, or fishing out some sort of rubber duck out of a tub of water.

Hardly worthy of these mock Olympics, yet thankfully the little shits were on our team and captured these obscure tests to put us slightly in the lead!

In fact this was a lot closer than anybody figured it would be. And though many of the seniors really didn't give a good shit whether we won or not, because most were planning to skip out on the days that we were supposed to clean anyway, you could sense the feeling that unlike the competition's recent history, we actually had the chance to snap the "senior/freshmen" decade long losing streak.

The final event was upon us, a relay race in which each side had twenty randomly chosen participants out of a hat, divided evenly between grades. The entire student body and faculty were in the gym for this one and, surprisingly, the energy level was quite high!

The object of this decisive event was that each team member would be given a plastic spoon and each team would receive one ping-pong ball.

The simple rule was, the first team to negotiate the obstacle course with all of its members ... wins! The only caveat was while the individual competitors wove their way through the course, the spoon's handle had to be in their mouth and the ball had to rest on the spoon's welled end, with no hands to be used except for the transferring of the ball to the next person on your team.

As the competitors of each team were being chosen, it was becoming apparent that we were about to lose, just on lineups alone.

Out of the twenty possible choices, all but three on our team were girls. In fact, the only senior boy was Hodgie, and the senior *babes* just didn't have what it took in the coordination department to win this thing. I mean, half of them thought that they'd never be chosen, and if they were, most of them were not in the mood or mind-set to forgo their heels. Therefore, this was not shaping up well for us.

Funny thing about this event, the administration was showing signs of anal retention, and for "general sportsmanship concerns," purposely put Frost, Pevia and the Gracie brothers in an upper level of the gym, where they were watched vehemently and out of harm's way.

Knowing that our fate was all but decided, in a last ditched effort, we sent Brian "rats hole" Galloway, over to their side of the gym to launch a little biological warfare.

Rats had the uncanny ability to pass gas on demand ... and not just a harmless bomb, but the stinkiest, grossest smelling emanation that you could ever imagine.

But his efforts kind of told what fate was in store for us, as the usually "sure shot" Galloway, was ... misfiring.

He tried so hard to make their eyes water, that his effort went beyond normal results and he had to quickly exit the facility because he shit himself. The look on his face was priceless, and almost made all of us shit ourselves, due to the fact that we were laughing so hard by the way he bolted for the door.

With nothing left to do but huddle up and encourage our futile team, a group of us proceeded to wish them well.

While giving them one last pep talk, senior girl, Paula Lupinski, who was about as interested in doing this as she was in receiving a root canal, just chewed gum and exuded the notion that she "just didn't care to be a part of this."

But, while staring off into space, this self-centered noncompliant bubble brain had the answer that we were looking for.

"Hey, stupid," Del yelled at her.

She just looked quickly at him and then rolled her eyes.

"Hey, stupid," he repeated.

"Fuck off," she blurted back.

"Give me a stick of you gum," he insisted.

"Get your own!"

Now in a more forceful tone he said, "Please give me a stick of your fucking gum!"

"Fuck off, Del," she followed, "anyway ... I don't have anymore."

A number of us looked over at Del as if to say, "We've got this situation on our hands and you're worrying about a stick of gum?"

All of a sudden, he grabbed her with the fervor that Michael grabbed Freddo on that ill-fated Cuban New Years Eve, he planted an awesome overpowering French kiss on her lips, to which she vehemently tried to push him away, but quickly succumbed to his force. With all of the commotion going on throughout the gym, surprisingly his actions went generally unnoticed, except to us in close proximity.

"Hey, Del," J.J. said, "isn't this a little early to be celebrating?"

But it was becoming evident that this wasn't a celebratory, preemptive or a "what the fuck … I'm going for it" kiss.

This had purpose! He was sucking on her mouth like he was sucking venom out of a fresh wound, until he finally came up with what he wanted.

Out of the clinch he prevailed with a smile on his face and a wad in his mouth. He was now the keeper of that over-chewn, flavorless piece of gum.

Shrugging my shoulders and with an incredulous look on my face, I asked him, "What gives?"

He just smiled at me with the gum now between his teeth and said, "Wanna win, motherfuckers?"

As if lightening had stuck all of us simultaneously, we now understood his actions and knew that our answer was now in his mouth. Our huddle suddenly got more intense and cloistered as we began to quickly break apart and distribute tiny pieces of the gum to all who had spoons.

"Quick, put this on your spoons and don't let anyone see that it's there," I said.

Some of the freshmen girls were concerned that this was cheating and that they'd be caught.

"We can't do this," one of the said.

"Why not?" asked Del.

"Because it's not right."

"Suddenly, the recently robbed Paula spoke up and said, "Sweetie, girls use makeup to hide certain things, that's not cheating, it's just assisting!"

Seemed Paula had things lined up for Spring Break as well and needed to win this to earn the time off, instead of risking the trouble of damaging an already fragile academic and attendance status that she had earned.

"Right," Del said, "it's just a little assistance."

The convincing had been accomplished.

"Just don't go too fast," I warned. "You don't want to give it away that we're … you know," and I just raised my eye brows to signify "mum's the word."

We now had the advantage and I didn't want to overplay it, by blowing the other team away!

Coach Lynch called the assembly to attention and ordered the two teams to line up. He explained the directions and went over the course. There was actually tension in the air and a feeling that something substantial was again, up for grabs!

Acting had to be employed; in fact, it was now the most important ingredient in what we hoped would be our road to victory.

Actually, there was little doubt that we would not win, because balance, coordination and the "dropsies" were all but eliminated from our tasks. While they were worried about keeping the ball on the spoon, all we had to worry about was not overplaying our hand ... make that mouth.

As the whistle blew, our first team member, a freshmen girl was racing to a clear-cut advantage. It was almost too blatant though, and luckily the ball teetered, giving indications that it might fall, though there was just enough gum beneath it to keep it securely on the spoon.

With arms spread wide, her pace modified and we instructed the rest of the team to follow suit.

Surprisingly, the juniors and sophomores were keeping relatively close in the early stages and nobody was really catching onto our angle. In fact, the best thing that could have happened was that their side was doing so well. Our conspiracy was safe, as was our lead through our first five-team members.

The only thing that started to become suspicious was that nobody out of first quarter of our line-up dropped the ball. So to keep the misdirection believable, we told our next two competitors to "nix" the gum and try to do the course on the "up and up."

This was a no-brainer for number six in our lineup was Edna the "weable" Wroble, known for bobbing from side to side when she walked in her usual gait. She was given the nickname after the toy ... you know, "weables wobble but they don't fall down."

She had the gait of an overweight grandmother ... it wasn't pretty, and if she would have went through the course without dropping the ball at least a couple of times, there would have been a criminal investigation.

This was a concession that we had to employ, just to make everything else look good; besides, we had an ace on deck.

On cue, she was fumbling away our advantage as if she were a running back on Lynch's football team. We had added legitimacy into our game plan at the expense of our lead, which had almost totally dried up.

"Come on, you fat fuck," egged one of the groups of freshmen that were trying to cheer us on, but were unaware of our hoodwinking.

Fortunately, Edna made it through without putting us in the hole and without killing herself.

Next was senior Tina Gregory, a girl that I went through all grades of school with, who was a good looker and a pretty terrific athlete. The latter being the much more attractive trait at the present time.

We were confident that Tina would give as a good run even if she were to drop the ball once or twice. Plus, she was up against some heifers on the other side.

The two teams were head and head now and despite playing it straight up, we felt that T could reinstate our advantage. Surprisingly though, during the transfer from the Weable, the ball got knocked under the bleachers on the junior side of the gym. Subsequently, there was no assistance to help Tina retrieve the ball, in fact a fight almost broke out when Adam and fellow senior Mike Whiting started physically clearing out a section of the junior side, trying to aid Tina's now desperate search.

She had finally retrieved the ball and repositioned herself at the head of the course. But instead of possessing her usual kick ass fighting spirit, she began weeping uncontrollably as if she had just found out that she had been sentenced to life in prison.

"Tina," I yelled, "calm down, babe, we need you!"

But this usually cool and cocky blonde was having a melt down right in front of the entire school, and our move toward legitimacy was now backfiring. Teary-eyed, she started her trek, fumbling the ball away more than Edna, and she was now getting raspberries from the stands reminiscent to a pissed off crowd of Philadelphians.

By the time she finished, we went from a being in the thick of it, to being two positions down and needed to go back to what got us this far … deception!

Like coaches guiding a football team's desperate attempt to get back into the game during the last two minutes, Del and I were working on the psyches of those of our team members who had yet to run the course. The way things had developed and considering what many felt was on the line, the use of a little stick'em was no longer considered an act of cheating, but a necessity.

Even those who were against such contempt were inconspicuously prepping their individual spoons for action.

Reminding them to haul ass, but not to make any noticeable mistakes was our job, and with the occasional fumble on the other side to help the cause, our gum-aided crew were once again asserting themselves.

Meanwhile, Tina was in the arms of Adam, and was being comforted by a couple other of the senior girls when word got back to us on the front lines that she was so embarrassed with her performance, that she was considering spilling the beans on the rest of us.

I saw Del jump into action and instruct J.J. to help Adam and Mike ushered her the hell out of the gym and quickly!

We were now about a full position in front with only three members left and Hodgie was to be our anchor. From the other side, jeers and trash talk were now coming in Hodgie's direction, most noticeably from his cousin.

Robbie Selby was going to be their anchor and he began to taunt his cousin, which, in all reality, was par for the course for these two. They cared for one another, but were always on each other's cases.

"Hodgie, you faggot, I'm gonna kick your ass," Muskie blurted.

"Pissant, you couldn't even wipe you own ass," Al responded, and they badgered each other with threats and innuendo while they laughed at each other. In fact, the worse the comment, the more the laughter intensified.

As the event was coming to its climatic finish, we had about a half course lead with our next to last entrant, freshmen Jenny DiVito barreling toward a hand off with Al.

As she negotiated the course's last obstacle, her shoelace got caught on the rung of a makeshift sawhorse used to support a hurdle that they were supposed to get over. Trying to free herself, she lost her balance, fell forward and lost the ball. Fortunately, the gum that she used remained in the well of her spoon and remained concealed. The bad thing was that her extra effort to recover the ball coincided with the exact thing that Al was trying to do as he waited for her handoff.

So, you have her going all out and headfirst to get the ball and Al also extending headfirst to do the same thing. Like two rams on a mountainside, they collided, noodle-to-noodle with Al taking the worst of it because of the momentum that she had going.

He landed straight back on his ass and lost his glasses, while the freshmen was sprawled out face down on the floor. Meanwhile, Muskie was awaiting the handoff for his team and laughing his ass off at what had just transpired.

The dilemma now was to either attend to the freshmen, or to get Al on his way?

A number of us jumped into the fray to assist the girl, but before I focused on her, I located the ball and affixed it to Al's spoon before handing it to him. I then helped him to his feet while Sue Vita rushed from her courtside seat and scooped up Al's glasses.

When she handed them to me, before I even looked, I knew that trouble was about to occur. The frames were bent and one of the lenses was shattered, while the other was missing.

In addition, Hodgie was completely disorientated as if he was on the receiving end of a Joe Frazier uppercut.

"Hodgie, are you okay, buddy?"

Staggered, he said, "Fuckin' ayyy, I am Joel."

"Joel? It's me, Moose," I said while slapping him on the face. "You ready to do this, man?"

"Do what?" he asked.

"The relay," I yelled. "We need you ... and now!"

"Yeah, yeah, yeah," he fired, "just gimme my specs."

He was woozy, but put on the useless frames, stuck the spoon in his mouth and began to chase after his cousin who had gained a short lead. Trying to urge him on, I quickly turned my attention back to the fallen freshmen and tried to assist in her recovery.

Suddenly, a roar broke out from the crowd, whistles blew and admonishments were coming from every corner of the gym as our blinded and off kilter warrior ambled his way through the center of the course. After all we did to conceal this deception and nurse along a safe but ingenuous lead, our anchor was running full out with the ball on his spoon ... and the spoon turned upside down in his mouth.

The juniors and sophomores began throwing whatever they had nearby at him while the teachers and administrators piled onto the floor to validate the infraction.

"If were not in zero gravity, your ass is grass, Mark," Sheddow said as she raced after Al.

I hated to admit it, but the pig was right ... I handed him the spoon.

After a review of what happened, a forfeiting of the event and a public admonishment was leveled upon those of us who participated. The punishment was simple, we had to stay and perform spring-cleaning with the goddamned freshmen. In addition, Coach Lynch, Sheddow and some of the other leftovers of Ann's Nazi group, wanted an additional punishment to be levied against all of us who they figured to be involved.

So, for the next two hours after the event, Hodgie, Del, Adam, J.J. and

181

myself, along with Frost, Pevia and the Gracies who in all honesty, were not even close to being involved, were confined in Sheddow's art room and staring down the barrel of an additional reprimand.

"You're going to finally admit to your wrong doings, you little smart asses," Lynch barked.

"Mr. Lynch, I will have none of that language," Loyola warned, while the group of us snickered at her lashing out at him.

"Listen," I said, "it was all my fault, the rest of these guys had nothing to do with this."

"That's not totally true," Del spoke up. "It was my idea; I'm the one who should take the blame here."

"You're all to blame in my book," said Sheddow.

"What … that coloring book that you're so proud of," J.J. said, as the group broke into laughter.

"This is what I mean," said Lynch as he looked in disgust toward Loyola. "If Ann were still here, all of your asses would be strung up." Which didn't come across too well with the interim principal, and if looks could kill, Lynch would have been the one getting his ass strung up.

"I think both of you have made your cases," Loyola said.

"Mr. Frost, Pevia and you two," she pointed in the Gracies' direction, "you're excused and are ordered back here tomorrow to commence spring cleaning with the rest of the losing team members."

The four of them filed out as if they just received clemency from the Governor and were getting nothing more than a slap on the wrist. Many were the times when the four of them were left standing alone waiting for sentencing, but on this quirky day, the usual targets were set free.

"As for the rest of you," she stated, "perhaps Mr. Lynch was correct, a just punishment is due, and I'm going to personally hand it out."

Lynch, Sheddow and the rest of the drones began to smile blissfully as the rest of us marched behind Loyola toward her office.

After standing in there for fifteen minutes and watching her confer with the teachers in the another glass enclosed area of the general office, we suddenly saw her raise a finger in Lynch's direction. There looked to be an exchange of words, but finally the session broke up and the teachers went on their respective ways.

Then, the noticeably irritated nun walked back into her office and proceeded to sit behind her desk. "Gentlemen," she said sternly, "I am not going to sit here and condone your actions. Cheating is despicable …" and then she paused, "but so is the childish behavior of certain adults. Sooooo, with that in mind, I'm going to agree with Mr. Lynch and levy suspensions against all of you. Three days, in fact … but, instead of enforcing it from the last day of school, I think I'll start it … tomorrow."

Without looking at anyone else in the room, you could just feel the tension lift, as a veil of joyful confusion must have come over each and every one of our faces.

"Umm, Sister," I peeped.

She looked up from signing some sort of form and said, "Yes?"

"Ummm, did you say that you're going to suspend us starting tomorrow?"

"Yes, I did. Do you have a problem with that, mister? Do any of you have a problem with that?"

In unison, we all answered, "No, Sister."

Then Al spoke up and said, "Is that all, Sister?"

"No, that is not all," she retorted. "I expect a large bag of pecans from you, Mr. Semko … and from you, Mr. Baker, a bag of oranges.

As for you," she said while looking at me, "grapefruit, and make it two bags, Mr. Instigator."

Then, like a mob boss who caught his crew with their fingers in the skimming the cookie jar, she told both J.J. and Del that they were going to take a couple of nuns grocery shopping before leaving on their respective trips. We were punished, I think … but we got what we wanted anyway.

"And gentlemen, be good boys down there and go to church on Easter Sunday! That will be all," she said and we looked at each other and began to file out of her office.

"Oh, one more thing, and this is for Mr. Semko. Seeing that you got caught red-handed … doughnuts … first thing in the morning, to the convent kitchen, and don't be late … now away with you … No wait, there's something else."

Uh oh, I thought.

Like a dictating godfather turned into the coddling grandmother, she came around her desk and gave each one of us a kiss on the cheek and a hug and implored us to be careful.

~ nine days, a few stops and a hell of a lot of baggage ~

Excited about the nine days off, but confronted with the prospects of the cost of transportation, lodging, food and drinks associated with Spring Break, Hodgie, Adam and I decided to pool our resources to try and get the biggest bang for our vacation buck.

One very large problem that we faced, was that Daytona innkeepers just didn't buy into the notion that we were these three incredible high school seniors from Detroit, who should not only get a last minute ocean view room, but it should include all meals and run us each about ten dollars a day. Instead, we went with our normal logic and called the day before we decided to travel to reserve our rooms.

"I'm sure we'll find something," Adam said to me over the phone.

"No doubt," I responded, "there will be plenty of space."

When I hung up with him, I knew that we were fucked and didn't have a snowball's chance.

In addition, Adam's nine-year-old LTD had a manifold problem and none of us could stand the thought of driving down the main thoroughfare of that sandy playground in mobile aquarium.

To make matters more complicated, Al was starting to waiver over the thought of going, because Koobs was in the midst of a month long funk that seemed to be getting worse instead of better.

At noon Thursday, it was an even money shot that we weren't even going to go, until I got a call from my uncle Chuck at about 3:00 that afternoon.

"Hey, numb-nuts," he greeted me over the phone.

"Choo-choo," I affectionately responded, "what's happening?"

"I understand that you and your two homo friends are leaving in the morning for the south?"

"Well," I hedged.

"What's the problem?" he responded.

"Ah … a couple of things, but nothing to concern yourself over though."

"Well, I got a favor to ask you fellas."

"Favor," I followed.

"Yeah, you remember my sister Dorothy down in Virginia, don't you," he asked.

"Yeah sure."

"Well, her daughter, Chrissie wants to move to Myrtle Beach, to shack up with her boyfriend who's stationed at the Air Force base down there … and you know the hard life that they've had … so, I'm just trying to do a good deed and be a good brother."

"So, whatcha getting at?" I asked.

"If you and your buddies help me out, move her down to the base in Carolina … I'll pay for your gas to and from Florida. Plus, the three of you can sleep at Dorothy's one night and if you decide to stay in Myrtle, I'll pay for your room and food there before you guys move on."

I remained silent for a few seconds, a trick that he actually taught me when you negotiate.

"Well, Chooch," I whined.

"Oh yeah," he said, "and I'll slip you each a fifty."

"Well, let me ask you something," I said with a bit more enthusiasm, "how much is there to move?"

"From my understanding, I'm gonna have to rent a twenty-footer," he said. "But with the four of us, we'll get it done in less than two days."

"Getting the truck down there?" I inquired.

"Actually, the truck will be packed and waiting for us when we get down there. All we're going to have to do is unpack it when we get to South Carolina. But, I'm taking the van 'cause Aunt Margo, Dana and the kids want to go down for a visit."

"Wait a minute," I perked up. "You're all going in the van?"

He had the hottest looking Monte Carlo that he just bought a couple of months earlier … and I thought, hot car, free gas, fifty bucks and a detour that would probably burn up two days that we wouldn't have had, if it were not for Loyola's loyalty anyway … let's go for it!

"Well, Chooch, if you'd consider letting us use the Monte Carlo, then I'm sure I could convince the boys."

He just started to laugh and said, "you little son of a bitch, you drive a hard bargain. Be here at six in the morning."

After I got off the phone with him, I called my two accomplices and told them of the offer, and even a lukewarm Alvin warmed up to it. After a number of calls back and forth to one another, we all decided to sleep at my house that night and get a good early start to the day.

Within an hour, I made arrangements for my dad to drive me down to Riverview, some twenty miles south of the city to pick up the car so that I could pack it that night and be ready to roll in the morning.

Plus, it was only a short hop over to Laura's to get a quick feel, a sandwich and a teary kiss good-bye.

From Laura's I drove right to Adam's, who was packed and waiting on the porch when I arrived.

"Where's your folks?" I inquired.

"He's watching the news and she's still at church (it was Holy Thursday), what did ya think?" And with that he sprung off the porch with his Army duffel in hand and jammed it into the open trunk. Then he said, "Come on, let's get the fuck out of here."

Three blocks over, we pulled up to Hodgie's house. Usually, somebody always showed up at the side door, but this time, nothing. So I laid on the horn and yelled "Hodge, let's gooooo!"

Lottie showed up at the door and said in a somber tone, "He'll be here in a moment."

"Everything okay, Mrs. S?" Adam asked.

"Oh yeah," she replied, but you could sense that all was not well. We both went up to the porch and hugged Lottie good-bye, and decided to wait in the car, instead of making our usual assault on the fridge, just in case something was wrong.

"What do you think?" I asked Adam.

"Don't know, but something ain't right."

I thought words or something happened between Al and Koobs, but if anybody was an authority on the wars of the father and son, I was sitting next to him. There always seemed to be an issue between Adam and his old man, but somehow they always seemed to work things out.

We just sat there for another a minute or two before Hodgie and his red eyes appeared. I popped the trunk, saw him kiss his mom good-bye and proceed down the stairs. Without saying a word, he dropped his bag in the trunk, turned again to waive good-bye and hopped into the car. I started it up, threw it into drive and slowly drove off.

We had gone about five or six miles and all Al had done was to stare out the window. Not a sound was uttered as we waited at the light on the corner of Vernor and Livernois.

"Hey ... umm ... Hodgie, what's the deal?" I asked.

"Moose ... not now," Adam responded.

"Listen, how long have we've known each other? There's something wrong and I just want to see if I can be of any help."

"Mark ... it's none of our business," Baker said.

Hardly out of the shadows of Hedwig's, Adam and I were already getting into a shouting match despite the fact that we only had another nine days and twenty-three hundred miles to be with one another.

"It's alright," Al shouted, "it's alright," his voice diminished.

Then as his voice cracked, he said, "I really don't think I should be going ... but ..." and he started to hyperventilate.

"Hey, man, do you want me to pull over?"

"Just go over there, Moose," Adam commanded.

"What is it, Hodgie?" I requested.

With a full-fledged flow of tears, he looked at the two of us and said, "It's Koobs."

"What?" I asked.

Baker followed by asking, "Did the two of you have words?"

He just shook his head no, waited a few seconds and said, "He's sick."

We had hoped that he was just over blowing a bad cold or something, but were fearful that his tears indicated something much worse.

"It's cancer."

We all froze up for a second and just gazed out the window.

"How bad, Hodge?" Adam asked.

"From the sound of it, it's pretty far along and all he wanted me to do was to go so that he could get some rest, but I just don't feel like I should be doing this."

"But he seemed fine the other day when he helped us with the switch with the twins during the race," I posed.

"They went to the doctor's last week … and today … well … they found out," Al said as he started to cry a little harder.

"Al," I said, "nobody loves their old man as much as you do. Besides, he's so fucking tough that you know he's going to kick the shit out of this thing. But, man, if your heart's not in it, then fuck it. We'll all stay home … because when it's all said and done, he's been like a father to all of us."

Baker added, "I'm sure he just wants you to have some fun and to let him get that rest that he wants. Anyway, they're so advanced fighting that fucking cancer thing, that they'll probably have a cure by the time we get back."

Al just smiled and wiped his eyes.

"Your call, man," I said, "it's one for all time …"

He just looked away and said, "Just don't let anyone know anything … okay?" And he motioned me on.

"By the way," I said "Don't you owe Loyola doughnuts in the morning?"

"Claudia to the rescue," he laughed, and onward we traveled.

We arrived to my house around 11:00 P.M., and considering the fact that Chooch wanted us in Riverview by seven, it was to the fridge for a quick bite, a little TV and then off to the sack.

After a groggy start, soggy cereal and burnt toast, we arrived at my uncles ten minutes ahead of schedule, at ten to six. Packed and ready to roll was Chuck, my Aunt Margo, who was my mom's sister, their daughter, Dana, who was a divorcee and her two kids, Becky and little Paulie.

After the greetings, Chuck's big ass Chevy conversion van was hell bent, southbound on I-75 heading for the Ohio Turnpike.

Chuck was the best driver that I had ever known. He knew all the routes and had just the right mix of caution and a lead foot. It also helped that he had a fuzz-buster and a state-of-the-art CB radio. So it was a pretty safe bet that we were going to blow through the northern tier of the Buckeye state, before veering off to make our southern trek on I-77 toward Owensbrough, Virginia.

Despite making seven pit stops, we would arrive at Dorothy's in less than nine hours. And considering that Paulie yanked our collective chains to piss every half hour, I was surprised at our pace.

"Doesn't this fucking kid have any kidneys?" Adam finally inquired.

"Funny thing," I said, "he seems to only be able to take a piss at Stuckey's?"

"Yeah … I noticed that," Adam followed up.

Usually they'd drop him off at the front door, he'd scoot in, do his duty and we would hop right back on the interstate. But after our fourth stop, still west of Cleveland, Adam decided to follow him in to actually see what this kid was up to.

As Adam trailed, he witnessed an old and storied form of theft being resurrected by this ten-year-old little con artist. While making his way to the bathroom, he'd case the joint by scouting out where the waitresses and the busboys were. Then, he'd see which tables were either finished or just about to, before he'd make his move and go for the tip money.

The way Adam told it he had down to a science. He was the innocent little boy who had to go to the bathroom and politely asked the restaurant's staff where the facilities were.

He'd then make a sweep of one side of the restaurant; grab the cash and dash to the head to calculate his *take* in a stall. Then he would duplicate the process after coming from the bathroom, working the other side of the joint before exiting.

The fascinating thing was that he had this process all timed out to make it look like he was actually using the head, when, in reality, he was just working the room.

Before we exited Ohio, Adam completely chronicled one of his jobs. After another grab and dash hit, Baker followed him into the head and snuck into one of the neighboring stalls. Then he stood on the toilet seat and peeked over the wall to see the little shit tallying up before packing it away. In the Buckeye State alone, he had amassed more than seventy bucks in heisted gratuities.

And if you thought that was bad, fucking Baker extorted half of it from him on the threat that he would rat him out, if he didn't fork over some hush money. So while Paulie rousted restaurants, Adam shook the kid down.

The fucking people that I ran with…oh my God!

It was late in the afternoon on Good Friday when we finally arrived at

Dorothy's house, which was a meager dwelling at best. The paint on the porch and façade was gray, chipped and brittle. The shingles faded and curled, the windows couldn't have been cleaned in years and the yard was simply a shit hole. But they were happy to see that we had arrived and emptied out onto the porch to greet us.

Dorothy was widowed for almost a decade and looked years beyond her age of forty-six. She was living off of state aid, and though I felt sorry for her, I was repulsed by the fact that she seemed to have her health, but didn't care about finding work or digging her way out of this fucking dump.

Plus, here she was with a Carlings in one hand and a cigarette hanging out of the corner of her mouth … looking like the white trash that she obviously had become.

But she seemed to have a heart of gold and was appreciative of the act of kindness that her brother was providing.

Also on the porch was her son, Luke, who at twenty-six was also living off of the fat of the land. Dawning a stained white … make that yellowing T-shirt, a pair of cutoff jeans and sandals, he had a full head of dirty blond hair and was one of those guys, who, regardless of how hard they tried, couldn't and shouldn't grow a beard.

The facial hair grew in patches with facial spots of no growth whatsoever. The only thing that looked in symmetry was the fact that he belonged on that porch, because like the house behind him … he was a fucking mess too.

To Dorothy's left stood the absolute misfit to this entire scene. Like Marylyn, the cast off normal looking niece of Herman and Lilly Munster, Chrissie was clean, bright-eyed and looked like the stereotypic farmer's daughter. From her tied-off checked midriff shirt, to her frayed cheeky revealing short shorts, she beamed with that combo look of half innocent angel and half back hills whore.

I thought Adam was going to need oxygen when he first laid eyes on her, and he purposely sat back in the car to suppress the tent pole that he was about to erect.

We all grabbed a bag to take in with us after the greetings had been exchanged, and to be quite honest with you, when passing through threshold of the house, a great smell was coming from the kitchen area.

Unfortunately, when we left the porch, we probably left behind the best part of the dwelling. The interior was abysmal.

To explain the setting and the absolute aesthetic disaster that was the interior would be redundant. But to paint a picture, if you took the Delta frat house, mixed in Grandpa's dungeon laboratory and doses of Bates Motel, this was ten times worse ... and these were our accommodations for the evening.

The enticing aroma was a southern fried chicken dinner with all the trimmings and Dorothy and Chrissie started to dish it out as soon as we sat down. However, when I saw the spread, I looked over at my Aunt Margo, a staunch Catholic for a ruling on what we were supposed to do ... it was Good Friday ... and eating meat was a no-no. Bad enough our travels made us miss services on this most solemn day of the liturgical calendar; but Aunt Margo was not going to allow us to do the improper thing here.

She just looked back at me with closed lips and a thinned look to her eyes and gave the entire traveling troupe a little nod to the affirmative, as if to say, "It would be a bigger sin to decline the gesture."

So we ate ... and the cool thing was that she served us beer, which is what we wanted, but didn't expect. Dorothy called it the unwritten law of the south, that "real men drink beer at dinner," but so did everybody else at the three different tables except for Dana's two little ones, and we expected little Paulie to pilfer a bottle or two before the night ended.

As far as the meal was concerned, the chicken was okay, and I think that one of the sides was potatoes, but if that thing that they put Wishbone Italian on was supposed to be a salad, then half of the shit that was in the bowl was picked from the side of the house just before we pulled up. At least, the beer was plentiful, cold and the need to open it gave you the notion that it was safe to drink.

It was hard to imagine that Chuck and Dorothy came out of the same womb, because they were as different as night and day. Chuck and Margo were meticulous and their home was a palace. In fact, the running bet between Hodge, Adam and me, was if Dorothy even had a broom.

As I sat in the dining area, I just leaned back and took in the entire splendor that surrounded me. Like the cobwebs that went from corner to corner, fingerprints that I guess that they considered part of the décor, and the hardwood floors that were splintered and hadn't been swept in ... well, who knew how long?

There were cracks in the drywall that were so large that you could see the stud work and what look to be the structure's support beams.

All of a sudden, I felt embarrassed that Alvin and Adam could remotely link me to this pigsty; I mean Chooch was my uncle ... (in-law), and this was his sister.

It was hard to imagine that we were going to actually sleep in this runner-up to a Turkish prison, let alone spend the night chewin' the fat in the sittin' room. When all of a sudden, Chrissie said, "Hey, ya'll wanna hit the bar?"

This was a question that didn't need to be scrutinized for long. In fact, if she was suggesting a gay country redneck bar, we were ready to jump at the opportunity, just to get out of this sequel to *Deliverance*.

Coughing to politely gain our attention, Margo was ready to reel us in.

"You know you boys have big day tomorrow and another long road trip to boot. Plus you have to move Chrissie into her new place, and let's face it, fellas ... I don't think any of you are of age."

"Well, wait a minute, Marg," Chooch interceded, "I don't think that one will hurt."

"Charlie," she said, "I promised my sister that I would look after them for as long as I could."

"Okay, mother," he conceded, "okay."

But it was not okay, and this was not a part of the bargain. Only one person could save what was now becoming a desperate situation, and she was the only one that Margo would cave into ... Dana.

As if she felt our pain, Dana spoke up and said, "You know, Mom, I could go for a little drinkie poo and some night life, I'll go with 'em and make sure that all is well." After a little himin' and hawin', Margo endorsed Dana's idea and parole was imminent!

Within minutes, Alvin and I were in the back of Chrissie's beat up Ford pickup, while Adam somehow worked himself a position in the cabin between Dana and Chrissie; enjoying the latest country hits from the radio.

"Hey, Hodge, you doing okay?" I asked my still subdued chum.

"Yeah, Moosie, I think I'm getting my second wind here. Besides, it's bet time ... and the action is: how long do ya think before Mr. Shades is in the driver's pants?"

"Hmm, sporting event," I said. "Okay, what's the wager?"

"Price is Right," he said.

"Yeah, why not," I responded.

Based on the longtime game show by the same name, we had to give a time that we thought he'd score, without overbidding. If he didn't score, we just considered that the action never took.

"Ten bucks says he has stinky fingers by 2:15 in the morning," Hodgie bid.

"And I'll say ... hmmm ... 1:45 ... just a hunch."

We shook on it and continued to sip on our beers as we were driven into the cool Virginia night air.

Within ten minutes, we pulled into a muddy lot that was jammed with every sort of pickup truck on the market. From a thousand feet away, we were starting to have trouble hearing ourselves think from the redneck sounds that were blaring from within Billy's, a Godforsaken place that seemed to double as an auto graveyard.

How were three assholes from Detroit, in the midst of the disco era, who were raised on the Motown Sound, Segar and Nugent, going to adapt to this country shit kickin' music?

At least we were dressed appropriately, in jeans and wrinkled shirts.

"Oh my fucking God," Al yelled as we walked into the front door.

Adam followed up with a, "Can you believe this frickin' place?"

There was no one at the door to check IDs, in fact, while looking around, I was convinced that one of the bar maids was still in middle school. The five of us found a table loaded with empties and decided to commandeer it.

Despite the place being filled over capacity, it was hard to imagine that the Fire Marshal had ever seen the inside of this establishment. But, everybody seemed friendly and Chrissie seemed to know everyone in the joint.

After choking down what seemed to be at least a half hour of the South's most indistinguishable music, the headlining six-member good ole boy band, finally played something that was actually distinguishable north of the Mason/Dixon Line, the old Righteous Brothers classic, "You Lost That Lovin' Feeling."

Adam immediately asked Chrissie to the dance floor, while Dana grabbed Hodgie's hand and left me sitting alone with beer in hand.

"Hey," a voice came from behind surprising me and almost causing me to spill my brew.

"Sorry," she said, "did I startle ya?"

I just shook my head no and signaled to her that we'd take another round. She beamed a sweet little smile back at me, which solidified the fact that she was going to get a nice tip upon her return. While surveying the room, I caught the little southern cutie on her way back to the table with our drinks and lifted one of the twenties from Dana's stack of four that she had taken out earlier from her purse. She put the beers on the table and I gave her the twenty.

In turn, she gave me back two fives and a single ... to which I raised the three bills back to her and said, "One of these is yours ... you choose."

"So, you're not from around here?" she inquired.

"Nope," I replied and cracked a little smile.

"Didn't think so. Five dollars is a Christmas gift around these parts … thanks!"

She turned her petite frame and before looking away, and gave me another one of those tantalizing little smiles from over her right shoulder.

Hmmm … interesting, I thought to myself.

The band followed up with another slow tune so all partnerships and positions remained the same. I found myself between pondering the prospects of returning to Dorothy's dive to crash for the night and wondering what Laura was doing back in Michigan, and pondering the severity of Koobs' condition.

As the song wound down, the four of them returned to the table with one additional member. A slightly overweight redhead named May was reeled in and placed right next to me. We exchanged introductions and greetings when she said, "So, I hear you're from Detroit."

Being the smart ass that I was, I responded, "Well, I summer there." To which, she just grimaced and shrugged her shoulders.

May had to be in her early twenties and was obviously looking for some company, even if it was with someone who was on the cusp of becoming eighteen.

Just then, Dana started looking on the table and then to the floor and said in a confounded manner, "I think I lost a twenty."

Nobody gave it much of a thought and she just dropped the issue.

"So what do you do in Detroit?" the redhead inquired.

Without missing the opportunity and illustrating that he was rebounding, Al used one of Koobs' classic set up lines by saying, "He studying astrophysics."

"Astro what?" she said.

"Astrophysics," he jawed. "He's studying to be an astronaut."

May then turned and looked at me in amazement. "An astronaut, wow!"

"Yeah," Semko said, "all day, every day, he just takes up time and space." To which, everybody at the table except for May and Chrissie started to crack up.

May was oblivious to the laughter and just looked at me and said, "Man, that's impressive." She was convinced that I was studying for the space program and didn't have a clue of what kind of a boob that she was being portrayed as. To save Chrissie from a similar fate, Adam grabbed her and whispered that this was a joke and not to take it too seriously.

When the band returned from their break, they began to play the Patsy Cline hit *Crazy*, and she got all excited and was laying hints that she wanted to dance. She was a split second away from making her move on me, when, all of a sudden, that sweet little belle who was our waitress came running up to me, grabbed my hand and said, "This is the song that I requested, and I want to dance to it with you."

What a stroke of luck I thought. Great song and as far as I was concerned, I was summoned by the best-looking girl in the whole joint! I jumped to my feet and said with a smile on my face, "Duty calls!"

As we walked to the dance floor I asked, "Aren't you supposed to be working?"

"We're not that formal around her. Besides, you know Billy," and I looked at her befuddled.

"Billy?"

"You know," she said, "the guy whose name's on the sign?"

"Oh, that Billy ... well ... no," I responded.

"Well that's my daddy, silly. So, consider this my coffee break, and I really don't want any coffee. So just shush and hold me!"

"Right," I uttered, "I'll just shush," and we both began to laugh.

"What's your name, honey," she asked.

"Mark ... and what do they call a fine-looking thing like you?"

"Victoria, but don't even think about it," she said with her brow furrowed. "Vicky's okay, but I prefer Vic ... got it, big boy?"

"Yes, Victoria, I do," and she gave me a shot to the ribs.

"Next time, I'll aim a little lower," she said.

To which, I responded, "I look forward to it," and we both burst out into laughter.

"I just love this song," she said.

"Yeah, it's a good one."

"So, Mark, you here with May?"

"What? Me? Nooooo, she just showed up at the table ... seems nice, but ... ummmm ... I think she's lost?"

"Don't get into a thither now," she said, "I was just wonderin'?"

We continued to just small talk our way through the number, when, all of a sudden, I saw raised eyebrows from both Adam and Chrissie as they continued to dance the night away, with what was becoming more than just a casual embrace between the two of them. The clinch that they had upon one another went way beyond, "Hey, thanks for helping me move."

When the song ended, Vic asked me up to the bar to join her in a drink.

We went all the way to the far end, and upon arrival, she informed a rather large fella that she was going on break.

"I'm a freshman at UVA and was studying Business Administration," she said as she raised her hands looked around at the establishment, "Yeah, Daddy wants me to take over the family business one day ... good ole Chez Red Neck." Then after a chuckle she asked, "And what about you, sweetie, what's your story?"

Somehow, I just couldn't get the words out that I was a senior at St. Hedwig's. *Half-truth time* I thought, "Oh, I'm in my second year at Michigan State."

"Cool," she said, "studying?"

"Umm, public relations, but I'm thinking about switching."

"To?"

Shit I thought, *why did I leave it open ended?* "Oh, either law enforcement or pre med ... I'm torn," and I just looked away to avoid seeing her response.

A few beers and an hour later had me stretching the truth just a weeeeee bit more, to include that my dad was a corporate V.P. at G.M., sis was studying law at an Ivy League school and mom was involved with charity work through the country club. *Goddamn, I lied good.*

"Hey," she said, "let's do a shot."

"Sounds good," I responded, not knowing what was in store.

Despite Dad's constant reminders not to mix drinks, I was currently Superman, and nothing could bring me down.

"Hey, Roy," she yelled to the guy behind the bar, "two bedspreads," she commanded

"Bedspreads?"

"Oh ... you're gonna love it, sweetie!"

What the fuck was I getting myself into? I thought. But the connotation was intriguing, maybe if you drank one, that's where we'd end up. I started to think about the possibilities, and immediately thought about Laura.

I would later come to find out that the aforementioned bedspread contained a shot of Southern Comfort, Wild Turkey and Kentucky Bourbon that could have also doubled as paint thinner or emergency fuel.

She downed it as if it were grape juice and ordered me to follow suit. It felt like I was sucking on something that the Gracies concocted. I tried to mirror her aggressiveness and down it in one full swoop.

"Goddamn," I murmured and began to cough and try to clear my eyes at the same time.

She just laughed and said, "Way to get it down, Yankee!"

I didn't know if she was genuinely saluting me or trying to poison me. I chased it down with yet another beer and was quickly on the approach to oblivion. You know, that point where your body just shuts down and concedes coherent, logical behavior and functionability waves bye-bye.

It was like I got blindsided by Dick Butkus and just went numb.

I honestly don't know how long it was before Dana leaned in between us and said, "Hey, cowboy."

"Deeeeeee," I dribbled, "come here and kiss me, baby."

"Time to saddle up," she said.

"Ahh … come on now, just one more … besides … I want you to meet Nicky." I was later told that she looked back at me and said, "That's Vicky, you asshole," and the next thing I remembered, I was being picked up off of the sticky and slimy floor of her soon-to-be-inherited kingdom.

It was my understanding that both Hodgie and I were laid in the flat bed of the pickup, by Adam and a couple of locals, just singing and babbling in some hard to distinguish manner. How we got home and what happened the rest of the night are all based on the accounts of those who supposedly helped us.

Upon arrival, Chrissie ran into the house to get her brother to help Adam and the two gals get us into the house. Supposedly, I was pulled out of the truck and dragged onto the porch and placed next to the support beam to which I had a death grip on.

They guided me to sit on the banister in effort not to wake the elders, and left me there with Adam while the two girls went into the sittin' room, to set up make shift beds for the evening.

Funny, but in retrospect, our beds were being made in a room where we didn't even want the worn and dirty soles of our shoes to touch the floor only hours earlier.

Luke then summoned Adam to come and help him with Al and left me on the porch to fend for myself.

Both were needed to assist the totally deadweight Hodgie from truck to sleeping area and the way Adam recollected, when he and Luke passed by the porch with Alvin, I wasn't there, so it was assumed that I got into the house on my own ability. They dropped Al like a wet sack of flour to his final resting spot when Dana said, "okay, bring in Mark."

"Bring him in," Adam asked, "from where?"

"Well, he was with you on the porch," Chrissie said.

"I thought he came in here on his own?"

"Oh shit," Dana said, "let's go find him."

With all of the commotion of getting Al settled and with the screen door banging on occasion, the worse case scenario occurred, Margo had risen.

"What the hell is going on here?" she loudly whispered.

"Uhhhh … weeeee … ummmm," Dana couldn't find the right words to say.

"Well?"

"Mom, we lost Mark."

"You what?"

"Well, we set him on the porch and now," she just shrugged her shoulders.

"Well get your asses out there and find him," she commanded.

They each staggered in a different direction, whispering my name into the cool early morning darkness, while the general waited on the porch for the results.

According to the accounts, Margo stood in the exact place where I was last seen and scanned the vicinity. While trying to keep an eye on everyone, she said that she heard grunts and groans from the bushes just beneath the banister.

"Mark, what are you doing down there?" she yelled.

Seems that I had become disorientated, and fell straight back off of the banister and into the bushes, trapping myself in the foliage in a position much like an astronaut's during take-off.

After they composed themselves from their laughing jag, the two guys tried to drag me out of the bushes, with very little effort to spare me from scrapes and gouges caused by the branches and thicket. They finally extracted me from the precarious position and deposited near Al's limp carcass in the house.

I honestly don't know what time it was when the human chess match ceased, but Chooch's promise to get us up at 6:30, was loud and had that hangover reverberation.

But, before we get too far ahead of ourselves, it was reported by Dana that Adam and Chrissie went hand and hand into the woods after all of the sleeping arrangements were completed, and didn't return until after 3:45 in the morning, with additional items to report. Margo told a story that remained one of the highlights of the trip and one of our all-time tales.

The room that Margo, Chuck and the two little ones slept in was adjacent to the now famous sittin' room. After our rather ruckus arrival she said that she was up for the duration and had a ringside seat for the rest of the late night activities. Including, Dorothy's admonishment of Chrissie's behavior for carrying on with Adam the way it appeared, especially considering that we were there to move her in with her boyfriend!

At first light, the three of us were still in our clothes, with yours truly looking as if I had been in a cat fight and sprawled out on the floor. Adam was spread-eagled and sitting on the overstuffed chair and Hodgie was actually laying in a fetal position on the kitchen table, quite displaced from where he was originally laid.

Now understand, nobody gave us a tour of this place before we split for the bar, so we had no idea that there wasn't any indoor plumbing or toilet. According to Margo, at about 4:45 A.M., Hodgie got to his feet, staggered over to the dark corner to where Adam was three sheets to the wind, dropped his pants and proceeded in his depleted faculties, to piss all over Adam as if he were a wide-open urinal. He then zipped his pants up and stumbled his way into the kitchen and went face first onto the table ... totally unaware of what he just did.

Now seven o'clock and conceding that we were in no condition to fast track it toward Myrtle Beach, Chooch just let us try to gain some sort of sense that we were alive, though barely, and slowly regain consciousness.

I was now sitting up against the wall and watched Adam regain consciousness, though still slumped in the chair and sensing that he was ... moist. You could hear him mumble, "What the fuck?"

Then he looked toward the ceiling to see where the crack was what could be blamed for his dampened condition. He then proceeded to lift his fingers toward his nose to confirm that there was something to this, more than just water.

Then Margo appeared by the entrance way to the room and said, "Adam, did you ever hear the expression ... piss on you?"

To which my classmate, half smiled and said, "What, did I snore?"

"Listen to me, Adam," she said again, "did you understand what I just said?"

"Yeah," he said in a ragged tone.

"Well, if you ever hear that from Alvin, believe it, because that's why you are all wet." She then proceeded to tell him the entire amazing story.

It was as if he had sobered up immediately and the look on his face told it all. He was in complete disbelief. Then he stood up; walked onto the front porch, found the hose that was hooked up to a spigot from the well, gave it a few pumps and turned the hose on himself ... clothes and all.

After Adam washed off and dealt with the fact that this really took place, he assisted me in dragging Al off of the kitchen table, outside and we placed him back in the flat bed end of the truck. I managed to crack a smile at him and listened to him say, "If you ever ..." and I just continued my laughter as I painfully worked my way back into the house.

To this day, Adam will deny that this ever took place, but it had to ... Margo didn't lie ... "it just had to."

— the three muscatels —

Remember the premise of getting to use my uncle's wheels and all of the other spiffs that went along with the deal…was based on the fact that we actually had to help move Chrissie.

Stage One: The drive down to Myrtle Beach was simply a lost cause. My uncle drove the U-Haul, Dana drove the van and Chrissie chauffeured the "three drunken muscatels" as my aunt so bluntly phrased it.

Myrtle was about an eight-and-a-half-hour drive from shitsville and among the three of us, not one-mile marker during the entire trip was seen. It was a brutal trek with excrements galore. Farting, burping and the occasional head out the window to heave, paved the way as we delved deeper into Dixie.

We were obviously dehydrated and food was not high on the priority list. What we needed were aspirin, a quiet dark room with a firm mattress and a comfy pillow. Instead, we got the deluxe suite at the Monte Carlo inn, with contorted accommodations going seventy-five miles per hour, with a driver who was allergic to air conditioning. So all of the windows were opened and the sun drenched and humid air was overheating our already sensitive body temperatures.

But what absolutely punished the shit out of us, was listening to nonstop country hick music from the moment we left to the second that we arrived.

"Can you please turn that horrible motherfucking noise off?" I begged.

"Are you kidding? That's the hottest song on the charts today," Chrissie responded. "Besides, I need it to help keep me awake."

"Death might not be that bad of a fucking option if we have to listen to this shit," I yelled.

"Oh, come on now … somebody's got their grumpy shoes on."

Fact of the matter was that if I could reach my shoes, I would have gone after the radio first and then after our driver for making that sweet little fucking comment.

Supposedly, we made three stops along the way, but none of us knew it. We were wacked and in some pretty bad shape.

When we arrived, Chrissie's new digs were of all places ... on the second floor of a two-story building, which was one of the strangest looking structures that I had ever seen. It was a Spanish style design with one of those half-mooned Army barrack's roofs. Plus, the frontage was brown with a green fucking crown. It looked worse than some of the shit that we left on the highway during one of those foreboding moments.

The capper was that there was no elevator or means of getting things upstairs, other than the stairs and us, and both were in bad shape.

If this was a move in a positive direction for Chrissie, the only move up ... was in altitude, for her beau didn't keep that clean of a shack. Lucky for him, he didn't have to live on base, because he'd never have passed inspection and his future bride didn't tote an impressive domestic housekeeping resume.

We moved in all of her stuff into a four-room palace that was in desperate need of a fresh coat of paint and a vacuum cleaner.

It had a prehistoric refrigerator, a couch with exposed springs, a thirteen-inch black and white TV that sat on an empty case of Miller High Life. There was an air mattress and a card table that acted as this putz's kitchen table, accented with a lawn chair.

There was no stove in this palace, but it did have a toaster oven and it was obvious that this guy ate out of bags and not off plates ... at least, there was no evidence that any plates were ever in use.

But she seemed excited, especially when my aunt and uncle said that they were going to take her to Sears to pick out a few things to help spruce up the joint.

Seeing us move her circus equipment into this disaster area couldn't have been a pleasant sight to behold, but within two hours, we had managed to get everything in and put some semblance to it.

"I don't know how you did it ... but ya bums did good," Chooch said.

We looked as if we had run a marathon with a car in tow, but we kept our end of the bargain and got Chrissie and her belongings into her new accommodations.

"Let's get you guys cleaned up and a room so that you can get some rest."

I responded, "Choo-choo, if it's all the same to you, I think were going to try and make it down to Daytona by nightfall. We'll grab a burger and splash our faces, but we're eager to get down there."

He nodded and said, "Okay, fellas, I understand," and he reached in his pocket for the money promised.

"Hey, Charlie," Hodgie said, "keep your money. You let us use the car ... and our little party last night ... couldn't have scored any points for us, let's just call it even."

"Bullshit," he answered, "you guys have fun ... and a deal is a deal," and he began to distribute fifty-dollar bills to the three of us.

We all hugged before parting ways and the focus was on Adam and Chrissie, who when they got together, hugged and she just gave him a little peck on the cheek. It had become official ... that last night was now a forgotten event.

So southbound we traveled along costal highway17 through Charleston, until we met up with I-95 in a town called Point South, South Carolina. From there we were still about two hundred and eight miles away from the sun, sand and the girls.

We changed driving positions before we exited the Palmetto state; with Hodgie replacing Baker in the driver's seat and I joined Al as shotgun. Adam piled into the back to commence what would be an extension of the sack time that was started in Virginia.

"Ya know, Moosie, he's gonna beat it," Al said.

"Huh?" I answered, still half asleep.

"Koobs ... he's gonna beat that fucking cancer."

I just gave him a thumbs up and issued, "Tell me something I don't fucking know."

"The old fart, smokes, drinks and gambles like there's no tomorrow. He's always in trouble and I know my mom is just gonna kick his ass one day."

Then he looked over at me and continued, "But you know why he's gonna beat that motherfucker? Love, goddamn it ... fucking love. No matter whatever has happened, I never went to sleep not hearing him say to us ... I love you.

"I'd see my mom and dad get into some pretty good doozies, but they always made up before the end of the day and they always took care of each other and all of us." He continued, "Besides Moosie, who makes us laugh more than that old bird ... who, Moosie, who?"

I didn't need to utter a word, because Al knew that I loved his dad as if he were my own ... everybody did!

But something felt different, despite Al's newfound enthusiasm about his dad's fate, there was something … strange … something you sensed that he was preparing for … I don't know what, but it was something.

Now somewhere between Brunswick, Georgia and the Florida line, I noticed an increased acceleration to the Monte Carlo and with traffic light, I was all for making good time.

A few minutes went by when all of a sudden, from in between the trees in the culvert raced a black and white car with its lights flickering in full working order.

Over to the side Al pulled and within seconds, the state trooper was arrogantly ambling toward the driver's side door.

"Officer," Hodgie nodded.

"Your license and registration, son."

"Certainly, sir, but is there a problem?"

"I'd say that going 97 in a 55 is a bit of a problem."

"97," Al exclaimed, "are you sure?"

The cop just looked at him with a "Don't bust my balls on this, sonny" look, and proceeded to walk back to his scout car.

"Ninety-seven, Hodgie, what the fuck," I said.

"Well, you were supposed to be looking out for me, you stupid son of a bitch."

"Looking out, I can hardly see my hands, you asshole."

Minutes passed like hours, until he finally got back to the driver's side door. "I'm gonna give you boys a break. I only wrote you up for going fifteen over, I could have busted you for thirty and hauled ya in."

"Well, that really nice of you, officer," I genuinely said.

He then bent down to look over at me as if I was mocking him and said, "What'd you say, boy?"

I suddenly got tongue-tied and didn't know how to answer. So, I just shrugged my shoulders toward Al.

"Ummm, he was just talking to me, sir, for … umm screwing up and going so fast," Hodge rendered.

Meanwhile from the back, Adam was moaning and groaning as if he were getting ready to puke his guts out. Then with his back turned to what was happening, he let out with a fervor "What the fuck are you faggots doing?"

"Ummm … shut up and just go back to sleep," I said and rapped Adam on his ass.

"Sorry, officer," Al said. "We're on our way to Florida and he worked all night, he's just really tired."

Then from the back, Adam bellowed, "Oh fuck, I'm never going to drink like that again," and he proceeded to burp and fart in unison.

I just rolled my eyes and thought that if this doesn't get us a night in the slam, nothing will.

"Make sure he doesn't drive, if he does, you're all going in. Got it?"

"Oh yes, sir, officer," Al responded, and the cop dropped a $125 ticket in his lap and made his way back to his car.

Al just scanned the ticket while the cop drove away, and seemed okay until he got to the bottom.

"A hundred and fucking twenty five fucking dollars!"

"What?" I responded.

Al just yelled out the window, "you fucking hillbilly motherfuckin' son of a bitchin' cocksucker!"

He then threw the car into gear, drove to the nearest exit, where he proceeded to the nearest gas station. Then he got out of the car, walked over to the station's dumpster and started to rip the ticket into tiny little pieces, accompanying each tear with an expletive.

When he finally cooled down and used the one time ticket as confetti for his personal ticker tape parade back to the car, I said to him upon his return, "How you going to pay for the ticket now, asshole?"

"Pay for the ticket? Are you fucking nuts? Fuck these rednecks! I'm never coming back to this state again ... so they can all just kiss my fucking ass."

And I just thought to myself, *I wonder how he thought he was getting home, if not through Georgia?*

Just for safe measure, I decided to jump into the driver's seat and take this little excursion the rest of the way.

Past the state line and through a congested Jacksonville, by the quaintness of St. Augustine and right into the heart of Florida's Spring Break Mecca and Gomorra, Daytona Beach.

Even at twilight, A1A was alive with activity as we approached hotel and restaurant row along the city's main strip. The honking of horns, the squealing of tires and the blaring of music were only background to the playful propositioning between the sexes.

The bars were packed, the hotels seemed over capacity and there were bodies for as far as the eye could see.

We were amazed at the banter between cars and how the fairer sex seemed to be the aggressors. Putting Adam in this setting was like reacquainting a fish to water, as he just loved the byplay and seemed to have a come back answer for everything that was thrown in his direction. I could have only imagined one other idiot in that back seat, who could have caused more trouble and that was Del. I figured if he had been with us, we would have either been in a hospital getting our wounds treated from some sort of scuffle, or would have all been getting head jobs within fifteen minutes of arriving in the city. But make no mistakes about it, Adam was a worthy understudy, in his element and was more than able to fly solo.

I wish that I could have admitted that I was as eager for pussy as the other two, but truth be told ... I wasn't. Oh, I was going to gawk, ogle and drool at all of the bikinis I could, and if the opportunity would have presented itself, I'm sure I would have gone as far as the moment would have offered. But I was smitten with Laura, and even without screwing her ... whipped. I just didn't have the burning drive or determination that Adam or Hodgie did.

My attitude on the possibilities of getting *some* on this trip could best be summed up in this fervent ditty, "if the fish goes for the worm, I'll reel it in from there!"

The three of us pledged that we were going to "pursue pussy," but nobody really defined the word pledge. And though Adam knew that my heart really wasn't in this mission, I was growing tired of his constant, albeit accurate insinuations that I was paranoid about the fact that Laura was somehow going to catch me.

"Fuck it," I said to myself while driving in, "if it happens, it happens and if it doesn't, lie about it to everyone back at school. What the fuck were they going to know?"

That was the one good thing about having the reputation that I did. Everybody thought that I was getting plenty of the snatch, and for the life of me, I couldn't tell you how that was manufactured. It would have been interesting to have been able to meet those expectations, but it wasn't happening.

In Daytona, all roads lead to the beach and in true Daytona style, the beach actually turned into a road! That's right, when the tide was out; the makeshift main street Daytona was just yards away from the Atlantic. It was a full two-way boulevard that featured gridlock and all of the bullshit associated with any big city's rush hour shuffle. The beautiful thing about this however, was that you wanted to be caught, locked and immersed in it!

Rarely was it seen where a car had a mixed crew of both guys and girls. It was usually one sex to a car, with the hope was that when gridlock occurred, you wouldn't be caught across from a car filled with your own kind.

Even as night loomed the headlights on the sand stretched for miles and we found ourselves right in the mix.

"Oh my God, is this fucking heaven or what?" Adam said. "Can you two dickheads believe all of the beautiful bush around here?"

"Moosie, I love ya, man," Hodgie said with a smile, "but thank God that we're in this ride and not your fucking Pacer."

I hated to admit, but he was right! Nevertheless, the best thing was that for the first time in days, Hodgie didn't seem consumed about his dad's health.

What we all should have been a little more concerned about though, was that we were still clothed in the rags that we had worn over the past couple of days. We not only looked a little out of place, but my two cohorts smelled out of place. And as luck would have it, our very first gridlock situation found us across from a Mustang convertible carrying four beauties, with two incredible lovelies perched up on the vehicle's recessed ragtop.

"Hey, ladies," Baker said, "how ya doin'?"

They returned some friendly banter, including a remark from one of the duo in the back seat. "Nice car, bet your daddy told you to be careful with it?"

"Daddy ... no way baby," Adam said, "we stole it!"

"Figures," she said, "aren't all people from Michigan thieves?"

Adam looked at me and I knew that something bad was going to happen here, because if there is one thing that he couldn't tolerate, it was for someone to bash his state. For some reason he loved Michigan and would often defend it to the extent of fisticuffs.

Before Adam said another word, Hodgie added, "You can kiss this car full of girls good-bye."

"Yeah, you know we are thieves, but don't worry, girls ... we wouldn't steal a kiss from you or a smell from your stankie fucking cunts! How dare you knock Michigan," and with that he ran out of the car and saw that they were from Alabama.

"Alabama," he yelled before jumping on the hood of our car, "couldn't your boyfriends ... oh, I mean your uncles and cousins get away from managing the general store to spend the weekend with y'all?

"No…no wait! I know, it's spring … when a young man's thoughts turn
to love … and in 'bama that means roll over, sis … I got me a boner!"

"Fuck you, Yankee," the driver said.

"Go back to the snow," another fired.

And I thought, *Boy … we're off to a great start.*

When you're around someone long enough, you get to know their little
habits and idiosyncrasies, but with Adam and for that matter most of the gang
I hung around, you became aware of one another's cues.

We came across yet another car full of chicks and surprisingly, they, too,
seemed to have an attitude.

"Are you boys lost?" one said while the rest laughed.

We just collectively looked back and smiled.

"They're not only lost, but they're fucking mutes," the brazen redhead
driving said.

As the cars ahead of me began to move along, Adam put his hand on my
leg and yelled out, "Hey do you girls like apples?"

A big-titted brunette riding shotgun said, "Yeah, we like apples."

Adam responded, "Wanna fuck?"

They responded with grimaces and a chorus of "ewwwws," when Adam,
said "How do you like those apples?" And that was my cue to hit the gas and
not allow them the last word.

Childish … yep, but the whole shootin' match was nothing more than a
cheap shot meat market.

I finally looked over at Adam and asked, "Do you have any subtitle pickup lines, Mr. Happy?"

"Chill out, Mark, I'm just having a little fun here."

I just raised my eyebrows and drove on.

We came to the end of the strip of beach designated for driving and the
cops were about to put today's sandy freeway to sleep for the night anyways,
so when I got to the main road I found a parking spot and pulled over.

"Uhhh, fellas, what are we going to do about finding a place to sleep
tonight?" I asked.

"Don't worry about that, there are plenty of places around here, we'll find
something," Baker said. "What we need right now, is a little drink and some
feminine company," he continued.

What we really needed was a day at the spa instead of a beaver hunt; we
were a sad fucking sight.

"I ain't going anywhere until I wash up, take a shit and brush my teeth," I proclaimed. "I feel like a fucking bum."

"And you look and smell like one too," Adam remarked.

To which I replied, "yeah, well not everybody can get pissed on and come out smelling like a rose."

"Blow me, dickhead," he fired back.

"Alright…alright," Hodgie interceded, "you're both fucking right. We can all use a drink, but we all could use a wash cloth too."

Then Hodgie pointed to the next block and said, "Pull in over there."

It was a public bathhouse and right now, it looked like the Taj Mahal. It wasn't the prettiest place in the world, but it served its purpose and in less than a half hour, we were all a little fresher and a little bit cooled off.

"Okay, one drink then we need to get a room … agreed?" Al said.

We were magnetized to a place called T.J's on the Beach, a place simply packed with wall-to-wall partiers. We never gave much thought to IDs, because we were basically told that during spring break week, nobody in Florida needed an ID, but that concept was about to receive its first test.

Adam had his brothers, but he looked twenty-five. I let my whiskers grow a little bit so I wasn't worried; the problem was going to be Hodgie. He was underaged and most noticeably … undersized and baby-faced.

We approached the three bouncers at the door who looked like they were members of Shula's Dolphin front line. They looked at Adam and waived him right by. Next was Hodgie, who even went for his licenses, when all of a sudden, they just waived him in as well. *Fuckin Ayyy*, I thought, *this was going to be great!*

I was strutting along and ready to join the two of them, when all of a sudden, one of the behemoth's grabbed my arm and said, "ID, let's see it."

"Umm, shit, man, I left it in the room, but those two are my buddies, they can vouch for me."

"ID, buddy…and now!"

"But …" and I was exasperated as Hodge and Adam watched me squirm from within.

"Moosie, we'll just have one and we'll be right out," Al yelled.

"Yeah, go back to the room and get your ID, we'll wait here until you get back," Adam smirked.

I just looked at the both of them and shrugged my shoulders, when the bouncer said, "Man, you gotta move it to the side."

I went out to the car, opened the windows and ended up just sitting there listening to the radio. Fifteen minutes became a half an hour. A half hour became an hour, which turned into two and I was spending my first night in Florida going up and down the goddamned dial.

All of a sudden, Al came strolling toward the car and in a mellowed tone said, "Moosie baby, how ya doing?"

"Where's Adam?"

"Oh, he's got one on the line. I think she's from Pennsylvania."

"Well, fuck this, you two are having a good ole' fucking time, and I'm out here waiting to chauffeur you two back to a fucking bed that we don't even have yet!"

"I know…I know, that's why I came out here, Moose, to help you find a place. Let's let him get lucky if he can."

He hopped into the car and we started hitting every hotel on the beat and path. Al would jump out and come back saying, "Nothing." Jump out again … nothing again. It was quickly becoming apparent that the only thing that there was plenty of … was nothing, until you drove to either St. Augustine to the north or Cocoa to the south.

"Are you fucking kidding me?" I yelled. "Now we don't even have a fucking room?"

"Well," a sobering Al asked, "what are we going to do?"

Now halfway between Daytona and St. Augustine and well after the midnight hour, I responded, "Fuck if I know, but we better go pick Asshole up."

As I drove back toward Daytona, I began asking Al about the action that I was missing inside of T.J.'s, when I looked over to see that he had become dead to the world. He was toast, and soon began to snore. I found myself beginning to think of happier times and yearning for the cozy confines of Dorothy's.

We finally arrived back in Daytona and with my drunken date totally out for the night; I drove up to T.J.'s, parked on the side of the building and approached my three friends at the front door.

"Any chance of me getting in to check to see if a friend's in there?"

"Got an ID?"

Fuck this, I thought. "Look … can you page an Adam Baker in there, and tell him to come out?"

They just laughed at me and said, "Man, there's fifteen hundred people in there, are you crazy?"

I just shook my head, turned and walked away.

Now what, I thought. *Do I wait around again for him or do I go look for a parking spot to call home for the night?*

When I got back to the car, Hodgie took up residence in the back seat and packed it in for the night. I decided to drive around and found myself following some cars, after I heard one guy yell to another at a stop light, that a group of them were going to park and crash on the beach for the night.

Beach, I thought, *well…it might be a little cramped, but it was ocean view and it was free*!

A number of cars seemed to be backing into the shadows of the break wall to secure a spot for the evening. "Well, Markie," I said to myself, "welcome home," and I officially joined the transient set. Then I turned to Hodgie and said, "Al, wake up, partner."

"Huh," he muttered.

"Let's go look for Adam."

"Yeah, ok, Koobs," he said and just turned and faced the window.

"Koobs," I laughed, and I left him fading back into his deep sleep.

I actually climbed onto the trunk and lifted myself onto the boardwalk area so that I would have an easier and closer walk back to T.J.'s, to reel in the third member of the troop.

Now 1:45 A.M., I figured Adam would soon be tossed out with the others by closing. So I waited … and waited … and waited until 2:45 A.M. and realized that Baker could have either come to the front door and waited for us, or he was given a reason and an attractive one at that, to go on his own. Either way, his time was up as I had my fill of being the worried parent.

When I got back to the car, the windows were fogged up from the inside and I made up my mind, that no matter who was in there, if they were in my spot, they were about to be expelled. But it was only Hodgie, curled up in the back seat with his denim jacket used for a blanket and sawing wood to beat the band.

The front seat was all mine, so I kicked off my tennis shoes, dropped my jeans and worked my way on to the bench seat here at the Hotel Monte Carlo. Not even my Bunkie's incessant sounds of slumber were going to disturb a blissful night of rest.

What would however, was General Motors lack of consideration for making its front bench seats accommodating for that inadvertent need to transform it into a cot! Especially, those prefabricated hard plastic and steel protruding female seatbelt receptacles that were digging into my fucking spine all night long! Between the rising sun out of the east and my need for a chiropractor, 6:00 A.M. sure made its presence felt in a traumatic way, and this seventeen-year-old stud feel like a seventy-year-old dud.

Like Dracula being awakened by the unwelcomed light of day, I wrapped my arms around my head and tried to bury my face into the fabric of the bench seat. But the sun and its warmth were prevailing and I started to feel as if I was in an oven's preheat stage.

Oh, how wonderful it would have been just to pop up out of a freshly strewn bed, open the drapes to greet an unassuming sun, scratch my balls, my scalp and then my balls again … stretch and yawn the way nature intended it to happen, wash my face, brush my teeth and make a sweet little call to room service to summon some morning nourishment!

But instead, from the Chevy's back seat came an elongated and loud beer fart, with all of its illustrious and lingering qualities, followed by an equally alarming burp that I sincerely hoped tasted as bad as the ass hiccup that preceded it. My senses were now taking over where my brain had dropped the ball.

Knowing that I couldn't erect myself because of the past evening's betrayal of my back, I lifted my foot to the passenger side door and with my toes, lifted the knobbed lock. Then, with that same foot, I felt for the handle to open the door and somehow was able to perform the operation to unlatch it. I then kicked the door open and began to inch my way to freedom, moaning and groaning with every movement.

I eventually got on all fours and backed myself the rest of the way to the end of the bench seat and realized that independence was only a step away. I reached back with my right foot for a sandy landing, when to my surprise, my foot hit the cold and unsuspected spring waters of the Atlantic at high tide.

"Ahhhh fuck," I screamed, and the shock of the coldness made me jump, causing me to pop my forehead against the curved and molded part where the chassis meets the roof, stunning myself and falling straight back on my ass into a foot of salt water. The car, which had been this trip's most reliable commodity had transformed from chariot to hotel and was now about to become amphibious.

Laughing as he looked at me from a fetal position in the back seat, Hodgie said in a gravely morning voice, "Hey, Moosie, gonna take a couple of morning laps?"

With my right foot, I lined up the door and pushed it with all of my might to slam it as hard as I could. I finally got my first feeling of joy from the morning when I heard him grimace in pain, "Oweeeeeee, you motherfucker, Moose, you didn't have to do that!" I had just launched the first attack on his morning hangover.

The slamming of the door actually sent two seagulls who were perched on the roof, high tailing it for safety. I got to my feet to discover that the roof and a good portion of the windshield were covered in bird droppings and it was at that time that I noticed that the city's bellhop had dropped off my bill.

There it was, tucked underneath the wiper, a juicy seventy-five dollar ticket.

"Goddamn son of a bitch," I screamed. Just then about four cars down from me a tow truck was on the verge of hooking and hauling a van away with multiple slumbering occupants inside of it. I looked around and saw a huge sign with large letters behind the van indicate …

PARKING ON THE BEACH IS PROHIBITED.
YOU WILL BE TICKETED, TOWED AND YOUR
VEHICLE IMPOUNDED – WITH FINES UP TO $500.00

For a fleeting moment, I thought *why not*? I'd love to see Hodgie's ass towed to the pound, but if Chooch ever got wind of this, I'd end up walking home.

The sound of the tow truck had an amazing effect, as ignitions were gunned and cars tried to slosh their way to the nearest beach exit. I rushed into the driver's seat, reached into the glove compartment to get the keys and quickly inserted them into start the car. But when I tried to fire her up, she moaned worse than Hodgie and wouldn't turn over.

The tide must have been higher during the night and caused trouble with the engine. I tried again … and nothing.

Now with a death grip on the steering wheel and my head bowing on it, I felt like I was going to cry. A seventy-five dollar ticket, a five hundred fine looming and God only knows what was wrong with the fucking engine, I was ready to pack it in.

Come on, God … GM builds tanks and other vehicles for the military that goes in to mud and rivers … this is only a little salt water? Please make this prick roar!

I turned the key again and it just slooooowly moaned until again … nothing.

"Fuck!"

I just shook my head, as I saw Hodgie in the rearview mirror roll over as I began to work on my list of excuses that I could tell Chooch, after he'd get that call from the City of Daytona, telling him that his brand-new car was not only impounded ... but dead.

With a Hail Mary going through my head, I launched one last futile attempt ... but alas, it just slooooowly moaned until it faded to ... a withering ... extinguishing ... dying ... "BANG!"

There it was ... an initial explosive backfiring of the engine, followed by a high wining pitch and white smoke billowing out from under the car, but it had turned over and was continuing to run! Despite Hodgie's bodily convulsions and pleas to "stop the fucking noises," I gunned the engine and tried to keep it from stalling out.

"Moosie, please ... my fucking head!"

"I'm gonna cut your fuckin' head off in a few minutes ... just shut up," I yelled.

Then I gripped the wheel, threw in into gear and proceeded to look for land ... dry land.

Praying all the way, I drove to the enormous beach parking lot, popped the hood and hoped that the sun would dry this thing out. I left the engine running, and the damn thing was coming back to life!

I felt like a combination of a boat captain and escape artist, convinced that I was responsible for conducting GM's first attempt at launching an amphibious line of vehicles. Any way, I let the car run for another ten or so minutes until it seemed totally resuscitated, gunned the engine a couple of times to rattle Hodgie's cage and decided ... operation successful!

I then popped the trunk, grabbed my bag and like a fucking bum, headed to the nearest public facility that I could find and stood in line to get my crack at a washroom that would have made any of Dorothy's outhouse look like the Ritz.

Here I was in one of the top spring break capitals in this country, a physical mess, babysitting a hungover boob, with a missing juvenile delinquent and not having the foggiest idea of what the next twenty-four hours were going to bring.

⏤ jail, bail and no sand in our pail ⏤

It wasn't a Four Star facility, but I ended up somewhat clean, was able to take a leak and ran a comb through my hair for the first time in three days. Now if I could have only worked up the nerve to use the water in that place to brush my teeth, I think I could have actually started feeling human again.

I put on a pair of shorts, a tank top and my flip-flops, and at least appeared to fit in.

When I got back to the car, Al was still passed out and Adam, for all practical purposes, was out of the picture. So I opened the trunk, placed my bag in, made sure everything was neatly stowed and with all my might, preceded to slam that motherfucker shut!

While walking away, I heard the lovely sounds of, "Oooooooo, stop it! PLEASEEEEE, stop all the fucking noise!"

And with a smile on my face I headed off to Denny's for a good ole grand slam.

I actually enjoyed the solitude of breakfast and the sports section, and felt free with no one to worry about and no time frame to work under. After my robust morning meal, I strolled by the Holiday Inn and thought to myself, *big hotel, with a big lobby, wonder if they have a pretty big men's room too? With clean private stalls and toilet paper too!*

How perfect, my belly was full and I had that feeling that nature was about to call, so into the Inn I walked. The lobby seemed appealing enough …

people were actually walking around with smiles, looking refreshed and happy. Could these individuals have enjoyed a good night's sleep?

Over in the corner was the men's room, and when I opened the door to my wonderful surprise, it was even better than I expected! It was spacious, clean and best of all, empty! I had found Nirvana!

I went into the far stall, closed the door and reveled in the pathetically, but tolerable sounds of the Beach Boys being played by some sort of philharmonic, and commenced on one hell of a movement.

It was about 10:45 A.M. when I came bouncing out, worked my way over to the rapidly filling municipal lot and the sight of Hodgie sitting on the passenger side of the car, with his bare feet on the pavement, bent over with his elbows on his knees and his face cupped in his hands. His hair was nothing less than an accident and he was still wearing the same clothes that he had on when we left Detroit.

"Hey, hey, it's a beautiful day," I shouted. "How ya feelin', buddy?"

He didn't even raise his head as he uttered, "Like I sucked the alcohol out of my fucking deodorant stick."

"Great," I needled. "For that incredible buzz and just totally abused feeling?"

"Fuck you, Moose."

"Ready for the nice hot sun, the beach and all of those babes, Hodgie?"

"Where the fuck have you been?" he said.

"Hey now, don't you use that tone with me. Especially since you and your date last night left me out in the fucking car! And weren't you only supposed to be going for fifteen minutes?"

He just waived his hand at me as if to say, "Alright … sorry."

"Can you just open the trunk and let me get my clothes?" he begged.

"No problem," I responded. And instead of opening the trunk with the keys, like he thought I needed to do, I just pushed him back in the seat, opened the glove compartment and hit the bright yellow button that indicated, "trunk release."

It was yet another beautiful thing to witness, seeing him just sitting there, looking at that button in disbelief. I knelt down in front of him, tapped him on the shoulder and pointed in the direction of the rest room; where it looked as if twenty or so guys were waiting in line to get their crack at morning freshness.

Besides, there was no way that I was going to reveal that it was clear sailing at the Holiday Inn.

Revenge, sometimes, is sweet!

While he staggered into line, I decided to call home and to check in. With the price of the beach ticket now hanging over my head, you knew that this was going to be a collect call.

Surprisingly after only one ring, Rose picked up the phone.

"Hey, sis."

"Where in the hell are you?"

"Daytona," I answered in a sarcastic tone. "What's the problem?"

"What's the story with Adam?"

"I don't know, I guess he might have gotten lucky last night … who knows? And besides, why are you so worried about Adam?"

Just then my mom grabbed the phone away from her and said, "Mark, what's Adam doing in jail?"

"Jail! Ma, what in the heck are you talking about?"

"Mr. Baker called us last night looking for you," she said.

"Wait a minute … you mean to tell me that Adam's in jail," I repeated with a faint laugh.

"Yes," she said emphatically. "Don't tell me that you didn't know that, young man."

"But, Ma, I haven't seen him since early last night."

"Then you haven't been to jail?"

"Me! No…no jail for me."

"Thank God! Your father was ready to kill you!"

"For what? I didn't do anything!"

"Well, you guys better get this jail thing cleared up," she said.

"Wait a minute, Mom, whatever landed that asshole in jail … I wasn't a part of it!"

"Yeah, but the Bakers are concerned and you better call," she said. "And call us tonight to let us know what's going on!"

"Yeah…alright. By the way, Ma, did they say what he's in for?"

"For some sort of fight or whatever the three of you were involved in," she responded.

"A fight? He was in a fight?"

I heard her start to cry. "Ma…Ma, don't cry," but she was just getting worse. "Ma, listen, Ma, let me call Adam's folks and I'll call you guys tonight, okay?"

"Alright," she said. "But promise me that you won't fight down there anymore!"

"Ma, I haven't been in any fights and I'm not going to get into any fights …" and she lectured me for another thirty seconds until I fired back in a quick tone, "Ma, I love ya … but I gotta go … bye." And I hung up on her while she was still going to town on the other end.

This was getting better by the minute. Al was mess, Adam was in the *can*, we were already low on funds, the was a seventy-five dollar ticket hanging over my head and we still didn't have a fucking room … "Happy Easter!"

I was beginning to think that those who stayed behind with the freshmen to clean the school were really the lucky ones.

Now the fun part, I had to call the Bakers … and collect yet. I was just hoping that it wasn't going to be Adam's old man, because he didn't like me and this was not going to be a "How ya doin', Mr. Baker," type of phone call.

No such luck though. When the operator asked if they'd accept the charges from me, the old man said, "For Christ's sake, now I gotta pay for the call? Yeah, put the little son of a bitch through."

"Hey, Mr. Baker," I said in a meek voice.

"Where is he, goddamn it?"

"Well, sir," I stuttered, "I was hoping that you could tell me?"

"What? You mean you don't know where he's at?"

"Well, sir … no."

"Wait a minute," he said. "He told me that the three of you had gotten into a fight and that all three of you were in trouble with the law?"

I didn't know what to do now. Was I supposed to tell the truth to find out where Adam was, or was I now supposed to spin a new web to protect his current lie? If I did, I speculated that I'd probably help Adam's story, but inevitably would add a new twist to this fiasco that would get back to my folks that I had lied to them about not being involved and spending the night in jail. Which in the long run probably would have worked out best, because I would have more than likely gotten some decent sleep.

So, I did the only thing that I could do. I ripped a page from the booth's phone book, and began to crumple it up against the mouthpiece faking a bad connection.

"Mark, what's happening?"

"Mr. Baker, sir … you're breaking up," and I rubbed the crumpled paper harder while holding the phone away from my mouth and faking that this connection was all but over. I verbally paused, while continuing to distort the sound quality of the call and said again, "we'll call ya later … hope you can hear me … bye" and I hung up the phone just as he was saying, "Don't you hang up on me, you little son of a …" click.

I had bought us a little time, but the fact of the matter was that we still didn't know where Adam was? So I drove over to Hodge, picked him up and told him what was happening while I went back on my own pledge and drove him over to the Holiday Inn, to expedite his cleanup.

While he refreshed, I called the police and found out where Dillenger was being held.

After getting past the cop at the front desk, I was transferred to the county detention area and asked about the status of our little inmate.

"Sorry," the officer said, "but we don't have an Adam Baker here. We have a Steven Baker in custody, but no Adam."

It just hit me; he had his brother Steve's I.D. and must have used it with the cops too.

"Uhh … well … ummm … no … well, thanks officer, but … uhhhh … that's not who I'm looking for … ummm, I'll a … call ya back later … bye," and as quickly as I could, I dropped on the cop.

We got to the county lock up about 12:30 and inquired about Adam's … make that Steve's situation. We were informed that his charge was reduced to a misdemeanor, but he couldn't pay his fine so he was being held until he could settle up.

"Well, sir, how much is the fine," I asked.

"Three hundred and twenty-five dollars."

"How much?" Hodgie rhetorically asked.

"Threeee twenty-fiveeeeee."

Al then pulled me over and said, "Fuck him, Moosie, let him stay."

I just laughed and said, "Yeah right." But it occurred to me that Hodgie wasn't kidding.

"Come on, man, you can't be serious?"

"How much you got?" Al asked.

"'Bout two twenty, not including the extra sixty that Chooch gave us for gas … you?"

"One eighty," he said.

"Well he's gotta have a couple of hundred on him, so we'll make him pay us right back."

"Goddamn him."

Fact of the matter, was between Adam's fine and the beach ticket, we were on the verge of turning right around and heading back to Detroit. I emptied my pocket and Al supplied the difference to post the bail to get Stevie Wonder out.

After processing and whatever else they needed to do, Adam walked out into a waiting room wearing a five o'clock shadow, a fat lip and looking as if he were the jailhouse bitch?

"Did you get that in there?" I said pointing to his mouth.

"Don't start with me," Adam said.

"Listen, Baker," Al interceded, "you just shut the fuck up or were all gonna end up back behind bars ... because were both ready to kick your ass."

"Yeah ... you're right ... sorry guys."

So we began to walk to the car when Al asked, "Well, what happened?"

"Remember those chicks from Alabama?"

"Alabama," Al said.

"Yeah, the ones we saw on the beach."

"They did this to you," I asked.

"No ... well ... no not exactly," Adam responded.

"You see, I saw them at that fricking bar, and they hooked up with their boyfriends; the next thing I knew, Bama was bashing good ole Michigan."

"And so you thought you'd defend the state's honor again ... alone?" I asked, "you asshole! When are you going to learn that you care for the state more than your own mother?"

"Hey, man, I wasn't going to let those hillbillies fuck with my state."

"For Christ's sake, Bakes, you're not Schembechler's son" (referring to the great University of Michigan football coach), "drop the fight to the death bullshit and grow up."

"Bullshit," he fired back.

"Well, listen, oh mighty warrior," I said, "your visit to the county lock up cost us three and a quarter, and we know that you couldn't come up with the cash to pay the tab, so either you find a way to fork it over, or we're saddlin' up and heading back home."

"Yeah ... well," he responded, "I'm a little shy, fellas."

"How much?" Al asked.

"Bout three hundred."

"What!" How much did you come down here with?" I questioned.

"'Bout three hundred."

"Wait a minute," I said. "My uncle gave you fifty, you scammed thirty-five off of little Paulie and you brought three hundred … and you only have twenty-five left?"

He just smiled, puffed out his jaw and nodded "yes."

"Where did all the money go?" Al inquired.

"Well, there was that night … the bar in Virginia … and Chrissie."

"Chrissie!?" the two of us exclaimed in unison.

"Well yeah, I fucked her."

"I kinda figured that one out on my own, Mr. Wonderful," I said. "You didn't pay her though?"

"Yeah," he said.

"What?" I raged on.

"She asked if I wanted to fuck … and I kinda said yes … when she was about to go down on me, she said that it was going to cost me … so I asked how much … and she said one fifty."

"You paid her to fuck," I admonished.

"Was she good?" Al asked.

I looked over at Hodgie and said, "Shut up!"

"Yeah," Adam fired back, "I paid to fuck her! I wanted to get my vacation off on the right foot." Then he looked over at Al and said, "And yeah, she was good!"

"Okay, you dropped one fifty on her," I said, "so you mean to tell me that over the past day and a half you dropped another hundred and fifty in bars?"

"Well, I bought a few drinks."

"For who … Florida State University?" I bellowed.

We arrived back at the car and I said to the both of them, "Look, he's practically bust and between the two of us we've got about a hundred and thirty bucks, no hotel and we're supposed to eat and party off of this for the next week?"

There wasn't too much said for the next few minutes until Al offered, "Look, let's go take a walk on the beach. We'll try and clear our heads, look at some broads and try to think of a way to coax one of our parents to send us some cash."

So we drove back to the Holiday Inn to let Adam get cleaned up, headed over to the golden arches for a Big Mac and then back to the sands of the Atlantic for that stress-relieving stroll.

We found a parking spot on the street, put some loose change in the meter and began our beachy trek.

"Holy fuck," Al said in response to the endless activity and sunbathers for as far as the eye could see.

"Wow," I laughed, "this place is incredible!"

The tide was out and the beach had to be at least three football fields from the now infamous break wall. The makeshift Beach Street was jammed with cars and I had never seen more people in one place just hanging out.

Though the Atlantic looked so impressive, equally was the sea of blankets, coolers and people who virtually covered most of this mammoth beach.

What was odd, however, was that there were very few people in the water. I knew that this was a place to lie around and flirt, but hardly anyone was cooling off and enjoying the splendor of the ocean.

Our collective attentions were constantly being dragged in different directions. From one hot looking chick to another, this was a feast for the eyes, mind and G-spot.

How could you pick just one?

We grabbed and clutched onto one another's arms or shoulders and taunted each other by saying, "Oh my God, did you see that one," or "Look at the tits on her!"

At least for the moment, leaving this female visual banquet was the farthest thing from our minds.

The problem with this place, especially for the guys was how were you to hide showing your excitement. I mean … I know there's self control and decorum, but with the provocative cuts of the bikinis and all of the smiles and the blatant forms of promiscuity, I was surprised not to see half the guys walking around with hard-ons.

If the eye candy didn't lather you up, the smell of lotion and the heat of the sun was sure to do the trick. It was a teenager's Magic Kingdom with the real Disney product only ninety miles away.

"I'd fuck anyone of them," Adam said.

"And if you were lucky enough to accomplish that," I asked, "where would you take her … to the men's room?"

He just sucked in his bottom lip and I thought the two of us were going to go at it … right there!

"All right, you two," Al said as he stepped in between us, "just move along."

Fuck it, I thought, *if I'm going to cool off I'm going to do it right.* I began to jog off toward the water, darting my way in between the blankets, coolers and masses as if I was going for the goal line.

I ran through the cars stopped in the beach grid lock, kicked off my flip flops, shed my tank top and picked up speed to impress any female observers that might be watching. And to my surprise, a few were watching and waving. In fact, the closer I got to the water, the more intense the waves from blanket dwellers got. So I picked up even more speed, into a full-fledged sprint and was about to take on the not so mighty Atlantic, head on … like a linebacker ready to make a blind-sided hit on an unsuspecting quarterback!

When I hit the water, I immediately knew the first reason why so few had ventured in … it was so fucking cold! The sound of my girlie screams seemed to gain everyone's attention and I thought I was going to freeze my dick off. There would be no getting use to this … at least not any time soon.

But the waves that I was receiving from the perceived well-wishers as I bolted for the water, were not of encouragement or support, but of warning!

I was about to be acquainted with *the* reason why the water was so baron. In my attempt to extract myself from the fridged waters, I felt a stinging pinch to the calf of my left leg.

"Owww, goddamn it," I yelled. Then before I could compose myself, it happened again on my lower back. The pain was excruciating and I looked around to find myself in the middle of hundreds of jellyfish that were part of literally thousands that had found their way to the coast.

Now jellies were obviously not uncommon, but this amount I came to find out the hard way, was some kind freakish thing called uplifting. A rare phenomenon that brings the ocean's colder floor layer to the coastal surface and attracts those stinging damned urchins, on this … the most important week of the year for the visiting coeds and the merchants of Daytona Beach.

I took two more stings before I was able to extricate myself out of the water, leaving myself at the center of this sandy stage, to thousands of eyes and their laughter.

I was dancing around trying to warm myself up while at the same time trying to walk-off the pain from the stings that I sustained. Jumping and contorting around like Curly of the Three Stooges, I started to welt up from the attacks until a lifeguard came up to me and said, "Hang in there, dude!"

He started to spray this shit on me and gradually the pain seemed to be going away.

"Ahhh … thanks, man," I sighed in a breathless tone.

"No problem," he laughed, "but I suggest you stay out of there for a while."

"Yeah ... I think I will. Thanks," and I started to walk back to collect my things.

During the retrieval process, my facial gestures began to react to the smells that were left on my body after the spraying from the lifeguard.

I smelled like salad for goodness sakes, as the miracle concoction that he had doused me with was of all things ... mostly vinegar.

So, not only was I a laughing stock for how I fared with the ocean plunge, but my body was covered with welts and while most smelled like Coppertone, I smelled like an anti-pasta.

I got jeered and ribbed along the way and just wanted to bury myself in the sand. In light of what had happened, the Monte Carlo's front seat was becoming a very tempting hangout.

I worked my way back to Al and Adam and was greeted by laughter and "Moosie, you looked like Jerry Lewis jumping around out there."

"Screw yourself, Hodgie," I countered.

"Oh man," he laughed, "you smell like shit."

"I feel like shit too ... it's a set."

Then he handed me some lotion and said, "Here, put this on before you get tomatoes thrown at you and a carrot stuck up your ass."

So I lathered up, composed myself and asked for a hit of the beer that he had pilfered from someone along the way.

"Where's Adam?" I asked.

He just motioned with his head up the beach, and there he was ... with the most beautiful, alluring and eye-pleasing black girl that I have ever laid eyes on.

If the adage was correct that most black fellas fantasize about making it with a white gal, then this girl singlehandedly, evened out the disparity.

I had often the thought of how erotic it would have been to *do it* with a black girl, and I know Adam ... he always wanted to do a black chick! But, regardless of pigmentation, he had found the prettiest girl on the entire beach!

"Goddd, Hodgie, she's gorgeous!"

"Yeah, I know," he said longingly.

We just stood there for a moment, gawking at our lucky companion before Al said, "Come on, Moosie, let's go check out some more of the sights."

So onward we marched, me in my black swimming trunks, tank top and welts and Al in his cutoff jeans, wearing a tee shirt with an endearing silkscreened message on it. You see, Al was a big Michigan State fan, and hated both the University of Michigan and our friends from Columbus, Ohio State. So this particular shirt said in big maze and blue letters on the front, "Michigan sucks," and on the back in huge scarlet and gray lettering, it followed up, "but Ohio State swallows!"

The shirt attracted jeers, laughter and even some threats from almost everybody who saw it ... and twice almost caused a fight.

After one of the close calls, I said to him, "Maybe you should take that fucking thing off?"

He responded by saying, "Are you crazy, this thing is great!" He continued, "You ain't seen nothing yet, I got a different shirt for each day!"

I just shook my head and said, "maybe we should go check on how bad Adam has screwed up the Civil Rights Movement?"

So we headed back in that direction only to be passed up by the paroled and unshaven one, hand and hand with the exquisite beauty just laughing and playing the afternoon away.

"How does he do it?" I asked.

"I don't know, Moosie, I just don't know?"

We walked for about a half hour when all of a sudden out of a cluster a loud voice yelled, "Hodgie!"

It obviously got our attention and when Al turned and saw who it was, he shouted, "Ziggy!"

Ziggy was the "moniker" given to a longtime friend, frizzy-haired Johnny Calvert, who earned it from using a famous brand of cigarette paper to roll his own joints. Al had known Ziggy from the cottage back at Estral Beach, and I had met him a couple of times there as well.

"What the fuck are you doing down here, man?" Ziggy asked.

"Just trying to party a little bit," Al responded.

"How long are you down for?"

"Well ... we had this thing that came up," Al offered, "that's probably gonna cut our stay short. This other guy that's with us got into a fight last night, and we had to bail his ass out, so we're a little light on dough and don't have anywhere to stay."

"Bummer," he said, and it became apparent that Ziggy had not only rolled, but had already smoked a couple of his own homemade doobies.

Then Al turned to me and said, "hey, Zig, you remember my buddy from school ... Moose?"

"Oh yeah, man, what's happening, mouse."

"Moose," I said.

"Yeah right," he issued and just turned back to Al and said, "hey, man, you gotta stay ... you can crash with us."

Al's face lit up with offer and he said, "You gotta a place?"

"Hell yeah, man, there's nine of us staying at the ... uhhh ... awww ..." and he turned around and pointed at a close by high-rise and said, "That fucking place right there."

And the place that he was pointing to was the Holiday Inn!

"Well, we're kinda short on cash," Al stated.

"What cash, it's only ten dollars a day, and if you and Mouse wanna join in ..."

"That's Moose," I said.

"Yeah ... whatever ... anyway, that means we're all gonna pay less ... dig it?"

"Well there's actually three of us," Al said.

"Fuck it, man, the more the merrier!"

"Are you sure, Zig?"

"Hodge, for you ... and you too, Maw ... uhhhh, I mean Moose ... anything!"

Al and I just looked at each other and shrugged our shoulders and nodded in approval.

"You know, Zig, I think we'll take ya up on that," and the two of them discussed how this arrangement was going to go down.

So why they talked, I just wandered down the beach a bit, wondering how this was all going to turn out.

Al finally caught up to me and asked, "Well, what do ya think?"

"I guess it's okay, at least we're gonna have a room for the night. But let's face it, man, even at those rates, we still don't have enough cash between us to last the week."

"Yeah ... I know," he said in an exasperated tone.

"Moose, I know we don't have much, but let's at least try to enjoy the day."

"You know, Hodge, you're right."

So the two of us proceeded to buy a couple of beers from a guy with a cooler and went in the direction that we last saw Baker, to let him know that we had some sort of accommodations for the night.

We walked for about an hour and a half ... up and down the beach and must have missed Adam and his newfound friend. Finally, as the afternoon was winding down we came by the area where they originally met and saw the two of them. We walked up to the group smiled and Al said, "Bakes, can we see ya for a minute?"

He got up and walked over to us and while he and Al began to chat, I found myself captivated by this light-skinned ebony knockout. Everything about her was perfect and her eyes were spellbinding. She just smiled back at me and I found myself froze with this dopey look on my face and unable to do much of anything.

"Hi, I'm Angela," she said.

I just smiled and sort of fumbled with my bottle and nodded.

"And you are?"

"Uhhh … ummm, me, sorry … I'm ahh Mouse … I mean Mark," I quickly corrected.

"You're Mouse?"

"No…no, Mark I meant to say," and I extended my hand, forgetting that I had my beer in it and out through the neck of the bottle came a rush of the beer, almost spilling all over her.

"Oh shit … I'm sorry," and I bent down to wipe up some of the spill, with my eyes still focused on her, and began dabbing the area where the beer fell.

"Ahhh, what you didn't get, I think went into the sand," she said, "so unless you're going to build a castle … you can stop."

The others around her laughed, and I said, "Oh yeah … right," and proceeded to stand back up and sheepishly headed back over to Al and Adam, while I looked back over my shoulder toward her.

I bumped into the two of them because of the distraction and Adam said, "Hey, Mark, wanna put your tongue back into your mouth?"

"Ummm … right," I said, "so what's the deal?"

"Well, lover boy over here is going to try to get into the Dark Continent, so we're on our own until about eight. Then we're going to meet up back over at T.J.'s."

"T.J.'s," I said, "are you out of what's left of you fricking minds? Hello … you were arrested in there last night and more importantly, I couldn't get in."

"Don't worry about that," Adam said, "I got to know one of the door men and he said any time I needed a favor, look him up."

"And how did it come to him owing you a favor?" I inquired. "Did you give him a blow job before the cops hauled your ass out of there last night?"

"No, smart ass, but he's from Michigan too and dug the cause that I was fighting for. So, when you get there tonight, just ask for Hank and tell him that I sent ya."

I just shook my head and hoped for the best, then Hodge and I parted ways with him and walked toward the Monte Carlo in effort to move into our new digs for the trip.

"So what's the story with the room, Al?"

"I guess they got a bunch of sleeping bags, some cots and a couple of big ass beds," he said as he shrugged his shoulders. "What do ya want for ten bucks?"

I just took a deep breath, raised my brows and hoped for the best.

It was up to the fourth floor upon arrival, and there was no mistaking that this was spring break week, just by strolling past some of these rooms.

The entrance to all the rooms in this place was from the open-air lobby that extended around the entire perimeter of each floor of the building. And with the drinking and horseplay that undoubtedly went on around here, there was a scary feeling that this place could be the perfect setting for a drunken co-ed to take a header to his or her death.

When we got off the elevator and headed down to 418, not one door that we passed along the way was closed. This was a mother's nightmare, as each room looked worse than the next, and no single housekeeper could ever be prepared enough to tackle the prospects of cleaning one of these disaster areas.

Fact was, this floor looked like one of those scenes in a war flick where the battle had concluded and the only way it could be resurrected was if the Army Corps of Engineers came in to clean up and rebuild.

And you just knew it … 418 was definitely the worst room of all.

First, I couldn't see the floor because there was so much clutter and shit thrown around, that it was difficult to see what color the shag carpeting was. The beds must have doubled as a kitchen table because there were wrappers, KFC chicken buckets, beer cans and pop bottles all over the fucking place.

"Anybody here," Al yelled. "Yoo hoo, anybody around?"

"Yeah, just hold on to your horses, I'm taking a shit … I'll be right out!"

Our eyes wandered from top to bottom as if we had just landed on some strange planet. Then the toilet flushed and without hearing the faucet turned on to wash any hands whatsoever, out of the bathroom walked this beatnik looking character straight out of the sixties. He had a full beard that extended far off of his face, wired rimmed circular glasses, and a flowered shirt that couldn't have been cleaned since coming off of the rack at K-mart.

"Yeah, so what can I do for you two?"

Al responded, "Uhhh, Ziggy sent me here … said that you'd have some extra room for the next couple of days."

"Ziggy huh? Well yeah, man, find a place for your shit and if it ain't movin', you can sleep on it! It's ten bucks a day and I'll collect from ya by noon of the next."

"Alright," Al said. I'm Alvin and this is Mark."

"Cool … I'm Thomas," and he extended his hand to shake. The dirty and long nails were bad enough, but thinking where that hand just came from … I just let Al consummate the arrangements with a handshake and I went into the corner and found a place for my things.

"Well I'm off," Thomas said.

"Hey," I said before he left, "what about towels or keys?"

"Towels are in the bathroom … if you ca find any clean ones. Housekeeping's supposed to bring some extra ones up, but that call was made two days ago. As for the keys …" and he just laughed and said, "Catcha later."

Well I had to bathe! Fresh water had hardly hit my torso in three days and I was starting to crust up.

"Fuck it, Al…I need a shower," I said. So I went into my bag, grabbed a shirt to act as my towel and proceeded into the bathroom to start the shower.

"Al," I yelled, "come here!"

The bathroom was an extension of Thomas and a fitting tribute to the rest of this dump. Water was pooled on the floor with towels and God knew what else floating in it? It was just a bad scene, but priorities were apparently evident among these sewer dwellers, as from behind the shower curtain, the tub was immaculate and loaded with cans of beer and cubed pieces of pristine ice.

"Jackpot, Moosie!"

Suddenly this place had a charm all to its own and despite the fact that I used some other poor slob's suitcase to stand on, much like the chivalrous gentlemen would provide for his maiden in the face of some aquatic peril, I stood in front of the basin in the bathroom and used my own soap and shampoo to bathe myself.

I could care less where the rinsed water and soap off of my body fell. Then I toweled myself off with a fresh shirt, slipped one foot out of a flipflop to climb into my underwear, and then the other, grabbed myself a cold one out of the tub and whistled my way out of the bathroom.

Al, too, cleaned himself up using the aforementioned technique and we indulged in a few more beers before getting ready to head over to T.J.'s.

While dressing I remarked, "Listen, Al, I promised my mom that I'd call to talk to my dad about this whole thing with Adam, so I'm gonna use the phone in the lobby. I'm also gonna ask him to wire me down some money," I said with a grimace.

"Then I'm gonna go over to the drug store to see if they got anything to get rid of these welts."

"Okay, Moose ... well then, why don't you just meet me over at T.J.'s, ask for that Hank character and we'll hang out there for a while."

"Sounds good," I said, "I'll see you over there."

"Hey, Moose, do me a favor?"

I knew what he wanted even before he asked; to see if my dad would call Koobs and tell him that everything was well. I just winked at him and walked out the door.

I told my dad the truth about Adam and that his shenanigans basically cleaned us out. I did lie to him however, when I said that we had found a nice room right on the beach and for him not to worry about us.

When I asked for the money ... he kind of laughed and said, "Don't tell your mother! I'll go over to the credit union in the morning and wire it down to your hotel on my lunch break, but you three are going to pay me back!"

My true best friend was about to bail me out again. I told him where to send it, then asked him to call the Semkos for Al and to let Laura know, if she called that everything was okay.

Then before hanging up I said, "Hey, Dad."

"Yeah?"

"Thanks!"

"Okay, son."

"Dad."

"What?"

And suddenly I put myself in Al's shoes and thought, *What if he had it...what would I do?*

And in a clearing voice that was actually held back the onset of tears, I said, "I love ya, Dad!"

And I could hear him clear his throat as well before saying, "Love ya too, son."

~ now that's room service ~

I had a good feeling going now, knowing that my dad and I were all square about the situation with Adam, and with the confidence that by noon tomorrow I'd have a few extra bucks in my pocket for food and whatever.

I picked up some antiseptic cream, found a bathroom to apply it and began to high-step it over to T.J.'s for what promised to be a much better night than the one before.

I walked up to the main door, which again had three large animals, two of which I remembered from the previous night. "Which one of you guys is Hank?"

They just looked at each other and the one in the middle said, "He was fired."

"Fired! When?"

"Last night."

"But why?"

"He helped some pissant out in a fight and was letting a lot of minors in."

"Well ... I was ... told to," and then I thought to myself, *Don't say another word*!

"If you're coming in, I need to see some ID"

"No ... I'm not going in, just wanted to see if Hank was in."

So I stuck my hands in my pocket, shrugged my shoulders and spun around before walking away. Here I was again, on the outside looking in. Stranded and with no course, it was off to ... where else ... Denny's, this time for dinner.

After getting something to eat, I decided to go back to the room where I had hoped to meet up with on of my two companions. I got back to the room at about 9:00 P.M. and this time the door was slightly closed with the TV's volume at an ear-piercing level.

I pushed open the door and saw two guys sitting in chairs with their feet propped up against the stand that was holding the television, eating pizza, drinking beer and watching a ball game from Atlanta. They were oblivious to the fact that I was there and were obviously in the midst of a pretty good beer buzz, which had them cussing at practically every pitch that was thrown.

Meanwhile, over in the corner on the stained shag carpeting, this rather hairy looking monsterish stud was in the midst of carnal knowledge with this attractive brunette in a missionary position, without any reservations of who was looking on.

I mean, from my position at the room's entrance, it looked like they were fucking … it sounded like they were fucking and as I edged a little bit closer … yep, they were fucking!

With her legs wrapped around his head, he grabbed them out of the way, turned and looked at me and in a panting rhythm over her moans of ecstasy said, "Hey, buddy, you mind closing the door about half way?"

I just pursed my lips, gave him a thumbs up and did what he asked. He didn't seem concerned about me, a total stranger looking on, but had scruples enough to at least veil what was going on from the general public.

And if that wasn't enough, being the perfect host, he turned to me and said, "You must be one of the new guys?"

With my hands in my pocket, I just gave a half smile back to him and shook my head yes.

"I'm Frank," he said, without missing a thrust. Then he added, "Those two over there are Mike and Kenny … and this," motioning his head toward the girl, "is …" then he looked at her with a blank look on her face and asked, "what's your name again, honey?"

Then from the floor came in between the grunts and passion-filled moans, in a New Yorkish dialect, "Geeee … geee … Gina!"

"Oh, that's right," he smiled, "Gina. Anyway, there's pizza over on the bed and plenty of beer in the tub … welcome home!"

"Mark," I said while pointing to myself. To which he just gave me a wave and I proceeded to grab a piece of pie … pizza pie that is and went over to the tub of plenty.

"Hey, Mark, can you grab me a cold one?" Frank petitioned.

"My pleasure," I said, though I doubted that anyone in the room saying that they were getting more pleasure than Gina at present was lying.

I brought it right over to him and like the gentlemen that he was, he said, "Hey, man, I appreciate that."

For the next half hour or so, I served this guy two more beers, a slice of pizza and watched him bang this little beauty for all she was worth. This place was really starting to grow on me!

I was watching the ball game on the tube, Frank's ball game, was eating pizza, drinking beer, saw one of those two idiots watching the game fall straight back in his chair to the floor, passed out and was suppressing a pretty good hard-on of my own. Plus, this Gina had the filthiest mouth I ever heard on a chick. In one stretch, she verbalized while Frank was drinking his beer and fucking her, a barrage of verbiage that would have even made Del blush.

"Fuck me, you motherfucking cock sucker. Let me glide over that big motherfucking tool! Oh yeaaaah baby ... fuck the shit out of this whore's slutty pussy and make me cum all over that huge fucking horse cock!"

You could tell that Frank was used to this kind of thing, because he'd go from laughing his ass off at her comments while looking at me, to getting his "game face" back on when he looked down at her.

Finally he reached the point where you knew that he was going to bust. You could hear it in his breathing and in the intensity of his moans. He was building for what promised to be an earth-moving climax, when suddenly the weirdest thing began to happen. Gina started doing a one eighty ... not physically mind you, but in attitude.

Frank's thrusters were reaching mach three when he began to say, "Ooohhh bitch, I'm gonna cum so deep in your fucking cunt ... you ready, whore? What's it gonna be ... in the snatch or down the hatch? Huh ... you ready, you fucking slut?"

To which Gina shouted, "Who are you calling a bitch and whore? Watch your mouth, you motherfucker!"

Then he said, "Shut up! I'm gonna cummmm!"

To which she replied, "Not in me, you're not!"

Then she got herself to her knees and saw him holding his swollen member. I thought her eyes were going to pop out of her head when she looked down and actually saw the size of the thing that only seconds ago was pumping away in her twat.

Without wasting another moment, she grabbed his tool and started stroking it with an incredible motion, and did yet another about-face in her Dr. Jeckyl and Ms. Hyde routine.

"Oooooo yeah, motherfucker, drop your seed on my fucking tongue and make this whore choke on your goooooo … give it to me, baby … give me your cummmm!"

I didn't know if I was watching a porno or a horror flick, but this had all the makings of one of those creative clashes that would bring together the likes of Marilyn Chambers from *Behind the Green Door* and any number of sick fucking possibilities from a Hitchcock movie.

But in the end, Frank simply gushed all over her mouth, chin and tits in a display that simply made me drop my pizza on the floor.

"Ahhh, that was good," Frank said. Then he raised himself to his feet and proclaimed, "I think I'll grab myself a cold one. Mark, my friend, what about you?"

I just shook my head yes and began to scan the room.

In front of me was the one character who had passed out and fell back to the floor; he was either dead or in one hell of a coma. Then slouched in the other chair was his buddy, also in an alcohol-induced stooper and finally there was Gina, scurrying around for her clothes.

Meanwhile, Frank, who looked to be in his mid to late twenties reappears in full splendor without a stitch of clothing on and his cock hanging down, tosses me over a beer.

"Can you throw me a towel?" Gina asks.

"Nope," Frank replies.

"Well, why not?"

"Because we don't have any clean ones."

"Well, why don't you call housekeeping?"

"We did," he said. "A couple of days ago … and still nothing."

To which she immediately walked over toward me, scooched between my body and the bed, grabbed the phone and pressed a button.

"This is Gina Angetti, the hotel manager, I want twenty fresh towels sent up to room 418 instantly, and get somebody up there now to clean up that room Then she slammed the phone down, slipped into her skirt and shoes, looked at Frank and said in a tender little voice, "That was fun … see ya around." She then kissed him, fluffed up her hair and walked right out the door.

Man, I thought, *now that's room service!*

~ this trip was going to the dogs ~

Thankfully the beer did its magic, and within an hour or so I was out for the night and didn't hear a sound. All I know is that at first light when I came to, I was hanging half off of a cot, with a pizza box on my back and Hodgie's feet to the back of my head. There were twelve guys in a room with two queen-size beds, four cots, two sleeping bags and one guy was passed out on the dresser.

The room door was still opened and two seagulls were just inside fighting for scraps that had ended up on the floor. What this room needed was either a mortician or an Army Drill Sergeant, whose wife was "PMSing."

When it came to slumber, even at ten dollars a night, this place was way overpriced!

The front seat of the car was looking mighty comfy again, and though it didn't have a bathroom, there were always the facilities in the downstairs lobby. Which by the way were cleaner and offered a lot more privacy.

Thankfully I slept in my clothes, because after I finally worked my way to my feet, it still took me fifteen minutes and some pretty nifty footwork just to find my shoes. I was surprised that I didn't trip and fall on somebody or kill myself in the process. I nudged Hodgie to try and get him out of his state of unconsciousness, but he was pretty tight.

With the alcohol that had run through his body over the past few days, it was a sure thing that this boy wasn't going to be pissing yellow for quite some time.

So I grabbed my bag, hurdled my way toward the door, chased the birds out and went to the car to stow my things.

When I slammed the trunk shut, I heard this, "Hey, what's with all the noise?"

Then I saw Adam's head pop up from the back seat looking a wreck.

I cautiously walk around to the passenger side door wondering how he got in, when I had the keys.

I open the door and said, "How'd you get in here?"

From the floor of the backseat, he raised a clothes hanger that he had modified to fit between the door and the weather stripping to hook and raise the lock.

"I thought you were with what's her name," I asked.

"Angela."

"Yeah right … Angela," I repeated.

He just shook his head and said, "I tried to score with her around three in the morning and when I tried to unzip her pants, she push me away and said, unless you have three hundred, you ain't getting any of this."

"Not again," I said.

"How could I?" and he showed me the empty linings of his pockets.

"How'd you drink last night without any cash?"

"Drink what," he said, "I didn't have a drop of anything that wasn't given to me."

"Didn't you eat?"

"I had some mints from the lobby of the hotel that she was staying at around 6:00 P.M., other than that," he just shook his head no.

"So, you couldn't take her out to dinner or pay her rate … boy, I don't know how you missed," I laughed. "So, did you ever hook up with Hodge?"

"I never even saw him; I thought he was with you?"

I just shook my head and said, "Come on, I'll buy you some breakfast."

He sprung to his feet so fast, that I thought he was going to knock the seat off of its track, "Denny's, here we come!"

We managed to pilfer a copy of the local paper and thumbed through a little of this and some of that. Suddenly, I came upon the weather forecast to see that skies were going to be clouding up today, and showers were eminent. In fact, rain and plenty of it was expected in the area over the next couple of days.

Great, gray skies, rain, shitty luck as far as the ability of getting into bars, and faced with the prospects of spending another night at Thomas and Frank's fuck and bunkhouse, staying just didn't seem all that appealing.

I mean, don't get me wrong, I enjoyed the live European-like fuck extravaganza, but in hindsight, I think the Monte Carlo, far and away offered the better of the accommodations.

After the late breakfast, it was now nearing noon. We found Al in the hotel lobby groomed and freshly changed.

"Hodgie," I yelled, "look what I found wandering around."

He just laughed and responded, "Mr. Baker, didn't think I'd ever see you again."

We all just laughed and small talked for a few moments until I went to the front desk to see if the hotel had received my dad's wire transfer. With the vagabonds looking on, the clerk indicated that the wire had been received and with the presentation of the proper identification, she began counting money in my direction.

"Hey, Moose," Al said, "good to see that your ID is good for something down here."

I just sarcastically looked back over my shoulder at him and whispered, "Fuck off!"

"Oh great," Adam exclaimed, "beer and food money!"

At that, the clerk just smiled and said, "Enjoying your stay?"

I just raised my eyebrows and offered, "Immensely!"

After getting the funds, we huddled up in one of the lobby's corners.

"Now look," I said. "I had to beg my dad to send this down."

"But we're in this together," Adam said, "You know … buddies … pals!"

"Well, listen, pal, you're already three hundred into us, you're busted and I've spent more time with those bums on the fourth floor this trip than I have with you. Plus, we're right back where we started again. We got no room and this is supposed to last us for another couple of days here, and we need gas money to get back!"

Then I looked over to Al and admonished, "And what about you, not only did you leave me outside T.J.'s again last night, but what did you drink on?"

He just gave me a casual smile, shrugged his shoulders and said, "Mommy, please don't yell at us any more."

To which, I just bust out laughing and fell back against the wall.

"Fuck it," I blurted, and I handed each of them thirty bucks, kept thirty for myself and pocketed the rest for the Shangri-La suite on the fourth floor, food and hopefully enough gas to get back home.

There we were ... the three of us, off to the sand on a beautifully cloudy Daytona Beach day.

It was business as usual, with or without sun. The beach was packed and the flirt factory was in full throttle. The crazy thing that was becoming painfully obvious though, was that there were many different ways of playing this game of sexual chance. Attractive people with active hormones, skimpy attire, alcohol, music, curiosity and worst of all, stupidity, were all present in this sandy mixing bowl, and the players were ready to take their shot at a host of possibilities, ranging from all out fun to an array of awaiting trouble.

Adam, for example was the bad boy. His come on lines and approaches were often crude and sexually orientated. It was the bombastic premise of finding out if a girl in close proximity who heard one of his lines would laugh, which, in turn, was Adam's cue that she probably didn't require too much in the way soft selling to coax her into the sack. But, considering his track record on this trip, his problem wasn't that he couldn't pick out any winners, he just was having trouble paying for them!

Hodgie's bait was a little more subtle. He let the message precede any oral attempt to attract the attention of the babes. If you recall, Al had a shirt with a message on it lined up for each day. Today's was especially endearing, because it was considerate, somewhat kind ... and let's just say, straight to the point. On the front would be the set up for the reverse side's punch line.

Today's message d'jour ...

HONEY, I LOVE EVERY BONE IN YOUR BODY ...

and on the back it read...

ESPECIALLY MINE!

These shirts were provocative, perverted and funny, but certainly got a mixed bag of results. The problem with Al's approach was that most of the time he was getting spun around by people wanting to get the punch line, and most of those people were other guys. He was quickly getting labeled as the funny little shirt guy and was becoming a favorite of all of the beach's male population who were basically losers.

As for me, I sort of had the prizefighter approach ... and not the aggressive, in for the kill from the opening bell style, but rather a counter puncher.

A girl would fire, and then I'd fire back. If she was sweet, I'm right there with the same tactics, but if she wanted to play rough, I could stand toe to toe in that ring too.

Plus, it didn't hurt that I had an athletic build, and modestly speaking was fortunate to possess the three basic sexual food groups: tall, dark and handsome.

But other than the waitress in Virginia, I was doing nothing but observing this entire trip.

As we walked down the beach, I was excited to be here, but related my stroll to the plight of sperm that, at that special moment, get released hoping to find that match … but usually end up just getting douched away.

There was however this beauty on a lounge chair just sitting back and soaking up all of the atmosphere. She was wearing a green and tan bikini, had brownish hair and even without the sun, looked stunning in her sleek framed shades. She was all alone despite having a couple of chairs opened beside her and she was grooving on some music that was coming from a nearby radio.

She was so intriguing that I couldn't take my eyes off of her and as I passed, the crowd in front of me had bottlenecked, and I tripped over Adam's feet and soon found myself with a face full of sand. Again, I seemed to become the beach's laughing stock as I was covered in full frontal sand blast.

Fuck, I thought and with a red face I ambled my way to the ocean to wash off … with the absolute awareness that I wasn't going to lend myself to the jelly fish target practice that I had the day before.

I found my way back to Al and Adam to some lingering laughs and jeers that resulted from the fall, but the one I was concerned about the most, didn't seem to care at all about what happened to me. So, I worked myself over in her direction, five deep into the cluster of seats and blankets that she was surrounded by and said, "Excuse me, but out of all these people, you didn't seem to mind my fall … Thanks."

She turned toward me and said, "Are you okay?"

"Yeah, thanks for asking. I'm Mark."

"Carrie," she said and she extended her hand, though she kind of made me reach for it.

"May I join you?"

"Sure, until my friend's get back," she responded.

"Oh, I'm sorry, are you here with somebody?"

"Well yeah, isn't everybody?"

I just smiled and thought, *finally somebody soft, pretty and without facial hair to talk to!*

"So, where ya from?" I asked.

"Georgia," she answered.

"Oh, one of those southern belles?"

"But of course," she said. "And you, let me guess you're from ... Ohio?"

And with that I turned toward her and just pointed to my shirt, which had the old English D emblem of the Detroit Tigers, but she seemed disconcerted and went back to grooving on the music.

"Quite a crowd, huh?"

"Yeah," she said and she reached for her Coke, but instead spilled it all over me. Shocked by the coldness of the drink I jumped and slightly screamed "Whoa!"

She kind of bit her lip and looked elsewhere as if to shy away from the incident.

I just looked over at her and said, "Hey, no problem." And she just fidgeted around and was reaching for her lotion. She got quiet and I was starting to get the impression that she was trying to distance herself from me.

Just then, Hodgie appeared and yelled, "Moosie, look!" He pointed down about twenty yards, where these two chicks were staging a catfight and one had the other's top off! The screaming, excitement and spectacle had everybody around, now on their feet and cheering for both combatants. When I turned see what kind of response this would generate from my new friend, I found her still seated and oblivious to what was going on.

Come on, I thought, even the most casual of observers would, at least, rise to see what all of the commotion was about?

The cops were soon on the scene, quelled tempers and restored attire and peace, much to the displeasure of those at ringside.

Everybody seemed to get a kick out of what had just happened and Al worked himself over toward us and was laughing over what had just transpired.

"Wow, Moosie, was that cool or what?"

"Outstanding," I responded.

"Gonna introduce me to your friend?" he asked.

"Oh yeah, Al this is Carrie ... Carrie Al."

Again, she offered a snobbish hand, making Al stretch to shake. He gave me raise eyebrows as if to complement me on my choice, while questioning her courtesies.

"Me and Adam are gonna go get us a burger at the stand, you gonna join us?" he asked.

"Uhhh, I don't know, ya hungry. Carrie?" I inquired.

She just shook her head no.

Just then Adam appeared in the walkway about twenty feet from where we were seated and yelled, "Hey, I'm hungry … you coming or what?"

Al stood up as if to leave and I said, "No, you two go ahead." Then I said, "Hey, Adam, this is Carrie," to which he waved. I then turned to her and said, "That's the third stooge, Adam." To which she waved in a totally different direction.

Simultaneously, behind Adam a girl and a huge linebacker of a guy came walking up hand and hand.

"Hey, Carrie, I'm over here," Adam yelled sarcastically. And in his asinine bluntness, he followed, "Are you frickin' blind or something?"

Just then it hit me, I turned to her and saw her beginning to shake and cup her hands over her nose and mouth.

So, I reached over to grab her hand when suddenly someone mouthed over in his direction, "Yeah she is, you stupid motherfucker," It came from the oversized guy that was now working himself toward the girl. Now on my knees, I reached toward Carrie to offer my apologies, when the big guy pushed me aside and said, "It's alright, sis, I'm back."

He continued, "Why don't you assholes get the hell outta here before I kick the shit out of you!"

Carrie was now crying at a vehement pace as the brother and his girlfriend tried to console her.

"I'm so sor …" and before I could finish my apology, the angry brother just pushed me again and said, "Just get out … go away!"

Then they raised Carrie to her feet and swiftly ushered her away, leaving all of their beach belongings behind. From my backside, I just looked at Al and saw him offer a bewildered look in response.

"Moose, who knew?"

I just shrugged my shoulders and sheepishly walked with Hodgie over toward Adam.

"Mark … I'm sorry," Adam said.

I just shook my head in appreciation and motioned for us to move along. We made our way toward the snack stand and not too much was said.

As the latter stages of the afternoon were now upon us, the clouds were thickening and the sea breeze rains began to kick in. This was definitely a saloon keeper's dream come true, not that they needed much help at this time of the year. So after snacking, we grabbed our bags out of the car, headed up to the ten-dollar-a-day suite and got ready for what I had hoped was going to be a more entertaining night than I had previously experienced down here.

When we got up to the room, Frank was just coming out of the shower alone, and surprisingly had the pigsty to himself. "Hey, fellas," he stated. "Hittin' the clubs tonight?"

We all nodded to the affirmative, when Frank said, "you ever check out Jubie's?"

"Nope, we've had a hard time getting away from T.J.'s," added Adam.

"Plus," Al laughed while gesturing in my direction, "we're be havin' a little trouble getting our son past the front door."

"Really, man," Frank asked.

I just shrugged my shoulders and indiscriminately smiled.

"Well leave that to me, my man," Frank issued. "I'll be your way in and I know all the guys there, it'll be nooooo problemooooo."

"I heard about that place the other night at T.J.'s," Al said, smiling and shaking his head, "supposed to be great!"

Frank just gave us a thumbs up and said, "I'm just going to need to wait for someone for about a half hour before we go, so if you guys wanna meet me there, I'll catch up with ya."

After waiting about fifteen minutes, the rain was here and though it started at a moderate clip, it was now at Biblical proportions and you could hardly see the street from the exposed isle outside the room door.

"Goddamn … what a storm," Frank said.

Just then a couple of sweet looking blondes from the next room over peaked in the door and said, "Hey, Frankie, you going to Jubie's?"

"You betcha," he responded. "Just waiting for someone and then I'll be ready to go."

They just giggled and I thought to myself, *Are they a part of his harem too?*

"You going to need a ride, sweetie," one of them said to him.

"He pointed to the storm and said, "What do you think?"

Which in and of itself commanded the question, *Didn't this sex machine, porno star of the Daytona strip have a car?*

"We're eager to go, Frankie," one suggested.

"Then go," he toyed.

Then he said while pointing over at Al and Adam, "Why don't you two go with the girls, and me, Mark and my friend will join you in a few minutes." Then he turned at me and said, "You do have some wheels, don't you?"

I just shook my head yes, and wondered if he was simply protecting my ego by not letting the girls know that I had been having trouble getting into other joints, or if he was trying to clear the room for just the two of us? *Oh fuck* I thought, *Frank, I'm not into that shit!*

Al, Adam and the two girls raced out the door leaving the modern day Caligula and me just standing around. "Let me get dressed, my man," he said, and I thought I'd never be so happy to hear those words, than at that moment!

We waited for another fifteen to twenty minutes, until he just gave up on whomever he was supposed to meet. "Ahhh screw this man ... let's get the hell out of here," he said, and off we were!

When we got to the main floor the elevator doors opened, and guess who was waiting? None other than the sexual split-personality Gina.

"Hey, Frankie," she smiled.

"Hey, baby," he uttered back.

"Sorry, I'm late."

"Hmm," he moaned while stealing a peak at his watch.

Then he looked at me and said, "Hey, man, do ya mind?"

And I didn't know if he was asking me if she could join us on the ride over, or if he was asking me if I wanted to join them on the ride going up? Honestly, I was ready for either option, but wouldn't you just know it, she leaped onto the elevator and this time neither of them were interested in an audience ... so, he motioned me to get out!

Now standing just outside of the elevator looking in, Frank rendered, "I should only be about a half hour or so. Just wait in the lobby and I'll be back in no time."

Then she pushed the button to take them up, went into his arms and grabbed his crotch, as the doors closed in my face.

Here I was sitting in the lobby of the Holiday Inn staring at the four clocks on the wall behind the clerks at the front desk, and wondering if there was an asshole like me, in either Los Angeles, Tokyo or London, (the three other locales that the clocks were set for), who were sitting around for what had now become two hours, waiting for the fuck machine to illegally get them into a bar?

No more, I thought, the rain wasn't subsiding, and the night wasn't getting any younger ... I had to get out on my own!

I decided to drive around and really considered just getting the hell out of town and letting my travel companions fend for themselves. I drove and drove, and some twenty minutes into it, I saw these big and bright neon lights inviting me like the burning bush.

At first, with all of the rain they weren't distinguishable, but as I got closer it read very clearly, DAYTONA BEACH KENNEL CLUB.

"No shit," I laughed to myself, "the dogs!"

I always wanted to see the greyhound's race, and with this not being a night fit for neither man or beast to be out … except at the track … why not?

I was used to the big tracks of Detroit, and the participation of either jockeys or drivers in the mix of horse racing, so this was a totally new form of pari-mutual wagering for me.

After passing through admissions, I noticed that the track itself was obviously much smaller in circumference. But the appearance of the facility was bright and a whole hell of a lot more appealing than those shit holes back in Detroit.

But I had the presence of mind to understand that I was out of my element here and that I needed to exercise caution, especially since I was relatively new to this form of racing and really didn't have much cash to burn.

So I bought a program and without making a single wager, watched a couple of races, hypothetically seeing what fate I would have enjoyed if I would have risked a bet. Truth be told, the two dogs that I would have bet in their respective races, finished dead last. So, I guess I saved some dough that I really couldn't have afforded to lose.

I knew how to read the past performances that the program had offered, and tried to relate them to what I had become accustom to from the ponies, but my experiences with the equines, were not coming even close to figuring out their canine racing cousins.

It wasn't that I was overly successful at picking winners on a consistent basis at the track, but I did enjoy a system and some sort of familiarity with the horses and quite frankly, didn't have a clue what was happening here. So, I grabbed myself a hot dog and Coke at the concession stand and watched as the rain continued to pound down upon the pound.

Actually, the best part about the dogs was the first turn of their races. They would come flying hell bent out of the starting box, chasing that mechanically driven hare down the straightaway into that first turn. Their speeds seemed incredible and when combined with the closeness in which they ran, the tightness of the turn and the slop that they were trekking on, it looked like a high-speed doggie battle royal!

They were banging, colliding and bumping into one another, knocking each other off stride or way off course. But, as fast as they were impeded and knocked down, these intense performers were back on their paws and in the chase. The greyhounds were a gas to watch!

No claims of foul or judges' inquiries here, just muzzle 'em up, send the rabbit and open the gates. It was thirty seconds of the wildest and purest forms of adrenaline that you could experience. But to bet on it, you'd have to be a fool. At least in my eyes ... it was just too tough.

This was a place where you brought twenty bucks, closed your eyes and flipped a coin or did something imaginative to be your source of wagering inspiration, and this poor boy didn't feel like risking what limited funds that he had.

I thought to myself, *if my dad only knew where I was currently at, after what I had asked him to do, he'd kick my ass!*

So I just sat and watched, race after race. What else was there to do?

I had just come back from taking a piss, when the trumpeters call to the post summoned the dogs to the track for the twelfth of the fourteen scheduled races. The track announcer indicated the conditions of the race just before getting ready to introduce the field of eight runners.

For the most part, I was just vaguely listening to his accounts, when all of a sudden, he introduced the four dog, named Laura's Cherry. Now, for obvious reasons, that name just happened to catch my interest and so I thought I'd pay just a little bit more attention to what was happening out on the track.

Then the last dog he introduced was one that went really struck a cord with me. Especially considering what I had been through earlier in the day. The name of the number eight dog was "Blind Ambition," and I thought to myself, *You got to be kidding me.*

I was missing Laura so much and looking forward to getting back to her, but Carrie, the blind girl was very intriguing and I just couldn't get her out of my mind ... how ironic?

Then I don't know why, but I was thinking about Adam and Al partying away, while I spent another night on the outside looking in. Just then, as if in an omen from the heavens, the track announcer's barking seemed to be on the same wave length as my thoughts, "ONLY TWO MINUTES UNTIL POST TIME..." while simultaneously I was thinking, *how are they always getting in, and I'm always getting shut* ... "PURCHASE YOUR TICKETS AND DON'T GET SHUT OUT!"

Laura's Cherry, Blind Ambition and this guy's telling me not to get shut out?

Besides, my rent was cheap enough and I was saving a shit load of cash from being stymied from the bars, so I raced to the mutual windows only to see huge lines in every direction that I looked.

"POST TIME IN ONE MINUTE ... ONLY ONE MINUTE UNTIL POST TIME."

This wasn't going to happen. The lines were too long and time was not on my side. I waited in one line, then found myself darting into another.

"AND NOW THE DOGS ARE BEING LOADED INTO THEIR BOXES."

Then from the teller in the line that I was waiting in I heard, "Damn it the hell! The machine's jammed again!"

"For Christ's sake," the guy in front of me blasted. Then he just threw his hands into the air and said, "If Patootie Princess wins this race, I'm gonna sue all of you assholes!"

I gave up hope too and thought, *ahhhh....just as well, I probably saved money,* when I heard the track announcer say, "HERE COMES SPEEDY!"

The rabbit was sent, the mutual ticket machine was down and I conceded the fact that fate didn't want me to wager on this event ... when I heard from behind the window, "Oh forget it, Jake, I fixed it!"

"Okay, Georgie," the machine technician said.

"Georgie ..." my dad's name too!

"I can take action here!"

"Laura, Blind, shut out" and now I just heard that the teller and my dad shared the same name.

I wasn't the overly superstitious type, but even I had to admit that this had a Hollywood ending written all over it.

I bolted back to the window and reached for the first thing in my pocket. When I looked at it, it was a twenty. "Give me a twenty dollar quinella 4 and 8!"

A quinella is an exotic wager in which you pick the two runners in the race, who you think will finish first and second. It's an automatic boxing of those two-ticketed runners that you have chosen. So, regardless of who's first or second, whether it's the four first and the eight second or vice versa, I'd win.

What I'd win, or how much, would be determined by the pool size (the amount wagered) and the odds on my combination, which I didn't have a chance to look at, due to the fact as I was racing back to the grandstands to watch the race.

The announcer said, "AND THEY'RE OFFFFFFFF!"

Unlike their horse racing counterparts who identify the runners by name, greyhound announcers, because the action that they're trying to follow is so fast and furious, usually just identify the runners by their number.

"IT'S THE 2 BREAKING OUT FOR THE FIRST CALL, WITH THE 5 A CLOSE SECOND, FOLLOWED BY THE 7 … 1 ON THE INSIDE … THEN THE 6 AND 3, AND ALREADY TRAILING THE FIELD ARE THE 4 AND THE 8."

They were only a hundred yards into the race, and my two dogs were already trailing by half a football field. As the rain pummeled the Daytona night, I just turned away from the track, grabbed the railing behind me and conceded that this was just about the quickest twenty that I had ever sent down the drain.

"AS THEY ROAR PAST THE GRANDSTANDS AND TOWARDS THE FIRST TURN, IT'S STILL THE 2 … PATOOTIE PRINCESS ON THE FRONT END, WITH THE 5 RIGHT ON HER HEELS AND IN CLOSE QUARTERS IT'S THE 7–1—6 AND 3, WITH THE 4 AND 8 STILL DISTANCED FROM THE LEADERS."

Ready to toss my ticket onto the floor, I heard an incredible crack of thunder resonate through the dark and gloomy Florida sky and literally shake the grandstands, when, all of a sudden, the announcer said…

"INTO THE TURN THEY ROLL, AND OOOOOOH THE 5 AND 7 TANGLE WHILE VYING FOR POSITION AND HAVE SCATTERED THE FIELD CLOSELY PACKED BEHIND THEM, SENDING A HOST OF RUNNERS WIDE AND OFF STRIDE TO THE OUTSIDE RAIL. SO THAT LEAVES THE FAVORITE, THE 2 PATOOTIE PRINCESS, UNCHALLENGED AND LOOSE ON THE LEAD WITH ONLY THE 4 AND 8 WITH A SHOT AT TOPPLING THE LEADER."

Did I hear that the only ones with a shot were the four and the eight? I turned back toward the track and saw my two dogs, blessed to be so far back in the early going to avoid the trouble of the first turn, actually gaining ground on the leader down the back stretch!

"Go, Laura … run, you blind bitch," I yelled.

"THEY'RE INTO THAT FAR TURN AND HERE COMES THE 4, LAURA'S CHERRY CHARGING AT THE LEADER … AND SUDDENLY THE EARLY PACE SETTER HAS BEEN COLLARED AND NOW PASSED BY THE 4, WHO'S AT 29 TO 1! INTO THE STRETCH THEY RUN, AND LAURA'S CHERRY WILL EASILY SCORE THE HUGE UPSET VICTORY, WITH THE BATTLE NOW ON FOR PLACE …"

And my attention was now turned to Blind Ambition, because my ticket would have been worthless without the eight finishing second!

"… THEY'RE DING-DONGING DOWN THE STRETCH, WILL THE 2 HANG ON, OR WILL

IT BE THE FAST CLOSING 8 … THEY'RE HEAD TO HEAD, MUZZLE TO MUZZLE, HERE'S THE WIREEEEE … OHHHH … AND IT JUST TO CLOSE TO CALL."

"Oh God, who is it?" I yelled.

I ran from monitor to monitor and tried to solicit opinions from anybody who was near the wire, but it was just too difficult to judge. Even with the benefit of the slow motion replay, it was just to close.

The photo sign was illuminated and remained lit long after the connections of the winning dog had gotten their winner's circle photo taken and had sloshed their way to cover.

"Oh I hope the duce hung on," said a lady standing near by, I got a two dollar place ticket on that little bugger!"

And I was ready to say, "Go fuck yourself, lady!"

Just then I looked at the odds board and saw that not only was the four a 29 to 1 shot, but the eight was 36 to 1! I was in line for a huge fricking pay off, but suddenly got the feeling that the broad with the two-dollar place ticket on the favorite, was somehow going to be the jinx.

Then a hush and a shit load of held breaths fell over the track and faintly beating hearts took over as the photo sign was removed from the tote board. I closed my eyes, tightened my grip on my ticket…and heard the track announcer say …

"IN A CLOSE BATTLE FOR THE PLACE POSITION, THE JUDGES AFTER REVIEWING THE PHOTO HAVE PLACED THE NUMBER 8, BLIND AMBITION SECOND."

And a little old man behind me raised his ticket and said, "Yahooooo, I got it … I got the quinine!"

I grabbed him and started jumping up and down with people looking at us as if we had just struck oil! "You got it too, sonny," he asked.

"You bet, pops!"

"Whooo whooo, sonny, look at that quinine pay off, will ya," and he just pointed at the tote board before running off to the mutual windows.

It was as if the board had exploded and was the most beautiful thing that I had ever seen in lights. The quenilla had paid $428.40 for a two-dollar ticket … and I had it ten fucking times!!

I rushed to the teller and when he ran the ticket through the machine, it registered a payout total of $4,284. The guy behind the counter looked at me with a pretty stern look on his face, and all I could think about was that guy was now going to question my age.

He started tapping his finger on the counter, looked down at the ticket and then back across the counter at me.

While swallowing the last of my saliva, I said, "Is there a problem?"

"Yeah," he said, "and I think you know what it is … don't you?"

"Look, mister," I said, "If …"

And he interrupted me.

Ready to run for the exits, because I didn't want to be nabbed for wagering as a minor, he said, "I don't have enough money in the drawer to pay ya."

"Oh," I nervously laughed. "Yeah, well that happens from time to time."

He rushed to the main teller to grab a stack of hundreds and returned to count off forty-two Franklins and change to me, and after giving him a ten spot for his troubles, I headed straight for the door with my pace increasing with each and every step.

Once outside, I was getting drenched by nature's continuing onslaught, but was so happy that it could have been the same substance that Al deposited onto Adam back at Dorothy's, and it wouldn't have mattered one bit to me … well … on second thought?

I drove right to the Holiday Inn, left the Monte Carlo double parked under the covered entrance of the main lobby and proceeded to the fourth floor. Upon my arrival, the door was in its usual half open position. I pushed it opened and found five guys in the midst of a hot poker game around the room's table, and over in the far bed, Frank and Gina under the sheets and each smoking a cigarette.

"Hey, man," Frank said, "sorry, but I got a little derailed here, if you know what I mean?"

"Wait a minute," I asked, "you mean to tell me that you've been up here all night long?"

He just smiled back and shrugged his shoulders while Gina spoke up and said, "When will you little ones learn, that a sweet flower like me can keep the fires of a good fuck burning all night long."

I just chuckled and reached for my bag over in the corner.

"Frank, man," I said, "it's been a pleasure. And as far as your companion is concerned," as I motioned over toward Gina, "she's quite special alright."

"Yeah." he said, "she's alright … for a bitch."

"Hey, who you calling a bitch, you motherfu," and he wrapped his rather large hand around her mouth and cited to her, "just shut the fuck up!"

I then reached in my pocket, pulled out a twenty from my stash and said, "Thanks for hookin' me up for the night, I enjoyed it!"

When the poker players saw my roll that I had broken out, they froze like fucking deer in headlights and before the first of them could speak, I said, "Sorry, gentlemen … but poker's not my game."

I then grabbed my bag, and before heading out the door looked back at Frank and said, "Hey, the two assholes that are with me, tell them that there will be a message waiting for them at the front desk in the morning." Then I waved, hoisted my bag and departed from Shangri-la.

I had gotten wind that the Hilton, a couple of doors down had some rooms available at premium rates, and unless they were reserved for heads of state, I was hell bent on the fact that I was going to be sleeping in the lap of luxury tonight!

I drove the car to valet parking, grabbed my bag and walked right into the mammoth Hilton lobby. When I arrived at the front desk the most sniveling little bastard that you could ever imagine was waiting to greet me. "Yes," he said.

"You have rooms?"

"We have many rooms here, but all of the frat boy suites are occupied, maybe you'd care to look down the street … way down the street," and he and two others working behind the front desk began chuckling in an authoritarian manner.

"Listen, meter-maid, I don't appreciate your tone! Now, do you have any rooms available?"

He tried to reestablish command of the conversation by saying, "Why yes, we do. But, it's ocean view and at one hundred and eighty dollars a night, probably out of your," and I began to count out six one hundred dollar bills and cut him off by saying, "I'll take it, for the next three nights … now, where do I sign?"

The prissy little cocksucker changed his tune post haste, and immediately asked, "can I have a bell boy take your bag, sir?"

"No!"

"Will you require any special services, sir?"

"Nothing from you, if that's what you're referring to?"

Then he handed me my change, the key and said, "have a pleasant evening, sir."

To which I just turned and walked toward the elevators that were about to whisk me away to heaven on the sixth floor. Then about twenty yards from the desk, I looked back and said, "Hey … you don't happen to have anybody on staff named Gina, do ya?"

The three of them gawked at one another and the sniveling one looked back with a confused expression and answered, "Well no, sir, we don't."

"Ahhh … well, just thought I'd ask," and I turned and continued my trek to solitude.

—   —

When I opened the door, it was spacious, clean, fresh, had plenty of towels, and no fucking creeps or slobs to share it with.

I dropped my bag, then my pants, stretched out my arms, yawned, scratched my balls, and proceeded to the window to see what kind of view that I had paid for. Though it was dark and rainy, it was hard not to be impressed with the digs and it's most impressive backyard!

I then proceeded to shit, shower and shave, order something off of the late night menu, watch a little Carson, and stretch out in my enormous fucking bed! It might not have been Buckingham Palace, but for the next three nights, it was the Moosie's Lair!

Now late in the wee of the morning, I dimmed the lights and began to say my prayers.

Thanks God, for Mom and Dad, the credit union, Laura and Carrie, a rainy night, denials at bars and for making Gina come at just the right time. Thanks for making me get lost, and for George's ability to unjam the machine just in the nick of time. Thank you for a little luck, that little collision in the first turn and though I could have done without the mini heart attack during that long review of the photo finish, I offer you four thousand two hundred and eighty salutes.

Oh … and Lord, thanks for this wonderful, kick ass room and those two little bitches at the kennel club for making it all possible … in the name of the Father, the Son and the Holy Spirit … AMEN!

I woke up about 10:30 from a blissful sleep, and stretched and yawned to my heart's content. It was a beautiful way to start the day.

After washing the sleep out of my eyes, I brushed my teeth and took care of all other bathroom activities. Then I had room service bring me up a couple of eggs, bacon, hash browns, toast and juice, while debating how long I would wait until I would let the other two in on my newfound fortune?

The rain was still relentless and the thunder and lightening displayed quite a show over the Atlantic. I finally decided to call over to the Holiday Inn and left the message to both of them … "You are invited to the Hilton for a little something different … room 622."

I then got dressed, and proceeded to the Daytona Municipal offices to pay the $75 ticket that we got for parking on the beach our first night, and went to pick up a twelve-pack of beer and a six-pack of pop. Funny how I wasn't asked for any ID this time, and how my confidence level was towering over the Daytona skyline.

Then it was off to get some gifts for Laura, my mom and dad, my sister and a little something for Chooch and Margo for the use of the car.

When I got back to the Hilton a little past one o'clock, there were the two lost little sheep, looking as if they were destitute, without a friend and ringing wet sitting in the lobby.

"Gentlemen," I said in a loud and cheerful voice, "isn't a lovely day!"

"What in the good fuck are you doing here?" Hodgie asked.

"And how are you able to look like that?" Adam followed.

"Oh, it's quite a fascinating story and I'm sure you'll enjoy hearing it, but I'm not going to tell it here. If you're interested, follow me."

With a smile on my face and a twelve-pack in my hands, I lead the way upstairs.

When I open the door, Adam just dropped his bag on the floor outside and walked aimlessly into the freshly made room, in front of the king-sized bed and fell face first onto the bed.

"Moose, how?" Al asked.

I cracked open a beer, sat in front of the window and began to tell my story.

The two of them would eventually get cleaned up, have a bite from room service until we decided to hit a bar and to see if my luck really had changed.

With no beach activities today we hit a place called Nick's Beach Club that seemed to be jammed to the rafters. Adam indicated that he had left his brothers ID back at the room, but since he hardly had to resort to it, we chanced it.

With a line waiting to get in, we filed along until we finally got to the infamous front door. Adam was first to attempt to get past the threshold, and with his beard and height, it was usually a given that he'd get in, and we'd hope to follow through on his older looking coat tails.

"Let's see some ID, pal"

Adam looked back in amazement and said, "What?"

"Let's go, buddy, and either get it up, or get out of line."

This seemed to be a great place, the music was enticing and the chicks waiting to get in were hot. But if Adam was being asked, there was little hope for the rest of us.

I was up next and without hesitation, the middle doorman said, "Come on, buddy, why don't you come on through so you don't have to wait through all of these games."

I was in! Adam was out there, but I was in! My luck really had changed! And again to my bewilderment, Hodgie was allowed in, no questions asked. He was too big to be considered a midget and too short not to be asked. This was the ongoing mystery of this trip.

So I threw Adam the keys, told him to go get his brother's ID and to meet us back there as soon as possible.

Within forty-five minutes, Adam returned and convinced the doormen that he belonged and the three of us flirted and played our way through the large establishment until late that night.

We had finally had the chance to all party in a Daytona nightclub at the same time, and really did live it up! It didn't hurt that I had a pocket full of cash either.

When we returned back to the hotel, it was about 10:30 P.M., and I decided to check in at home. Everything was fine with my folks, but my mom informed me to make sure that Al called home, for Koobs was not doing that well.

When Al got off the phone, you could see him start to tear up. "Guys, I gotta get back," he issued.

He continued to tell us his story and we instantly agreed on the fact that we had to cut our trip short, but instead of doing what Al asked, to leave immediately, I interceded and said, "Hodge, we're in no condition to leave right now." Much to Al's dismay, Adam supported my position and we convinced him that we'd leave bright and early in the morning.

We got something to eat and then hit the hay as Al and I shared the bed and Adam sacked out in the cot that we had ordered up. By 6 A.M., I had settled my tab at the front desk and had ordered up breakfast for the three of us. By 6:45, we were on the road with me starting off and Al riding shotgun. It was about a one hundred and seventy-mile jaunt to the Georgia border and where we were to pick up I-75 for the straight shot home.

Before leaving Florida, however, I pull off to one of those roadside stands and loaded up on the payoffs promised to Loyola. Al begged me right then and there to take over behind the wheel and you could see that he was in a rush to get back to Motown.

Obviously, he was pushing the speed envelope through the Peach state and as we roared through the Atlanta city limits, there it was again, the blue flashers of a state trooper's car. After a check of all of the particulars, the trooper came back and said, "I see you've had a ticket here for the same violation within the past thirty days."

Al nodded and the cop proceeded.

"I'm sorry, but you're going to have to either pay up right now, or I'm going to have to detain ya until payment is received."

"Sir," I interceded, "we can't deal with any delays at this time, my friend here has a family emergency that we're trying to get back home to. How much would the fines be?"

After some calculations, the cop indicated $260, to which I forked it over. He gave us a receipt, Al an admonishment, but sympathized with our plight and was cool enough to also wish Al good luck with the troubles that he faced.

Even with the delay from the ticket and all subsequent stops there after; we had dropped Al off at home some sixteen hours and forty-five minutes after we left the Daytona Hilton. Both Adam and I wanted to go in and see for ourselves how Koobs was doing, but realized that this probably was not the right time.

I then proceeded to drop Adam and asked him to run all of the goodies over to the nuns in the morning, to which he agreed.

The weather was noticeably cooler and despite our collective concerns for Koobs, I found myself warmed and laughing as I reminisced about all of the events both in and around our nearly twenty-four hundred miles of springtime fun.

~ motivation ...
motivation ~

Shortly after our return, Koobs began chemotherapy treatments and it was immediately evident that this was going to have a devastating effect on his life. He went on disability from work and slowed considerably. He lost his zest to do almost anything and that alone would spur significant changes.

Al remained strong, but you could see that he was preoccupied with sharing the rigors of caring for his dad with Lottie and his siblings. School and all of its requisite activities would become secondary for Hodgie, and thankfully his grades were such, that Loyola and the rest of her staff were able to take it easy on him and allow him to focus his attention on domestic needs. His high school days were now set on cruise control and whatever he needed from the gang to make things manageable, we did.

We were now heading into the home stretch of the year, and despite the thought that things would be slowing down, on the contrary, for me things were just starting to heat up.

On the home front, Mom was prodding me on what I thought I was going to do after graduation. Though she had hoped that I was going to continue my education, I think that she resigned herself to the thought that I wasn't, and that I'd probably be joining my dad on the docks of Allied Chemical. In addition, she would occasionally lay hints about employment and the need for me to start monetarily contributing to the house.

But my dad wouldn't stand for it and would quickly squash my mom's attempts to get me started in the work force.

"He's going to college, plus it's baseball season … and my son's playing ball!"

Despite the fact that my dad was living vicariously through my sporting endeavors, baseball was indeed my strongest sport. I had a kick ass junior campaign, leading the Catholic League in hitting with a .398 average and in RBIs with 72. I was voted to the All League team for the second consecutive year and was All State, class D catcher of the year. Defensively, I was even amazing myself, and had not allowed a pass ball in my junior season and had gunned down attempted base stealers against me, at a clip of 89%.

I had a couple of smallish, regional type schools that started taking an intense interest in me during my junior year, but the knock against me was that the competition that I faced was weak and not a true indication of how I would stand up against a better talent pool of players.

Plus, some critics said that my weaknesses would be exposed in my senior year, because opposing teams could just key upon me, now that we lost a sizable sum of players, off of a pretty damn good team that won the divisional championship, to graduation.

Then there was the continuing fallout from last year's football fiasco. With most of the athletic department sustaining an overhaul, the only holdover coach, was in fact, the best coach that I had ever had.

Len Herzack was an incredible instructor who could always get the most out of his players. Unfortunately, Len had ties to Paul Owen's gridiron failures from the year before, and though exonerated from any involvement it was pretty much a given that his days were numbered and that the welcome mat would not be extended by the new régime.

He was responsible for the success of our 1977 ball club, and had deflected some of the school's fragile and damaged athletic reputation away. But alas, just before training camp was to begin, Lynch and Coach Lenny had a major difference of opinion in philosophies and in a letter that was released to us only days before camp was to begin; he wished us success … but announced his resignation.

This sent shock waves through the pool of players who were going to make up the team and there was an air of defeat even before we got started.

Though I had little in common with Lynch, and the fact that he and I didn't see eye to eye on anything, I appreciated the way he took the time to come by my house and ask me for some leadership and help in assisting him make the transition while a new coach was sought. If he would have used this sort of diplomacy earlier in the year, I think that both the football and basketball programs would have enjoyed much better fates.

The process to replace Herzack had to be expeditious, due to the fact that we were already falling behind in pre-camp related issues. So the filtering through of candidates had to be both thorough and speedy.

Now I don't know how many people actually applied for the job or what the requirements and qualifications were, but literally, from out of the shadows of obscurity came Ollie Alhambra. A 5-foot-nothing, stocky pigmy whose hair protruded through his tight polyester clothes, like straw through a burlap wrap.

He had the gait of a polar cap pregnant penguin and was always trying to make us aware that he successfully converted to Catholicism from being a Muslim, whatever the hell that was supposed to signify?

It wouldn't take long for comparisons to start to be drawn between Coach Ollie and his predecessor. When you came out of a Herzack training camp, you were in the best shape of your life. It was regimented and mirrored a military boot camp. Len Herzack's teams focused on the little things … those incidentals that you really didn't plan on, but would be prepared for if the situation ever arose. You looked the part and performed it if you played for Coach Lenny!

Ollie's take on preparedness was a little more laid back to say the least. Stretching took place twice a day according to the new coach, when you got out of bed and stepped out of your car. He took a Ruthian approach to getting ready for a game, throw the ball around, field some grounders and make sure that you go to the bathroom before we start.

Where a Herzack player had to earn his spot on the roster, breathing was Ollie's prerequisite. Thankfully we had a pretty good core returning that we were able to build upon.

It is said in baseball, "If you're good up the middle, everything else should fall into place." We were good up the middle with me behind the plate and our ace hurler, Maxie Boughton, on the mound. Maxie, if you recall, for some reason was able to gain the fancy of Becky Lorenz, who without a doubt had the nicest set of tits in the entire school.

Maxie wasn't anything special as a pitcher; his fastball wasn't that fast, his curve ball didn't break and his change-up was basically his fastball, with just a little taken off the delivery. But, he got the ball over the plate and he was able to get the other team to hit it right at one of our fielders, when he needed a crucial out.

Simply speaking, he got the job done and won ball games. I don't know how he did it; all I know is that he did.

At shortstop, we had J.J. Lambert. Now you're obviously well aware of the fact that there was no love lost between Joel and myself, but I had to admit, if I was going to start a team, he'd be my first pick. He was a solid little player who could do it all, and played the game the way he lived his life, like a sneaky, taunting little shit, but always with the will to win!

At second … it was newcomer, sophomore David Berlez. I knew that he was going to be a good one, because I saw him develop … and that was easy, because he grew up as my next-door neighbor. In fact, all of his brothers, and there were five all together, were pretty good athletes. David was a gritty one who didn't mind doing whatever it took to get the job done. He was a welcomed addition.

To complete the up the middle trek, I give you Rudy "Smiles" Velez. Dubbed "Smiles" due to the fact that he had the worse case of bucked teeth that you had ever seen. Regardless of whatever his facial expression was, Rudy always appeared to be smiling.

In addition, he had this frizzed out fro of a hairdo, which he had to have thinned out to allow his baseball cap to fit. Even then he looked like a fucking Latin circus performer that you just couldn't resist laughing at.

But, he carried a good stick and anything hit in the park between left and right center, would usually end up in his glove. After that, all bets were off, for Rudy was the game's first dyslexic player when it came to throwing the ball.

He knew where it had to be thrown, but getting it there was a whole different issue.

You never knew where the ball was going to end up, if he had to throw it.

I saw Rudy make the greatest catch that I had ever seen in a ball game, which initially saved the contest, and seconds later he turned right around within the execution of the very same play, and blew the game.

We were playing out in Marine City, the scene of the football fiasco. With one out and runners on first and second, we enjoyed a one run lead on the Crusaders in the bottom half of the seventh inning. Their next hitter lined a 2-2 pitch into the left centerfield gap that was sure to have ended the game if it had fallen safely.

Rudy raced toward the gap and lunged in a flat out dive to haul it in, and actually ended up snow coning the ball in his mitt. Even the opposing squad applauded the catch and were about to concede the distinct possibility that one of their base runners would be doubled off with a game-ending throw to either first or second.

But instead of making a controlled throw back into one of the middle infielders; Smiles comes up firing a dart, over the right fielder's head, and into the corner. This allowed both runners to get back to their respective bases, tag up and motor onward. There was little doubt that the runner from second would score, and with the speed, or lack of it that we had in right field, this throwing away of a victory was a foregone conclusion, as the runner from first would also cross the plate.

I saw Rudy throw the ball into dugouts, bullpens, stands and his most memorable blunder, was during another close game that we had against St. Florian's.

With two outs, in a tie game at old Wisner Stadium in Hamtramck, Florian had a runner on second. One of their lower placed hitters dribbled one through the box and just past outstretched glove of J.J. into center field. A hard charging Rudy came up with the ball and had plenty of time to hit one of the cutoff men for a relay peg to the plate. So, I got rid of my mask, kicked the bat away from the plate area and positioned myself in front of home, anticipating a game deciding play.

The runner was getting waved around third and Rudy at least was headed in the right direction. Now with ball in hand, he gunned it toward the plate, but not the plate that I was standing by. I took three steps forward and conceded that the winning run was going to score.

The amazing thing about this play was the trajectory and flight of the ball. It went way over my head, over the screen and into the second story press box, beaning an unsuspecting beat reporter from the Detroit News who was eating his lunch while covering the game.

We seriously tried to concoct a number of alternatives to address Rudy's liability, including having him roll the ball into J.J.'s direction, and just pray that if a play needed to be made, that we'd have enough time to make it.

Even with having to deal with his shortcomings and Ollie's relaxed style of coaching, this year's edition of the diamond Knights defensively were going to fair well, if the opposition didn't hit anything to either corner of the infield, or into left or right fields. For away from the middle, we were pathetic.

Case in point, the Aurelia brothers, senior Eloy and sophomore Hector. In class, they were geniuses, on the field ... they were novelties.

They were inseparable and only spoke Spanish to one another, so half the time we didn't what the hell they were up to? Baseball-wise they were an ongoing blooper act; especially Hector who had the attention span of a five-year-old. Like a little one just being introduced to the game, Hector could be found kicking at dandelions or watching a cloud formation pass by at crucial stages of a game.

In a pre-season affair against neighboring Melvindale High, he was stationed in right field and just having a jolly ole' time out there. While in the midst of one of his usual fogs, a lazy high fly was lifted in his direction. This would have been a routine play for most many years his junior, who simply would have had their heads in the game.

"Up in the air," was collectively screamed from our entire defensive alignment, which included pointing to the ball and yelling at him to get ready to make the simple catch.

"Hector, heads up!"

"Hector … it's all yours," were just some of the warnings issued in his direction.

But in true Hector fashion, though he was physically in position, mentally, he was in Disneyland. He honestly was lost at the crack of the bat, and when yelled at to gain his attention, he would look bewilderedly to the ground and then into any direction where a sound came from, until his befuddled posture and perplexed arm flailing put him on a collision course … that would allow him to either catch the ball or eat it.

It was like trying to help the beloved and renowned master of the keyboards, Ray Charles, out in the field. If a ball was hit in his direction, we had to verbally guide him into making a play.

"Hector," Ollie yelled.

But it was too late. As soon as the younger Aurelia looked up, the ball popped him right square in the head, laying him flat out on the ground after the contact. Rudy rushed over from center and David ran out from second to get the ball, hoping to avert an inside the park homer. Meanwhile, brother Eloy ran to his sibling's aid.

"Hector, puedes escucharme … can you hear me," Eloy yelled.

He then proceeded to shake his brother, who eventually came to, giggling in the goofy manner that we usually expected from him. He was eventually taken out of the game, and we played a two man outfield with Rudy camped in right center and freshman Billy Patalka moving from straight a way left, into left center. With the general consensus that we were probably better off in this alignment any way.

Eloy wasn't much better, but at least he could catch. So he was positioned at first base, where running could be kept to a minimum along with the rest of his diamond liabilities.

Eloy's troubles came at the plate. For what his brother was to fielding, he was to hitting. If they pitched grapefruits to this guy, he still couldn't hit the side of a barn. In fact, he would get to base only three times in seventy-four plate appearances over the course of the entire campaign ... and he was walked once and was hit by the pitch on two other occasions. He did ground out three times, but struck out the other sixty-eight times.

He tried everything from prescription glasses to rubbing garlic bulbs on his bat. We even tried to convince Father Felix that his lumber was possessed and asked him to perform an exorcism on Louisville Slugger product, but even the whacked out priest couldn't buy into that one.

Unfortunately, this was all a sign of things to come.

Now a little shy of two weeks into the season and we had lost our first seven games. Nothing was working.

Hodgie, who was on the roster, played sparingly because of Koobs' up and down condition, and our core players were sluggish.

J.J. was sterling in the field, but struggling at the plate. Maxie's heavenly intervention that had carried him for years on the mound had deserted him, and the rest of the staff was getting absolutely shelled.

Rudy actually was splendid in throwing the ball, but suddenly couldn't catch anything out in center, and that superstar catcher that I bragged so much about earlier, simply sucked.

I had one hit in the losing streak and defensively couldn't throw out Mama Cass Elliott, if she were trying to steal while toting one of her infamous ham sandwiches. I had no confidence and any hope of college scouts looking my way, was fleeting fast.

One evening while I was sitting up in my room, my dad came up, "Hey, son, quite a rut you're in."

I just shrugged my shoulders and said, "I just can't figure it out, Dad? I can't hit, my fielding stinks and I'm just not having any fun."

"It's a long season, you'll figure it out." Then he gave me a pat on the shoulder and said, "Sometimes when things are not working out, you gotta shuffle the deck and get a fresh start."

I just looked at him curiously. "What do ya mean?"

"You gotta get away from the ordinary ... I dunno, but you seem to need some sort of release ... some sort of shock to your system." Then he stood up, gave me a wink and walked out of the room.

I didn't have the foggiest idea of what he was leading to. *Release? What was that all about? Did he think I should whack off or something?* I just couldn't get a handle on what he was referring about.

Not one for the psychological approach, even I began a mental inventory of what was fucking me up. Everything was cool on the home front. I was doing well in my studies and my college entrance exams and national tests were fine. The only thing that I could attribute to my current doldrums was that I just didn't seem to have any motivation.

I mean, for Christ's sake, it was getting so bad that everybody was trying every and anything to try and get us jump-started. There was even a rumor that Ollie was thinking of rescinding Catholicism in effort to call upon Allah for help.

Laura and I were still doing well. The relationship seemed strong, as were my feelings for her, I knew it was love, because I just enjoyed hanging out with her just as much as I wanted to have sex with her. Granted, that I would have enjoyed a little bit *more* in expanding our carnal realm, but I conceded that we would eventually get to that point.

The thing with Laura was the proximity issue. Which was really a double-edged sword. It was great when I wanted to do something with the guys or play cards and stuff like that, but when I got the urge to indulge in the dirty deed … she was sure a long way away.

The other thing that started to come into play in our relationship, was that we started guessing each other's moves and the freshness and spontaneity aspects were getting stale. But how do you say that you would like to try something new, without hurting the other one's feelings?

With Koobs not feeling all that great, the Friday night card games were starting to fizzle out. So, on this one particular Friday, Laura and I went out to a movie and to grab a quick snack. Around ten o'clock that night, we found ourselves at a favorite late night hang out spot in the area, Wyandotte's Bishop Park.

"You seem distant," she said to me, "anything wrong?"

"Nawww, it's just me. The baseball thing and …"

"And what?" she smiled as she reached for my crotch.

"Ahhh … nothhin," I stumbled.

"Markie, come on … I know that something's wrong."

"I don't know, Laura, it just seems like nothing changes. Everything's the same … even when we get together … it's a movie, something to eat and a drive … I don't know?

I found myself flustered wanting to tell her what I really wanted. Problem was … that I didn't know myself?

She began to tear up and started to back off, probably anticipating something along the lines of me trying to break up with her, but that was not the case!

"I thought you and I could always talk out whatever we needed to," she stated.

I just nodded and starred out the window.

"And I hope you could talk freely to me about whatever you wanted," she added.

"I don't know … it's just me, I guess," I responded.

Then she scooted close to me and put her head next to my chest. "You know I'd do anything to please you … anything," and she began to rub my inner thigh.

I didn't know if I should ask her to give me a blow job or to see if she would throw me some late night batting practice under the street lights, to see if she could help out of my slump.

And just when I was probably going to make a fool out of myself, this straight-laced, sweet and innocent, good student, who was an exemplary young citizen, rocked my world!

"Can I share something with you?" she whispered.

"Sure."

"While you were away, Tracy and I were hanging out," (a girlfriend of hers) "and one of her brothers left out this copy of *Penthouse*, so we started to thumb through it … and I couldn't believe some of the things in there. Have you ever read it?"

Interested, I said, "Yeah … ummm … I…I've seen it … so?"

"So, I got kind of got embarrassed looking at it with her," she said in an innocently sly manner.

And I just had to laugh.

Then she unzipped my pants and said, "But I snuck the issue home with me."

I'm sure the unleashing of my member and the physical contact was part of the reason for its sudden arousal, but I was hinging on her every word about the reasons why she pilfered the guy's fuck mag?

Laura was on the verge of turning seventeen, came from a pristine home and seemed way beyond even comprehending being interested in a gentleman's publication.

These were inferences that I would have expected from a Shelley, and in church yet, but not from this sweet little blonde who was inches from swallowing my cock. She then began to stroke my unit, and said, "Those stories ... in that forum section ... they're just so...so ... fucking sexy."

I couldn't believe what I was hearing, but I didn't want to interrupt the flow ... of the story or the sensation!

"And those pictures ... oh my God," she uttered and she began to lick my shaft. "Those girls are just so...so ..." and she started going down on me.

"So what?" I blurted, with my right hand starting to cinch up in her hair.

"What baby?" she sighed as she continued to work on my little buddy.

"You...uhhh, you...you, were saying ... they're so ... uhhh ... so."

"You mean those beautiful girls," she softly spoke "... they're so beautiful, Markie, that I couldn't ..." and she went down again.

And I found myself thinking about a million different scenarios, from her being in a layout to her being laid out with any of those hot fucking chicks in *Penthouse*! I mean, long before catching Shelley with Gainer, the thought of two women together was really high on my short list of sexual fantasies! And the thought of Laura, my sweet little schoolgirl in that position ... well Holy Mother of God!

I found myself totally lost in the thought as she went down on me again and again.

I realized that my sweet and oh so pure little angel, had mastered the art of the mind fuck. She *had me* and she knew it!

I was in this erotic ping-pong match, and my cock and brain were working in unison in this wonderfully epic new game!

If getting pushed and pleasured by the incredible blowjob itself wasn't hot enough, she was toying with my psyche in a way I never thought she would, and was proving the theory ... that the mind was the true erogenous zone!

I couldn't help myself; I grabbed her by the hair and implored her, through my grunts and moans to continue her story.

"Ohhh," she sighed, "baby, don't keep me from this beautiful dark and stiff meat."

"But you...you ... were saying?"

And she began to laugh, knowing full well that she had me compromised in both mind and body.

"Goddamn it, Laura!"

"You know," she smiled "I had to, Markie, I just had to."

"Had to what?"

"You know ... finger myself."

"Oh my fucking God," I thought, *she was turned on by those girls*?

And before I could go on, she looked at me and said, "Baby, can I tell you about something else that I saw?"

Nothing could have interested me more, as I felt like a panting dog.

She then proceeded. "There was this one pictorial, where these three people ... you know, a guy and two girls were in this hot tub ... and," she went down again on me.

"And what!?"

She continued to bob up and down on my prick, and came up in a breathy voice and said, "And ... they ... the two of them shared this guy's cock ... you know sucking it," as she continued to stroke my already purple joystick. "And they ..." and there she went again!

"They what?"

"They ... took turns sucking ... and licking ... and their lips ..." and she submerged again.

"Their lips! What about their lips?"

"Markie," she said, "their lips...their lips met right at the tip of his cock, and...and they kissed until he ..." and she didn't have to say anything else, because I unleashed a stream of cum that saturated her mouth, tongue and chin.

She just smiled and stroked my unit, begging for more and moaning as I descended from erotica heaven.

What just happened, I thought to myself. *Did this under aged angel just pull me through the perverted twilight zone? Or did I just have one incredible fantasy lived out ... at least in mind*!

The legendary late great Packers Coach, Vince Lombardi once said, "Football, like life, is played hard and for keeps. But most of it is played in between your ears. Get that part straight and the other part will come pretty easy." Coach was right!

And maybe Dad was too? I can't really say what he was eluding to that day he came into my room, and I don't think he was promoting promiscuity, but as the adage goes, "any port in a storm."

The next ten games I hit almost six hundred. Even the outs that I made were shots! Defensively, I was torrid, not allowing a past ball and throwing out any and everybody who had the nerve to steal on me.

I was back, and the team was starting to gel at just the right time. It was as if most of the team had gotten this incredible oral satisfaction that sucked the venom out and left the good stuff in!

In team sports, "you win as a team and lose as a team."

It isn't always easy to understand how a streak begins or gels, but when it happens, "Don't fuck with it!"

And if it's true that behind every great man there's a great woman, I wonder if they ever mentioned that she was occasionally on her knees?

~ more motivation ~

We finished with a flurry, and though we didn't win the divisional crown, our second place finish in the Catholic League west, earned us a return trip to the post season. The format was the same as in years past where number one team in the west would play the second place finishers in the east, and as the second place finishers in the west, our opponents would be the eastern division pennant winner. Those prevailing in those two games would square off at historic Tiger Stadium for the Detroit Catholic League crown.

The venue for these semifinal match-ups was the venerable old complex on Detroit's east side, Memorial Field.

The late May Friday afternoon was sun drenched with temperatures in the mid 70s … there wasn't a cloud in the sky. Only a hint of a breeze prevailed and perhaps the most pleasant thing about the entire setting was that Koobs who had been rebounding nicely and was complying with doctors orders, was in terrific spirits and on hand to root us on.

And we were going to need all of the help and positive karma that we could muster. For our opponents were not only the eastern division champs, but they also were the number one ranked team in the entire state, the undefeated Eagles of Orchard Lake St. Mary.

A solid club throughout their lineup, who were impressive and flawless the whole year. But what really made this team special was the fact that they featured the state's most sought after player, High School All American, Jim Pepper, whose brother, Tom, was already a big leaguer with the White Sox.

Pepper was a thoroughbred, standing 6'-5", a lean two hundred pounds and everything he did … he simply did well. He had a stoic look and seemed to intimidate all opponents as soon as he stepped off of the bus.

Though rugged, this kid was the darling of the metro Detroit media, and had features that could have landed him on the set of a Hollywood movie. During warm-ups, not only were our cheerleaders captivated with him, but I think half of the mothers in the stands were wet gawking at him.

He was *all state* in football, basketball and baseball, and was being recruited diligently since his freshman year. This kid was a *stud* and deserved every accolade given.

Though he was a standout at shortstop, as a pitcher he was 7 and 0 on the season, with a 0.72 ERA, with 48 strike outs, he only walked 3 batters all year long, recorded 4 shout outs and threw two no hitters.

Hysterically, he was considered the number three starter on their staff, and we didn't know if we were lucky in drawing him in their rotation or not?

Oh, and for good measure, he hit .411 on the season, with 17 homers and 81 RBIs. He was a one man wrecking crew, and a sure bet for the bigs!

But he had this problem … you see, he was carrying a 4.07 grade point average and was on the wish list of every major college in the Midwest, for both academics and athletics.

"Jesus fucking Christ, he's a monster," J.J. said.

"No shit," I answered while stretching in the dugout. "Okay, fellas, who's ready to rock this primadonna pussy," I said, cringing that he might hear what I was yelling to my team in hopes of motivating them. Just my luck, I would have probably ended up pissing him off.

It felt like we were ready to face off against the Yankees.

We were the visiting team, so we'd soon know what we were facing, as the plate umpire yelled, "Play ball!"

J.J. led off and fouled the first pitch back to the screen. He was so pumped up, that he jacked his fist toward our dugout and said, "He ain't got nuthin'!"

The next two offerings were fastballs that J.J. never saw; though he swung at the middle one … he went down on strikes.

"Hey, man, what does he got," I asked J.J.

"Shit, M, I've never seen anything like it," he said with a shocked look upon his face.

Likewise, it was the same results for our second and third place hitters. Nine pitches, three strikeouts and the Knights were three up and three down in our half of the first.

Maxie had been regaining his groove over the last half of the season, and was undefeated in his last six starts. But it was conceivable that his best might look like batting practice to these guys ... and then again ... stranger things have happened?

He went two and two, to their lead off hitter, until he popped a fastball to David at second base for the first out. The second place hitter lined a lead off fastball on one hop to J.J., who gunned it over to Eloy for out number two.

The monster then strolled up to the plate and surprisingly greeted me with a smile and said, "Hi, catch."

I just nodded and went into my crouch. I called for a curve ball low and toward the outside of the plate, but Maxie hung it belt high.

It landed somewhere near the Grosse Pointe city limits.

As advertised, Pepper, crushed the ball and trotted around the bases to a barrage of shutters clicking ... St. Mary's 1 – Hedwig's 0.

After their cleanup hitter, roped a double to the left center wall, Maxie got the next hitter to fly out to Hodgie in left, inning over with minimal damage.

I was first up in the second inning, and took Pepper's first pitch just under my chin. J.J. was right, I never saw anybody bring it this hard and this fast on this level ... *Holy shit!*

He then threw two fast balls right by me for strikes and had me set up for an offspeed floater that I was so far out in front of, that I almost twisted myself into the ground chasing strike three.

Through four innings, the wonder kid remained virtually untouchable. He had no hit us and only relinquished two ground ball outs, while fanning the rest.

In the bottom half of that same inning, a two out double to the second placed hitter in their lineup, gave Pepper another RBI opportunity and forced Ollie in to a decision making process. From the dugout, he motioned me to intentionally walk Pepper to set up the force and most importantly, take the bat out of his hands. We were stunned at this sudden stroke of brilliance from our manager and as ordered, walked the menacing presence.

It was really sound strategy, but it would go by the wayside, as the next hitter up lined a single to right scoring the runner from second; St. Mary's 2 – Hedwig's 0.

The next hitter popped out to J.J. at short and though we were still in the game, unless we figured out a way to start connecting against the All Stater, the season would be coming to an abrupt end.

Joel led off the fifth for us and seemed intent on jump-starting our club. In all my years of playing ball, J.J. was the best leadoff hitter that I ever saw. Sooner or later, he'd figure out a way to break through and he was tenacious.

Quickly he was down two strikes in the count and began to dig in even more intently at the plate. He fouled a couple of pitches off, and then drew three straight balls. Now with the count full, he fouled the next five pitches back to the screen and was putting up one hell of a battle. In baseball parlance, this was a kick ass at bat, no matter what happen.

The next offering, J.J. let pass. The catcher framed the received pitch adjacent to the outside corner, but there was no call. The plate umpire ruled ball four, and J.J. had broken through … becoming our first base runner of the game!

In an effort to try and manufacture some kind of a run against the fireballer, Ollie had Rudy lay down a sacrifice bunt and moved J.J. down to second, into scoring position. Then little David Berlez, who was making quite a name for himself as a freshman, and batting third in the lineup, was hit by a curve ball that got away from Pepper. Suddenly we had two men aboard and the *phenom* was starting to show a human side after all.

I had my chance … but I must admit that I wasn't relishing the opportunity. In fact, I was scared, with so much on the line and trying to stare down the behemoth, I would have rather been somewhere else. Everything that helped me rebound from such a shitty first half of the season, Laura's motivation, my dad's encouragement and all of the generated confidence seemed to abandon me as I stood center stage in front of what had to be a crowd in excess of three thousand people.

I suddenly remembered something that my grandmother told me before she passed almost a decade ago, "Diamonds shine brighter because of the pressure."

I dug in for my second plate appearance with the stakes much higher and the tension at a fevered pitch. I raised my hand to ask for time from the plate umpire, planting my right foot in first and then my other into the right-handed hitter's box. I waggled my bat and relaxed, then re-tightened my grip on the handle awaiting the first offering. He gave me a steady diet of fastballs for the most part during my first time up, and that was his bread and butter pitch. So what's to think that he wouldn't do the same thing?

"Fastball…fastball … quick bat, Mark … he's gonna bring the fastball, I prodded myself.

Wrong. He gave me a big sweeping curve, the same kind of pitch that he struck me out earlier with, and again I was way out in front of it and missed it by a mile. Now he had me really guessing. Was he going to switch gears on me and feed me nothing but junk, or would he now bring the gas?

I dug in again, went through the same routine and was just hoping for something big, fat and juicy to be delivered into my wheel house, so that I could drive it somewhere in a gap. It was a fastball, letter high and by the time it got to me it had risen to the bill of my helmet. Despite the fact that it was way out of the strike zone, I chased it and didn't have a chance of making any contact. Here I was again, quickly down in the count and not knowing what to expect.

"Marcus ... come on, man, we need you now," J.J. yelled from down at second base.

"Moosie ... one time now babe, one time," Hodgie yelled from the dugout.

The crowd had picked up the chants and the intensity was really starting to build.

I stepped out of the batter's box and went down to get a little dirt to soak up some of the sweat that had pooled in my palms, and to get a better grip. I took a deep breath and repeated my entering ritual.

Just make some kind of contact, asshole, I implored myself.

Again I dug in, choking up on the bat a little more than usual and leaning in more over the plate ... the 0-2 pitch ... was a heater, but this one was headed for my chin and forced me to drop on my ass to escape getting a face full of fastball.

"Hey! ... Watch that shit, asshole! ... Come on, ump, give him a warning about that," were just some of the blasts that were coming from a crowd that seemed to be responding to our plight.

I picked myself off of the ground and saw the catcher kind of snickering while looking at me.

"Find that kind of funny?" I said.

"What's your problem?" he fired back. "Can't take a little brush back?"

"Brush back? You mean like brushing back the hair off of your mama's chest?"

"Hey fuck you, dickhead," he levied.

"Suck my cock, queer bait!"

"Fellas…fellas," the umpire said. "Watch your mouths, besides, this the Catholic League, or I'll throw both of your asses out!"

I brushed myself off, picked my bat up and walked in front of the plate to stare the pitcher down. "Bring that shit again, and my fucking bat goes flying, asshole," I blasted in his direction.

"Hey," the umpire said, "didn't I warn you about your mouth?"

On my way back to set up, I looked into the crowd and saw my dad motioning to watch my mouth, while many others around him in many different ways, basically wanted me to jam my bat up Pepper's ass before sending one into the street beyond the center field fence. I then looked towards Ollie in the third base coach's box, when suddenly I saw Koobs. He looked better than had been and though in a wheelchair, you could see him trying to rise to his feet. He gave me a thumbs up and then put his hands together as if he were swinging a bat, and indicated … "swing away."

I then looked back at my dad where I found a wink and a smile, and the feeling that this was now my place … and my time.

Here were all these influences in my life. These supporters, battlers and givers who invested in my well being and growth, hoping to see if I could meet a challenge and rise to an occasion.

I reentered the box an awaited the next pitch. His leg kick was high and his stride toward the plate seemed to put him halfway home. The ball had a lot of spin on it and broke a little more than the hurler wanted. It short hopped the plate and got past the catcher allowing both J.J. and David to advance.

In a show of sportsmanship I picked up the catcher's mask, but decided to spit in it when the ump wasn't looking. When he got back from retrieving the ball from the fenced area behind the plate, I tossed it to him and said, "Nice stop, asswipe."

Without listening to his response or any of the crowd, I was back in the box and keying on what I had hoped would be a fastball right down main street.

He checked the runners and from the stretch and delivered the two-two pitch. Most of his prior offerings were like blurred bee-bees, but suddenly something had changed once the ball left his huge right claw … I guessed right … and it looked like a huge grapefruit. It was exactly what the doctor ordered and the closer it approached the larger it appeared.

I was told that the crack of the bat was solid, but from my perspective it was all feel. I knew I had solid contact with it, and my only concern was if it would have enough trajectory.

It was on a line heading for the left center field power alley and had the distance to clear the fence, but as I rounded first I could see that it just wasn't going to have the lift to clear the ten-foot barrier. It couldn't have been more than a half-foot away from disappearing for a three run homer, but instead, it caromed of the fence for a two run double that had tied the score and sent our fans into a frenzy.

Our bench was ecstatic and I felt like I had just hit the motherfucking lotto! I saw my folks getting hugged from those around them, our bench was ecstatic and Koobs on his feet, with fists raised saluting me. I pumped my fist into the air, acknowledged the crowd and felt on top of the world!

Now I was just hoping that somebody could now bring me in. But it was to no avail, as I was stranded at second when Maxie went down on strikes.

The game remained tied into the last of the seventh, the final inning in high school ball. And wouldn't you know it; Pepper was the first scheduled hitter in the St. Mary's half of the inning. Ollie grabbed Maxie, J.J., Al, Rudy and me and chatted with us before taking the field about how we were going to handle the heavy part of the Eagle order.

"I think we pitch to him," I said, "but we have to keep everything to the outside and not give him anything to yank."

"Walk him," J.J. added, "one swing and we're out of here." Then he looked at Maxie and stated, "It's late, and you probably don't have your best stuff, man, so let's try to keep him at first."

Al and Rudy tended to agree with J.J., but Maxie wanted to pitch to him and convinced Ollie to allow him to try to bag the superstar.

Up strolled the star and in a classy gesture, he looked at me and said, "Hell of a game, man, and that was one hell of a hit you had … thought you were going to touch 'em all."

I just nodded in appreciation and knew that he really was something special.

I wasn't going to allow Maxie to throw anything off speed or anything that he could have hung over the plate. So it was to be a steady diet of Maxie pads, J.J.'s nick name for his fastballs low and away.

But … wouldn't ya know it, the first pitch was belt high and right down the middle, and the MVP ripped a shot down the left field line for a lead off double.

"Goddamn it, Max," I said, "low and away … I thought we agreed low and away?"

He just hung his head and asked for the retrieved ball. I knew that he had pitched a hell of a game, but the heat of the moment just got to me.

It was a given that even though their cleanup hitter was up, that the smart move here was to try to bunt him over to third. Which they attempted. On a 2-1 pitch, the batter squared to bunt and instead of laying it on the ground, he popped it up to an on-rushing Eloy who broke in on the ball from first. The wacky Mexican snared it in the air … no advance of the runner, and one down in the inning.

The next hitter in the line up was a guy by the name J.C. Dillard, a left-handed hitter who would have led the Eagles in every hitting category, if it wasn't for the guy who was currently standing on second.

Dillard, like the hitter before him ran the count to 2 and 1, so Maxie went to the stretch to keep the runner as close as possible to the bag. When he delivered the pitch, his spike caught awkwardly on the pitching rubber, which made him short hop a pitch up to the plate, forcing me to slide to the inside corner to try and block the pitch; which I did, but it bounced about three feet to my right, giving Pepper an ample opportunity to break for third.

With speed to burn also a part of his athletic resume, he gassed his large frame toward third base.

I rushed to the ball and had him within my sights, planted my feet and gunned the ball … only to throw it off of the helmet of Dillard who was in my line of sight. The ball deflected into right field allowing Pepper not only third, but to easily scamper home with the winning run.

I went numb and what felt like a slow motion cell, I fell to my knees, gazing out to right field where the ball laid untouched.

The Eagles celebrated jubilantly, prevailing and earning a trip to the Catholic League finals at Tiger Stadium, while our season and the careers of the senior's came to a crashing conclusion.

Though the team was supportive and tried to console me, I just couldn't bring myself to my feet. Finally, I was unknowingly lifted to my feet, and by of all people, Jim Pepper.

"Incredible game, man," he offered.

We just hugged and I wished him the best.

"You're fucking awesome, man, good luck downtown and in the pros," I said, and we just both started to laugh before parting ways.

After shedding my gear and bonding with the guys in the dugout one last time, I made my way back into the crowd, hugging Koobs and Lottie along the way and some of the other parents and students before finally working myself over to Mom and Dad.

I hugged and kissed my mom and my dad laid a big hug on me and said,

"I'm proud of you, kid, and I don't care who was out there, today my son was the best player on that field."

Suddenly a nearby voiced concurred with my dad, "Sir, you're absolutely right ... your son was the best player on that field today, and I want him to be the best player on my field ... every time he suits up!"

We looked in amazement and in disbelief as he handed my dad his card and extended his hand to me saying, "Mark, I'm Coach Antonio Pappas, of Wayne State ... can we talk?"

Hmmm ... motivation ... motivation!

~ high hopes ~

One of the great Detroit warm weather traditions was to load up the gang, drive downtown to the foot of the Ambassador Bridge and hop on the old Columbia steamer for a leisurely voyage of some twenty-five miles to the neighboring Canadian island of fun and games called Bob-lo.

Located on the water, this parcel known as Boise Blanc, Bob-lo was southeastern Michigan's and southern Ontario's family amusement park of choice. Most kids our age would have rather ventured down to Sandusky, Ohio's Cedar Point for the best coasters and thrills in the Midwest, but the school said that Bob-lo was all that they would spring for, both monetarily and from the aspect of chaperoning the senior class.

This was the Parrish's way of saying to the seniors, "Thanks for all those years of tuition and special interests that we asked you to support with thousands of dollars, now we'll treat you to a $9 boat ride, give you a day of amusements, a picnic lunch and call it a wash." But, it was the day off and that probably was worth its weight in gold to most of us.

Accompanying the seniors would be about half of the school's nun population, some of the lay teachers and a group of parent chaperones.

Per instructions from Loyola, a bunch of us were responsible to pick up ... what else, but "doughy treats" and morning drinks for the elders and hand it off to some of the girls to set up and serve at the Bob-lo docks.

The Columbia was a four-tiered, two hundred and twenty-foot vessel that sported many of the features of a New Orleans steamer that was headed down the Mississippi, minus the distinctive paddle wheel. Whether seen on the water or from land, the boat was unmistakable, as it would transport visitors to and from the island, by splitting the two countries down the Detroit River to the park, which sat at the mouth of Erie.

The boat itself was a wonderful experience. One would enter from the plank onto the craft's lower deck that was a holding area for strollers, bikes or wagons filled with provisions that families or groups would bring and picnic with on the island.

But aside from that area, the ship's lower level offered the perfect view of the loud, hot and mechanical engines that drove the mammoth craft. Forget about carrying on a conversation when the boat was in motion down there, because you couldn't even hear yourself think, let alone talk.

From that point, there were three ways to ascend on the boat. An elevator for the elderly and handicapped, the refined stroll of the inner wide elegant stairwells or the get the fuck outta' my way bull rush of the narrower steel stairwells that fed up from the vessel's outer port and starboard sides.

The second option was so aesthetically appealing, that it was worth risking the loss of a seat on the top deck, that the bull rush tried to accomplish.

The mid-ship's staircase was its showcase. It was a highly polished combination of oak, mahogany and teak that would have done the Queen Mary proud. Up the fifteen-foot wide passage, the second level featured the ship's concessions, souvenir shop and a large quiet area for seating, where the nuns, teachers and parent chaperones usually sat during the sail.

The store's most endearing keepsakes were the island's crested captain's hats or Bob-lo's famous sailor caps, making the younger guest feel as if they were part of the ship's crew.

Continuing up the stairs that were lined with southern art and wall lamps, deck three housed the ship's dance floor and a stage for live entertainment. Though dancing would take place, this was usually where the eight- to fifteen-year-old crowd ran wild. Playing tag or chasing down somebody, which on this level was pretty commonplace.

What was amazing ... was that with all of the running around on this floor that nobody ever took a header overboard?

Oddly enough, on this same deck where all of the youthful animals rough housed it, the ship's bar majestically stood, offering the simple but necessary selections of either Molson Canadian or Labbatt's on tap, or for those who needed a little more of an oomph, Canadian Club whiskeys and mixes.

Usually while the moms shopped on the floor below, the kids were left in dad's care on the dancing deck. So while the younger ones were urged to make new friends on the floor, Dad did the some mingling of his own standing at the bar.

Finally, there was the top deck. A haven for sunbathers, pot smokers, spitters ... and those who preferred to cuss at, offer the bird to or expose the occasional bare tit or ass at passing vessels.

It was the ship's smallest deck and only had a seating capacity of about 150. This is where the bull rush came into play and the outer passages were the quickest route ... with the assistance of the right kind of people and a game plan.

You could spot the seasoned riders of the Columbia, because they'd form huddles at the gate area devising schemes to secure a location for their group on the top deck.

There was a respect factor involved too, as representatives from one group, would be sent over to the other's to see what route that they were going to secure. Agreements in principle would be reached and if one group promised not to infringe on the other's passage, similar considerations would be passed along.

The strategy was to get about twenty seats secured for your assembly, anything over that would have been a coup ... anything less a failure.

Ours was a twofold plan. First, to employ the assistance of the biggest guys that we could find, to log jam the turnstiles. Three of those bearers of interference came from our dead weight offensive line from the football team. *Finally*, they became of some use.

One of the other large groups taking this sailing was from Cass Tech, a Detroit Public school recognized for students who excelled in the fields of technology, science and mathematics. They also had a damn good football team and when their student leaders heard of our plan, they offered to send help in the form of some extra girth, if we promised to go along with a little something that they had planned. But, they insisted that they needed top deck seats for at least thirty ... which was no problem.

The absolute key to the plan though, was to clear out the front of the line in the most devastatingly civil manner possible.

To insure enough of a head start that top deck seats would be guaranteed ... we need something full proof ... something bankable ... we needed rat's hole!

Yep, once again we would turn to the human anal sewer to unleash one of his potent explosions, with hopefully better results than he enjoyed during the All Stars competition. It was one thing to have the muscle to run the interference necessary, but Rats needed to be on his game to stun the senses, water the eyes and clear the way.

Brian's diet the night before was groomed for success, with his full proof recipe, White Castle burgers, or in his parlance, "enemas in a bun." And if what was coming from his ass in a preliminary form was any indication of what we were going to be able to expect, success was assured!

He was at his best ... or worse considering your position in proximity to his pooper, when digesting those little square burgers.

Task number one, to clear out the hundred or so individuals who had already assembled at the front of the line. We couldn't exhort any physical force, so a couple of us detracted the nuns and other adults who accompanied us, to execute getting Brian to the front of the line.

So, while the diversion was being employed, we put the Rats in a wheelchair that was used for either the elderly, injured or handicapped, and wheeled him to the front. Thank goodness for the kindness and consideration of unsuspecting strangers.

He was left at the front of the line and allowed a moment or two for those who wheeled him up to clear the area. Once he unleashed the madness the six large blockers needed to re-secure the front of the line, like marines that would be sent in after an initial artillery barrage.

At first, there was nothing. Then you could sense that something was billowing as commotion built into queasiness—queasiness turned into superlatives—and the superlatives ensued a panic, and a need to run for relief.

The *ass* was firing on all cylinders and Rats was hitting a new high ... or low as it turned out to be! He had some pretty impressive accomplishments in the past, but this was his sphincter's pinnacle.

In an open-air venue such as this, Brian was a lion! This was the nuclear winter of flatulence and for some unknown reason; it just hung in the morning air.

I had witnessed him, in the past, clear out classrooms, restaurants, a movie theater, make a dog throw up and even make a priest pause at mass, but this was his finest hour.

This even surpassed the time that we took him down to Olympia Stadium in an attempt to get us into a big sold out hockey game between the Red Wings and Toronto Maple Leafs. With not a ticket to be found, the objective was to gas the ticket taker, in hopes of making him leave his post, to allow us to hop over the turnstile to get to the standing room only area.

That in itself was an unfair situation, as Rats made the guy actually tear up and sent him barreling for the bathroom for liberation. With nobody at the entrance, we just strolled right on in!

Despite its obvious effect, the fun of a Brian Galloway special, is in the visual.

To be *in the know* that something is in the works and to be able to prepare is to be privileged. But to be able to see the facial expressions change from happiness or contentment, to this troubled look of "oh my fucking Lord, what is that," is an experience that is always good for a laugh and hard to forget.

The only glitch that occurred was that the blast was so potent, that it made one of the studs from Cass Tech, pass out. And not just stagger, I mean this guy who was almost standing at full attention, fell stiff, face forward to the floor.

This could only be classified as injury due to friendly fire.

The other funny part to this is the reaction the ticket takers had. For as bad as it has been illustrated, they stood their post and in all honesty, should have been rewarded for their commitment to duty.

In the brief time that they were subjected to the onslaught, they turned different shades of color and were on the verge of ralphing all over the place … which simply proves, that those Canadians can really handle their pong!

But, the damage had been done and the objective accomplished. The Cass crew headed up the port passage, while our gang hightailed it up the starboard side. The final count, sixty-one students

Once there, everything that we had scammed for seemed to be hanging in the balance, as thunderheads became more evident in the distant southwestern skies. And though the top deck offered a terrific view, it was not the place to be if Mother Nature decided to turn the tables.

The route that commenced in downtown Detroit, gave all passengers a special look at many interesting sites on both sides of the river. From the scrapers on the Motor City side, to Windsor's quaint European-like scape, our voyage worked its way south.

Under the Ambassador Bridge we continued, toward historic Fort Wayne, named in honor of one of Detroit's revolutionary heroes and the site of one of its earliest settlements.

There was Fighting Island, located in Canadian waters; this, too, was a parcel that saw its fair share of battles and also housed wartime settlements.

Continuing, our path would lead us past the industrious ports of Detroit.

Home to steel makers, marine merchants and chemical producers. From a development standpoint, along with the auto industry, this area helped manifest Detroit as one of the nation's leaders in manufacturing and employment opportunities, at a time when our nation began to take its place in the spotlight of the world.

Yet aesthetically, this area became an aquatic eyesore and a casualty in Detroit's national perception and appeal. It was nothing to see the blatant dumping of waste and byproducts into the river and even at our age, it was easy to ascertain that this was a hazard to the entire area's eco-system.

"Can you believe the fucking shit they're dumping into the water, Moose," Del said.

I just shook my head no, as he screamed out, "M o t h e r f u c k e r s!"

What was even harder to believe was that the fishing fraternity would still drop their lines in this area on a daily basis? They couldn't possibly eat this shit … or could they?

The general playing around and prodding that one could expect from groups our size was happening. Basically, it was all harmless and there was little need for the chaperones or the boat's security people to keep too much of an eye on us. But, there was a notion that something was going to happen, especially considering the earlier plea from the brethren from Cass Tech.

Curiously, they had with them a rather large duffel bag that they were obviously transporting something with. There was a good-sized group around the bag and the farther we traveled, the more this group seemed to huddle around whatever they were trying to conceal.

We had now made our way into neighboring Ecorse, another industrialized suburb of Detroit and the home of the giant steel producer, Great Lakes Steel. The complex was so large, that it actually spanned back into Detroit Proper and onto yet another endearing section of the Detroit waterway, Zug Island.

Zug was named in tribute to one of the many Native Indian Tribes that had first settled the area, who had succumbed to the forces of the later arriving settlers.

This was yet another favorite spot for anglers, especially an older contingent, which always surprised me, because

A) as previously mentioned, were they eating their catch?

B) The shipping traffic in the channel forced the smaller boats to frequently feel the effects of heavy wakes, and

C) the verbal abuse alone from the Bob-lo sailings had to drive these guy nuts.

Let's face it, smart ass remarks from a younger crowd, didn't sit well with this age group regardless of its origination.

In addition, there's something about verbal communications on the water. The sound was clearer, crisper and carried further.

"Hey, you old fuck, quit playing with your dinghy," Del yelled.

Then from a lower deck you would hear in a gruff and gravely femalish voice, "Watch your language, Arroundo," which spurred laughter from the lot of us.

But Del went on, "Hey, gramps, that's your pants pocket, not your bait box … the only worm that you'll find in there is probably shriveled up!"

And, of course, he must have raided his mom's adult toy chest in planning to say, "Hey, try this worm!" To which he hurled three rather large dildos overboard to complete his verbal barrage.

He had us all cracking up, but stacked up against what was about to occur, Del's pranks were really child's play.

"Hey, Moosie, what do ya think is goin' on over there?" Al asked, as we both looked over into a little nook huddled around by at least seven or eight of the fellas from Cass Tech.

"Don't know," I responded, "but where's Shelley?"

He just started to smile and smirk as we both suggested that she could have been in the corner earning a little extra spending money for her day on the island.

"Hey, whatcha you two homos looking at," Del said as he split and put an arm around each of us.

"I don't know, man, but neither one of us can figure it out," I said.

Hodgie added, "They keep switching up on whatever it is they're doing?"

"Where's the slut?" Del inquired, and immediately Al and I gazed at one another and began to laugh.

All of a sudden, one of the guys who we struck up a conversation with earlier looked over at us. Giving a wink and nodded his head, prodding us to "Sit down and get ready for the show!"

About a minute went by when their huddle broke from over in the corner, and made its way to the rail about fifteen to twenty feet away from us … with one additional member more then they had going in.

"Maybe they were getting head jobs," Al suggested, for out of the pack came this frame, with a blonde mane, red T-shirt and shorts. To be honest with you, they had surrounded her so well that the Secret Service's Presidential detail could have taken some lessons from them.

They sat around a group of their fellow classmates who seemed to now become in sync with what this *core group* had started in the corner. More of us started to become aware that something was brewing, and it compelled us to sit and pay attention.

The way they had arranged their seats, they created a cove that seemed to double as a staging area … opened, yet guarded.

Then the blonde stood up and screamed, "You son of a bitch, I just knew you were fucking around with her."

Was this the Act One … the opening scene?

"Oh shut up, you fucking whore," this rather large guy said back to her.

This, in turn, made Del and Adam rise to their feet, thinking that they needed to intervene and come to the aid of the attractive damsel in distress. A couple of us just grabbed their arms and told them to settle down, not really knowing for ourselves *where this was leading*?

She screamed again, "I hate you … I hate you," as tears started to well up in her eyes.

The two of them went on for about thirty seconds and those who were around them began to stand, making it more difficult for us to see what was going on. Then we heard some screaming, followed by obvious sounds of physical contact, more or less … slapping.

"You fucking bitch, don't you ever touch me again," the guy said.

"Fuck you," she shouted back, and again slapping sounds could be heard.

"I'm gonna kill you, you fucking bitch," resonated loud enough that you could see people from the lower decks trying to look up to see what was going on from their vantage points.

In addition, the fishing boats in relative proximity became interested and were focused on what was taking shape on the top deck as well. The maze of people that surrounded them started to thin out as we made our way closer to the gathering, now fearing that this was more than just an performance.

When the two embattled lovers seemed to reappear, the guy was choking the blonde and rendering her helpless as he dragged her toward the rail.

"Isn't this great man?" the guy who signaled me earlier said.

"What … are you crazy," I responded. "He's gonna kill her!"

"Well, actually, he's gonna throw her overboard."

"What?" Del raged. "Let me at that motherfucker!"

"Ease up, buddy, look," and he pointed at the floor where the girl was comfortably curled up, smiling and waving back at us.

Then with confused looks on our faces, we focused our collective attentions back at the guy who was masterly executing this staged assault and noticed that the blonde who was in his grips was actually a mannequin, who, we would subsequently come to find out, was smuggled aboard piece by piece.

The dummy was dressed identically to the lovely who was on the floor, but we still didn't know why this charade was being carried out.

What in the hell was going on?

Soon, all would be made aware. With a vicious lunge, the award winning performance would hit its climax as our villain wrestled the mock girl over the rail to a watery plunge. To all those unaware of what was happening, this had now become much more than just an altercation, it was an attempted murder ... but of a what ... a mannequin?

Screams of horror and shock came from every deck level as the dummy plummeted into the water! The boat's alarm went off and its engines were shut down, as the crew pressed into action.

First on the scene were a number of the anglers who were drawn into the pretense by the byplay of the two actors, who incidentally were once again swarmed over by a mass of people, who were providing cover to allow them the opportunity to change their clothes and dodge possible accusation.

Four local fishermen, three from one boat and one who was a solo, pulled the fake chick to safety, when all of a sudden a voice said, "Now, Jack, do it now!"

After being summoned, a small geek emerged with a device that looked like a remote control. He flipped a switch and began to count, "Three ... two ... one ..." and he pressed a button.

With all eyes focused on the water, the mannequin exploded with just enough force to release a fluorescent red paint that covered all four rescuers, their gear and boats.

"You motherfucking kids," one yelled while holding a dislodged arm and shaking his fist at us, while the entire top deck broke into hysterics.

It was an incredibly well-perpetrated prank and before security could even arrive on the scene to investigate, it was as if we were all attending a garden party. Idle chitchat was commonplace and not a stitch of evidence could be found. Best of all ... nobody was talking.

But the boat had been stopped, and that, in itself, commanded the presence of the Ontario Provincial Police, who would be waiting upon our arrival at the festive island along with the complainants.

The entire boat was emptied except for the top deck, which was quadrant off by the boat's security team. While the lower levels were ready to enter the park, those of us top deck dwellers sat under cloudy skies and waited as the police conducted their investigation. One by one, we were filed down the port staircase, passing by a checkpoint at the boats plank, to be stared down by the OPP and these four paint-covered doops.

Sure of their identification abilities, the four swore that the guy was wearing a green shirt and that the girl in question was wearing a red top. Yet the march by didn't find anybody with those colors and the police seemed to have more of a problem dealing with the obscenities from the fluorescent four than with the cooperative passengers of the top deck.

Curious however, was the fact that fat-ass Valerie Sheddow was at the front of the line ready to point out to the OPP, who she thought may have had a hand in the matter, based on reputation alone.

"Him ... him ... that one ... there's one ... those two ... oh, absolutely you should check that one," she offered in her *Third Reich-like* manner, which had most her homeroom class lined up for questioning.

If looks could kill, we would have placed her smug fat ass at the end of a plank, but it probably would have cracked from all of her weight.

There was no love lost between the senior class and Big Red. She banked on Ann's regime to insure her longtime tenure, but with the picky principal's exodus, she and her cronies were left out on that limb.

There wasn't a day that passed by that she didn't try to bust our balls, or one that would have us trying to fuck her over. And considering the fact that a Catholic school instructor received shit for wages, what was she trying to hang on to?

Which validated the point that shitty pay, no respect and even less of a future made Big Red one mean bitch with a chip on her shoulder.

The final result of this upper deck hi-jinx, *something happened*, but with no witnesses and no evidence except for a mannequin's left arm, because the rest of the dummy sank ... even the cops agreed that it was time to *shrug the shoulders* and to just let it go.

"Awww, this is bull shit," one of the dooped anglers declared, "those fuckin' kids ruined my boat and you're not gonna do a goddamned thing ... fuckin' Canadians ... you're all pussies!"

Those pussies, who both stood over 6'-4", didn't take too kindly to those less than pleasant nationalistic comments.

"Excuse me, sir, what did you say?" one of the cops inquired.

"Nuthin'," the mangy boater responded.

Then one of the girls from Cass Tech said, "He said that Canadians were pussies."

"Why you little bitc …"

"Hey … watch your mouth, mister," the other cop said. "I think the young lady is right," the cop said to his partner, and the two of them preceded to run him, his mouth and his freshly painted boat in, for what I'm sure was a little bit more of Canadian hospitality.

Too bad that they didn't have extra room for the other *red* menace … Sheddow.

The thing that Sheddow never learned or for that matter was ever concerned to realize, was that if she would have been straight with us, we would have forgiven her for her alliance with Ann. We forgave Gainer, and not just because she had a nice ass and pretty face … well … mainly because she had a nice ass and a pretty face … but she understood that we were kids, who were becoming adults … albeit reluctantly … and to get respect, you had to give it!

We didn't want to be shaped or molded, but preferred to be guided, and yes … nurtured.

No matter what kind of a façade we were putting on about how being treated as an adult was cool … it was actually a very scary proposition and a little understanding would have gone a long way.

I think that responsibility and independence were things that we wanted to test drive for a little while, with heavy doses of the independence and an easy as she goes portion of the responsibility part.

I couldn't quite pinpoint Sheddow's general disdain, but I think it went far beyond the halls of St. Hedwig's.

⚊ ⚊

Our stay on the island was pretty simple … enjoy the rides, meet for lunch and stay out of trouble. The island itself wasn't very large, so it wasn't a matter of having enough time to enjoy everything, but rather how many times you could actually go around the park.

As far as lunch was concerned, two pieces of cold chicken, served with warm potato salad and a dinner roll in a box was not going to make or break anybody's day, consumed or not.

So that left trouble, and I think that we all felt that we had enough of a brush with it, and had already filled our daily quota on the trip down.

On this less than Chamber of Commerce day, the clouds continued to thicken and you suspected that sooner or later, rain was certain. So we just went from ride to ride, hoping to make the best of it for as long as we could.

Our groups would break up with some going to the coasters and others going to the water rides. Around mid-afternoon, I happened to end up on the park's sky needle with sixteen elementary students, their teacher, the Kinovich twins and fellow senior, Marcia Walters.

What Sue and Laurie were to *sweet* looks, Marcia was to dowdiness. She was a tall drink of water, with a long face that was without an affect, with a personality to match.

It wasn't that she was a prude; she just didn't have any appeal. For some reason, the twins took a liking to her and often, where you found them, you found Marcia.

She was kind of like the player to be named later in a blockbuster baseball trade ... where you'd say, "Oh yeah, I forgot about that one."

The sky needle was a two-tiered, rounded-glass enclosure that lifted some 327 feet into the sky while rotating at a very slow pace. At its summit, it provided one of the most incredible panoramic views of the entire region. In fact, on the perfect day one could see as far away as Cleveland in the southern horizon, and to the mouth of Lake Huron to the north.

It was really breathtaking to be able to pick out all of the sites from this bird's eye view, but today was not going to be one of those *cherry* days where you could see forever. In fact, we just made it into the comfort of the enclosure, before the rain finally made its presence felt.

So today, it was more of an escape from the elements, than a "Wow ... what a view" thrill.

Once in and secured the operator sent the ride into motion and we began to ascend. The smaller ones ohhhed and ahhhed as the earth began to get smaller and their outlook on the world changed.

"Can you believe this weather?" Laurie said, "one minute it wants to rain and the next ... who knows?"

"Beats class though," I countered.

"I don't know ... I'm kind of bored," Sue added, as we continued our way upward.

Suddenly, a bolt of lightning flashed through the sky and a horrific crack of thunder accompanied seconds after. Screams and tenuous laughter filled the air of the glass compartment, as the rain began to pick up in intensity.

I tried to keep a calm demeanor as I looked out the window, only to see that the weather that was on again, off again was definitely "on!"

The clouds were darkening and it became swiftly evident that whatever was brewing outside … we were ascending right in the middle of it!

The rain was pelting down against the glass and allowing for a skewed and blurry image of our surroundings. It wasn't hard to figure out that instead of going up, this ride should have been on the ground and its passengers seeking cover.

What had become evident, was that the needle didn't have a kill switch to stop the ride. It had to go through its cycle, and we were just reaching the top, where it was supposed to circle for the next thirty seconds before starting its decent.

In what was virtually seconds, the heavens had become shrouded in total darkness and erupted with a force that would have been terrifying on the ground, let alone being suspended 327 feet above it.

There were no tentative acts of behavior going on now. Instead, just one form of conduct … full-fledged panic!

You could hear the teacher trying to calm her class, by expressing to them that "Everything was going to be alright," but even at their age, she wasn't fooling anyone.

Even the twins clutched each other's hands wondering how this wrath had suddenly come upon us and were noticeably concerned and eager for the safety of the ground.

Then, after another thunderous blast, the worse-case scenario became a reality. The needle suddenly stopped … and its interior lights went dark.

The wind became more of menacing presence and absolute danger was upon us!

I was scared shitless, but thankfully in this case, my dick overpowered my brain and instead of cowering, I thought, *Man, I could score some major points with the twins if I was able to squeeze in between and comfort them!*

But with another ferocious rumbling, I was frozen, terrified and actually looking for someone to comfort me. This had become surreal.

The storm was relentless and the teacher who was dealing with her distraught students, started to demonstrate her own vulnerabilities, as she started to come apart at the seams.

We had now reached full-fledged terror and no end was in sight.

The lights had not only failed, but now the air-conditioning system was not functioning and the compartment was becoming incredibly stifling.

Suddenly over the intercom we heard, "Please remain seated, the sky needle is completely grounded and is saf ..." zap! With another flash of lighting, now the intercom went dead.

The magnitude of the situation finally hit home, when I saw Sue Kinovich make the sign of the cross and begin to cry.

"Suz, easy now ... we're gonna be okay," I said in between the cracks of thunder, as I put my hand on her knee while looking into what had become a pitch black sky, at a little past three in the afternoon. Her sister took her into her arms and tried to console her.

This scene had moved way past the traumatic stage, and something had to be done ... and quick!

Then, in what could only be described as life imitating art, in a script that Hollywood would have been proud of, an *angelic intervention* occurred.

In a soothing and lyrical tone came the softest, beautiful and most comforting sounds I ever heard ...

"GUESS WHAT MAKES THAT LITTLE OLE ANT, THINK HE CAN CLIMB THAT RUBBER TREE

PLANT, EVERYONE KNOWS AND ANT, CAN'T, CLIMB A RUBBER TREE PLANT ..."

And as Marcia stood up, she walked toward the younger kids and continued...

"CAUSE HE'S GOT HIIIIIIIGH HOPES, HE'S GOT HIIIIIIGH HOPES, HE'S GOT HIGH APPLE PIE, IN THE SKYYYYYYY HOPES."

She had made her way into the huddle of terrified youngsters, sat in the middle of them, and like the Pied Piper, captivated their interests and deflected most of their fears. While she continued, she gestured for us to come closer and to join her in consoling the group, by cozying up to the kids.

Though the storm was raging on, she had singlehandedly defused the fears and anxieties of everybody in the compartment. There was no blandness and no pettiness of character, just a glimmering and radiant angel who had risen above the adversity to calm, comfort and protect.

Red eyes and anxious dispositions were rendered into submission, and though the occasional clap of thunder was cause for alarm, there was a definite feeling that everything was going to be okay.

Moments later, the lights kicked back on, the A/C began to cool things off and the needle began its descent, floating to safety.

It was during this controlled spiral that I looked at Marcia in a manner that I was never before able to manage. I saw a smile that was captivating and eyes that were warm and inviting, and though I knew that this was not anything physical, she truly radiated!

I knew that I could have never gone for Marcia, which was just as well, because I could have never held a match to her internal beauty and brilliance of heart.

Nobody at Hedwig's ever cemented my respect the way she did, in that critical moment of need.

When we arrived back to ground level, we were met by the park's officials to check on our well-being, and a couple members of the gang who were aware that the three ... make that the four of us were trapped in the needle during the storm.

"Hey, you guys okay?" Del asked the ladies as they were the first to exit after the little ones disembarked.

They responded by nodding and Sue lunged into his arms clasping onto the first one that she saw back on land.

Then Hodgie pulled me aside and said with raised eyebrows, "Moosie, you and the twins ... trapped up there!"

I just shook my head and looked back toward the needle's summit and responded, "Yeah, man, it was heaven ... and you're not gonna believe me when I tell you this, but I met a real-life angel."

"Yeah ... I bet you did," he laughed, "which one?"

And when I turned to give credit to where credit was due ... *she* was gone.

I found myself spinning around to find her, but she was nowhere to be seen. Then I took a step back and looked up to the place where ... "little ole' ants ... can!"

Thanks, angel ... I mean, Marcia.

～ devilishly tempting ～

As the final weeks of my high school career began to wind down, I found myself reminiscing about great times and strange occurrences. The people that I had shared with, the trouble that I somehow dodged, and yes ... even some of the girls that I would have enjoyed nailing.

I thought about some of the classes that helped to shape my outlook on life and some of those people that I probably would have been better off not knowing.

Case in point, Wednesdays with Father Felix.

The course was titled *Life Studies*, but should have been subtitled ... *Felix's totally fucked up view on how everything in life is manipulated by Lucifer!*

This was supposed to be a class examining how wholesome Christian values *should be* the basis for a healthy, happy and prosperous life. How a family *should be* started and how God *should be* at the center of all matters.

Instead, it was a two-year sentence of chocking on Felix's compulsion that everything from sex to food will bring you down.

You sneezed in class ... "The devil made you do that!" Cold weather, "the devil's doings!" Pens running out of ink ... "the D E V I L!"

For Christ's sake, he even thought the devil invented potato chips and were nothing but sadistic temptations.

Felix was not only unfit to teach us about life, but instead of a collar, the only thing white he should have been wearing, was a jacket with long and restraining sleeves.

Even his appearance gave us the willies. He resembled and often sounded like acting legend Peter Lorie. His eyes were bugged and off center and you couldn't quite tell if he was ever looking you in the eye or not?

He always wore a long, black cassock, and preached as if he were at the pulpit on Sunday.

In winter, he wore a heavy wool cape and what looked like a woman's pillbox hat.

But what was most annoying about this strange creation of God was the way he delivered his message. Every sentence started off with him talking very fast and very high pitch, which would gradually subside in tempo and descend in timbre at the end.

It didn't matter if it was a question, statement of fact or a decree...

"ifFelixdeliveredit that was t h e o n l y w a y h e k n e w

h o w

t o t a l k."

I often thought his delivery was some sort of sterilization process to render all of us impotent. Because in his warped mind, we were all handmaidens of the devil and destined to a life of sadistic service.

The incredible thing about this class, was that in the entire two years that I was in it, I never once remembered taking a test, being responsible for any homework or even taking a note.

He just rambled and we either tuned him out or slept. He preached and we daydreamed, he hypothesized and we passed notes. No matter what he did, I doubt if anybody had paid much attention past attendance.

But, if you were one of the lucky ones ... like me, you sat close to and were mesmerized by the vision of Wendy Kutzko's incredible legs!

Oh my God, the girl had legs ... and ass ... and body ... and face. If her cheerleading colleague Shelley was considered to be the total package, then Wendy was her equivalent, with one added ingredient: a personality.

Where Shelley was saucy and a bitch, Wendy was sweet and considerate.

She was the kind of girl that you wanted to take home to meet the folks and walk hand in hand with to church.

While you were afraid that if Shelley petted your dog, you'd need to take the animal into the vet to get a distemper shot.

Wendy was an auburn-haired beauty standing about 5'-6", who looked great in heels and next to J.J., was the best-accessorized dresser in the school.

Especially considering that she only had four styles of uniformed skirts that she could wear, and two of those were plaid.

She was not only a dream to look at, but also a delight converse with, and never had an ill word about anyone. She was even able to tolerate Felix's rambling, without being caddy toward him like the rest of us were.

But those legs ... they were absolutely perfect!

I couldn't even imagine her shaving those magnificent mechanisms of movement.

Angels must have been deployed during her slumber to remove any signs of tresses or other forms of unsightliness. Only a maestro of podiatry could have been worthy enough to have given her a pedicure ... that's how perfect those legs and her feet were!

Oh ... and she knew how to show them off too!

She must have had, at least, fifty pair of shoes to perfectly complement everything.

From flats to pumps, she looked good in them all! And truth be known, I would have given my left nut to trace those legs with my tongue from her toes to the crack of her firm little ass.

I used to love when she wore open-toed heels, for her feet were just as flawless as the rest of her frame. She'd always have her toenails painted and they seemed to be buffed to a high gloss, with the nails impeccably manicured to the perfect length.

It was at this time that I conceded that I had a serious problem ... *foot fetishamania.*

We sat in the farthest row away from the door, against the room's windows. Wendy sat in the first seat and I was in the second.

She had a wonderfully nasty habit of always sitting with her back to the windows, with her legs delightfully perched out to the side of her desk and always crossed. So, I had a front row seat to stiletto nirvana!

There were concerns that she was going to eventually put me into a trance, because I would just sit there for most of the class period and look intently at the one foot that she dangled over the other. She would nervously twirl it around and around, and well ... it was memorizing.

But the thing that absolutely enthralled me, was when she'd let her shoe slip off of her foot, still with her legs crossed, and would suspend it on her toes ... for Christ's sake I used to think, *Is there something wrong with me?* I found myself getting a hard on just by being visually affixed to her feet!

We had a pleasant kind of conversational relationship, but I always thought that there was some sort of sexual tension between us. We'd flirt with one another, but she knew that I was involved with Laura and I knew about her relationship with this football stud who had already graduated from Holy Redeemer, and was currently in his first year at Eastern Michigan.

I can honestly say though, for as much as I enjoyed ogling over her feet and gams, I really didn't desire any carnal knowledge with her. And not because I was committed to Laura, I just didn't think of Wendy as anything more than my own personal Playboy Bunny, of whom I glimpsed at three times a week.

In a way, she confirmed to me Felix's commitment to his order and his vow of celibacy, because those legs could have easily tempted the Holy Father himself.

Sitting right behind me was another tasty little morsel in the form of junior Nickki Dobeleski. The operative word to use when describing Nickki was that she was "perky little."

She had a perky little Dorothy Hamel style haircut, with a perky little smile, a perky little body and a nice set of perky little tits.

The only thing that was not perky about her, were her conversational skills. One, two and on the rare occasion, three word responses were the norm with her. But, on those infrequent instances when I would turn away from the legs, she was a more than ample diversion. Truth be told, I had the occasional fantasy or two of her giving me a blowjob!

Behind Nickki, was school boob, Mike Whiting. You were first introduced to Mike as the over-sized, stumbling and bumbling idiot who entered the ill-fated, mud bowl football game without as much as a spec of dust on him, and before he hit the huddle, he had fallen like a cartoon character face first into the slop. As clod-hopping as his abilities were on the gird iron, his classroom standards left even more to be desired. He made Robbie Selby look like an Ivy Leaguer.

Even in appearance, Mike was a misfit. He towered over all of us and was the only human that I ever knew who could be totally clean-shaven at the start of the day, and damn near had a full beard on his kisser by the end of it.

Not only did he have thicket for a beard and moustache, he had this mono-brow over his eyes that was in even more of a need of grooming than the whiskers below his peepers.

He was St. Hedwig's answer to Big Foot, and thankfully had more of a little boy …playish way about him, that made him both lovable and tolerable.

He'd run for a football pass down the hall, and would unknowingly take out four or five members of the student body while he looked back over his shoulder for the pass.

He would stick four or five White Castle burgers in his mouth at once, just for the attention and a laugh. His eyes would bug out and he would turn three shades of red, but he wouldn't spit out a morsel, just to get them all down and a rise out of us.

But Big Mike's signature novelty was anything that dealt with fire. He'd stick his hand out like some sort of swami and hold it over an open flame for what seemed to be minutes at a time. Undoubtedly a torture for us mere mortals, but for Mike, he'd just giggle and say, "Isn't this cool?"

His masterpiece though, was a day that I wished never occurred.

With just a little over a week left in the senior class year, I arrived in Felix's class before anyone else, because I had cut the class before to run over and see how Koobs was feeling.

There for a few minutes prior to the others filing in, I saw Nickki and a group of her junior friends make their way into the room. She had the cutest damn smile, and according to Robbie Selby, an ongoing crush on me that she was afraid to act upon.

Though I was committed to Laura, my problem … which was an ongoing failure of mine, was my flirtatious nature. I was a fucking wolf, who was a sucker for a pretty smile.

"Geeez, doesn't someone look scrumptious today," I said as she walked into the row.

Her smile just grew and she responded by saying "Thanks!"

She was dressed in uniform, just like any other day during the school year, but today she looked out of place. The reason being was that it felt more like late July than early June, and short sleeves were the attire of choice. Especially considering that there was no air-conditioning in this part of the school and the only fan was on the fritz.

But Nickki was wearing a cardigan, which intrigued me as more of the class filtered in. I found myself repositioning to get more of a glimpse of the junior, and kind of turned my torso and legs to sneak frequent peeks.

Trying to be as inconspicuous as possible, she slid a blue folder from her desk's storage space, opened it and began to write something on a sheet of paper inside of the folder.

She had now bent over the paper that she was scribbling on, giving me the most perfect view to her cleavage and allowing me to notice that the top two buttons of her blouse, normally latched to cover her bra, were wide open.

She had now erected the folder and blocked out everybody's view except mine. Instantly, I found myself at a full stare, noticing that not only was her blouse loose, but so was her laced fringed bra, giving me a privileged view of her ever-hardening nipples.

I know that my jaw had dropped and I had the dumbest look on my face.

Then I found my eyes following the movement of her head until I seen her baby blues. I had this tentative smile on my face as she innocently looked into mine and said, "I'm looking for someone to take me to the prom."

"Have anyone in mind?" I stupidly asked.

Just as I was about to get her response, *Legs* strolled in, out of uniform and was quite a sight to behold! The aspiring model and actress was dressed in a skintight black spandex jump suit, with a Capri pant cut and loose-fitting black and gray blouse. And to accent the outfit, what else ... black pumps!

Between Nickki's nipples and Wendy's incredibly seductive outfit, I thought my cock was going to jump right out of my boxers.

"If you're modeling next year's school uniforms, I'm submitting my desire to be held back," I mumbled.

"Like it?" she pirouetted.

"Try love it! You look fantastic," I exclaimed.

Meanwhile, I could see Nickki backing off like a turtle retreating back into its shell.

"What gives?" I asked Wendy.

She proceeded to tell me that she was chosen to represent Hedwig's in a photo shoot that was slated to promote the Catholic League cheerleading guide, and recruitment process.

"Holy Christ," I said to her when she told me of the opportunity, "you're dressed like this to recruit and promote Catholic cheerleaders?" And we both laughed thinking about the possible perceptions.

Fully engrossed in Wendy's story, I had totally blown off the bold attempt by the underclassman behind me.

"Devil dresser," Felix the heathen hunter exclaimed. "Miss Kutzko, what in Heaven's name are you doing out of uniform and dressed in those immoral garments?"

She simply walked over to him and gave him some sort of permission slip that Loyola approved for her to adorn this garb prior to an early dismissal.

"You children, I can't believe some of the clothes you dress in," he remarked.

Then, as if God himself set this one up, in walks Whiting.

"Holy shit," Mike blurted out. "Wendy, you look so freakin' awesome!"

"Whiting, you satanic boob ... watch your forked tongue!"

"Sorry, Dad," the towering giant responded to the priest, "but you gotta admit, she looks hot!"

The class was roaring as the priest stood with hands on hips and reprimanded the bearded side show. After taking Felix's brow beating, Mike continued to make his way across the front of the room and toward our row. Still scoped on the auburn-haired fox, he tripped over the legs of Felix's desk and fell flat on his face in front of Wendy and those lovely legs. Another chorus of laughter sounded out while the priest just shook his head and seemed to summoned help from above.

"Wow ,Wendy, you sure do look pretty," he said.

Now bending over from her seat, Wendy replied, "Are you okay, Mikie?"

"Yeahhh," he said with a shit-eating grin on his face, "I'm doing great!"

"Up, you idiot, up," Felix commanded.

Mike picked himself up and while passing by, he whispered to me, "Moose, she looks so fucking hot ... dragon hot ... don't you think?"

While laughing, I look up to him and mouthed, "I know, big fella ... I know!"

But what didn't register to me from the circus act that had just occurred was when Mike said "dragon hot," he was implying much more than just a metaphoric opinion.

This was his signal that he was about to turn into his version of Puff the Magic. When I turned around to try to discourage him, he was already sucking on the emissions from his butane lighter.

"Mike, noooo," I pleaded in a loud whisper.

He just smiled at me and waved. I had seen him exhibit this insanity before, but never in doors and never in the presence of someone in authority, let alone God's number one firefighter.

Nothing was going to stop this loveable nut job, from becoming an oral flame thrower now, so I just sat back, folded my arms and in a facial expression encouraged him to "fire away!"

The giant rose to his feet, brought the lighter to his mouth and ...

"Whiting, sit down, you fool," Felix implored.

It had to be one of Felix's worse dreams, fire coming from the mouth of someone he already considered as one of the devil's disciples. Mike flicked the lighter and blew, what was a prolonged stream of flames that were fueled by the fluid in his mouth.

"Whiiiiiiiiiiting! Are you maaaaaaddddddddddd?"

The priest was beside himself as the girls in the class were screaming out of shear fear, while most of the guys were egging the giant on!

"Devil boy, stop, d e v i l!!"

For what seemed to be at least a dozen seconds, the fire breather was actually showing Wendy how "hot" he thought she was, with a constant flame that seemed to shoot between three and four feet.

Cute, funny, hilarious, comical … no matter what it was, it was about to become hazardous … and …

Who knew that Mike was ever going to go through with this? Worse yet, who knew that the idiot was going to sneeze halfway through his performance?

His nasal itch forced him not only to lose control of the directional flow, from straight out to straight down, but when he sneezed the flame went from a stream to a burst!

Subsequently, Nickki who was cowering in my direction was hit with the flame in the back, igniting her sweater and singeing her hair.

When she was hit, she panicked and initially lunged in my direction.

Unknowingly, my hand went into her already loose blouse and bra area and when I saw that her sweater was on fire, I reached to remove it from her body, but in my attempt to lend aid, I ripped all of the latched buttons off of her blouse and dislodged her bra enough that when I turned to rip the sweater off, "everything came with it!"

No longer was the fire the issue, but it was now Nickki, standing there topless with her clothes in my hands.

"You asshole," Wendy screamed at me.

"What?"

While Nickki stood their crying, Wendy like a cat, removed her own top and proceeded to push me out of the way, cover the junior and quickly escort her from the room.

Without any conception or premeditation, I had gone from trying to stop Mike from even attempting this stunt to becoming an accomplice and holding the evidence right in my very own hands.

Felix in his warped perception, linked me to this attempt to humiliate the junior and held both Mike and me in contempt.

The chaos had spread to other classes in the adjacent area and Loyola and her staff were summoned to the scene. Felix simply unleashed this doozie of a story that Whiting and I had planned this whole thing out, and despite my attempts to defend this bullshit rap, I ended up in the main office.

It seemed like a parade of witnesses were ushered in and out of the Loyola's office and the crowds outside of the glass enclosed main office picked up by the minute.

There was little doubt that the rest of the school was starting to get wind of what had happened and Whiting and I were sitting in the glass-enclosed cage like two exotic animals on loan from a foreign zoo.

Fat ass Sheddow was next to stick her nose into this mess, when she came into the office for something obviously non-related. She took her expected shot at me, shaking her head and making that "tisk…tisk…tisk" sound.

Figuring that if this was it, what did I have to lose, and not counting on much support from my rotund homeroom teacher, I decided *What the hell*, and I flipped her the bird.

Through the shear curtains I could see Al, Del and Adam milling around, trying to avoid being sent to their next class and missing any of the action.

Next one in, Coach Lynch. "Perversion, huh, you two make me sick."

The waves of support were astonishing, "Yeah thanks, coach," I said. "I knew that sooner or later your ways would hit home with me."

And though this sarcasm seemed to be appeasing a giggling Mike, I was making advisories even angrier.

"You little son of a bitch," he said, "you don't even know what kind of trouble you're in?"

"That's right, I don't! How can I be in trouble, when I didn't even do anything, and how can you accuse me when you weren't even there? You know Lynch," and he interrupted me and sternly said, "that's Coach Lynch."

I just paused for a moment, shook my head and replied, "Like I was about to say, you know Lynch, the only one missing from this lynching is your girlfriend Ann." And before he could utter another word, into the office walked Nickki, Wendy, Miss Gainer and Nickki's mother.

Now, I was getting a little worried, because I not only figured that suspension was imminent, but the cops were soon to follow. But the thing that scarred me the most was what my dad was going to do when they would have eventually got him involved.

I loved my dad, but his kind of justice in these types of matters was to swing first and question later.

Strangely, while waiting, over the intercom I hear McCartney singing "Let it Be," and thought maybe a little S.O.S. to Mother Mary couldn't hurt right now?

Emerging from Loyola's office was both Gainer and Wendy, with the later looking in our direction and lambasting, "You stupid asshole! How could you do something like this?"

I just put my head down, and shook it in disgust. I thought *this is it, I'm fucked.*

"I'm so disappointed in you, Mike," she said, and I remember becoming a little shocked by this exchange.

"Me too, Mr. Whiting," said the sexy blonde teacher. Then she said to me, "Mark, they want to see you in there."

I rose to my feet and as I was about to walk by the two of them, Wendy grabbed me by the arm, forcing me to look at her and then she started to cry, softly uttering, "Sorry."

I didn't know what to think now, *was she sorry that she had to suggest turning me in, or was she sorry that she got the whole thing wrong?*

When I walked into the Principal's office, it quickly became apparent. Nickki ran up to me, threw her arms around me and said, "Thanks for being there; I know you didn't mean for what happened to happen."

I just hugged her back and looked at her mother smile with a couple of tears in her eyes and Loyola crack a little grin as well.

Then I looked into her eyes and said, "I'm sorry that you had to go through that, Nick, and I'm glad that you know that I'd never do anything to hurt you."

Then I reapplied a bear hug to her and whispered, "You know who I'm taking to the prom, but if she wasn't around, I would have loved to have taken you."

It was a genuine statement and I believe sincerely accepted.

With her still clutching on, I turned to Loyola and asked, "What's going to happen to him?"

She just shook her head and said, "He'll graduate, 'cause I couldn't force him on those young teachers another year."

I released Nickki to her mom and was about to exit the door when I heard a voice clearing. I turned back to the Principal who handed me a note and said, "Take this to your parents."

"Yes, Sister," I responded. Then I waved to Nickki and her mom and walked out the door.

Before I left the office, I heard, "Whiting, get in here now," knowing full well that the dragon was about to be slayed.

What was only minutes earlier a jammed hallway was now empty, and the perfect spot for me to see what was on the note.

There was no greeting, no body and no salutations, just a request … "It's been a long day, some Big Macs and french fries would sure hit the spot around five o'clock!"

I just smiled, folded the note and headed to my next class thinking that, *Whew, a great future almost went up in flames before it ever got started.*

― squeeky floors and bi-fold doors ―

The nice thing about the sex drive of a teen is that it is resilient. Despite all of our adolescent tendencies and geeky execution, this is where determination supersedes style. Let's face it; at this age it's the touch that counts, especially if you can get it from somebody other than yourself!

There are certainly other factors in this civilized quest for teen sex, like mood, sensual settings and the all important moment. But none of that stuff means anything until you get by the classic standards … such as the time honored real estate theory of location, location, location … or the ever present issue of timing, because, for teens the *time* is always right, but too often when you have the time, you don't have a decent place to do it.

But greater minds than the horny teen have wrestled with such dilemmas and have come up with answers to such questions. Not necessarily the right answers mind you … but answers nonetheless.

Take Einstein for instance; who was credited with the summation that genius was somehow linked to the delicate balance of inspiration and perspiration.

Well now, who better than a horny teen could counter and conclude that his conjuncture was nothing more than a crock of shit!

Genius huh? Let's test his hypothesis, shall we?

He proclaimed that you only needed 10 percent of the brain part of this premise to qualify for the status. If that were the case, everybody in my graduating class would have fit. What they cumulatively generated in inspiration, you could have squeeze into an eyedropper, let alone extract 10 percent. So as a class, we were well within the Einstein's range.

I do believe however, that ingenuity is subject to perspective.

What I might consider ingenious could be different than another's view of the same situation. So, I guess that it simply comes down to results, and, in this case, what ingenious ideas did I come up with to assure Laura and I a place where I could get a little *piece* and quiet.

And then there's perspiration … what a joke!

Between thinking about sex, dreaming about it, masturbating, trying to avoid getting caught in the act, and actually having the pleasure of doing it, I've sweat enough on my own to float a Mississippi River Boat.

So who's Albert fooling here? Or … am I some sort of closet genius and smarter than I gave myself credit for?

Well I seriously doubt the latter, but regardless of how you worked the calculations, Laura and I still couldn't come up with the right answers to these questions.

Desire, lust and intimacy were commodities that we had in plentiful supply. In addition, Laura's "Don't fuck me till I'm a senior force-field" seemed to be dissipating … so our problem became finding somewhere to play the game!

However, even if the moon and stars were in perfect alignment, and the timing concerns came in sync, the location always seemed to be in the back of my car, and it didn't take a genius to tell you that those accommodations grew old … and quickly!

Now let's take this moment to examine the pros and cons of exploring the art of making love in the 1977 AMC Pacer wagon. On the positive side, when the rear seats were folded down, there was plenty room for two or more. So, if I were ever able to persuade Laura into extra participation, accommodating it wouldn't have been a problem. And though we'd test the limits of headroom on occasion, it was ample enough, so the space was there.

Where it got a little tricky was in the field of climate control.

In the colder months it was the delicate balance of knowing when to rely on nature's warming ways in contrast to the employment of man-made devices. We would just leave the heat running until our own kicked in, but you didn't want to leave it on too long, because it would eventually get too hot. Which brought into play the modifying of temperature, because once you were into trying to make each other's thermostat rise, you didn't want to get interrupted by having to screw with the car's controls.

Plus, it required leaving the engine running, which was bad on two fronts.

First, it wasted gas, but most importantly the exhaust would send smoke signals to possible third party intervention ... namely the cops. So even if you were in a secluded spot in the woods, you were basically giving your position away. Therefore, engine off was the way to go ... or was it?

Reason being was that when we finished, if the car was off and our naturally produced heat started to free-fall, our sweaty bodies not only helped to ice up the windows, but also had a similar effect on our frames. In fact, the car became like a thermos, keeping an already cold pair, (her tits and my balls) ... frosty!

In retrospect, the really chilling part was the post-climatic realization that when the blood reverted from genitalia back to other body parts, that impervious feeling that you had toward the elements while in the throws of passion, dissipated quicker than the Superman's ability to fend off kryptonite.

But all of that other whining and complaining was *nothing* when stacked up against the worst possible sensation of all ... having to restart the car and restarting the vehicle's blower to heat the car and defrost the windows.

There might ~~not~~ be no greater deterrent to the satisfied teenager, than to experience the shock of a car's cold fucking blower, on an already cold and wet body ... clothed or not!

Mind you, we tried to incorporate experience into our post session dilemmas by bringing along blankets, but when the body's energy is sexually spent and you're in a frozen fish tank, bear skin wouldn't do the trick.

Which speaks volumes for the resiliency notion of lustful teenagers, and brings into play doubts about what another giant of science ... Pavloff was trying to pass off with that fucking dog.

Come on, Saturday night at 10:00, if there was nowhere else to go, we could have been in the Yukon and despite knowing what we did, it was into the back for another round of sex and the Artic aftermath. Modifying behavior ... *my ass*!

It wasn't any better in the spring and summer either. In fact, it was probably worse, because the Pacer was without air-conditioning, which took our rendezvous from the frozen tundra into the mobile sauna.

Note that the same logistical problems applied. Beyond kissing, if discretion was a priority, it meant that it was back into the woods for carnal exploration ... the mosquito-filled woods!

At this time of the year, it was keep the windows airtight, turn up the passion dial and while dropping a little cum, you were more apt to drop five to ten in water.

Suddenly, we went from horny teens, to nutritionist concerned about imminent dehydration.

And it was inevitable, that when mixing the lethal combinations of carnal heat and confined space heat, that the need would occur to crack the windows and … to chance it.

Which was wrong, a bad choice and simply ouch…ouch…and ouch!

Sweaty bodies and bloodthirsty winged predators do not bode well for humans in the woods.

God can occasionally flex a mean streak at teens whose desires overcome common sense, in the form of zillions of needle pricking sexual deterrents.

One Friday afternoon I rushed out to see her after her classes had concluded for the week, and you could feel that both of us were ready to take this relationship to its ultimate physical level.

So, we decided to quell our urges and play a little tennis, but less than a set into the match, we decided to ditch the court activities and head for one of our favorite places of wooded seclusion. By the time we disappeared into the woods, she was already giving me head and had one of her hands in her pants, prepping the muffin.

"Today's … the day … right," she said, while she bobbed up and down on my erect member.

"Oh yeah, baby, today we fuck … long and hard," I answered in a breathy manner while I was scraping the shit out of my car on the branches just off of the narrow tree-lined path.

"Just promise me something," she begged.

"Anything, baby, anything!"

"You gotta promise not to cum inside of me!"

"I promise, I promise!"

"I mean it, Mark, I don't want to get pregnant!"

"And you think I want you to?"

"Just bail out … okay!"

Without any condoms, bailing out was a no-brainer. I wasn't any more interested in becoming a seventeen-year-old daddy, as she wanted to become a sixteen-year-old mama. And without regard for leakage, spillage or any other kind of age, leave it to two horny teenagers to trust in the highly successful bail out method of birth control.

I'm aware of the cliché for guys when their small head outthinks the one on their shoulders, but what's the characterization for this with the gals?

When we finally got to a secure spot, we vaulted into the back seat and proceeded to grope one another into submission.

As we attempted to forego with most of the foreplay, our temperatures were rising quicker than the price of a target of a hostile Wall Street takeover.

We were dripping wet in no time and soon it felt like we were trying to get it on in the bowels of a steel-producing boiler.

"I'm burning up," I said in a gasping voice.

"Me too, baby, I want you to fuck the shit out of my wet little pussy!"

I just laughed for a moment before saying, "No, Laura, I'm burning up, I gotta get some air," as I felt on the verge of blacking out.

I opened one of the windows and panted like a dog for air, simultaneously opening the floodgates for the bloodsuckers buffet.

I know it's a pun, but after getting my second wind, I worked my way back to Laura's open legs and anxious trap. I started to rub the underside of my cock on her swollen clit and began to feel the surge of passion grow between my legs.

"Oh yeah, baby, I'm ready to do this," she insisted. "I need to feel your long thickness inside me!"

I grabbed my member and was ready to enter the *real hot spot,* when all of a sudden; she slapped me on the face.

"Hey, what's that all about?" Before she could answer me, I was twisting and turning and must have looked like a whirling dervish. Literally, a split second from bliss we found ourselves rolling around, swatting wildly and losing to an Air Force that was way beyond our ability to defend.

Oh, and by the way YES, in the past we tried a repellant, but using OFF as a stimulant or sexual tool doesn't feel, smell or taste right, if you get my drift?

Nature had thrown us a contraceptive curve ball that we just could hit, and suddenly the only thing that was swelling on our respective bodies were the welts that we were receiving from the bites of those little motherfuckers.

The trick was going to be, how we were to explain looking like we both picked up a wicked case of the mumps just from playing tennis … long story short, we did.

If conventional thought enters your mind, understand that …

1	It's a Pacer; it's got more windows than an Amsterdam red-light district's storefront display, so trying to score in it, especially in locations that are not remote defeats the notion of needing to employ a little discretion. I mean, if privacy weren't part of the equation, we might as well have just done it on her front lawn.

2	Hotels are expensive and if I had trouble getting into a bar in Daytona, how do you think I was going to fare in a motel lobby, and…

3	I don't know why parents always stay home?

— —

Despite the aforementioned failed attempt, Laura was putty in my hands and went absolutely nuts when I'd kiss her neck and run my tongue inside of her earlobes. Her back would begin to arch and even through her bra I could see her nipples ripen to a nice size and texture!

On those occasions when I'd go over to her house and we'd be in her basement watching TV with her folks, I used to pine for commercials because her dad would bolt in one direction and her mom would go in the other. That would leave the door open for at least sixty seconds of petting opportunity, and we would go at it.

I'd work her back and ears and she would immediately respond by spreading her legs just enough to allow my hand to start rubbing her muffin through her clothes. She would put a leg lock on my arm and start humping it, as if she were riding Secretariat!

Her moans would increase and I would occasionally either have to go back to kissing her or would have to actually cover her mouth to avoid being questioned about "What was that noise?"

Thank goodness for squeaky floors, because it would always be a dead giveaway that it was time to wind down the ultra quickie.

The foolproof in her house were the stairs coming from the main floor. The basement would be full of sounds that somebody was on the way down when that first step was hit. We'd quickly compose ourselves and act if we were in the middle of some kind of small talk.

Her basement, despite being finished was always cold, promoting the need for a blanket, which her parents would allow us to share one, though I'd always get the occasional "Don't try anything under there" look.

Though we'd take what we could get in the drilling in the dwelling department, the car seemed to be our best bet for romping. But like most things in life, time has a way of earning trust ... and trust turns into allowances and allowances into liberties!

Plus, I'm fairly positive that her dad was of the mind-set, that if they're going to do something, do it in the basement so that I can at least stop it, if I hear something going wrong.

On the contrary, I was even more confident that her mom's take on this was, "Don't do it!" But, if you do, make sure it's on another continent, because I don't want to even to get the feeling that my baby is anywhere near or possibly getting violated by that scumbag!

That's where I knew that we'd eventually miss the Pacer, because first of all, we were both pretty good in the grunting and moaning departments.

Then, there was focus. That special kind of focus that only comes from great sex ... you know, the kind where the house can be burning down around you, and you wouldn't notice it kind of focus.

In the car, after we would tear each other's clothes off, and I'd start working from one direction to the other, like from head to toe, or vice versa, making occasional stops along the way. And when I'd hit one of those special locations, my sweet and innocent baby, had the tendency of mimicking Daytona Frank's friend Gina, minus the major psychotic pornographic swings.

Laura would have the inclination of begging for things, with a bit of extra volume kicked in for good measure. When I worked my way up from her feet, I'd kiss her ankles and trace the heel of her foot, up to her calf and purposely slow myself as I approached the inner part of her thighs.

She'd start to sigh and laugh in more of a slow guttural and sultry manner and reach for the hair on my head before she would begin to moan.

"Oooo baby ... you're making me ache! Mmmm ... that's it," she'd croon.

"Like that baby?" I'd prod.

"Ohhh fuck ... what do you think? That's it, baby, come on and lick that sweet little dish."

And I'd find myself drawn to her musky and swollen clit, and when I hit it, there would be no mistaking that I struck honey pot oil, because she start to moan even louder and her hips would begin to sway like a magnolia in a hint of breeze on a hot Georgia night.

"Oh yeah, baby, come on and give it up ... gimme the stuff, Laura!"

"Yeah, my Markie, lick my stuff ... make my pussy burn ... oh yeah, y e a h, Y E A H motherfucker, suck on my gash!!"

Those are always nice words to hear, but when incorporating the decibel level that she had the tendency of employing, out in the woods in a sealed vehicle and not within earshot of her parents and papa's sawed off was the only place to be!

And though, I would assume that most woman enjoy having their pussies eaten, Laura wanted to make a vacation out of it. The girl loved getting head and quite honestly, I enjoyed doing her!

In turn, for such a young girl she gave great blowjobs. She had a wonderful way of using her palms and fingers in perfect unison with her tongue, teeth and mouth that would just drive me crazy. Add her beautiful blonde mane and those innocent turned devilish blue eyes into the mix, and mouthfuls were destined to be deposited!

What was amazing to me about her was how she could go from the naïve, pure and innocent little girl into a seductress. Furthermore, it would blow my mind when she'd start to beg for me to cum all over her mouth and chin, while she would increase the strength and stroke of her grip on my cock. Girls just shy of seventeen were not supposed to be this proficient in the art of fellatio, but my nymphet was!

We would have our moments when it would seemingly appear that we would have a house to ourselves, but for some reason, it always seemed to slip from our grasps at the moment of truth. Her parents weren't to keen on the fact of her spending too much time at my house, and the few times that we did, my folks tended to be nosier than hers.

Once I remembered being up in my room with her, with yet another possible block of alone time, being that my mom went to the grocery store and my dad wasn't expected home from work for at least an hour. As we started to disrobe, the lock on the front door was opened ... and wouldn't you know it, *he* had the chance to take off early, and just my luck ... *he did*.

In his typical style, he came in and said, "Mark!"

To which I replied, "Yeah, Dad!"

"You home?"

I just looked at Laura and answered in an exasperated voice, "What do ya think, Dad?"

There were also a number of times back at her house that our passions turned into extremely close calls of being caught, and one time that ... well ... this one's worth detailing.

It was the Thursday before my prom and I had gone over Laura's house to compare some of the frills of my tux to some of the extras that she was going to accessorize with.

Now approaching 9:30 P.M., the customary situation was at hand … the four of us in Laura's basement, watching some crappy show on the boob tube, when the old man said, "Well, Manya," (an ethnic pet name that he had for his wife), "I gotta be in by six, so what do ya say … wanna hit the hay?" (He was a butcher for the A & P).

I thought, *Yes, they're going to give us a little time for funzies*, while Laura inconspicuously squeezed my hand in hope that the two of them were about to *vamoose* for the night.

"Naw," she said in breaking our collective bubbles of hope. "I think I'll wait up for Cin."

The Cin that she was referring to, was Laura's twin sister who was at her boyfriend's folks' house across town.

"Ah, Mom, don't worry about her, I'll wait up," Laura insisted.

"No, that's alright," she said in a matter of fact tone. "Besides I want to watch the end of this program."

Truth be known, she was sleeping through the most of it, so it was obvious to me that she really just wanted to detour us of the possibility of being able to fool around.

Laura would frequently tell me about all of the times after I would leave, by the time she got back into the house from seeing me off, her mom had the basement lights off and was already upstairs and in the process of brushing her teeth prior to going to bed. So this wasn't that big of a shock to me.

Furthermore, though she was always nice to me, I'm quite confident that Laura's mom extended to me the same cordial, "I trust ya about as far as I can throw ya," attitude that my mom seemed to have toward Laura.

So it was a given that as soon as I'd hit the road, the lights would be off and she would be on her way to the sack. But as long as I was around, even if we had to pull an all-nighter to guarantee admittance for Laura into an Ivy League school, she'd sleep in front of that goddamned TV and fake some interest in whatever was on … including reruns of a PBS presentation of the Portuguese National Farm Report, which we once saw on the tube late one night while she had fallen asleep, waiting for me to split after one of our study sessions.

The old man on the other hand, though intimidating and demanding in respect to certain aspects of our relationship, gave us our space. When he called it a night, nothing short of a military attack was going to wake him up.

Proof positive was the fact that Laura's parents in the warmer weather months installed a window mounted air-conditioning unit that sounded like it was churning out about a billion BTUs. It sounded as if you were standing in the flight path of a jet when this thing was in operation.

So, between his sleeping habits, the volume of the unit and the squeaking alerts of the stairs coming down into the basement, those rare and infrequent times that we had the lower level to ourselves, we at least had ample notice if someone were on the verge of interrupting us.

It was some thirty minutes since her dad had retired for the night, and right before our eyes, her mom was drifting away in the recliner and began a subtle round of snoring.

While sitting side by side on the floor, we looked at each other in hope that she might reconsider and decide to turn in for the night.

"Mom," Laura gently whispered while nudging her slippered foot, "you're snoooring."

"I'm okay, just gonna wait for Cin," she said in a partially startled and fatigued state.

It was painfully apparent that the Mark factor was in effect and she wasn't going to give any ground … conscious or not.

Knowing that I had an eleven-thirty school night curfew and that anything past ten was pushing the envelope in Laura's house, the chances of getting *some*, were fading fast.

Feeling the futility of the moment, I whispered to Laura, "I better get going." To which she said with fervor while digging her freshly polished nails into my thigh, "No!"

I made a silent gesture to her, to which she grabbed me by the hand and led me to the stairs, saying to her mom, "We're just going to go over some things upstairs before Mark leaves."

The thing that she was planning to go over was my cock, and when we got into the kitchen she devilishly grinned at me and said, "You're not leaving until I swallow everything you got!"

"Where, next to the fridge?" I sarcastically countered with a furrowed brow.

The kitchen would have been the worse possible place to have performed this act. Reason being, that this was the Times Square of the dwelling. All rooms seemed to lead to it and sooner or later everybody passed by.

There were no less than four entrances into the kitchen, with the present danger being a blind access from off of the bedroom hallway. Obviously, her papa was the number one concern, and despite being a sound sleeper, there was a first time for everything, and it would have been just my luck that he would have developed a hankering for a late night snack.

Besides, the triple threat thought of having my pants down around my ankles, my cock hanging out in the same room where they keep the knives, and her butcher father only seconds away, unquestionably would have interfered with my focus and enjoyment.

Concern number two … Mama! Though she had nodded off in the basement, she was sneaky quick and was quiet as a church mouse. Being only a few squeaky stairs from her daughter's insatiable mission, which was far too close for my comfort.

The house's back door was also an element of the kitchen, and though the thought of her twin sister walking in and then joining in, was mildly exciting, it would simply remain just a deviant contemplation in my mind.

Then there was the living room entrance, partitioned off by a bi-fold door that remained closed to avoid being in the direct path of the air-conditioner's arctic blasts and noise.

In spite of my concerns and lack of suave debonair Bond-like sexual spontaneity, the blonde nympho still dragged me into the living room, through the bi-fold and next to that monstrous producer of cold air and excessive noise. Then falling to her knees and with the precision of an international jewel thief, she extracted my stiff member, and began to kiss and lick it.

"Are you crazy?" I whispered in an adamant manner, and actually pushed her away while I backed off.

"Your father's sleeping thirty feet down the hall," to which she responded with a crooked smile and those dreamy eyes, "You know that he'd sleep through a bomb."

"But your sis…your sis…ter," I said in an ever weakening state as she began to stroke my lick my shaft more vehemently.

"Won't be home for hours … probably getting a little cock of her own," she laughingly said.

"Laura," I begged as my eyes started rolling back in my head, "it's cold here!"

not possible ✓

To which she remarked, "Not for long," and she went to town, bobbing up and down on my little general, while cupping my sack in one hand and in a rhythmic piston like fashion, sucked my dick while she jerked me off simultaneously with the other.

She had raised my T-shirt over my sternum and had my jeans and boxers down to my ankles. Conceding a joyful defeat, I occasionally used my left hand to assist in directing her head and to help force the issue as deep as I could. Then, if the excitement of getting head in this potentially dangerous spot wasn't bad enough, she began to unbutton her blouse and loosened her painter's pants. She then proceeded to take the hand that she was working my nuts with and buried it in her own sweet little nether region.

Soon she was working herself off almost as furiously as she was working me, and began to moan in such an enticing manner. Then adding fuel to the fire, she brought that off hand up from her pussy and rubbed the freshly recovered sugar all over my hooded peg. She then looked up at me, smiled and preceded to savor the nectar of her sweet spot on my bubbling purple volcano!

I thought I was going to come apart at the seams. There I was, standing with hands on hips, like Yule Brenner as the King of Siam, getting the blowjob of my young life and seeing my girl work me as if she were a seasoned pro schooled at the famed Cherry Patch Ranch!

I was oblivious to everything around me; the drapes were drawn, and I suddenly found myself affixed to the shadow that was being cast upon the wall of Laura's performance. It was as if we were transformed into an orgy of blowjobs that allowed me to not only participate, but to gawk as a voyeur as well … what a turn on!

I was practically naked, standing in the equivalent of an Alberta clipper with most of the blood from my large frame now housed in my dipstick" enamored in the negatives projected on the wall and ready to bust my nut, when all of a sudden … the bi-fold opened from the kitchen.

There she was, in all of the splendor that curlers, a housecoat and fuzzy slippers would allow. Like an unsuspecting stag frozen in the glow of a car's headlights, I found myself shocked and fixed upon the disapproving eyes of Laura's mother. The visual clinch, which seemed to last for a decade, probably was in play for less than three seconds and my hard-on dropped like a free falling sack of flour that was thrown off of a delivery truck.

I was caught, dead to nuts, by the judge herself, and I thought even if Jesus Christ were my defense attorney, I was headed for the chair.

She had turned away and I could just feel Laura looking up at me, in a look that spoke for itself, "Did what I just think happened … happen?"

Without saying a word, Laura ushered me in the unmade shape that I was in, out the front door and practically pushed me into my car as I was fumbling for my keys.

"Iloveyou, I'llcallyou, don'tcallme, bye," she hurriedly recited. Then she turned and sprinted back into the house.

I would have rushed into a burning building to rescue that girl, but truth be told and as much as I adored her, I was sure glad that it was her and not me running back into that place.

Suddenly fearful that her father might have been awaken with the troubling revelation, I fired up the ignition and burnt rubber in hightailing it the hell out of there.

I had often heard of the theory of phantom conscience taking over for you when you're performing one task, while dwelling on another. I experienced it that night. For with the concerns that I might soon be gelded, fears that our relationship would soon come to an end, and worried about what Laura was going through, I couldn't remember driving from Trenton back to Detroit.

I don't remember getting much sleep that night and with the prom in less than forty-eight hours, I was going through that rolodex in my head as to who I could possibly hook up with at the eleventh hour. But without Laura, I really didn't desire to go.

School wasn't much better, as most of the student body was brimming with the anticipation of what the weekend would bring. I on the other hand found myself nonchalant when others would address the impending gala with me, and even hinted that other possibilities might be explored.

I didn't even want to think about showing up there stag, and then started to conger up excuses that I might have to call upon if I did.

Later that afternoon about 3:30 P.M., I got a call from her. She was at a pay phone and told me that there was no dialogue at all during breakfast, and that she didn't know whether or not her mother had or was going to tell her father.

Other than the million reasons and excuses that were going through my mind, I tried to understand this matter from a parent's position. And though I postured that sooner or later a parent concedes that their child will dabble in the realm of sexual promiscuity, they probably didn't want to have box seats to any of the performances.

I was certain that she was going to tell me that she wasn't going to be joining me, but to my surprise she said, "If I have to escape out of the window,

I'm going to be there with you. Besides, you're not going to get out of taking me that easy."

Then after some small talk, she said to me, "Mark, I love you ... and I'm always going to love you!"

It was at that time that I just knew that Laura and I were going to be ... *forever*.

~ the rippling effect ~

Here it was, Prom Day 1978 and my main concern was how was I going to get Laura into the car without seeing her mom. I thought about a quick drive by and pick up at the curb, but conceded that with pictures and the formality that the event commanded, that wasn't going to fly.

Then I thought that I could have one of the guys pick her up, and make an excuse that I was having car trouble or I had to do something for my mom, but the realization set in that half of them would have kidnaped her for ransom or sex, and the other half were still having problems lining up transportation for themselves.

Hell, I even thought of asking her to coax her older sister into dropping her off at the hall, just to avoid the inevitable.

Around noon though, I got a call from Laura, who insisted that everything was going to be all right. "It's not the best of situations around here, but she said that she wouldn't tell my dad because she feared that he might kill you."

"Well that's comforting," I commented. "But that still doesn't solve the problem about what she saw. You did tell her that this was your idea ... right?"

There was silence on the other end of the line.

"Lauraaaa ... tell me that she understands that this was all your idea."

"Uhhh ... sheee ..." again silence.

"Oh shit! Come on, Laura, I'm not coming over there if she thinks ..."

"You got to," she interrupted. "My dad's going to take pictures and he's insistent that you be here at least a half hour before we're ready to leave!"

"A half hour, I don't even want to drive on your street!"

"Oh, don't worry about it ... everything's going to be okay," she insisted.

I didn't even want to go to this Godforsaken prom, let alone now through the gates of a pissed off mother's hell!

I mean for the most part, the theme of this prom could have been best described as *who cares?*

Even the student planning committee's focus left a lot to be desired. In fact a month prior, there was a pretty strong consensus among the cash-strapped senior corps that favored a modified sock hop in the gym as opposed to this upper crust shindig.

But the small contingent who actually cared about this event, some of the faculty advisors and especially Loyola, insisted that it was going to receive the formal setting and attention that it deserved. This despite the fact, that for an event of this magnitude, it hardly receive the pre-billing and in-school build up that you might have expected.

I was on the fence with this one. I felt that I needed to attend to fulfill some rite of passage, but I really wasn't all that cracked on the path that I needed to travel to get there.

In fact, it was Laura's insistence that we had to attend, despite my warning to her that she was not going to be the most welcomed guest among the locals, especially my fellow female classmates.

So here I was at about 5:00 P.M., standing in front of a mirror, about to clip on a an ugly velvet bow tie to an even uglier frilled shirt, beginning to come to grips with the knowledge that Laura had actually allowed her mom to believe that she was the victim, and that I was the driving force behind what she had witnessed. Which from her perspective probably bought her some time and a little compassionate understanding.

Regardless, my main concern was how long would the truce hold up, before big mama laid the news on her spouse.

In addition, whether she did or not, I was about to walk into a situation where in her mind I was labeled the perpetrator, and her sweet and innocent little daughter was nothing like the cock hungry nymphomaniac that in essence she really was!

The thought of this, not only gave me a couple of nights of bed-sweats, but at present, I saw the perspiration pool on my face in the reflection of the mirror that forced me to re-blow dry my hair.

But I considered ... her mom wasn't stupid! There wasn't a gun being pointed at her daughter's head and I didn't have a couple of cinched hands full of blonde hair forcing Laura to engulf my dick.

Unless she thought her offspring was on her knees in some sort of religious expressionism, she had to know that this was an official blowjob and that her daughter was an active ... and not a passive participant.

So then, I guess you go with the lesser of two evils and mentally persuade yourself that if it's an us against them scenario, I'll stick with our team! Consequently, in her mind Laura is good, and Mark is evil!

No matter how I did the math on this one, I saw myself coming out on the short end.

Before leaving, I got the white glove treatment from both Mom and Dad. "Heyyy, looking good there, son!"

Smiling on the outside, but still contemplating my fate on the inside, I just continued my grin and said, "Thanks, Dad."

"Oh, you look wonderful," my mom added as she came close to me for a hug.

I noticed my sister passing by, when suddenly she flinched and developed a puzzled look upon her face. "Little heavy with the aftershave, don't you think?"

"Well ..." I just responded with a disconcerting grin on my puss. I was afraid that I was sweating so much that sooner or later it would turn to stench. So I upped the deodorant and cologne applications to try to combat the ill effects of possible B.O.

After I got her *Good Housekeeping* seal of approval, my mom shoved the corsage and her camera in my hands and said, "Now make sure her parents shoot plenty of pictures for us." To which I obviously thought, *that's not the kind of "shooting" that I'm worried about* ... and contemplated that this might be the last time I'd ever see these guys.

While in route, I started talking to myself ... out loud ... on what I might say.

"Hi, Mrs. L., you sure look nice tonight ..." nawww, too kiss assish, she'd know I was groveling.

"Hey ... how's everything?" Nope, why tee-up an open-ended question to let her run wild on!

"Wow, the house looks great! Did you paint recently?"

I found myself laughing at my own suggestions and toying with the idea of again faking auto problems. But if I knew Laura, she would have sent a cab for me.

About halfway there I saw a florist who appeared to be open and considered a little floral and aromatic olive branch. She was probably going to shove these up my ass, but I felt like I needed some sort of help and I was a bit too late in calling the Forty-Second Airborne.

When I got to the door the guy waved at me as if to say, "Sorry, but I'm closing."

My whole body must have appeared to go limp and as I turned to walk away, I heard the door unlock.

"Hey, my friend, you look like you can use some help?"

I turned back around with a half smile on my face and he motioned me in.

"Prom night?" he inquired.

I just shook my head yes.

"Forgot the corsage?"

"No," I answered, and I proceeded to say, "I got this little problem."

Without going into too much details, I gave him what I thought was enough to go on. It didn't take long to surmise that this guy was taking this to a level, a bit beyond the budget of a seventeen- year-old.

"I know exactly what you need to smooth over things … leave it to me."

Roses were flying out of one cooling unit, carnations out of the next. Then he threw in some of these pointy things, added a little of this color and some more of that … and before you knew it, he seemed to be creating the blanket of flowers that you'd present to the connections of the Kentucky Derby winner.

"Hey look, I'm just trying to come up with a little something to cool down this misunderstanding, I'm not trying to patch up the riff in the Middle East," I insisted.

"Son, trust me," he said, "by spending a little now, you'll be farther ahead in the long run."

And while he continued with his task, I found myself reflecting upon a lesson that my government and civics teacher, Mr. Brevard had once taught. "The world is rapidly shrinking, my young friends," he said, "and because of that, everything sooner or later related to one another."

And who would have thought that at this place and time, his words of wisdom would suddenly click into place for me?

It was the old theory, that for every cause, there was an effect, and damned if he wasn't right!

Even one simple blowjob could have a profound effect on the lives of hundreds.

Consider … when she walked in on us, Laura's mom immediately got the migraine of the month award which forced her to eventually visit the medicine cabinet. To which she needed to switch on the light before opening the mirrored enclosure to make sure that she was drawing the right relief, from the right bottle.

Once she found the correct container, she popped the protective cap, which not only kept the contents of said bottle out of harm's way of youngsters, but obviously provided proper content storage to avoid premature product expiration.

Of course, she needed to chase the pill with a cup of water, so she reached for a Dixie cup, turned on the faucet, filled the cup, and then turned off the water.

She then swallowed the pill, followed it with some water, crumpled up the cup (imaging that it was my neck), and proceeded to throw it away in the wicker waste paper basket, adjacent to the basin.

She then shook her head in disgust, paused for reflection, looked into the mirror to see if she was really awake and that this was not all some crazy nightmare, grabbed a tissue to dab the duct of her one eye that was starting to tear up ... again, disposed the used paper product, turned off the light, and proceeded to her bedroom where she removed her robe, kicked off her slippers and climbed into bed.

But that's not the end ... not just yet. For next, she would look out into the star-filled night sky, through the blinds that were opened just enough to allow for the glimpse, so that she could say to herself, "Where did I go wrong?"

Then she started to say her prayers ... hoping to find *the answer*, but more likely was thinking about driving to church after her morning toast and coffee, to pick up enough holy water to bring back home to have Laura gargle with, in hopes that it would quell, redeem and purify the mouth that she and her hubby sunk all that fucking money into with nourishment and braces, only to witness it being soiled with that ugly, vein-ladened, good for nothing, piss producing, inter-city, Pacer driven ... for Christ's sake of all cars, cock!"

Now ... if you're keeping score, consider all of the good that came from this act ... of ... charity ... yeah, this designed act of charity!

First of all, thank goodness for all of the researchers and staffers, who painstakingly pinched and dabbed their way into creating a pill; that would help relieve cerebral discomfort and tensions.

And let's not forget all of the equipment, fixtures, gauges, controls, levers, and devices used by those researchers, chemists and scientists to make that tiny stress reliever ... which were created by designers, engineers, die makers, production staffers, and marketing specialists, all an intricate part of those who contributed in the crafting process, engineering, retrofitting, modifying, production, distribution and assembly of the aforementioned.

Then, how about that electric company! God may have said, "Let there be light," but it's ConEd who's pushing it through the wires that are connected to the substations and grids and generators that are located at the power plants … blah, blah, blah, blah …while God's working his magic with the sun on the other side of the marble.

So, when you flip the switch at midnight, there it is! But behind the scenes, there's the gang at plant where the turbines grind coal and other byproducts that were mined, refined and transported by rail, freight and ship to the plant, so that the process of conversion can take effect.

Which, of course, is carefully monitored by another group of engineers and technicians, who also use more equipment with gauges, controls and blah, blah, blah, to push the power through all of that previously mentioned shit, that was either laid or strung properly by trained professionals, before the juice can hit your house's fuse box and be available on demand at the flick of a switch.

Same thing for the water! There's all that processing and filtering and monitoring and pipe laying, just so that we can turn a lever and have nice clean, refreshing water, to push that little fucking pill down the same passage, that only moments before saw your precious little girl jamming ten inches … okay, eight and a half … oh fuck it already, alright, six inches … "but I'm still a growing boy" of cock down her throat.

The Dixie cups and tissues don't just appear on the grocer's shelves from the paper products fairy. They need trees and mills and foresters and processors and a whole bunch of other shit so that you can pull a Kleenex and blow your honker or dry your eyes.

And somebody's got to pick up all of that shit and take it to the dump. How about a little recognition for the garbage men and sanitation crews … they got a stake in this too!

Who wove that wicker wastebasket? Who made the windows that you could look into the night sky through, and the blinds that you wish were in front of your daughter's genuflected body instead of being on those motherfucking windows?

Let's not forget those bean pickers and sack makers who do whatever the fuck that they do so that you can have a caffeine overload. And if you take cream and sugar in it, well then, that just opens up a whole new roster of players.

The auto companies are in this from the transportation of goods to service support.

You want holy water and the church is a couple miles away ... you know what that means ... you need a car, and the car needs gas ... and blah-blah-blah-blah-blahhhh.

And Heaven forbid, don't discount the role of the church in this thing. Because the blessing of the water may be free, but somebody's headed for the confessional in this mess, and though there's no meter to get into the fess-up bin, there is this thing called a collection basket that they pass around on Sundays, and they expect you to put in something, no less than 10 percent of your entire household income.

Not too shabby for spreading a little ceremonial water and some ecclesiastical psychiatry.

Which brings me back to this putz who, with the entire floral industry behind his efforts, is song and dancing me into a thirty-dollar arrangement, so that there can be peace in our time.

So, my friends, I offer to you the concept, that beyond the mere conception of this being a "simple blowjob," that I have sketched for you a diagram, complex as it may seem, of one of the many economic principles that has made this country great!

In fact, dare I say, that if all this productivity and inter-connected manufacturing can be generated to benefit the multitudes from the results of a "simple blowjob"... can you imagine the stimulus and windfall that a threesome would deliver?

Now, how do I get that across to her mother even if she does accept the flowers?

I even thought of driving back home to see if Rose would let me borrow her new Mercury Cougar. It was a soothing forest green in color and compared to the aquarium; well, there is no comparison ... the Cougar looked the way a car should look.

I also thought it would somehow make her think about change, and the concept of starting over. In addition, I figured that if Mama was going to crack and say throw a brick at the windshield of whatever I was driving, better Rose's insurance woes than mine.

But after circling the subdivision four or five times, I drove the red tortes at the pace of the same onto Woodside Street.

From down at the corner I could see Laura posing for pictures. I could also make out that her twin and older sisters were there, her dad and a number of neighbors were also on hand in front of the house as well.

Her dad was taking pictures, *Hmmm, that was a good sign.* But from my current angle, no sign of you know who.

Maybe she's sick, I thought. *Or maybe she's lurking in the bushes ready to attack at first sight?*

When I finally pulled up, I noticed that dehydration from all of that sweating had finally set in, because when I tried to swallow my own saliva, I couldn't … there wasn't any. And though I was scared enough to piss myself, that reservoir was pretty much dried up too.

"He's here," yelled Cindy. I didn't know whether to smile or duck.

Hail Mary, full of grace … I began to silently pray as I extracted myself from the car as if I were an eighty-year-old man.

I was greeted first by Cindy, who with a smile on her face and whispering through her teeth, said to me, "Where in the hell have you been so long?" She resolutely linked arms with me and said, "Get your ass moving."

We walked by next-door neighbor, Janet Wallace, who was standing in front of the house and said, "Oh, don't you look handsome." To which, I just smiled and continued on with this dirge of a procession.

Here came the old man, holding his camera. He looked at me and bellowed, "You weren't planning on standing my daughter up, were you?" And I thought to myself, *Oh, if you only knew?*

Finally from the driveway side of the house, *she* appeared, looking like a high-ranking politician, diplomatically smiling, with one hell of a fire raging beneath the surface.

I couldn't tell if she was doing this for Laura's benefit, or the fact that the neighbors had foiled her plans by appearing, and thus became instant witnesses, but so far … so good.

"Hello," she said.

"Hhhh," I sputtered. Dry mouthed and all I managed to say, "hi."

We just kind of looked at each other, with hers being much more of a searing and burning stare than my meek, obedient puppy dog response.

I raised the bouquet and in a broken voice said, "For you."

"Oh," she responded and she nodded in approval, before quickly handed them off to Laura's older sister, Debbie.

Breaking the silence, the old man said, "Well, let's make some memories," referring to picture taking, and I thought, *No memories … bad choice of words there, pal … no memories!*

Her mom grabbed the camera and said, "Laura, why don't you stand over there and let me take a couple of you by yourself."

To which I thought, *Probably the way she wants to see the relationship end up anyway.*

Then after she took a couple of shots, she turned back and in a general malaise remarked, "He did get you a corsage, didn't he?"

Caught off guard, I said, "Oh ... here it is."

"You mean you didn't give it to her yet?" she belted out in a condescending manner.

After placing it on her wrist, I was once again told to move aside and was relegated to watching her snapshot after shot of her victim princess in front of her perfectly manicured foliage.

While the shutter clicked on, I reflected while standing in the background, and thought to myself, *Look at that pretty girl!*

From kneeling private porn queen to public image prom princess, *Oh, what a difference a dress and a day makes.*

Careful not to call me by name, she finally turned and said to me, "Okay, why don't you jump in there."

I rushed to Laura's side and she snapped off one picture.

Then she turned and handed the camera off to Debbie and said, Okay, Laura, let's get some with you, dad and me."

A little shocked, I thought, *Why rock the boat,* and I exited as Quick-draw McGraw would say, stage left.

I just kicked my shoes around the lawn and tried to maintain the lowest profile that I could.

All of a sudden, Cindy spoke up and quipped, "Hey, don't you think that we should include Mark in some of these?"

"Yeah ... get in here," her father emphatically said.

As I approached the trio, Laura's smile was bright, but you could see on her face that she was aware of this uncomfortable situation. Her father seemed to be enjoying the moment, especially the way the neighbors were gathering around and making his palace the center of the neighborhood's attention.

As for her mom, well, she remained affixed to Laura's left side with the affirmation of a Great White Shark.

I was placed between Laura and her dad, when just before the next photo was taken, Laura turned, looked at me and whispered through her teeth, "Just a few more and it will all be over, then partying, sex, fun and more sex!"

As much as I wanted to always hear that from her, now was neither the time nor the place.

When the last shot was taken, the old man looked at me and said, "A little bonus ... two o'clock."

Simultaneously, I saw her mom kiss her and say, "Try and have a good time."

Try, I thought, *give me a break.*

Then I said, "Well, we better get going," and I escorted Laura to the car.

Among the random well wishes, I looked one last time in Mom's direction and offered up my most sincere smile, to which I received a half smile back, along with a nod. But those eyes, oh if those eyes had Superman's laser beam capabilities, I think that they would have cut a hole in my belly, on their way down to searing off ... need I say?

After getting Laura in and settled, I walked around the front of the car and heard, "Hey, pin head ... thanks for the flowers, they're beautiful."

Pin head, I thought. *She couldn't have been referring to ... nawwww.*

I just decided to smile back and wave.

~ the prom ~

The gala was actually much closer to Laura's neighborhood than it was to St. Hedwig's.

Southgate's St. George's Grecian Center was the venue, a beautiful huge complex that could accommodate many different events at one time. The façade of the structure itself sat only a hundred yards or so off of the road, with parking and the main entrance located to the building's rear.

This would be Hedwig's first prom ever at this site, and if it were not for a cancellation six months prior, and the fact that Shelley had some sort of an *in* here ... which, in and of itself, congers up visions ... we never would have been able to get this place.

The facility was so huge that on the marquis alone it indicated that there were two weddings, two proms and a family reunion that was being serviced simultaneously that evening.

Arriving in the area designated for parking, we were stunned at the size of the lot that seemed large enough to handle a packed house at the Pontiac Silverdome for a Lion's NFL game.

We quipped back and forth for a while about the different people that we saw getting out of their cars walking into the hall. Next to us a couple got out, both smartly attired, and Laura inquired, "Which one is in your class?"

"You little smart ass," I laughed. Reason being is that they both had to be either in their late sixties or early seventies, and obviously were off to one of the wedding receptions or the reunion.

"Actually, he is," I added. "Wonder what your mom would have thought if she would have walked in and saw you on your knees in front of him?"

"Funny," she responded, and I got out to get the door for her.

I don't know if it was all of the concern over the impending confrontation with her mom, or the worry I had that her dad was in the know about what had happened, but I never really noticed how stunning my date for the evening was. Even more than usual, Laura was lovely and impeccably attired. Her dress was strapless and off the shoulder, pearl in color, with tiny pale colored roses accenting, and the more I looked at her, the more entranced I seemed to become.

When she turned to exit the car, she led with her slightly postured right foot that was adorned perfectly with a soft color-matching heel that picked up some of the accents of her dress. And even her glow somehow made my joke of a car actually carriage-like.

I offered my hand and really felt privileged that she was going to be on my arm this evening.

Before I closed the door, she said to me, "That white bag in the back seat."

"Oh … I almost forgot. Thanks for reminding me."

If she thought it was for her, I was sorry to disappoint her, but this was for another lady in my life. I grabbed it and then closed the door.

As we started walking toward the facility, we notice this huge all in one mobile home being driven into the lot. "Holy shit, can you believe the size of that?" I said.

We just laughed and I added; "Now that's what you call an optimist!"

"What do you mean?"

"Well it's one thing to pick up a girl for the prom or a date and have certain intentions, but my man even brought the hotel room with him."

"Hey, Moosie," was yelled from across the way. It was Hodgie, arm and arm with his date for the evening, diminutive Kelly Pixter, the sophomore who he slipped the Exlax Mickey to during the All Stars competition.

When they caught up to us, he gave Laura a little peck on the cheek and said, "What gives with the mobile home?"

I just shrugged my shoulders and remained silent.

"How's your father doing, Alvin?" Laura inquired.

With a smile he said, "Ah, he's doing better, thanks for asking. In fact, Moosie, I think he wants to do the ponies next week … you in?"

I followed with a thumbs up!

"By the way, Laura, you look great," he said.

"Why thanks for noticing," she sarcastically said in my direction.

"Didn't I mention that you looked great?" I asked.

"You haven't said a thing!"

"Moosie ... shame on you," Al toyed.

"I'm sorry, I forgot!"

But they were right, I was so preoccupied with my return to the scene of the crime, that I totally omitted any complements that were due Laura, who again, really did look incredible.

"I thought you were bringing Rose's Cougar."

I just furrowed my brow and said, "Naw, decided to go with the limo." Which brought laughs from everybody.

"Kelly, you look quite fetching tonight," I remarked.

"Fetching, what's that supposed to mean?" she blasted. "Are you saying that I look like a dog?"

"Whoa...whoa ... wait a minute," I pleaded while I raised my hands in defense.

"It was meant as a compliment," Hodgie argued.

Just then, the driver of the Holiday Inn mobile opened his door, and who walks out, none other that Polish exchange student, Yahdic Stempedich. A blond, fair-haired fella, rather smallish in stature, I'd say somewhere around 5'5" ... maybe 5'6", who was dressed in a powdered blue tux with tails, with a corresponding frilled shirt and all perfectly accented with a matching Abe Lincoln styled, color coordinated top hat and a walking stick. He looked like he should have been in a chorus line instead of stepping out of that movable suite.

As debonair as one can be in a get-up like that, he strolled around to open the door for his heroine, to which we were all awaiting the identity of. Who could this fair maiden be? Cinderella, Snow White, or maybe even some damsel in distress that he rescued?

The door opened, and despite her best efforts to appear graceful, the decent from the passengers seat to ground should have required a pick and a mountain climber's rope to come down from. Due to the darkened tinting of windows and the time of day that it was we still couldn't get a line on who this young lady was.

We'd see a heeled foot or a little calf, but then it would disappear again out of sight. Then she must have repositioned and tried to back herself down off of the vehicle's running boards or something, but again, the drop must have seemed too intimidating. If she was from the storybook world, it looked like she could have used a hand from either needed Romeo's ladder or Rapunzel's hair.

Now please understand that if Del, J.J., Roger or Adam would have pulled up in something like this, there would have been some sort of symmetry to it. You'd expect something like that from those deviants, but Yahdic, no way … in fact, we never even seen him drive a car, let alone this fucking bus.

Yahdic was now actually standing at the bottom of the opened door, like a firefighter, with his arms extended upward, trying to encourage a cat to take a leap of faith.

"Hey, Al, wouldn't you just shit yourself if it were Shelley," I said. I thought he was going to fall over splitting a gut.

Finally, as if you were watching the rewinding of a video of a jockey being assisted onto his mount, the mystery date was about to have her identity revealed. It was a struggle, and you saw his knees buckle, but she seemed to avoid tumbling to the ground or worse yet, falling prey to the dreaded run in her nylons.

From the opposite side of the door you could see her straightening out her dress and trying to compose herself. It even looked as if she was pushing him away, despite his genuine efforts to help her tidy up after the landing.

The door was now about to close and the true identity revealed.

Towering over him, Yahdic's date for the evening was Marcia, the true hero of the storm incident in the Bob-lo sky needle.

The sight of them together was indeed comical at first; seeing that she did, in fact, stand at least a head taller than her date, compounded by their chariot and the dismounting act.

But I can't tell you how good it made me feel to see her have a chance to attend this function. She wasn't the most graceful thing in the world, and would probably not end up on anybody's top ten list of good lookers, but in my eyes, she had a radiance unto herself, and tonight, she was a welcomed sight.

The four of us turned and entered the facility's main entrance, mesmerized by the majesty and stunning beauty of this extraordinary palace!

"Oh my God, baby, this place is beautiful," Laura said.

"Yeah, lovie, this place is a real keeper," Al said as his eyes gazed toward the peeks of the vaulted and impeccably detailed ceiling.

"Wouldn't this be a great place to have a wedding reception?" Laura remarked while squeezing my hand.

"In about ten years," I replied, which garnered me a glint and furrowed brow from her.

Between the gold and silver trimmed walls, the high glossed Mediterranean marble floors, the fountains, chandeliers and the presidential red carpet that adorned the staircase, the foyer alone made this an awe inspiring experience.

A hostess greeted us in the lobby and indicated that our room was to the far right. As we approached the doorway, it was wonderfully trimmed in our blue and gold school colors, with a white runner paving the way for us into what promised to be a fairytale type of an evening.

Through the doorway, the host room was perfectly ornamented and the lights dimmed to the ideal level. Glenn Miller's "In the Mood" was being piped in through the facilities sound system, the many aromas were enticing and there was actually electricity in the air.

Very few of the throng that were going to pass through this entrance had ever been exposed to this type of refinement.

To the right was a fifteen-foot long bar stocked full of everything … except alcohol. To the rear of the room was the dance floor and stage, where the band was beginning to set up. Each round table featured fitted linens, attractive place settings, and a centerpiece … the room had an air of majesty to it!

Like any formal occasion there was a reception line, and at the head of it was simply the only person who to deserved to be in that position … Loyola.

"Sister Mary Loyola, it is my pleasure to introduce you to my girlfriend, Laura." And as I looked into the aging nuns smiling eyes, I continued.

"Laura, it is my pleasure to introduce you to our Prin … no wait, to my…my…my buddy … my pal … my dear friend … Sister Mary Loyola."

"I feel like I already know you, he has told me so much about you," Laura said as she extended her arms to embrace the nun.

"Welcome, my dear," Loyola responded. Then she pulled Laura closer and whispered something to her that just made my beautiful date smile from ear to ear.

I decided to get in on the action and give the Principal a squeeze of my own.

"You know I love ya, don't you?" I said.

She just smiled back at me.

"Here, being that this is more of a formal occasion, I thought I'd go a bit above a jelly," then I handed her the white bag that Laura noticed was in the back seat. Earlier, I had stopped at her favorite bakery and picked her up a couple of Napoleons for dessert. She then pulled me close and said, "She's absolutely a lovely girl!"

"I know," and I wanted to say "That she gave great head jobs too," but I just decided to wink at my dearest Loyola and move on down the line.

Following the principal, were Sisters Erasmus, Loraine, Patricia, Anastasia and Ann Marie. Also in the line was Father John and good ole Felix too. Following the priests were representatives from the parish council, and the lay teachers: Gainer, Sheddow, health teacher Ron Kelly and Coach Lynch and his wife, Ingrid. Why she was in the reception line sure beat the shit out of me, but now was not the time or the place.

The line was then completed by the senior elected officials, which included President Billy Bednarik, Shelley the VP, and the Kinovich twins

I must admit I was interested to see how Laura was going to be received by a few of these trouble makers in line, namely Gainer, Big Red and Shelley.

I got hung up in the line talking to some of these so-called dignitaries and had noticed that Laura was getting a bit ahead of me and into dangerous territory, despite the fact that she seemed to be working the line like a debutante.

As she was getting closer to Gainer, I kind of blew by the parish reps and the priests to re-join her, just as she was about to meet the bisexual blonde instructor.

To be quite honest with you, I started to fantasize that a hand shake would lead to a prolonged holding of the hands, while the two would gaze into one another's eyes, smile and exchange some sort of womanly ESP hint to meet in the powder room at some time during the evening for a stolen kiss, and a plan on how to make me their object of affection.

But when I regained my focus, I got a fright as she was about to shake hands with Sheddow.

"Hey," I rushed in. "See you've met Ms. Pickasshole," an artsy slap and tie into the great Pablo, mocking the remote connection between her profession and her affection for the famed impressionist.

Then I grabbed Laura and rushed her away from the human plague, fearing that something from Red would have rubbed off onto her.

We worked our way down to the class officials, and were about to be greeted by Billy. He extended his hand and said, "Hi, you must be Laura?"

To which she smiled and said, "yes."

"Bill Bednarik, Class President. Mark's sure told us a lot about you, and it nice to finally to put a face together with all of the publicity!"

This made her beam, as she looked back at me as if to say, "Wow, you must really like me?"

"Yes, heeee hassss," emanated from the slithering gutter slut to his right.

"Laura, let me introdooo …" and before Billy could get in another syllable, Shelley stuck out her hand and said, "Shelley. Shelley Hench, class Vice President, Captain of the cheerleaders and verrry, verrry close friend of …"

All of a sudden from behind, Del appears squeezes in between us and puts one arm around me and the other around Laura, and cuts off Shelley by saying, "Yeah, yeah, yeah … friends of pimps, dykes and anybody with a fuckin' bed between here and Toledo."

"Fuck you, Del," Shelley lashed out while giving him the bird.

"See, what a dedicated performer," he responded, "she's already working the room."

Unable to resist riding on Del's ribbing coattails, I added, "Actually, Shelley and I were very close … very, very close until … you know, Sheeel."

And with a retracting look on her face, I said, "Until the better woman won. And oh, by the way," I said as I leaned back and looked into Gainer's direction, "Your date is sure looking good tonight."

And with that I pulled Laura out of the reception line and led her to our assigned table.

"Anything you want to tell me?" she said.

"Yeah. Welcome to the dark side! Honey, she's a bitch and tonight you're a target, so be careful."

We continued toward our table, when all of a sudden, I received a tug on my left shoulder, it was Billy. "Hey, Mark, before you go tonight, I need to talk to ya … OK?"

"Sure, Bill, everything okay?"

He gestured yes, but there was obviously something amiss.

We arrived at table six to find Hedwig's resident basketball nut, Joey Ochuba, sitting there with date, Annie Vita, who had hounded me to take her months before the prom was to take place.

I liked Annie, who was a natural double for the heroine of the Underdog cartoon series, "Sweet Poly Purebred." She was cute, and had these lips that poutiness and botox injections couldn't even come close to rendering!

But I really don't think that I could have kept up with her sexual needs or what motivated her. Annie always seemed to be on go when it came to sex, and according to Del and Adam, she was willing to drop to her knees for a cold beer!

She also was *always* flirting and that *always* seemed to be followed up with a poke or a prod in a region meant to tickle, but close enough to the cock to gain your attention. If this girl performed these little gestures of fun and to gain one's interest fifteen years later, she would have had a laundry list of harassment suits to deal with.

On the other hand, she may have actually met her match in Joey, who even before I knew what the psychotherapy definition of a type A person was, I had experienced in him.

He was always jumping around and fidgety. Plus, everything that came out of his mouth or that he was involved with had to deal with the game of basketball. When he came to school, he had his books and classroom things in a backpack, while he dribbled a basketball. At lunch, he'd be reading something about the game while balancing his sandwich on his ball.

I even saw a teacher resort to comparing the Celtic/Laker rivalry, to the ongoing struggles in the Middle East, just to get him to understand what the situation entailed and the degree of its importance.

And though I grew up in a multi-cultural neighborhood and had many Blacks as friends, I had never experienced or noticed the effects of one culture's traits or influences on another, acted out with purposed or adapted as second nature, the way he literally became Black.

Joey had mastered certain flamboyant Black playground tendencies and traits in his jive talking sentence structures and the way he expressed himself, that even the Blacks in the school would question him about it. But he had the charm of a little boy, was harmless and really pure of heart.

Also at the table was Tina Gregory, my longtime classmate, who as the story has it, hooked up with Del at the eleventh hour. While most of the girls at the event were dressed in formal, schoolgirl eveningwear, Tina, who looked as if she were ten years out of high school, was in this incredible, black, clingy, spaghetti-strap thing, whose hemline was barely above the crack of her ass. To this day, I think she actually forgot to put on her dress and just came in her slip.

I always liked Tina, but she kind of scared me. First, because of her appearance … she always looked out of place. She looked like she should have been night clubbing while most of us should have been still at the malt shop. Her reputation was dragged through the mud, and there were rumors that included everything from prostitution to her need for an abortion.

I know that she had been into drugs, and not just token on some joints, she was doing a lot of hard shit. It was with confidence that I knew that after twelve years of school with her, that this was going to be one of the last nights that we were going to be together.

I always hoped that she would find her place.

But, if there was one guy that would be able to fit the bill as her escort that night, Del was the guy! In fact, it was even money that Tina and the A man would be trading bodily fluids by sunrise.

Couple number three was Al and Kelly, and they actually made a very cute pair. The only thing that I could tell you about Kelly was that I wondered if she ever knew that Al was responsible for giving her the laxative prior to her All Stars' running event. The little prick never answered that question for me and made it a habit of not incriminating himself. But, considering the situation with Koobs and all that he was dealing within relation to that, Al was happy, and that's all I really cared about!

The table was rounded out by the evening's most interesting couple, senior Cal Visorich and his date … someone older.

Simply speaking, Cal was an incredible physical specimen. He never played any athletics and as far as I could tell, never picked up a ball or a helmet … nothing! But, if you were to line Cal up against anybody in the school, this guy looked like a perfectly engineered champion thoroughbred.

Reason being, he was a martial arts freak. The guy lived and breathed anything to do with multiple disciplines of the Asian art forms. He worked the weights and could often be found in meditation. And while we were throwing down Big Macs, fries and a shake, Cal was countering with grilled chicken, fish, carrot sticks and maybe fruit juice or something like that.

He was a Polish Adonis, thirsting to be in the land of the rising sun. And though the coaches were killing themselves to convince him to play conventional sports with Hedwig's, Cal had no interest whatsoever.

Nobody fucked with Cal, because nobody wanted his ass Kung Fu'd to death. But, like most who trained and adhered to the martial arts, Cal was not aggressive, but rather passive. In fact, I had seen him use his abilities and reputation to actually diffuse trouble; and could honestly say that he was quite the gentleman.

His mane was platinum blond, and I would have hated to have been the tailor that had to prepare his tux, because everything had to be taken out to accommodate his impressive physique.

I went around the table introducing Laura to all, and purposely came to Cal and his date last. She was a dark haired attractive woman, who made Tina even look young. In fact, while most seemed to be sipping on punch or pop from the bar, this one was enjoying something poured from a flask and was puffing on a Newport.

"Cal, this is my girl, Laura, hon … this is Cal."

The gentleman that he was, Cal was the only guy that rose to his feet to greet her and extended his hand.

"Hi, nice to meet you," he said. "This is Angela…Angela Kinney."

"Pleasure," I said. "What did he say your last name was?" I asked as I ducked in to hear.

"Kinney," she said adamantly, "K I N N E Y, ya'll got it?"

And I backed off with a furrowed brow. We had a Kinney who was in school with us. A pretty cute looking … dark haired ……. .sophomore ………….. named …………….. *oh my fucking God; she couldn't have been ... Francine Kinney's mother! Nawww!*

I glanced with a stunned look on my face over at Del, who had this tight-lipped grin on his face, as he just nodded his head, "Uh huh, you got it, I got, but nobody else got it!"

To keep things moving forward, Del looked over at Laura and said, "So, how did a good looking thing like you end up with a bum like him?"

"Bum," she responded as she looked over at me with a half grin, half frown on her face. "You know, maybe you're right, I think he is a bum … but, I'll keep him," she said as she gave my knee a squeeze from under the table.

That brought out courteous laughter from all at the table, and a comment from Tina. "I've known him practically all my life, and he may be a lot of things, but he ain't no bum. So if you're gonna hold on, use both hands." To which Laura just nodded with an attentive look.

Small talk prevailed for a while, until Del asked Tina if she wanted a little something stiffer to drink. For that matter we all wanted something with a little more of jolt to it, except for Cal, of course. And though his date was packing her own wallop, she wasn't offering anything to the table.

So Del summoned Al and me over to the bar area where we got glasses and mixes for all. After delivering them to the table, he asked both of us to join him outside to assist in smuggling in some hooch.

When we got outside he looked at me and said, "So, what do you think about shit-hole's rap on Billy?"

I just shrugged my shoulders and said, "What gives? He asked to speak with me before I left tonight, but I'm in the dark here."

Del proceeded to tell us that when the planning committee finished selling the advanced tickets for the prom, they turned the money over to fat ass to pay for the hall rental, food and band. "Well," Del added, "six hundred is fucking missing."

"What!"

"Yeah, and that motherfuckin' bitch told Loyola that it was all in fucking cash and that Billy was the one who deposited it."

"Well, not that I'm gonna take the side of that bitch, but …"

"Don't even start with it, Moose. You know that Bill would never scam like that," Del admonished.

Sheddow was the teacher/advocate who was in charge of student affairs and special events financing.

Del continued, "Now she's threatening to bring fucking charges against him, because when they counted the money together before taking it to the fucking bank, she filled out the fucking deposit slip and then got called away for something. When she got back, they packed up the money, then he had to run and do something and when he got back, she handed it off to him to make the deposit.

"Long story short, the bank called and said that the slip was off and that the amount would be adjusted."

"Oh fuck," Hodgie exclaimed.

"Hey," I added, "we all know Billy, and can vouch that he'd never do anything like that!"

"Fucking thing is," Del followed, "if she goes through with the larceny charges, you can kiss fucking Notre Dame good-bye."

Billy was an exceptional academic wiz, and earned a full ride to South Bend. Hedwig's first ever to study at the golden dome.

"Son of a bitch," Al remarked.

"Well we can't let her get away with taking the money and screwing his life up like that," Del issued.

"Could she have?" I posed to the other two, inquiring if Sheddow stole the money.

"Listen," Al said, "the way we fucked with her this year, maybe it's a way of getting back at all us?"

"Then do something to us … all of us … not just him," I suggested.

"So what are we going to do?" Del asked.

"What about a collection? Ten bucks from each class member should do it," Al said.

"Supposedly, the money's not the issue." Del continued, "she's had it with all of our shit and she's going through with this fucking thing."

I countered, "No, the money is the issue. If it didn't go bye-bye, then there wouldn't be any fucking problems. Return it, and the issue should go away … right?"

335

"Anyone talk to the prin?" Al asked.

"Yeah, Shelley told me that Loyola said that her hands are fucking tied, and even though she talked to that fat fuck, it's up to Red and she's basically going for his fucking balls," Del responded. "Besides, the bank's involved too."

"The bank," I excitedly inquired.

"Yeah, he was the one who took the fucking sealed envelope to the bank and dropped it into the night depository," Del said.

"Sealed envelope," I exclaimed. "Did you say sealed?"

"Yeah, that's what fucking Shelley told me. When the bank caught the error, they called fat ass, and that's when she went off on a nut."

"Hey, wait a minute," I surmised. "They both count the funds, she leaves, then comes back and they pack up the money together. Then he leaves and she makes out the deposit slip, seals it in an envelope and hands it off to him to deposit, without him knowing the true contents of the fucking envelope ... come on, she fucking did it!"

"Anybody else help them count the money?" Al asked.

"Shelley said that she was there for a while, but left way before they were done," Del informed. "Plus, here's the kicker, Loyola called his fucking parents to let them know, and though his folks believe him, they're offering to pay back the money just to keep this from turning into something that could cost him that fucking scholarship.

"But, that fucking redheaded cunt refuses to talk to them. On the flip side, Billy said 'no way' to his parents when they offered to pay back the money to Loyola, because that would make him look guilty of something that he didn't fucking do."

"Well then," I said, "sounds to me that somebody's trying to set one of our own up. Who else knows?"

Del proceeded to indicate that Shelley, the twins, Loyola, Billy's parents, and that he just told Adam before laying the bomb on Al and me. He didn't know how widespread it was through the faculty, but he offered suggestions.

"Anybody let J.J. know?" I asked.

"Nope," Del said.

"Better let him in on it, we'll need his sneaky fucking ideas on what to do," I commented. "But that's it, don't let nobody else know ... at least not yet. Especially Frost or the fucking Gracies ... it wouldn't take much to set those assholes off."

We grabbed the flasks he prepared and then went back into the hall for more of the evening's festivities.

When we got back to the door, we were greeted by who else than Big Red herself.

"I was about to turn the lock on you degenerates," she quipped.

"And fuck us out of our dinners, like you're gonna fuck my man, Billy?"

"Watch your mouth, Arroundo, I'm not some tramp that you're trying to pick up!"

"You're right, my tramps are way above your standards, porky," and the three of us walked away from her toward the table.

I was detoured however. Getting waved over by the Principal, she summoned me to her side.

"Where were you three?"

"Out for a breath of fresh air."

She paused for a moment and seemed to think while her mouth puffed up as if she was licking her own teeth with her lips cinched shut. "Let me tell you something, avoid the Bednarik matter or you'll end up in trouble too."

"Bednarik matter, Sister?"

"Okay, have it your way" she said, "but I warned you," and off I went.

When I got back to my seat, I turned to Laura and said, "Sorry, but now I'm all yours!"

She responded, "Mark, what's going on?"

"Ahhh, it's nothing," and they started to serve dinner to our table.

Actually, the spread was quite plentiful and good. Served family-style, there were two entrees, roast beef and chicken. The accompaniments were red-skinned potatoes, green beans, a pasta dish and salad.

While we enjoyed the meal, I stole a glimpse over at Billy and his girl, a long-timer who he had been with, at least, since sophomore year, she attended St. Andrews. It wasn't the happiest of settings and the two of them just seemed to be going through the motions.

"You know, I gotta be honest with all of ya, I thought that this was going to be a big bust," I said, "but the hall, the way it's decorated and the food have all been first rate!"

"Dig it, Moosie, my man," Joey said, "You takin' it to da rack wid dat chit, baby!"

I just smiled back at him and winked.

Just then the aforementioned Francine Kinney came up to the table, next to her mother and without any reservations said, "Hey, Mom, can I bum a cigarette from you?"

Laura, upon hearing that, practically choked on her current mouthful, and even spit some out on my lap and pant leg. Joey's eyes almost fell out of his head, and Annie Vita knocked over her drink, as she looked stunned when she heard what we all did.

Laura looked into my eyes, and said, "Oh, I'm sorry, baby ..." then while trying to clean me off she whispered to me, "Did she say Mom?"

I just nodded yes, and whispered, "I told you ... the dark side." I then backed away from the table and said, "I better go clean myself off."

My heading to the bathroom seemed to draw a contingent of other fellas as if they were all coming back to the huddle after a poorly executed football play.

When we got there Al said, "Holy shit, Moose, Francine's mother and Cal?"

"I know," I laughed, "can you believe it?"

Just then Del walked in laughing his ass off. "Did you see Joey; I thought his fucking eyes were going to pop out of his head."

Al followed, "Are you sure he didn't shit himself?" and with that we all laughed like crazy.

Suddenly, Billy walked in ... "Hey, fellas," he said. Then he turned to me and said, "Can I have that minute with you now?"

"Yeah, man, let's go outside."

"Hey, Bill, we all know, and we're with you, man ... don't worry," Del said.

I just shook my head in agreement and followed, "But, Billy, be honest with us ... did you?"

With tears in his eyes, he sternly shook his head "No!"

Del then asked, "What's the latest?"

Sniffling, he said, "She went to the police last night and while I was out running around doing things today, a detective came over and talked to my parents. I gotta go in and see them Monday afternoon," he said as he started to cry even harder.

"Billy, it's only six hundred bucks," Al said while rubbing his shoulder.

"No, Alvin, you don't know. They told my dad that they were going to book me for larceny, embezzlement and theft."

"Bull shit," Del rifled, "we gonna get that fat fuck."

"Easy ... everybody just take it easy," I said. "Bill, you're our class president, pull yourself together and know that everybody's behind you. We know she did it and we got some pretty good ideas on how were going to take care of this ... so enough tears. Don't worry, we're gonna get tons-o-fun."

Then I turned and looked into the mirror and said, "If I don't get my ass out there and dance with that blonde that I brought, I'm the one who's going to be in deep shit … so let's go have some fun!"

Over in the corner, I saw Hodgie just laughing to himself. I shrugged my shoulders and said, "What?"

"Her fucking mother," and he just shook his head and dried off his freshly washed hands.

Dinner plates were being removed and dessert was about ready to be served.

"Hi," I said to Laura.

"Can I ask you a question?"

"Sure, baby."

"Am I your date, or are the three of us (referring to Tina, Kelly and herself), just fronts for the fact that the three of you are queers?"

"Huh?" I responded.

"Mark, you've hardly been around! And not only do I know who the Pistons draft pick is this year, but I know that he's really gonna take it to the hole or something like that, because Joey's the only one who seems to be taking an interest in me tonight. Now either stay or I will have Debbie come pick me up!"

"You're right … I'm so sorry, but I had to take care of something. I promise, the rest of the night is yours," and I raised my right hand as if I was taking an oath.

Then I saw her look over my shoulder, and get this odd look on her face. She just pointed and I turned to see six scruffy looking guys that were dressed in back jeans, big black ass shit kickin' boots, who were bare chested and donning open black leather vests.

What the fuck I thought, as I started to back my way toward Cal. I didn't know if we were about to be taken hostage or if the Hell's Angel's decided to slide by for dessert?

This gang made their way toward the stage and began picking up their instruments.

This was the age of "Saturday Night Fever," and these guys weren't the Bee Gee's or KC and the Sunshine Band. And though we were all into a good rock and roll band, these guys looked like nothing that we had ever seen before.

One of the members walked up to Sheddow, whispered something into her ear and they hugged before he made his way the rest of the way to the stage.

"What the fuck's this," I said to Del, while motioning over to Sheddow and this guy embracing.

He couldn't have been her boyfriend, because the heifer actually had brought a date. So then, who was this?

When the last guy got to the stage, the entire room went dark. I grabbed Laura's shoulder to let her know that I was there.

" Y Y Y Y Y E E E E E A A A A A H H H H H bbbbbbaaaaaaabbbbbbyyyyyyyyyyyyyy," was screamed and amplified. "Saint Henry's are you ready for a bitchin' party!"

"St. Henry's," Tina said.

All of a sudden, their downbeat blasted and reverberated through the room as if a bomb went off. It was followed by what could only be described as an excruciating, irritating and deafening set of sounds. We were teenagers and used to all of the latest groups and recording stars, but this was nothing that we could recognize. We were in the midst of a hair raising, acid rock rehearsal at best, when we were expecting jump to your feet dance music.

We were actually standing as far away as we possibly could from the band, and we still had to yell at the top of our lungs to a person standing next to us, just to be heard.

From the indistinguishable lyrics to the migraine producing accompaniment, this was a fucking nightmare and the only thing that I could think of was Felix running through the hall screaming, "devil...d e v i l...D E V I L!!!"

Two questions immediately came to mind, 1) who were these assholes, and 2) who were the fucking idiots who booked them?

After seven and a half minutes of musical penance, the punishment finally came to a stop. Out of the entire hall, only two people were clapping for this shit, Joey, who was admonished almost immediately by a number of people, and Sheddow, who was cheering as if she had just hit the lottery.

"What in the good fuck is she cheering about?" asked Del.

A number of us seemed to be wondering the same thing before Del took the initiative to do what the rest of us didn't have the nerve to. He screamed at the top of his lungs, "Take a break!" Which not only brought out laughter, but also brought over a flaming mad redhead in the form of Sheddow.

"Quiet, Arroundo, not another word from you," she commanded.

"Hey ... lay off, Valerie, they suck," I said.

"They're terrific! You little smart asses wouldn't know talent if it fell out of the sky and hit you in the head."

"Just like this musical egg that those assholes are laying," Al added.

"For Christ's sake," I said, "they greeted us as St. Henry's, and did you get a final count on how many people got up to dance? … doughnut, kiddo … a big fat zero!"

You could see that she was getting flustered with this barrage, when out of the blue, Cal spoke up and fired the most decisive shot yet, "Sheddow, why are you defending these guys so much?"

She just shook her head and turned to walk away.

She was emphatic about backing these so-called musicians, and it had become very apparent that with the earlier hug and her adamant support, there was more here than met the eye.

In fact, it was becoming increasingly disturbing as the night went on, how Sheddow's shadow was casting a dim light over this event.

I motioned to Laura to sit tight as the band went into another rage, grabbed Al and Del, and asked them to pull J.J. and Adam aside and to meet me in the foyer. Then I went over to the President's table and summoned Billy, Shelley and the Kinovichs to join us out of the line of fire, and in the diminishing solitude of the lobby.

In somewhat of a place of refuge, nine of us stood out there, still in need of earplugs or something to drown out the shit that was filtering out of our hall. But the problem was only beginning, as other events were starting to complain about the overpowering sounds that were interfering with their galas.

"Billy, what I the hell is going on in there?" Adam asked.

The twins followed with an "Oh my God, this is horrible!"

Inundated with one question after another, our beleaguered president said, "Okay … I hear ya … enough! It's Sheddow's brother's band. She insisted that they could play everything."

"At the same time," J.J. interjected.

Approaching our little huddle was somebody in the Center's management, and Laurie snuck away to summoned Loyola to help.

"Billy, they gotta stop," I issued.

"Yeah, I know."

Then J.J. asked those officers who were present, "How much did we pay these assholes?"

"Twelve hundred," Shelley said.

"What," Hodgie whaled, "are you kidding me?"

Del followed up with, "I just want to know, did any of you listen to these fuckin' guys before giving them this gig?"

Red faces gave way to embarrassed facial denials.

When Loyola got out to the grouping, she raised her hands as if to say, "This is not good!"

"You people are going to have to do something about this, or they're going to kick us out!"

Then the ultimatum came. It was a middle-aged gentleman representing the facility. "Are you the organizers of this party?"

Billy responded "Yes."

"I giving you fair notice, that if you don't immediately lower the volume of your music, I will be notifying the authorities. The other events are complaining about the excessiveness and it will not be tolerated."

"We'll be taking care of it immediately," Billy said.

"Please do," and with that the man walked back to interested members of the other events, I'm sure to inform them that actions were being taken.

When we got back into the room, the band had just finished with the second song of their opening set, and there again Sheddow was leading her own little cheering section ... of herself. Not even her date was applauding for these hacks.

"Hey, man, doesn't anybody in this school dance," questioned one of the band members over the microphone.

To which J.J. responded, "Doesn't anybody in your band play?"

"Joel, you hush," warned Loyola.

"But, Sister," he pleaded.

"Not another word," she issued.

"That's right, quiet, Lambert," Sheddow said.

"No, you take a step back, Ms. Sheddow," the Principal implored.

"Hey, Sheddow, Is this really your brother's band?" I threw out.

"That's none of your business," she lamented. "They're good and none of you seem to know it!"

"Yeah, it is my business, and, in fact, it's all of our business," I countered.

"You're not part of the planning committee," she barked back at me.

"Yeah, you're right, but they are," I said as I pointed to the class officials, "and together, it's my understanding that we have twelve hundred reasons to question you and them."

Just then the band went into another tune, but somebody in the building management's employment bypassed the band's sound system and had greatly reduced their volume.

Noticing the change, Sheddow turned around and said, "Hey, what happened to the sound?"

"They stink, and everybody's complaining about them," Billy said as he closed in on her and adamantly got into her face!

"Oh, I know what this all about," she responded as she took a step back and addressed us all.

"We all do, fat ass," Del fired back.

"Arroundo," Loyola yelled. "Enough of this language and tone, not another word!"

"That's okay, if you think that this is going to change my mind, you're wrong. He took the money and now you're trying to embarrass me, my brother, and his band! He's going to pay, and if you little boys and girls want to join in, I'll take care of the rest of you as well."

"Did you just threaten us shit-hole?" came from a voice that was anything but masculine.

Shelley stepped forward and gave the redheaded teacher the dirtiest of looks.

"I know about your attitude toward these guys. Opinions are one thing, threats are another. These are my friends, and if you threaten them, you're threatening me," the diminutive harlot belted out.

Then she walked back to her table to be with her date.

Coach Lynch, some of the elders, big Mike Whiting and even Cal got involved to break things up and to allow cooler heads to prevail.

When I got back to the table, Laura said to me, "This is becoming a nightmare."

"Don't worry," I answered, "let's just try to enjoy." After another undancable tune, the band finally took a break … leaving the hall, and being accompanied by Sheddow and her escort for the evening.

When it was apparent that they had left, J.J., who had earlier, ran to his car to retrieve some cassettes, popped one into the facility's sound system. It was the popular soundtrack from *Saturday Night Fever*, and with a mad rush, the dance floor filled up with the music-starved guests, like a hoard of ants attacking an abandoned picnic lunch. It was hilarious to see all of this taking place, once the live entertainment stopped.

There was merriment and finally a party atmosphere, and for about a half hour, we reveled in the popular music of the day! Gradually, I became aware of the fact that shortly, I would no longer be seeing many of these people who over the past four years, I shared with, and quite honestly, probably took for granted.

The sad thing was that many of them, I blew off as fillers in my life who just happened to be coasting along in my world, and now I started to realize how wonderful most of them really were. They added to my comfort zone and were my equals, though often they were not given the respect from me that they deserved. And now they were about to become categorized as yearbook window dressing in the form of, "oh yeah" I remember that person ... wonder whatever happened to them?"

The disturbing thing was that for a small school like Hedwig's, my heir of snobbish behavior and isolation just didn't belong. Which made me wonder, *What kind of a fucking person was I?*

Why didn't I get to know more of these people intimately, and not in the carnal sense, but rather to know what they liked, or wanted or expected out of life?

Instead, I just kept putting everything else on hold, figuring that tomorrow was a long way away, suddenly realizing that tomorrow was here.

Oddly, this makeshift disco brought my past, present and future, closer than it had ever been. There were no flashing of life passing me by and no tears, but I couldn't help thinking about Mick ... or about what was happening to Koobs, when Al came into view.

About the rivalries with J.J. and the sexual tension with Shelley and some of the other girls. The witnessing of Marcia's magic and the satirical fear that Frost, Pevia and the Gracies would one day rule the world.

While I danced, I looked to the side of the large room and saw the penguins cloistered, enjoying the sight of all of us dancing and realizing that they had in some small way, prepared yet another group of young adults for the world.

And then there was Loyola, carrying on the spirit of Emolina. She, too, guided, assisted, steered, shielded, reprimanded, mothered and taught all of us. I then visioned, when we're gone, who was going to get them to the grocery store, run them around to do their errands and get their occasional snacks ... who was going to bring doughnuts?

Then I turned and locked eyes with Laura. They were simply inviting; and more perhaps than either one of us knew.

We smiled at each other and I began to drift off in the thought that there would be college and a job and whatever else was headed in my direction, but I just knew that I wanted her to be a part of it all ... for she was my future.

It was a thirty-minute purging of the past, embracing of the present and a hint at what was to come. But more than anything, it was my chance to somehow redeem myself and to take the stand that I needed to take. For

344

though I missed many of the battles that my fellow classmates endured, while I fashioned my own wishes, the one that needed to be resolved before we left, was to make sure that Billy's life was not going to be fucked up by that self-servin' bitch.

As the band returned to the stage, my visions began to dissipate, and the floor emptied.

Even the nuns, who were drawn closer to the activity by the sight of our enjoyment, retreated to the opposite end of the room in anticipation of the band's second set.

When we got back to the table, Laura grabbed her purse, excused herself and went to the power room. This was my greatest concern of the evening. Laura was an outsider and she was headed for a place that I couldn't lend any aid. Yet, I must admit that I was ready to park myself just outside of the woman's room entrance just in case something was to go wrong.

But, J.J. picked me off. "Hey, what are we going to do about this shit with Billy?" he inquired.

Just then, I looked around the room for Big Red, but she was nowhere to be found.

"Hey, man," J.J. fired back in my direction, "you listening to me?"

"Uhhhh ... yeah ... J.J., well ... uhhhh ... you see, it's his word against hers ... and ... uhhhh," I continued looking around the room for her. "Where is the bitch?" I said.

"Hey, man, am I talking to a brick wall here, or are you going to listen to me?"

"I'm sorry, man," I said as I refocused. "Yeah, Billy. That's why I asked the guys to get you involved! I don't know what to do or how to do it ... got any ideas?"

He just drew an exasperated deep breath and said, "No ... fuck ... no!"

"Well think of something, because we only got until Tuesday, and if you do ... call me as soon as possible!"

The senior's final day of classes was Tuesday, with graduation to take place during the following Sunday's ten o'clock mass.

I just went back to my seat, grabbed the concoction that Del had recently made for me and started sipping while I looked over at the forlorn and embattled president.

"Your girlfriend is very pretty."

"Huh," I said as I turned and noticed that it was Cal's date.

Smiling I said, "oh, thanks, Mrs. ... uh, I mean."

"It's Angela ... just Angela," she said. "I noticed that you were a little shocked when my daughter walked up and revealed my identity."

"Actually," I said, then I paused and decided to just smile and to keep my mouth shut.

"You're the baseball star that Francine talks so much about, aren't you?"

"Well," I chuckled, "I don't know about star."

While I looked around the room, she must have scooted a bit closer to me, because my eyebrows raised and I began to get a sensation that I didn't expect to get from her. She had slid her left hand on my right thigh and all indication was that the experienced hand was headed for my Louisville Slugger.

"Uh...ummmm...uh," I fumbled, thinking all along that despite the fact that this was exciting as fuck, Cal was somewhere within the state, and I didn't feel like becoming his prom night sparring partner.

"You know ... you're very handsome," she whispered, and I found myself now looking directly into her seductive eyes and her very persuasive smile. This was more than a compliment of an interested fan.

"You are going back to the hotel after this, aren't you?"

Despite the missing money that was plaguing Billy, the class had budget for adjoining suites at a near by hotel, for an after-hours get-together.

"Uh ... I really don't think we'll be," I mumbled.

Just then she covered my unit with her hand, and I heard Del call, "Moose!"

I jumped out of my seat as if I was launched off of the pad at Cocoa Beach, in the direction of his voice.

He motioned me into the corner and when I got there he roared, "Are you fucking nuts, motherfucker?"

I just shrugged my shoulders and raised my hands.

"Remember that big motherfucker ... Cal?"

"Yeah!"

"Well," he said.

I must have broke into a little sweat, because he dabbed my brow with a napkin, as I said, "It wasn't me!"

"Yeah, I know," he said. "Just stay away from her ... she's trouble. And besides, he said already with a good buzz working, she's really not that good of a fuck."

I just looked back at him in amazement, laughed and gave him a big hug.

Things seemed to be loosening up, even to the point where the band kind

346

of played something that was sort of distinguishable. Thankfully, Laura came back into view and was in one piece, though she had an incredulous look upon her face.

I greeted her with a "What?"

"You're never going to believe what just happened to me," she remarked.

And I almost said the same thing back to her, but decided to keep quiet and pulled her off to the side to avoid Angela. "What gives?" I asked.

"Boy, did I just get an earful. While I was in the bathroom, that redheaded teacher that seems to be the focus of attention approached me."

"What?" I blurted as I felt my blood start to boil.

"She asked me, you're Mark's girlfriend ... aren't you? And when I said yes, she got aggressive with me and said, what's his problem ... and why doesn't he like me?"

I was fuming now and was looking around the room to attack that bitch.

"That's it," I said, "I've had it with that no good cunt!"

I was ready to go off full throttle, when Laura grabbed me and said, "No, babe, not here and not tonight. Don't let her spoil your fun."

I took a deep breath and looked over at Sheddow, just shaking my head and watching her snicker back at me.

For the remainder of the evening, we just mingled and watched and listened to twelve hundred dollars go down the drain and danced when the band took breaks. Thank goodness for Del's libations, for they really were needed to take the edge off of this roller-coaster ride of an event.

It was getting to that time when there was a lot of glad-handing, hugging and parting shots being taken.

Those who I mentioned earlier ... those people, who were for the most part stiffs, had either worked up enough nerve or consumed enough booze to feel free enough to speak their minds.

"You know, Moose, you always thought that your shit didn't stink," Andy Uvalde, a squirmy little asshole, came up and said to me. "But I always knew you were an asshole," he finished up with.

And if it weren't for the fact that his bow tie wasn't being used as a headband, and that his shirt was completely untucked and that his fly was opened, I would have decked him. But I couldn't ... any way the little shit was probably right.

I just patted him on the head and said, "Andy, I'm sorry that I didn't tell you this earlier, but every girl in the senior class wanted you to fuck their brains out ... and now, it's too late. Sorry, bud," and I just moved on.

There were a couple of more like Andy, and every one of them who took a shot at me, received my undivided attention. It was a harsh medicine, and though I probably deserved most of it, those earlier mentioned sincere thoughts seemed to be fleeting away.

Then there was Tina Gregory. She came up to me, and we embraced.

"God, Mark," she said, "I've known you all my life. You always made me feel safe for some reason … and you've always been a friend. What the hell am I going to do without you?"

We began to laugh and there was even a tear or two developing in both of our eyes.

"Me too, sweetie," was about all I could muster.

"Laura seems to be something really special … don't let her go, and … I'll try to keep Del away from her as long as I can," and with that we both burst into laughter and hugged for the last time.

I gave her a kiss on the cheek and we parted for the next bouts of farewells.

Laura was engaged in what seemed to be a pretty good conversation with Al, Adam and their dates when I strolled over to the bar for a breath of fresh air and a little water to clear my head. I was small talking it with one of the bartenders and minding my own business, when next into my view, came Annie Vita.

"Annieeee," I said as I extended my arms to take her in.

Her smile was playful and her eyes were dreamy. There was little doubt, that she, too, was hitting the hooch with a bit of regularity. As I stood leaning against the bar, she mirrored my pose and began to mimic my gestures.

"Markieee."

"You okay, sweetheart," I asked.

"Uhhhh huhhhh," she giggled. Then she followed up with, "Why?"

"Why what, sweets?"

"Why?" she repeated more forcefully.

"Annie, what are you trying to say?" I slowly asked.

"Why … haven't you," and then she hiccupped. "Why haven't you seen how much I've wanted you … didn't you see how much I've wanted you?"

"Sweetie, you flatter me … but you're with," and before I could get another word out, she stopped me saying, "Yeah, yeah, yeah, don't remind me, Mr. Dribble. Probably what his dick's like too."

"Now, now," I said. "Joey's a great guy and you two make a nice couple."

Then she slurred, "And now you're gonna tell me about how great Miss…Miss Wonderful is."

"Huh?" I interjected.

"You know, Miss Perfect over there … the suburban princess."

"Annie," I said in a lingering tone, "that's not fair."

This was a conversation that was not going to end on a happy note and one that I wanted to get out of quick!

"Annie, you know that I've always liked you and always thought you were attractive."

Then she raised her pinky finger on her right hand to the side of her mouth as I continued, "But, for whatever reason, we just never had a chance to make it work."

"Well," she said with a belch, "oh," then she giggled and went on, "better late than never, huh…huh?"

Then she incoherently rambled, "'Cause, think you … know I will … and uhhhmmm … ready to immediately … uhhhmmm … for you to fuck me now!"

I just curled in my bottom lip, looked over at the bartender, who went from washing some glasses, to staring right back at me, with his specs now down around the lower bridge of his nose, with a look that said, "Fella, I know you're trying to be nice, but it's there for the taking!"

"Annie come here," I invited and I extended my arms to give her a hug.

"I know…I know, but I had to try … shit, I had to try." Then she said, "Have a great life you big lug," before she turned and staggered back to the table.

I turned and directly faced the bartender and laughed slowly as I shook my head. "What a night," I said. Thinking that I was finally rid of trouble, I hear another familiar voice say, "Well…well…well Marcus, aren't you the center of attention?"

Now what I thought? I turned to see the icing on my prom cake.

"Miss Gainer, don't you look luscious tonight. Enjoying your evening?"

"Except for the shitty music and the fact that this seems like a night at the wrestling matches … why yes, thank you," she responded beaming that incredible smile.

"Excuse me," I answered playfully, "but did you just say shitty? Did you, my always precise, my always well-dressed and my always hot looking English Comp Teacher … just use shit in a sentence?"

She just responded with a guttural laugh and said, "Cute … very cute." Then she continued, "What are you … seventeen?"

To which I nodded "… about to turn eighteen!"

Pointing to herself, she said, "Twenty-two. You know we've been through quite a lot this year, and you're concerned with a little shit from me," and we both laughed at her comment.

"I guess you're right, Miss Gainer."

She rapidly fired back, "And it's Carol!"

"Okay then, Carol."

"By the way, I know that you were behind a lot of the things that happened this year, both good and bad, but I could never bring myself to confront you."

I just looked backed at her and smiled.

Then she continued, "You see, there are sneaky fucks who are finks, like that one," she commented while pointing at J.J., "and that rat over there," and she was about to raise the bar, because she was now pointing at Sheddow, someone that she was considered to be in cahoots with throughout the year. I was all ears, and probably easily led astray by this one, but suddenly I drew concerned at her unexpected openness.

"Yeah ... I said it, she's a rat. Always looking out for herself."

Was she fucking me, or giving me ammunition that I needed to get back at Sheddow and to help Billy out of this mess?

"You," she continued, "you're the one that everyone wants to be like ... the one that everyone wants to see get away with things ... the troublemaker that everybody cheers secretly for."

Laughingly, I said, "Yeah, right."

And without missing a beat, she countered, "The kind of trouble that excites a woman."

I cracked a glint of a smile.

"You know exactly what I mean, don't you?" she urged. "Your smile, your look, and your refusal to even challenge me speaks volumes."

Then she hit me with the most dynamic comment of the night.

"Mark, you have exactly what it takes to get anything out of life that you want." Then she purposely brushed by me as she walked away, pausing enough to give me a gaze that sent oh so many fucking images through my mind.

I went over to Laura, grabbed her hand and said, "What ya think about you and I taking a drive?"

I didn't know if I was indirectly ready to take out on Laura what I wanted to explore with Gainer, or if I just needed to head for higher ground, but I knew that if I didn't take care of that little thing that I was toting around between my legs soon, it might go off by itself!

The one o'clock conclusion of the event was quickly approaching, so we went around the table and said our good-byes and it was obvious that Laura made quite the impression.

Just before leaving the table, Cal grabbed me rather rigorously and pulled me aside.

"Hey, man," he said, "sorry about Angela. Heard she laid some heavy shit on you, and … well … ya know it was the booze, man."

I just shook my head, and listened to him say, "Thanks for handling it the way you did … thanks."

We just shook hands and parted company.

At the door, Loyola smiled at us and said, "You're a lovely couple and I hope that you had a good time."

"We did, Sister, thank you," Laura proclaimed before embracing her.

"Who's taking you back?" I asked.

"The parish council members," she said.

"Well, don't let me hear that you all stopped off at some after-hours place," I issued to her while playfully waving my index finger in her direction.

"Oh you … get out of here," she laughed, and I grabbed her and gave her a big kiss on the cheek.

Out of the corner of my eye, I saw Sheddow and asked Laura to give me a minute. With purpose in my step, I walked up to her and stated, "I'm not going to let you bring Billy down."

She countered by saying, "I told you, he did it to himself."

"Bullshit," I responded, and then walked away for the final time that evening.

While walking through the parking lot, Laura said, "It's gone!"

"What's gone?" I asked.

"The mobile home … it's gone." I just raised my brows and we both laughed. Then she said, "You know, that really wasn't a bad idea."

"What?"

"The mobile home … pretty smart if you ask me."

"You know … you're right," I said, "bet you there's no big ass air-conditioning units and no bi-fold doors in it."

Then she smiled back at me and said, "And no mothers either."

~ sorry, but your call to god has been diverted ~

The next morning my folks let me sleep in until nine, but insisted that I get cleaned up and get to church for the 10:00 A.M. mass. After dropping Laura off and with getting a late night bite to eat, I didn't arrive home until almost three and really didn't hit the pillow until four, so despite the wake-up reprieve, even answering the nine o'clock bell was going to be difficult.

It was a slow motion performance, as everything I did was in low gear. But somehow I managed to get to a pew for the start of mass.

With shades in place, I looked like an unmade bed trying to sit as far in the rear of the church as I possibly could. But this must have been the mass of choice for prom night victims who like me, probably would have opted to sleep the rest of the day, with an embalming fluid chaser.

If you didn't have a scorecard, it wasn't that difficult to tell who the players were. They were the ones who were dressed in something wrinkled, whose hair looked like it was combed with a wet fish and were slumped in their pews.

An interesting side note was to see Marcia being escorted into mass by Yadich, both looking fresh, clean and very happy. The kind of happy that came with either eight good hours of blissful slumber or that other kind of bedtime activity ... which I pondered, *Do ya think?*

Still before mass has even started, there I sat in God's house, when, all of a sudden, an eager Roger Frost raps me on the shoulder and says in a pretty impressive volume for church, "I'm gonna torch that fucking fat bitch's ride," to which I just sunk deeper in my pew and shook my head no, as the others around me looked at us in an admonishing manner.

Thankfully the opening processional music commenced from the choir loft and everybody's attention seemed to refocus on the mass.

For the most part, I just went through the motions, remaining in a slumped position in one of the cathedrals darker corners, until I was abruptly pushed down by big Mike Whiting to make room for him, Del and J.J.

"Wake up, motherfucker," Del said to me.

"Go away," I replied. "I'm praying to God to somehow erase the memory that I ever knew any of you," which just made Arroundo giggle.

"Shut up," he responded, "dickhead has a pretty good idea."

Then he summoned J.J. to practically crawl over all of us to get to my other side.

"Check this out," he whispered; "you know that we all have to go to confession on Tuesday for next Sunday," to which I just nodded. "And when I say everybody, I mean everybody … including the teachers."

"Yeah, so what?"

"Well it's a long shot, but I got this small tape recorded and I know that the Gracies have one too. We're thinking of bugging the confessionals."

"What … are you fucking Nixon?" I lashed out. "You wanna bug the fucking confessions of everybody?"

"He said it was a long shot," Del interceded. "Has anybody else come up with anything? Maybe we'll catch her saying something?"

I just stared and shook my head no.

"And what the fuck," Del laughed, "if nothing else, I'm sure we'll have some juicy shit to talk about round the poker table."

I just shrugged my shoulders and said, "fuck it, why not? What do you need me to do?"

"Nothing! J.J. and the G-twins will take care of everything tomorrow after school," Del whispered, and they got up to split out of mass early.

"But," I issued as I grabbed Del's sleeve, "nobody can know … nobody!"

So after school on Monday, the three of them wired the last known vestiges of assumed trust and confidentially, for an attempt at gaining anything possible against the Big Red machine.

On Tuesday, the morning notices were given over the public address and we were told that we were also supposed to report to church, with our homerooms by ten thirty, which meant that parameters were needed for one of the three break-in artist to get to the church and to activate the devices before the rest of us arrived.

At ten o'clock, we reported back to Sheddow's room in preparation to head over to the church. When we got there, she was in the midst of shuffling some papers and was coming and going, probably to avoid as much contact with us as possible.

"You heard that the cops formally charged Billy last night, right?" Al said to me.

"Yeah ... it's not looking too good, is it?" I replied.

All of a sudden, Sheddow entered the room slamming the door shut in her wake. It was quite the attention getter.

"Listen up," she ordered. "You may be going to confession, but we're going to set the record straight, right here and right now!

"I have put up with your shit all year long. You have disrespected me, belittled me and have tried to humiliate me every chance that you could. The other teachers and I have dealt with your pranks and it's no big surprise that you ruined the career of Sister Ann.

"None of you, and I mean every last one of you could ever be trusted and I hope all of you get what you really deserve out of life. And to do my little part, I gave every one of you who had me for Art, a D minus, just to make your transcripts a little more colorful, because it was the lowest grade that I could give you and still get you the hell out of my life."

The room remained dead silent, until ... Del began to applaud in a sarcastic manner.

"Lovely," he voiced, "just lovely," as we all began to snicker. "Fuck Billy's life up and just for kicks, maybe muddy up someone else's life too, and you're preachin' to us about what we deserve!"

"Quiet, Arroundo," she said, "or I'll turn that into an F."

"I'll tell you what, you can add a $u - c - k$ to that f, and that would be fffffffine with me ... bitch!"

"You got it, loud mouth," she shouted.

"Add me to that list then too," I said, "you have some nerve; protecting Ann, defending spying on us, and linking us to shit in the past that we weren't even behind, and you weren't even here to witness."

"That's enough from you," she shouted at me.

"The hell it is," I fired back. "I want to know why you cornered my girl in the restroom the other night and questioned her about things that you had absolutely no reason to do?"

"That's a lie … seems your girlfriend has the same virtues that you have!" And with that I jumped to my feet and was ready to go after her. Fortunately, Adam and Al restrained me.

Just then, Marie Ricci, a silent and introverted girl who was always either reading or writing something down, astonishingly for one of the few times that I knew her, spoke up.

"Really, Miss Sheddow, that was you who I heard while I was in one of the stalls, attacking Mark's girlfriend. And you're calling her a liar."

The silence was deafening.

"Tell you what, I'll take one of those Fs also, and you can explain to my father why you did it." Then Marie just looked out of the window and started to cry.

"So this is what it's come to," I blurted out. "Leadership by example!"

Sheddow started to speak, but was now quivering in her delivery, "It's all about trust, and none of you … not one single one of you could be trusted."

I began to laugh, "Trust … are you kidding me? Most of us have known each other for at least four years, and probably longer. We've laughed, cried and shared our way through this place and you think that you can just come out of the blue and judge us? We care for this place and we care for the nuns. This is our neighborhood and this is our school!

"You and the rest of these fucking junior Nazis came into this place to cut and slash us down to size, as if we were attempting to take over the world. What did you expect, no resistance when you tried to muscle us around?

"Yeah, we fucked around, but never with the intent to hurt anybody.

"But you…you fucking bitch, you want to bury Billy for something that he couldn't have done and for a measly six hundred dollars yet! Then you blow twelve hundred dollars of our money on that fucking joke of a band that your brother's a part of, and for a farewell present you want to give us all failing grades because we didn't kiss your fat ass!

"Well you reap what you sow … and I'll tell ya what, I'm a little low on Sheddow love and respect.

"So Miss Sheddow, for my last official act as a part of this class, I proclaim that you… can kiss my ass! And remember this, you can fool us, but you can't fool God, so may I suggest, that you clear your conscience," hoping that she would bite on the bait and spill the beans in the confessional.

"Now seeing that I'm gonna get an F anyway," I walked over to Marie, "would you do me the honor," and I extended my hand, motioning her to accompany me to exit the room … arm in arm, to the cheering of our classmates.

That started a mass exodus out of Sheddow's room.

In the hallway, I stopped and turned to Marie and said, "Hey, you just got the big balls award of the day."

And she smiled back at me and said, "I always wondered what that would feel like," and we both laughed as we walked to church.

Funny, here I was moments ago defending practices and defining trust, when in a matter of minutes, I was going to be a part of the most blatant form of distrust, by breaching the sanctity of the confessional.

Now half way to the church, I saw Dickey standing next to his car giving me the high sign that everything was set. The moment of truth, or for that matter a lot of truths was close at hand.

Candles dimly lit the church as the sun's rays protruded through the gothic cathedral's stained glass windows. Some of the community's older parishioners were all ready on hand to receive the sacrament as the church began to fill with the senior student body.

Forgoing sitting with my class, my pre-confessional examining of conscience turned to the thought of *Would we have enough tape to catch what we needed?* I mean, between Frost, Pevia, the Gracies, Del and Shelley, if they were truly compelled to tell all, that alone could have chewed up a couple hours of tape!

I looked over toward the seniors and reflected. *There was a lot of fucking sinners in that bunch!*

The procession of senior confessions commenced and I kind of chuckled to myself, as I thought about some of the possible things that we were going to become privy to. Such as the cleansing of consciences of the likes of Shelley, the Kinovich sisters, Gainer and I was dying to hear what both Marcia and Yadich had to say for themselves in wake of the prom.

Finally, after about a half hour Sheddow entered the *box*. We were hoping for gold, but were kind of afraid that if we did hit the jackpot, how were we going to be able to reveal our source, without incriminating ourselves?" If we thought Billy was in Dutch, we were on the cusp of some big time turmoil.

We just looked at one another and hoped for the best. Sheddow was in seclusion for what seemed to be only a short amount of time, but was hopefully admitting to a windfall of wrongdoing. She finally emerged looking solemn and from my view and a bit teary-eyed.

The plan was for everybody to go about their business and J.J. would come back later and gather up all of the data and equipment.

After confession, a group of us gathered in the parking lot and came to the realization, that *this was it*. There was no ticker tape parade, no fireworks and no formal sendoff. And though Sunday was to be the official graduation ceremony, this was our last day and it concluded pretty much the same way it all started four years earlier, in the parking lot and unsure of what to do next.

I pulled Al aside and asked what he was going to be doing, and he informed me that he was going down to Cobo Arena to pick up some concert tickets to see Mitch Ryder.

"I'm gonna run over and see how your dad is doing," I said, and with that we went in our different directions.

Upon arrival, I walked in unannounced as usual and saw Lottie tending to some kitchen chores.

"Hi, sweetie," I said.

"Hey, Moosie, how's my baby?"

"Good," I answered, "where's Koobs?"

"Sleeping."

"Sleeping?" I questioned.

"Yeah, he gets tired … some days that all he wants to do," she responded with a tear in her eye. "Now come on and sit down, I'll make you something to eat."

"Lottie, tell me something. If you're fighting a losing battle and the odds are against you … and you know that you're not going to win, when should you give up?"

"Never! Mark, how can you say that … you of all people know that you can never give up! And what about my Koobs? You know what he's going through and do you think that he'll ever give up? Now none of that kind of talk from you!"

But I just couldn't help thinking that we were on the verge of getting some bad news, as she put a sandwich and a glass of milk in front of me. I found myself reflecting about everything that had been happening in a place where I had nothing but wonderful times. Yet, I had the worst feeling that the near future was not promising.

I finished my little snack, stretched for a moment and asked if she needed help with anything before splitting for home.

My mom had a full list of errands that she needed to have me do, and what I thought was going to be a simple afternoon, turned into five hours of running all over the fucking place.

I got back home at about twenty minutes after five, to the admonishment of my dad asking, "Where the hell have you been?"

With bags in my hand and a shit load more in the car, I responded, "I was running around for Mom!"

"Well, call Hodgie for Christ's sake! He's already called here three times and he keeps saying that he's got gold for you."

"What!?"

"I don't know, something about gold … what the hell does he mean by that?"

I ran outside to get the rest of the bags, dropped them off in the kitchen and vaulted up to Rose's room to make the call.

"Hodgie," I eagerly said when he answered.

"Moosie, get your ass over here."

"Tell me now, is it good?"

Al answered, "oh, it's good alright! Just get you ass movin'!"

I bolted down the stairs, ran into the kitchen and grabbed a piece of bread that my dad was buttering for himself and said, "I won't be home for dinner … I'll call ya," and as I ran out the front door I yelled, "Bye!"

I drove like a bat out of hell to get to Al's and when I walked in the door, the first thing I saw was Koobs sitting up in a kitchen chair with a blanket covering his legs.

"Hey, Koobie, what's up?"

"They're upstairs, and they're waiting for you. What the hell's going on, Mark," he inquired.

"Ahhhh … it's nothing, Koobs, just probably some fucking pictures of some tits and ass."

"Pictures, my ass, they got a broad up there," he said.

"Huh?"

"Yeah, I'm not bullshitin' you, they got some little cutie up there with 'em. And fuck, if you little bastards do anything, at least' let me come and watch," he issued, and with a smile on my face, I patted him on the shoulder as I passed on by.

This had to be big, because when I got into Al's room he was joined by J.J., Adam, Del and even Shelley was on hand for this one

"Finally," Del said as I walked into the room.

"Just shut up and listen," J.J. ordered.

He clicked on the device.

"Bless me, Father, for I have sinned, my last confession was about three weeks ago."

There was no doubt, it was Sheddow.

"Father, I have frequently taken the Lord's name in vain during this period and have used it when arguing with family, friends and my students. I have been terribly unforgiving, as of late, yet I seem to want forgiveness from everybody else.

"And I have sinned in my mind and in unholy ways of the flesh. I am sorry for these and all of the sins of my past life, because they have offended Almighty God."

I looked at them with shrugged shoulders and said, "Big fucking deal, there's nothing there?"

"Quiet," Al ordered.

"Then I hear Felix, who presided in the confession ask, "Sinned against the mind and flesh?"

"Yes, Father," she answered, "the lord knows what pains my heart."

"This is true," he said, "but it will never be a true confession until you get it out into the open. For only true penance is achieved through opened admission. It is time to cleanse your soul."

She began to cry and said, "I used my position to force a minor to have carnal knowledge with me." She cried more fervently now and continued, "Bbbbut ... it only happened once and I have dealt with the matter in full ... I...I...I'm sorry for these and all of my sins."

And with that J.J. shut off the unit.

There was nothing but silence until Hodgie asked, "Whatcha think ... we got her?"

"Well we definitely got something," I followed, "but what?"

I couldn't help thinking that we really crossed the line here and had raped the sacrament.

"Moose," Adam said, "when she hears this, she's gonna have to let Billy off of the hook."

"Is Billy the one she had sex with?" I asked.

"Who knows," said Del.

"Who cares," Shelly said.

"The fact," J.J. spoke up, "is that we got some shit on her and we think that it's enough to get Billy off of the hook."

"Probably, but she didn't mention anything about taking money or the shit with Billy," I suggested.

"Hey, listen, Al said, "she's smart enough to know that Felix was on the other side of that shade. In confidence or not, if she were to truly fess up, Felix would have to do what's right."

"But what is right?" I posed. "Felix, regardless of the confession, is supposed to zip up. And yes … she's smart enough not to sing about certain things, but I think that we can all agree that she told a whopper with this sex thing!"

"Fuck you, Moose, are you chickening out?" Del asked.

"No, goddamnit, but I'm concerned how this shit is all gonna shake out!"

"We sit her down and play the tape," Adam said.

"But if you do that, then she's going to know that it was us," J.J. followed.

"She's going to know that it was us anyway," I said. "The trick though, is to get everything and everybody else off of the tape, so it can't be said that we fucked the whole school over. Can we get everything else off?"

"You mean edit it," J.J. asked. "Uh huh!"

"Then do it," I urged. "Now we need a typewriter. Hodgie, you got one?"

"Are you fucking kidding me," he laughed.

Shelley spoke up, "I do."

"Great," I said, and while J.J. took off with the tape to handle the edit, Shelley, Adam and I went over to her house to compose.

"And what the fuck are we supposed to do," Del asked.

"Play euchre with Koobs, sweetie, go play euchre with the man!"

When we got to Shelley's, I told the two others that we needed to keep this message short and sweet, but we needed to scare the shit out of Sheddow!

We went through draft after draft, until we came up with something that we all agreed was straight and to the point.

It read as follows…

THIS MAY NOT BE ADMISSIBLE IN A COURT OF LAW, BUT IT WILL GO A LONG WAY IN THE PUBLIC'S EYE. LISTEN CAREFULLY TO THE ENCLOSED TAPE, AND KNOW THAT WE WILL RELEASE IT TO ANYBODY WE THINK WILL USE IT TO BRING YOU DOWN, THE WAY YOU DECIDED TO TAKE THE CLASS PRESIDENT DOWN.

YOU WILL DROP THE CHARGES, AND YOU WILL REPAY 50 PERCENT OF THE MONEY TO THE SENIOR BANK ACCOUNT. WHEN WE HEAR THAT THE CHARGES WERE DROPPED AND YOUR SHARE HAS BEEN PAID, THIS ISSUE WILL GO AWAY…FOREVER.

YOU WILL CONTACT BILL BEDNARIK AND MEET WITH HIM AT THE POLICE STATION TO DROP ALL CHARGES, AND TO INDICATE TO THE POLICE THAT THIS WAS ALL A MISUNDERSTANDING AND THAT IT HAS BEEN WORKED OUT. THEN YOU WILL INFORM THE BANK THAT THERE WAS AN ACCOUNTING ERROR AND THAT THE SENIOR CLASS WAS GOING TO RESOLVE THIS MATTER ON ITS OWN.

FAIL, AND WE WILL ACT WITHOUT FAIL! YOU HAVE MADE TRUST A BIG PART OF YOUR VOCABULARY, NOW IT'S TIME TO EXHIBIT SOME!

ARE YOU READY? WE ARE.

YOU HAVE UNTIL FRIDAY NOON. AT 12:01, WE RELEASE THE TAPE, AND IT WILL FOLLOW YOU FOR LIFE.

At nine o'clock that evening, we all met back at Al's.

An edited copy of the tape and the indistinguishable typewritten note were placed in a large yellow envelope and we even took precautions to avoid leaving any fingerprints on anything. Then J.J. got in touch with Wally the janitor and by midnight, the envelope was on Sheddow's desk for a morning review.

Was this our handiwork? No doubt! But, there was no way that it could be traced to us, unless somebody in the know ratted us out.

Who knew that we would be so adept at extortion?

By 3:30 Wednesday afternoon, Billy had called Adam to inform him that all the charges were indeed dropped and that she would not interfere with his plans to attend South Bend.

And though it wasn't a textbook boardroom resolution of the issue ... the problem was resolved nonetheless.

On Thursday morning, a money order for three hundred dollars with instructions on what to do with it were dropped off to Loyola in a similar undetectable fashion in which Sheddow also received her notice.

By noon on Thursday, I had received a call from Billy.

"Hey, Mark, just wanted to say thanks for all of your help. You know that Sheddow dropped all of the charges!?"

"I heard that, man, congrats. But, I didn't do anything."

"Yeah, right ... well okay then, thanks for nothing," he laughed.

"Bill, just know that we all believed in you and that friends always help friends!"

As bad as I felt about how we gained the results that we did, it was great to hear the swagger back in Billy's tone!

And to be honest with you, I really wanted to ask Bill if he were the one that submitted sexually to that fucking cunt, but I realized that we had already passed way over the line.

The objective was met; and pushing the envelope would have brought nothing but trouble. We had successfully completed our mission and all was good ... or so we thought.

Saturday night I was on my way over to spend some time with Laura, knowing that everything had been taken care of and that her mother and I were at least on speaking terms again. But, when I arrived, she told me that I needed to call Al as soon I as got this message.

So, I was provided a little privacy in Laura's basement and followed through with the instructions.

"When can you get home?" Al questioned in a solemn voice.

"Home, I just got here. I want to spend some time with my girl!"

"No ... I think that you better get back here."

"Can I ask why?"

"Moose, just meet us back at your house by nine, okay? That'll give you a little time to spend with Laura and enough time to drive back."

Despite the fact that Laura and her family were going to be at the graduation in the morning, she was pissed that I was summoned home so early. But, like the trooper that she was ... she kissed me goodnight, gave me a little feel and sent me happily on my way.

I got back to my house around 9:15, to find Al and J.J. sitting on my front porch and visiting with my folks.

I walked up the porch steps already asking the question in my posture, and following it up with, "So?"

Al insisted, "Let's go inside."

J.J. had a satchel with him and when we got into my room we closed the door.

"Okay, motherfuckers, this better be good," I inferred.

J.J. spoke up, "You know me," he said sheepishly. "Always snoopin' around and looking for things." Then from his shirt pocket, he revealed the original tape from the confessionals.

He then grabbed the chair from my desk and Al nudged me back onto the bed. Then out of his satchel, he removed his tape player and said, "You gotta hear this!"

I was ready to start listening to the rest of the tape, hoping to hear something in the area of Gainer or the Kinovich twins or even Wendy wanting to get fucked by me in such a deviant way that they were compelled to summoned me home so soon!

But when I told them my thoughts, Al said, "Quit dreaming."

"So, you sick fuck," I said to J.J., "what did you discover?"

"Something that I think you're going to be quite interested in hearing."

Then I looked at Al, and he proceeded to say to me, "Moosie, you ain't gonna fucking believes this one."

J.J. pushed the button, and it was no different from any other standard opening to a confession. "Bless me ,Father for I have sinned, my last confession was one month ago."

It was a male's voice, but I wasn't too sure who.

Again it was pretty standard shit, "I lied, I said goddamn too much … blah, blah, blah, blah, blah, blah, blah …"

All of a sudden the voice started to crack and shutter more than what a standard fessin' up session would command.

"uhhhh…ummmm…uh, Father, I also stole something and … uhhhh."

"Yes, my son," Felix said, "go on."

"I stole some money and I made a lot of people think that it was somebody else."

And with my head postured down toward the floor and my eyes affixed upon the rug next to my bed, it suddenly clicked in!

"Oh my fucking God, is that Billy?"

I looked up to see J.J.'s lips cinched and him nodding to the affirmative.

"That lying fucking son of a bitch," I screamed, "he did it! I can't believe that he used us! That rotten piece of shit! He cried and told us straight out that he didn't do it!"

"Moose … what are we going to do," Al asked.

"We," I yelled. "We! I don't have the fucking foggiest about what we're going to do! But I know what I'm going to do … not a goddamned thing! I'm so sick and tired of bailing fucking people out and I'm even more tired of that fucking school!

"It's the same old fucking thing, trying to turn a mountain back into a molehill. Well, tomorrow it all comes to an end, fellas … at least for me it does.

"Sheddow's a fucking cunt, there's no doubting that, but we went wayyyyy over the fucking line this time. We fucked her big time, when all along, she was telling us the truth!

"We thought we were good guys, but, fellas, we met our match!

"Billy fucked all of us over and he beat us like a cheap set of fucking drums. So what am I gonna do tomorrow, I'm gonna tell them what I'm telling you right now … good-bye!"

"Moosie," Al begged in a disbelieving intonation.

"Get out … please, just get the hell out of here," and the two of them honored my request.

I just laid back in my bed, with my hands crossed behind my pounding head feeling as if I was going to throw up. I had plenty of personal reasons to detest Sheddow, but I knew that we had had really screwed her.

But truth be told, I really didn't know what I was angry about? Getting fucked by Billy … actually feeling shitty about screwing over Big Red … having my time with Laura interrupted to hear this bullshit … or not having any of my fantasies realized, by hearing one of the cuties from the school fess up that she masturbated when thinking about me.

Oh fuck, who was I kidding? I was petrified over the fact that I was a major part of a conspiracy of the highest degree. A robbery from the vault of God and a severing of trust that I knew that I could never be mended.

How could Sheddow ever trust the confessional again, knowing that what she expected to be safe was actually used against her. And having a modicum of scruples, I also realized that this would continue to haunt me.

Now aware of the truth, I felt like I had been immediately sentenced and that my conscience would act as my cell.

I had enough presence of mind and enough clout with my peers to nix this fucking idea, but I failed. And despite the fact that we all had relatively good intentions about what could come of this whole charade, the fact remained that we trivialized the cherished and sacred bond between God and penitent.

Considering years of friendship and trust that are built between people, why shouldn't we have believed that Billy had given us the straight and narrow? Furthermore, Sheddow's track record was one of antagonism and spite, so what grounds other than the obvious did we have to work with there?

One thing kept resonating in the back of my mind though, without their knowledge of what piracy was perpetrated, all truths were told. And if I thought that confessing that I was a part of said piracy was going to be difficult, squaring this mess outside of the box was going to be even a greater task.

I found my passions transforming from guilt to anger and I needed to get out of the house or I was going to blow up!

I was so hot under the collar, that despite my dad requesting that I slow up and answer some questions, I pushed through his meek attempt to restrain me and headed out for a drive. I decided to motor down Vernor Highway and found myself reflecting on everything that had happened, from startling Laura's mom to prostituting the confessional.

I felt like I ran the full gamut ... from publicly getting sucked off, to privately getting fucked over.

I did have a purpose to my quest however, and I found myself now only a couple of blocks away from Billy's house. Though it was closing in on eleven o'clock in the evening, I felt like a hawk ready to close in on its prey. At the end of his street, I stopped my car, turned off my headlights and suddenly found myself numb.

This was all about assisting a friend, and now I wanted to kill the one that I actually wanted to help. This was getting messier by the second and I found myself justifying that this had become all about me, instead of realizing that most of this occurred because of me. I was ready to add fuel to the already embattled fire, when I should have been trying to put my efforts into the only thing that mattered right now ... reconciling with Sheddow.

Regardless of her escapades and as despicable as it was that she forced herself on a student, she did recognize her error, indicated that she tried to right the wrong, confessed and exhibited remorse.

Sitting there I came to grips with the fact that I needed to get to the campus early in the morning, find her and to apologize for my actions. But for tonight, even if I were to see Billy crossing the street, the only action that was going to be taken, was to put my tail between my legs and quietly drive back home.

— absolution needed, but not from you, lord —

Though the sun had trickled through my drawn shades to greet me good morning, I was awake peering at the darkened walls in my room long before it had decided to make its grand appearance. The gentle early morning breeze was ruffling the clear laundry bag that covered my freshly cleaned and pressed blue suit that was hanging from my slightly opened closet door.

I heard my dad's seven o'clock alarm go off and heard him try to whisper to my mom, "Come on, we got a lot to do before he gets up!"

I laughed to myself and realized that although I thought that this was my day, that their stake in this was pretty lofty as well. I knew that they had prepared a congratulatory banner to surprise me, but couldn't erect it because of my flying off the cuff the night before and not hitting the hay until after 1:00 A.M.. So I just sat tight, and when my dad peeked in the room to see if I was still asleep, I played along and just closed my eyes.

Off the two of them scampered and I could hear the rustling of the banner and them arguing where to hang it. Thankfully, after fifteen minutes of noncompliance my dad said, "The hell with this … I'm going to go start the breakfast."

My dad made the worlds best scrambled eggs … fluffy, with just enough *rum* to them, and they were one of the few dishes that ever looked appealing coming off of the stove in that house. The bacon's aroma was just perfect and Mom even put a little good morning Sinatra on the RCA Victor.

366

I washed up, brushed my teeth, threw on a shirt and some shorts and was greeted at the foot of the staircase by the two of them.

Like the selfish asshole that I was, I just played along that I was pleased with all of this ballyhoo and tried to amuse them, genuinely missing out on the true meaning of the moment and their efforts.

Here I go again I thought, *taking for granted another sincere gesture of love and kindness, and ready to blow my parents off. I rarely gave them what they truly deserved ... a heartfelt thank you for everything that they did for me!*

My dad handed me a card and insisted that I opened it on the spot. Actually, it was quite a simple card, white with "Congratulations, son," written in raised cursive lettering on the front. But, it was what was inside that counted!

"You cried on your first day of school (which was true) out of fear, and today we cry for what we know ... that our son has honored us with his graduation."

There was no little boy looking up to his dad while clinging on to his mommy's leg, but rather a young man, albeit a confused young man, looking his father in the eye and towering over his mother, realizing that a lot had changed since I was pried out of my mommy's arms, that first day in Mrs. Wilk's Kindergarten class ... some 4,380 days ago.

My eyes swelled up and I embraced them both. It also didn't hurt that there were two crisp, one hundred dollar bills inside either!

I had a lot of friends, but my two best were standing right in front of me.

Then my mom handed me a smallish rectangular box, perfectly wrapped and said, "Go head...open it!"

It was a handsome Boulava with leather straps and a gold faceplate, and it fit *oh so well* on my left wrist.

We proceeded to the kitchen for breakfast and were finally joined by my sister, who also gave me a little something, that happened to be a handsome pen and pencil set.

"So, Laura's folks are coming, right?" my dad inquired.

"Yep, I told them to be there a half hour before mass started," I responded.

"Good ... it's high time that we met," my mom followed up.

After going over some brief details of how the morning was going to shape up, my mom got on the phone to Choo-Choo and Margo, to see if everything was on go with them. They volunteered their beautiful house and patio to host my graduation shindig, and my mom, Margo and my other aunts were in charge of making it a blast!

"Well, listen," I said, "I got some running around to do before mass, so if you'd excuse me," and I dabbed my kisser with my napkin, smooched all at the table and bolted back upstairs to gussy myself up for the big event.

In less than fifteen minutes, I even impressed myself with the debonair results. Every hair was in place and the dark blue suit accented with my highly glossed wing tips and the perfect tie, made me feel confident enough to audition for a shot to be the successor in the 007 series ... nawww ... not really!

I raced down the stairs, grabbed my keys, a freshly laundered hanky, my money and was about to hit the door when all of a sudden the phone rang.

"Yes, honey," my mom uttered, "he's here and he's looking very handsome!"

Smiling, she handed me the phone and whispered, "It's Laura."

Feeling a little spry, I thought I'd have a little fun with her, "Hi, baby!"

"Just wanted to say that I love you ... and that I'm proud of you ... and that I can hardly wait to see you ... and that I miss you!"

"Oh, Laura, it's you?"

There was nothing but dead silence on the other end of the phone. Then I started laughing, but there was still no response from the other end.

"Laura ... come on now, I was just kidding!"

"Oh, Mark, I'm sorry," she said, "I dialed the wrong number," then she hung up.

I stood there with the phone in my hand and was completely dumbfounded. *Holy shit, what did I do,* I thought.

I hung the phone up and leaned back against the kitchen counter, thinking that I just fucked my own future ... when all of a sudden the phone rang.

"Hello," I sheepishly answered.

"What did you say to my sister?" was yelled through the earpiece. It was Laura's eldest sister Debbie, admonishing me and telling me that Laura was crying her eyes out.

"But, Debbie."

"Don't you but Debbie me! This poor little thing is heartbroken ..." and she went on and on about what kind of a shit I was ... until I said, "alright already! I didn't mean for this to happen, I'm gonna drive out right now to show her that I was wrong and that this was nothing but a little prank!"

"Well before you do," she said. From the other extension in their house, a voice said "... gotcha," followed by the rest of the family laughing in the background.

I was stunned!

That little blonde beat me at my own game and I just found myself laughing at the fact that instead of being the stinger, I was the stingee!

"Remember, two can play at that game," she said with a little laugh. "But I meant what I said ... I love you and I'm sooooo proud of you ... and I'll see ya soon!"

"Love you too! Remember, no later than 9:30 ... and one more thing!"

"Yeah," she said.

"Tell Debbie to kiss my ass!"

"Naw," she responded, "think I'll keep that job for myself."

And we both laughed before saying good-bye.

I stormed out of the house to the old Woodmere Florist and picked up a bouquet of flowers. This one was special, and it wasn't for Laura, or her mom or mine, but for the only one I deserved flowers on this day ... my redheaded advisory. *who*

I purposely left early for the campus to secure some one on one time with her and to sincerely try to make amends.

Driving toward the school, I used my rear view mirror as a point of contact and tried to format what I wanted to express.

"Miss Sheddow" ... *naw, to formal,* I thought.

"Valerie," nope ... too disrespectful!

What about, *"Heyyyy, don't you look great today!"* *Nawww, called her a fat fuck too many times to sell that one.*

I didn't want to seem too weak, but then again she deserved my very best. I didn't want to admit that I was a part of the recording brigade, but I had to let her know that I knew that she really was telling the truth all along.

Then again as cold feet started to set in, I thought *what if the others see me resorting to this? Then again, who fucking cared what they thought anyway!*

I had debated and doubted myself right into the parking lot at 8:45, far before any of the expected pre-graduation activity. In fact, the lot was pretty full with cars of those that were attending eight o'clock mass.

I popped out of the car and surprisingly was amazed at how beautiful the area seemed to be. It wasn't just sunny; it was drenched with beams from above. Even that fucking ugly Cadillac plant seemed to shimmer in the sun.

This was just too good not to work out.

Whatever it took to display my regret for any role that I may have played, that caused her any grief, I had to get that across to her.

With my floral present in hand, I was ready to adlib my way back into her good graces!

I raced past the athletic department, down the hall and past the office, made that right turn one final time and saw that her room door was opened and that the lights were on!

I stopped, took one of those cleansing breaths, buttoned ... then pulled down on my suit coat and slowly, but confidently walked on. This was exactly the scenario that I was looking for, quiet and alone.

I'm ready for this ... I can make this happen, I coaxed myself!

I turned into the room wearing a smile, not concerned about lobbying for an eleventh hour grade elevation or anything else ... all I wanted to do was to extend a genuine olive branch.

The room was meticulous, but seemed to be empty. I peeked into her cloakroom, but nothing.

Okay then, I thought, *she'll walk in on me.*

I came back into the main classroom from her personal area, and heard footsteps lumbering toward the room, *this had to be her*! But instead ... it was Loyola.

"Morning, Sister, she's not here yet ... guess I'm a little early?"

She just smiled at me as I continued in a bit of a fidgety manner, "Sorry, no doughnuts this morning ... flowers though ... great day, isn't it!"

"Mark," she somberly stated while walking toward me.

I just cocked my head and looked back at her in an inquisitive way.

"My dear boy," she preluded, and I just knew what she was about to say, 'she's not here and she's not coming back. She resigned late Friday afternoon.'"

I just started to fill with emotion and my arms went limp.

"I called her to invite her to join her class at graduation, but her mother indicated that she was ill and chose not to cause any further trouble by attending."

"Goddamn it," I said as I turned away from the nun, and began to hang my head in shame.

She came close and put her arm around me and said, "I know about everything ... the tape the note ... everything.

"Shame on you for what you did, for if anybody had the power to stop it, it was you. And now you're getting exactly what you deserve."

I was crying inconsolably and wanted no part of the rest of the day. I just tossed the flowers on a nearby desk.

"This is your punishment, you deserve to cry and you deserve to feel sorrow" Then she paused and said, "But you must let it go, Mark."

"Let it go? How can I? I'm ashamed of myself and I…I tried to help, but I ended up hurting … how can I just let this go?"

"My son, you let your heart blind your mind … and it won't be the last time that it happens."

Then she said, "It's like a nun, lying to her superior that the two boys who rang the Friday mass bells are not really skipping school, but actually running errands for me … or concluding for the Arch Dioceses that the sudden rash of unfortunate incidents during Ann's important inspection couldn't have involved any of our students. It had to have been motivated by rivalry and those hooligans at Holy Redeemer."

My shocked expression must have said it all. Then she smiled and said, "I often find my heart playing tricks on me too. Sometimes, my dear, no matter how hard you try or no matter what you do, there are simply no answers … in those instances, you must trust in God's Providence and just let it go!"

She then chuckled and said, "You feel empty, like a doughnut without the center."

"Spare me the doughy metaphors please," I countered.

I just shook my head and smiled as she continued.

"Valerie will recover! We both know that she is not without sin, and has some pretty big problems of her own to deal with. Besides, she wasn't going to be asked back next year."

I just took a deep breath and leaned back on one of the desks.

"Mark, you're a leader and you know right from wrong. And here you are trying to right a wrong, but still fate won't let you finish. Sometimes it's like that … your efforts are true, but your fruits are few. But your heart is absolute and your mind is clear.

"You have experienced the ultimate in affirmation and know God's most blessed lesson of all, to receive forgiveness … you must forgive those who trespass. Your confession is complete, and my dear boy … the day is yours!"

We embraced and I said, "Oh, I'm going to miss you."

Then I turned back, picked up the bouquet and handed them over to her saying, "I actually got these for you!"

She just looked back and with a halfhearted grin responded, "A beautiful confession … right down the drain with another lie."

I left her standing alone in the room and slowly took my last stroll down the senior hall, trying to use every sensation and feeling that I could to capture all the sensory souvenirs that I could. And though physically empty, incredible images of fun, laughter and lasting recollections of both good and bad times came back to life … if only for a fleeting moment … they all came back to life!

~ crossing the double-crossed altar ~

It was now twenty minutes past nine and I had made my way in front of what was an ever-growing crowd on the church's front apron. I began mingling with classmates and their families, as we were encouraged to pick up and don our cap and gowns.

There was still no sight of Laura's or my own family as of yet, and decent parking seemed to be dissipating by the second.

"Hey, Mark!"

I turned to see Nickki Dobeleski, the victim of the flawed pyrotechnic show back in Father Felix's class. "Hey, Nic," I responded.

She was wearing a terrific smile as she greeted me and said, "I couldn't let you go without saying good bye. I'm really gonna miss you."

"Me too," I responded, and she opened her arms and gave me the warmest of hugs. Then she said, "Hope you get everything out of life that you want."

"Thanks, Nic," I replied. Then from out of the crowd came one of the areas most renowned high school athletes, Preston McCollum, a three-letter man from Holy Redeemer. I was surprised to see him at our ceremonies, for any number of reasons, but I was really puzzled when he walked up to me, or at least that's what I figured.

With Nickki still embracing me, I looked over to him and said, "Hey … how ya doin'?"

To which he just smiled and stood there in a gentlemanly fashion, nodding to me in a congratulatory way. Not knowing what I owed the privilege of him stopping by, my answer came as soon as Nickki released me.

"Oh hi, baby," she said to him, "where'd you find a parking spot?"

The two of them grabbed hands, and despite the fact that most of this ethnic, blue collar crowd probably was frowning upon the fact that this attractive neighborhood girl was holding hands with a black fella, regardless of how handsome he was, they looked great together and a happier couple couldn't be found!

He extended his hand to me and stated, "Congratulations, man, you were one hell of a ball player."

I just smiled back and said, "Takes one to know one!" Then I followed up with, "She's a keeper, so take care of her!" And you could see in his eyes that his feelings for her were as genuine as it got.

I excused myself as from over their shoulders; I saw Bednarik, his parents and his brother walking up toward the crowd, but noticeably absent was his longtime girlfriend, Mary. I was compelled to confront him and ultimately give him a piece of my mind, especially over the entire chain of events that recently occurred.

He saw me approaching and, in return, I saw him flash a smile and wave to me. What was strange, however, is that besieged class president had a large white piece of medical tape, obviously concealing a wound over his left eyebrow, and a shiner that seemed to circle that entire side of his face.

"What happened?" I greeted.

"That frickin J.J., for no reason whatsoever, did this to me last night outside of Big Boy's."

Suddenly, I got this big grin on my face and exclaimed, "Really!?"

"Well, I don't see any reason for you to be happy about this," his mother admonished.

"I turned to her and answered, "You know, Mrs. Bednarik, you're right. I would have been much happier, if I could have popped his ass myself!"

"What?" his father exclaimed.

"Well, I never," the Mrs. Frowned.

"You piece of shit," I said, "you deserve this, and you know you do!" Then, looking at the parents, I continued, "Your son is a conniving thief who got away lucky, but worst of all, he deceived his friends.

"Instead of Notre Dame, he should be headed for the University of Penn … pen-iten-tiary that is." Then I turned back to him and said, "All this for six hundred dollars … fuck you," and I turned and walked away.

I intently searched for my parents, when I suddenly caught my dad in the distance being hugged by Laura. She was wearing a sleeveless sundress that hung from her sweet little frame and truly billowed in the morning breeze. Her heels were perfectly matched and I was breathless knowing that this incredible looking girl cared so much for me.

Behind her were her mom, dad and her twin sister, all smiling, as they were about to finally meet my beaming folks, Rose and her boyfriend, Mike.

I just stood back and took it all in, because that was the picture that I wanted to be in!

I finally walked to the contingent and smiled saying, "Finally, north meets south."

Her mom broke out into laughter and to my surprise, was the first one to greet me with a hug and a kiss!

"There he is," said Laura's dad and he gave me a hardy handshake as both families greeted one another as if they were reuniting after a long absence. It was almost too good to be true, there was peace ... harmony ... and everything seemed like it should have been.

"Seniors, it's time please! Take your positions," Sister Erasmus called. Sixty-seven of us were summoned for entry of pomp and circumstance, as all witnesses and well-wishers started to file into the massive church to take their seats.

It had started for me. I was fanning through the visual recollections of my schooling. Laughing about that first day, when I clung onto my mother like a cat on a tree in a ferocious windstorm.

Then there was my first grade teacher, Mrs. Pollard, whose shapely legs haunted me throughout all my years in elementary school.

I recalled being the errand boy for my third grade science teacher, Mr. Jackson, who constantly would shuttle messages up to another good looker, Mrs. Slouth. Even at our tender ages, we were aware that they had a thing for one another. We just didn't know that it wasn't right for her to be married and conduct a school time fling.

In sixth grade, I was the captain of the safety patrol, the most exalted position that a little guy at Higgins Elementary could have achieved.

Then there were the discoveries of rivalries, male territorial needs and that girls were more than just the last to choose from and throw-ins when you picked teams for softball in gym class.

I remembered my first crush on a flamboyant Jewish gal named Maya Saperstien, and the way we'd tease each other to death, without ever exchanging as much as kiss.

I also recalled the shock I felt when she suddenly didn't show up to school, and it was revealed that she and her siblings were taken by her mother's sister, on the news that her parents, both doctors, were jointly arrested, charged and subsequently convicted of writing more than 2,800 fraudulent prescriptions.

And I remembered my first day at Hedwig's. The regimentation, the uniforms and the initial disdain for the nuns, who, in the end, were the only ones who I really found it hard to let go of!

I became lost in the past while being enraptured with the present, and despite the events of the past week and a half, I finally felt that there was a logical end in sight.

Presiding over the mass and ceremonies was Pastor John Gatalski, who quite honestly I couldn't tell you much about, because he hardly was around the school scene. The man had a beak on him though, which warranted the handle of Parrot Head, and not because he was a fan of balladeer Jimmy Buffet.

He always seemed to be in distant thought and even if you'd pass him on the street and offered him a greeting, you could be up to ten paces past him before he'd look back and acknowledge you.

The thing that was most strange about him, however, was that like his associate, Felix, he had a peculiar habit in dialogue, as he would end each thought with a tentative laugh, followed by a sigh ... strange dude!

Joining him on the altar was a throng of altar servers, Felix, Loyola, the battered looking Bednarik and class valedictorian, Eddie Gasiewski. Unlike a non-secular institution, the mass took precedence at these proceedings, not the graduation.

But instead of conducting a normal homily, this one would recognize the graduating class and their accomplishments, and would mark one final revelation of an incredibly tumultuous year.

John preached, "For those of you moving onto higher education or to jobs, or to whatever the Good Lord has planned for you ... you cannot forget the roots placed and the knowledge that you obtained from here at Saint Hedwig's. For those gifts come with a price ... and a continued debt that you must repay by supporting those who will follow in your foot steps."

And I could hear my dad saying to himself, "Debt! Who the fuck do you think paid for the last four years of tuition, fees, books, field trips and we can't forget the gifts of benevolence that the parish required once every three months. Which didn't include the weekly envelopes!"

John continued, "As young adults of this community, each one of you is obligated to financially support this parish and to honor your debt of a rich Catholic education."

Which I'm sure went in one ear and right out the other, like a lot of that rich education that you just were talking about.

After he went for the cash, John's direction did an about-face.

"Many of the graduating young men today have aspirations of becoming leaders in many of the different walks of life ... medicine, the legal profession, perhaps the military and even running businesses of their very own."

Funny, not once did he mention anything blue collar, which 95 percent of our fathers were.

"But gentlemen, I would like you to consider life's most rewarding career path. It is also, life's most challenging and, at times, the most difficult and dangerous."

Just then, I got nudged on the shoulder and was instructed to look behind me and three people down. It was Del.

In a loud whisper, he said, "Moose, he's fucking talkin' about us ... pimps, man ... pimps!"

Which brought out a good amount of laughter from those close by.

The Pastor's appeal went on, "Of course, I'm referring about being in the service of the Lord. True, the hours are long and the money and other earthly possessions are few, but the grand reward promises to be heavenly!"

But Zig Zigler he wasn't. His pitch was falling on deaf ears and it wasn't because of the lack of earthly possessions part.

What was missing was the pussy part, and though God was high on our priority list, I don't remember seeing the trim part listed on any of the clergy's recruiting literature.

Let's face it, pussy to most of the guys ... and Shelley, at least at this juncture in life, nudged out God at the wire.

He proceeded, "And though I know it's not for everyone, when one of our very own decides to follow the path, it becomes very, very special!"

Yeah, I could buy that. Someone would have had to be very, very special to chose that path.

But one of our own?

I knew that hell didn't freeze over, so that left out Del, Al, J.J, Adam, Frost, the Gracies and me. Eyebrows raised and shoulders shrugged as square headed, tassel dangling graduation caps were pivoting like crazy to see who it was that got hooked by the Fisher of Men?

John paused and then continued by saying, "I hope you will join me in praying for and wishing the very best of luck to the young man whose studies will be focused upon the Lord, and who will commence seminary matriculation at the University of Notre Dame, your class president, William Bednarik."

For most in attendance applause was at a fevered pitch, but for those of us in the know, our fucking jaws dropped as a subdued Billy rose to his feet for the acknowledgment.

I turned back to look at Adam who was a longtime friend of Billy's, but the shocked look on his face said it all. With palms up, Adam looked befuddled and simply speaking, the lot of us were not expecting this news.

"I mentioned dangerous," the Priest said, "seems like William has already been introduced to a lesson or two," which drew some laughter from the packed assembly.

"My dear William, may I suggest a class or two in pursuit of the finer aspects of pugilism. In fact, I know of a couple of my fellow priests who handled themselves quite well in the squared circle."

"Besides," the priest pontificated, "they don't call them the fighting Irish for nothing!"

And like a South Bend pep-rally, the congregation broke out into a gregarious cheer!

"But seriously, a select few who have been close to William, especially since he had made his intentions known, realize that this young man had been dealing with a number of complications and adversities and through perseverance and family support, he has prevailed."

Suddenly, I found myself looking toward the only one who seemed to be able to link this whole thing together ... Loyola.

Like a Gypsy fortuneteller, she was anticipating my visual dismay, and she was waiting for my facial inquiry.

"Complications ... adversities," what did she know? What did this "select few" know that we didn't?

She mouthed the words once again that she earlier emphasized to me ... "Just let it go."

But something else was missing ... was this adversity tied to the missing funds?

Again my attention was diverted, this time to Adam, who directed me to look at Billy's older brother, Brad, who mocked shooting up with a hypodermic, and then he rubbed his fingers together to indicate money, while nodding toward his younger brother.

It wasn't till after graduation that we would find out that Billy was an addict and took the funds to pay for a private form of treatment that he was involved in, unbeknownst to all, except for this "select few," that included both priests, Loyola, the proud but ashamed parents, Brad and, of course Billy.

When J.J. blackened his eye the night before, he did so in front of Billy's girl. Supposedly, J.J. left a verbal exclamation point at the end of the shot, saying, "That's for lying to us, you cock sucker!" In turn, that prompted Mary to question Billy, who fessed up to more than what precipitated the punch.

In the meantime, while the guilt pendulum was swinging back and forth between Sheddow and the confession busters, the "select few" were also dealing in a little Hedwig hypocrisy of their own.

By pure stroke of luck, we not only helped the administration find the ammunition that they needed to get Billy out of trouble, but also did their dirty work by dropping the bomb (the tape and the demands) on Sheddow, that forced her to cave.

Felix, meanwhile, hears the confession, is able to maintain discretion and eerily … another one gets chalked up to look like Divine Intervention.

So for those of you keeping score … Billy, gets exonerated and Notre Dame. Sheddow gets her walking papers and the promise that her confession disappears. The "select group" fills their quota, by sending someone to seminary, and the rest of us … get our diplomas and one hell of a lesson about "now you see it … now you don't."

For in our attempt to get justice, we perpetrated a crime so heinous against the church, that we should have been considered for excommunication.

Yet, somehow it was just treated as collateral damage.

Everybody *kind of* got what they wanted … with a golden parachute chaser.

So then tell me, why was J.J. crying down the row from me?

Was it because he knew … as did Al, Del, Adam, Shelley, the Gracies, and that "select few" that the lessons we learned, about truth, respect and honesty in this exalted Catholic Education were really bullshit and based plainly on the means justifying the ends?

What happened to the concept that the church was uncorruptable?

How did back room deals overtake the truth?

And how did we as children of God compromise the commandments?

We felt like shit, as we witnessed the church … not Christ and not God … but the fucking church conforming instead chastising to meet an agenda.

It was painfully apparent that we were the only ones who were truly feeling the pain and contriteness that this whole charade commanded.

If Loyola's advice, that personal solace and reconciliation were possible by just letting it go, it just wasn't sinking in. For no matter how vindicated that I was supposed to feel in my failed efforts to clean the slate with Sheddow, I fell right back into the fucking vat, when it came to my disdain toward Billy.

But what hurt the most, was that our model for true happiness … the church was illustrating a weakness and a susceptibility that quite frankly … mirrored us.

It was at that time, that I not only grew aware, but conceded that I was wrong all the while in my blame and disdain toward the Almighty for Mick's shortsightedness.

For *He* is so truly wise and loving, that in spite of his powers and his all-encompassing abilities … he made it as simple as can be … the choice is yours.

One thing was crystal clear though, today … at this moment, I had the chance to deal directly with Billy and this time I wasn't going to fail.

The valedictorian had completed his address and it was now time for the ceremonial distribution of diplomas.

Father John issued, "Will the graduating class please stand!"

After some rearranging on the altar, Loyola retrieved the mic and said, "Father John, distinguished guests, family members and friends. I am proud to proclaim that standing before you are students who have met and surpassed the requirements necessary to graduate from an accredited high school in the State of Michigan, which, of course, includes Saint Hedwig's.

"Joining me on the altar, in our traditional salute to the graduates is, of course, Pastor John and Associate Pastor, Father Felix and senior class President, William Bednarik.

"Ladies and gentlemen, it gives me great pleasure to present to you the 1978 graduating class of Detroit St. Hedwig High School."

The microphone was then passed to Billy, who stood at the far right corner of the altar.

With a bed of musical accompaniment, he would introduce each graduate and without the need for a script, provided a little bio on each of us to the audience. We were not in any specific or alphabetical type of order, but like a seasoned pro, he gave a little insight on each and every one of us that was warm, detailed and concise.

One by one, he was honoring each individual, cognizant that possible trouble still lurked. Each graduate commanded applause, with some receiving more than others.

Finally, J.J. appeared in view and was next to be announced.

"Ladies and gentlemen, here's graduate Joel James J.J. Lambert, who is not only St. Hedwig's Mr. Fix-it, but he undoubtedly sports the best male wardrobe and the flashiest wheels on campus."

And while the applause rang out for J.J., Billy, who had the chance to fire a verbal counterpunch of his own said, "Close … and I mean very close … observers say, that he also possesses one of the best haymakers in the class."

J.J. was about halfway through the altar, when he suddenly turned, smiled and walked back toward Billy. Fearful of a repeat of last night's sucker punch I held my breath, when all of a sudden, J.J. appeared to gently point in Billy's direction and said something to him.

I don't know what it was and the crowd didn't seem to have the foggiest, but the two began to embrace to the cheers of the packed house. The same was offered for Del, Hodgie, Shelley and his close pal, Adam.

I stood next to receive his accolades. He simply stated, "He was voted most likely to succeed, best all around athlete and if you ask anybody here …" and his words began to be drowned out with the chant of "mooooooooooose………mooooooooooose…………."

I was embarrassed by the incredible reception and acknowledgment of the crowd and I purposely stopped on the altar, turned toward the audience and specifically looked for two souls in the crowd.

When I meet eyes with the Bednarik's, my hands formed two fists that I placed on my heart and mouthed to them "Please forgive me, I was wrong."

Then I turned and walked up to Billy and said, "You're a son of a bitch, but you're gonna make one hell of a priest! I know your choices were tough and you strayed a bit, but we need you, Billy … we need you to lead us to what's truly right. Lead us to him!

"You may be humbling with your words right now, but I expect you to astonish me … and hopefully my kids one day, Father."

Now standing toe to toe with him, I grabbed his head and placed it against mine, temple to temple. With the church in an all out applause, I said to him,

"Know that whatever you took, paled in comparison to my theft ... and there's nobody in this place who can absolve me today except you ... so, Father, what do ya say ... please forgive me?"

He just smiled and winked back at me with his good eye and laughed, "I don't believe this, I should be asking you for forgiveness, and instead ... you're my first confession."

— a lot of new and a little no —

Weeks later, as the euphoria of graduation started to wear off things began to settle down.

One factor that really hit home was that for the first time in my life, the future was unclear. Not that everyday didn't already bring with it a host of uncertainties, but when September was to roll around, there wouldn't be that comfort zone of friends and facilities that I had become so accustomed to.

Suddenly, baseball, hanging out with the fellas and just being able to fuck around, seemed to be slipping out of reach. I felt like I was space walking, and my umbilical cord to the ship had broken loose ... and slowly, regardless of my efforts, that part of my life was getting farther and farther out of reach.

To compound this severing of what was, my folks decided that they wanted to live near the rest of the family, most who over the years migrated to the area's southern suburbs.

In what was a whirlwind decision, by July, they had sold the house and purchased a large condo in of all places, Trenton. Convenient to family and, of course, ... Laura!

The new digs were just that, new, or at least a lot more modern than the old house back on Lawndale. The only thing that seemed kind of weird, was that back in the city we had this buffer. You know ... those twenty-five miles or so that, in essence, was a stone's throw away from the extended family, but far enough away to dissuade too many visits.

Don't get me wrong, both sides of our extended family were cool, but like most things in life, only when taken in moderation.

Call it the newness or a honeymoon period, but every fucking day seemed to bring somebody new over, and when they came, they stayed ... all day long.

What became funny was the fact that when my dad came home from work, he'd usually just like to lounge around in his boxers, and it wouldn't be uncommon to catch him scratching his nether region while he read the paper or watched the tube.

But his style, was becoming cramped and you could see the frustration starting to build in his demeanor every time he walked in the door.

Eventually, however, the visits lessened and some sort of normality soon followed.

Likewise for me, there was the excitement that Laura was only two miles away, instead of that long drive. A lot of pluses for me, but, there were some questionable issues that crept up as well.

This unfettered access allowed her to bike over any time she practically wanted.

Then there was the fib factor! That ability, to say that I wasn't feeling well and then perhaps bolt over to play cards over at Al's or head over to the track or to just do whatever I wanted ... without the fear of the drive by verify.

And maybe ... just maybe she felt the same way about me being so close.

But as time would tell that I was more paranoid then practical. For what I could only imagine was any number of reasons, she had her restrictions and despite the fact that we saw each other everyday, there were few, if any expectations and we each enjoyed our liberties.

One of the things that I was looking forward to was the invitation that was extended to me by the baseball coach from Wayne State. It was to be a day of glad handing it with some of the current team members, checking out the facilities, becoming orientated with the campus and grabbing a little lunch to discuss my future.

I knew that as an incoming freshmen that I'd have to bide my time, but I was confident that they had a strong interest in me. Strong enough to pick up some scholarship money and hopefully able to work myself into the starting line up as soon as possible.

Plus, what really sounded great was that the team usually took up residence in Florida for a month in February. And anytime that you can exchange the sun of Florida for the soot-covered snow of Detroit in any month ending in a "y," you better jump all over that!

It was the Wednesday after the Fourth of July and I got to Coach Pappas' office as scheduled at 10:30 sharp. Dressed in a comfortable pair of khakis and a Polo shirt, I thought that I was attired casual as requested, but showed enough respect by not coming in like some sort of a beach bum. Speaking of which, while sitting in the reception area of the University's sports department, now at 11:15, in strolls Coach Pappas.

He had on a wrinkled T-shirt that couldn't have seen a washing machine since it was purchased, a pair of blue jean cutoff shorts, where one pant leg was longer than the other, and a pair of sandals that clearly showed that this guy hadn't washed his feet in days. Even the length of his overgrown toe nails were disgusting as was evident on the face of the girl who was working the department's reception desk.

His hair was a mess, he hadn't shaved for a while, and I couldn't rule out the fact that he might have just returned from an all-night drunk.

"Coach, your ten thirty," and she just pointed in my direction.

"Oh yeah," he laughed, "ten thirty ... right ... Matt isn't it?"

"Uhhhh, noooo, it's Mark."

"That's right. Mark...Mark. So, how's it been hangin'?"

"Okay, I guess," I answered.

"So, what are you here for?"

With a confused and exasperated look on my face I said, "You invited me ... to discuss my future here ... about playing baseball?"

"Yeah ... right, right. Well okay, what do ya say that we start off with some lunch ... you hungry?"

He procured a golf cart and the two of us started to drive from the University's sports complex, onto one of Detroit's busier streets, Warren Avenue, during midday traffic. So, here we are motoring along, in a cart that like the coach was messy, sluggish and something that I didn't really want to be seen around. And the crazy thing about this ride, was that the University had emulated a craze seen in Major League Baseball, and had outfitted the cart to look like the head of school's mascot, a Tarter.

Which, to be honest with you, I always thought was slang for the cream and relish based fish dressing, but came to understand that it was actually warrior figure, that I'm not quite sure had anything relevance with Detroit.

It was one of those hot days where the pavement radiated, reflected and magnified the sun's heat. Plus, it was humid and the only breeze that was being generated was the stale air that the vehicle passed through as it made its trek. To make matters worse, it was compounded by the hot exhaust of the passing busses, car emissions and the stench of those rancid fucking feet.

And if that wasn't bad enough, before we took off, he asked if I didn't mind riding in the back of the cart, whose seat faced to the rear, so that he could stretch out. That image alone, rendered laughs and finger pointing from both transients and pedestrians alike.

"So, Mike," he said.

"It's Mark."

"Oh yeah, sorry. You like Greek?"

And before answering, I thought to myself, *for Christ's sake, don't tell me that the only way I'm going to get a scholarship from this guy is if I take it up the ass.* "Yeah, it's alright," and that was the extent of our conversation for the two-and-a-half-mile trip that we made across campus, to a place called the Circa.

For the next two hours, I sat and watched this slob eat two gyros, a couple of pieces of spinach pie, a slice of mosaka and for dessert, and a gigantic bowl of rice pudding. All washed down with two super-sized draught beers, which promoted a hardy rendition of burps, belches and farts.

The other thing about this guy that became so repulsive was not just the size of his nose, but the untrimmed nasal hair that protruded from it. I swear, if he sneezed, he would have looked like a fucking feather duster.

He rambled on and on about the program, and frequently indicated to me that I'd be a welcome addition to the outfield, which I just kept shaking my head about. We never once discussed checking out any of the training facilities, the fields or what was expected from me. For that matter, we never even touched upon anything related to academics at all. Finally, he dropped the ultimate bomb on me.

"As a freshmen, of course, we really couldn't use you at all. Probably for a couple of years, in fact, but you could go out for an intramural club on campus."

Feeling like I hit a brick wall, I reflected for a moment, then said, "Ya know, you gotta let me think about this ... and ... uhhhhh, I'll call ya. Thanks for the lunch!"

Then I gave him a two-fingered salute and hit the bricks back toward my car. I needed to walk the distance back to clear my head and to try to figure out how I was going to tell my dad that this was probably not going to work out.

My first impression of college is that it left me yearning for Hedwig's. So to quench my void, I decided to drive down to the old gal, to gawk, gaze and savor. It was a fifteen-minute drive from Wayne's campus back to my Alma Mater, and it would be the first time that I had returned since graduation.

The grounds to the courtyard were locked and chained, and in the distance I saw a couple of windows opened and heard the hammering associated with some summertime fix ups. The church, too, though basking in the heat of the day, was dark and seemed … cold for some reason.

The nuns had retreated to the motherhouse for a bit of R and R, and I felt for the first time like a stranger on these hallowed grounds.

Well, this trip wasn't going to be a total loss, for I was committed to drop over to Al's to pay a visit and to spend some time with Koobs. If there was one place where refuge could always be taken and sanctuary found, it was always with the Semkos.

I pulled up and vaulted from my car eager to see the gang, talk about what was going on, grab a bite to eat and maybe even get in a couple of hands.

I got to the kitchen door, gave a little courtesy knock and walked in saying, "It's just me … hello … anybody here?"

I heard the shower running and decided to sit tight until somebody emerged. After some ten minutes, and while I was skimming through the Free Press left open on the counter, into the kitchen in a pair of shorts and with a towel around his neck was Al's older brother, Gary.

"Moosie," he said, surprised to see me.

"Hey, man, where's everybody at?"

"Al, Claudia and Mom took Dad in for a treatment."

"How's he doing?" I inquired.

"Honestly, Mark, not good. He hates the chemo, he can't stand the fact that he can't drink or smoke. He misses work and he says that everything he eats, tastes like shit. Now come on now, Moose, Mom's cooking tasting like shit?"

"I know, man," for nothing could be further from the truth.

"When they coming back?"

"His appointment isn't until three thirty, so I wouldn't expect them home until after five thirty … closer to six."

"Shit, I really wanted to see him."

We continued with some idle chatter, he asked me about the new place and what I was planning to do come September, but soon, we ran out of things to say, and before he excused himself to get ready for his afternoon shift at the

Rouge Plant (of Ford Motor Company), he asked, "You know were kicking off the summer league at Rotunda this weekend."

Rotunda was a large softball complex in neighboring Dearborn and a group of us were going to join in with some of Al's older brothers and their friends to form a summer team.

"Yeah, Al called and told me all about it. I'm not going to be able to make any of the practices this week, but I'll be at the game."

"You're playing Legion ball, aren't you?"

"Yeah," I answered.

"With as much ball as you play, I wouldn't worry about showing up for the practices," he said. Then he ducked into the fridge for a moment, pulled out a Pepsi, and said, "Well, Moosie, I gotta get ready for work, hang out as long as you want."

Then he went toward the bedroom area and I heard him shut his door.

Some fucking refuge? Was I just having a bad day, or was this a sign of things to come. I hadn't played cards with these guys for almost two months, and according to earlier conversations with Al, Koobs, the lifeblood of the game had hardly played either.

I just sat there, leaning back in the chair and thinking. So far today, my future looked glum, Hedwig's was a ghost town and my second home had the numbing sensation of a funeral parlor. Oh, the memories that were had at this table ... suddenly, I felt like an abandoned pet, who was lost and without a clue on why he was left behind.

I also felt that out of the blue, that I was no longer impervious, but rather vulnerable to life. That instead of being able to impose my will on the world around me, that I was now being shuffled around in life's giant deck of cards.

I kind of got the awareness of what Koobs must have been feeling, certainly not in the physical sense, but how fucked it is to be broken in spirit. It was time to move on.

— the last to know —

Thankfully it was a pretty slow paced rest of the week, I played some Legion fast pitch, went out with Laura on Saturday night, and on Sunday, she accompanied me to Rotunda for opening night of the softball season.

What should have been a relatively quick and easy trip was gummed up by an accident on the northbound Southfield Freeway. I wove my way from the fast lane, over to an exit and took the service drive to side streets to try and make headway.

At three minutes before the six o'clock start, I finally got into the parking lot, drove up to the field's entrance, grabbed my bat, bag and spikes and told Laura to park the car. Then like a lame horse who threw a shoe, I limped my way to the furthest diamond away from the lot, where we were scheduled to play.

"Hurry up, Moose," yelled a couple of the players.

Though winded, I got there in time and to avoid the team forfeiting the game. "Sorry," I weased, "but Southfield was a bitch!"

"Yeah, yeah … okay, Moose, we got the field and you're in Left," barked Al's oldest brother, Donnie.

"Kay, skip," I said and I bolted into position. *Fuck, what an attitude* I thought, *it's only a game and it wasn't my fault Southfield was all backed up.*

But that didn't seem to be the only problem, because there was no hop, or excitement about playing the game. Before you knew it, Donnie, usually an excellent softball pitcher, had already walked the first two batters that he faced.

"Come on, D, find the plate, babe … no free passes," I shouted. In fact, I was the only one who seemed to be talking it up on our team.

389

From bad to worse, Donnie walked the next three in a row, before the sixth place hitter launched one about forty feet over my head that had cleared the fence by some twenty feet for a grand slam.

When you measure an inning by time, it usually means trouble for the team that's out in the field. It was 6:28 P.M.; they had scored eleven runs and still had the bases full with two outs.

The same guy, who earlier cleared the bases with that shot over my head, was up again.

This time on a three and one pitch, he laced a shot into the left center alley that I got a decent jump on. Just when it looked like it was going to fall in, I laid out for the ball and snow coned it in the webbing of my glove, for the third out and quite honestly one of the nicest stabs that you'd ever want to see. Even the other team congratulated me on the catch, but nothing, not a word from our guys as I came into the dugout.

"Goddamn, I make a catch like that and not even a fart from you fucking guys ..." I just shook my head and wondered why I had even committed to playing with these lames.

Donnie had yelled out our lineup as Al walked over and said, "Hey man, nice catch."

"Yeah right," I sarcastically barked back, "I never seen a more dead fuckin' bench then this in my life."

I was batting third and when I turned to talk to Hodgie, he was walking toward the bathrooms to take what I assumed was a leak.

"Come on, fellas," I implored, "let's get some back!"

Donnie led off and on the first pitch, grounded one between short and third for a base hit.

Returning from the john, Al worked his way through the dugout, with sunglasses in place went to coach first base. Our second place hitter, Kenny Calvin, popped a two and one pitch into short right field, where it was easily hauled in for the first out.

As I walked to the batter's box, I saw that Laura was behind the bleachers on the first base side of home plate, involved in what seemed to be a pretty serious conversation, but I couldn't make out whom the other person was.

I placed myself in the box, and with a faint chant of "Come on, Moosie," coming from the bench, I prepped myself to put a little life back into this team, by putting one into the night sky and over the fence myself!

I had taken the first two pitches and was ahead on the count, two and nothing. I stepped out of the box to grab some dirt to take some of the moisture out of hands, when again; I looked back at Laura, who seemed to be disillusioned at what she was hearing.

Whatever it was, she could tell me later, because I was about to touch 'em all! The next pitch was right in my wheelhouse and I roped it into left center for a solid single. I rounded first and held my ground as Donnie was forced to stop at second.

"Ah shit," I exclaimed as I clapped my hands once in frustration. "I got all of that one, Hodgie, but I just didn't have any lift to it!"

When I walked to the bag, at first I saw Al, bent over with his hands on his knees and spitting on the ground, oblivious to what was going on around him.

"Hey, what's your fucking problem? This team is so fricking dead, I wish you'd never had called me to play!"

I just shook my head and caught Laura out of the corner of my eye all teared up, standing aside a sad demeanored Claudia.

"Hey wait a minute, time out here, ump … time out," I yelled.

I took a couple of steps into foul territory and was about ready to run over to Laura's aid, and saw others in the crowd who knew us begin to turn away, when all of a sudden, Al grabbed my left arm and said, "Moosie," and he began to choke up. "Moosie … ahhhh, Mark … we…we didn't know how to tell you."

"Tell me? Tell me what?"

"Koobs … Daaaaad … he's gone."

"When … uhhhh what … uhhhh when," I jumbled my words as I began to cry.

"Moosie," he cleared his throat, "we found him yesterday morning."

Then he grabbed me and said, "Mark, he…he…he hung himself!"

I couldn't tell you how long it took or what my condition was, but I had fallen to my knees and began to feel like I was going to get sick. I started to dry heave and dropped to my side in a fetal position. Al quickly came down and grabbed me and pulled me closer to his chest.

"Is he okay?" their first basemen said in a concerned manner.

Donnie immediately went over to the umpire and forfeited the game as the entire field became as silent as a Nebraskan cornfield on a late June evening.

I remember shaking in the dirt and chalk line of the first base side of the infield, hearing Al tell me, "God, Moosie, he loved you. You were like his fourth son."

That was all I needed to totally break down and sob inconsolably.

I don't know how long I was down for, but the other team had all ready cleared out and only a handful of our players had still remained.

I finally worked myself back to my knees and then with the help of Al and Donnie, back to my feet. They got me over to the dugout and quite frankly, if they hadn't, I really didn't know how I was going to move, I felt that weak.

"Moosie … you gonna be alright? Donnie inquired.

I just shook my head and looked into his eyes and as if he knew the answers to every one of the million questions that I had in my head, he just looked back at me and said, "I know, buddy, I know."

After what had to be at least another ten minutes on the bench of just staring aimlessly into the outfield, Claudia and Laura came and sat next to me.

Claudia spoke, "Mark, I just want you to listen to me. We have cried ourselves out over the past twenty-four hours trying to understand why he did this. Donnie thought that we needed some kind of diversion and to let Mom and Auntie Marianne take care of some loose ends. Obviously, we were fooling ourselves."

"With tears streaming down from our faces, she continued. "Honey, we called your folks last night, you and Laura were out.

"We told them and asked them not to tell you." And she began to cry harder, "Because as crazy at it seems, we all felt that we had to tell you in person, that you deserved nothing less. This just happened to be the time and the place."

She just joined me in staring out into the field and said, "There was no note, no nothing to let us know why … and now…now the house is a crime scene and it's just not the place to be … and my daddy … my poor daddy, he's going to eee…ee…end…end up in hell because of what he did," and she began to cry before falling into my arms.

"Bullshit, Claude, bullshit.

"How can a man who brought so much joy to so many, who just didn't want to be a burden … go to hell?

"No God that I know, who understands what truly is in a pained heart could ever sentence someone, who meant so much to so many others to a fate like that.

"No … that soul lives … and if there's a fuckin' poker game up there, they better look out, 'cause the Koobs is comin' to stake his claim!"

We held hands and laughed for there were no more tears to give, when something compelled me to say,

"I know you want answers, but regardless of how close that you thought you were, this one was between Koobs and God. Trust me ... he made the decision he had to and I'll betcha he had a pure heart and a clear conscience when he discussed it with the guy upstairs."

Then she turned and said to me, "Even money says that Mickey was the first one there to greet him."

"No doubt!"

After an autopsy, the body was cremated and his ashes were released over the same waters where his nephew perished a little over a year earlier.

~ oh, by the way ~

It was mid-August and I found myself driving south on I-75 and somehow compelled to turn off on the Luna Pier Road exit, about six or seven miles north of the Ohio border. I drove into the little cottage and port community, past its gas station and country store, by the post office and down to the village's namesake ... the pier.

It's far from the most glamorous protruding walkway on Erie, in fact, the cement, steel and stone path and break wall was crooked and really kind of ugly. But it provided a great view of the lake and was the perfect place to reflect and clear the air!

Under threatening skies, I sat down on one of the many benches that lined the pier. Alone and with nobody else in sight, I said aloud, "I just don't fucking get you. There is not one good reason you can give me to justify what you allowed to happen, not one! But I'm just supposed to trust in your ways and heaven forbid, never question you. Well, fuck ...you know me better than that ... or at least you should?

"I have a billion questions about a billion issues, and rehashing the past with you, why bother? Quite frankly, I think you screwed up; and you know you did!

"Mick is gone, Emolina and now Koobs. This whole damn thing disgusts me. This lake disgusts me and carrying the thoughts of how you took them disgusts me. They couldn't have just gone behind a door or off to some place to cross over, nooooo, let's give 'em a gut wrenching drowning.

"No, wait, how 'bout tarnishing an impeccable career and sending a gentle soul out to pasture to ponder why she saves an asshole before you took her.

"Even better, the climatic show stealer ... suicide! That's it! A horrific death and survivor humiliation! Perfect! Well, screw you!"

394

As the clouds thickened and the rain started to increase in intensity, so did the volume of my voice as I became irate and began to cry.

"Hey, what's keeping you from stopping me from running off the edge … huh? You think you're so fucking powerful?"

I began to sprint along the crooked barrier, seeing the faces of Mick, the nun and Koobs flash before me as I fixed my sights on the pier's end.

"I can do this, ya know … I can give you another spectacular ending! Fuck the future … what could you possibly do to stop me? God's will, the hell it is … this is my day … I'll call the shots from here on."

And as I approached the end, on one of the remaining down-boards, there it was … simple, scuffed and always there just in case.

My sprint diminished to a jog and then a crawl as everything around me slowed and my eyes were affixed to it. I stood in the pouring rain and within its preserving circumference was shown all I needed to see.

There, reflected back to me were my folks, my family and my friends. Images of the past and a hint of why I had to stay. There was Laura and a yet to be completed portrait of life that compelled my spirit.

And as I gazed at the circular refuge I saw it all … then as I chuckled … "How did I know you'd show up?"

I put my hands on my knees and momentarily stared at the pavement.

Then I looked back into the ring and said, "I've been wondering where you have been … and if you'd ever come again?"

I found myself now falling to my knees, not out of reverence, as much as it was out of exhaustion. "But you've been here all along."

I saw what I had failed to see, not on a crucifix or in a billowing cloud, but within the weathered yet inviting life-ring that was there … all along.

A doughnut … who would have believed it?

This product is based on real life experiences. The author has employed discretion in some cases to protect individuals and situations via modifications.

Printed in the United States
20458LVS00002B/145-153